CHRISTY SMITH

Expecting to Fly

Fallen · *Book Two*

SECOND EDITION

Penakiuppi Press

Penkaluppi Press © Second Edition
USA

Book cover design by Ana Grigoriu-Voicu

ISBN 13: 978 0692723166

Football references are courtesy of Steven Mead.

For I do not do the good I want to do, but the evil I do not want to do, this I keep on doing.

Romans 7:19

This book is most lovingly dedicated to my Mother, my creative and

spiritual inspiration

Table of Contents

Expecting to Fly
Fallen

"Time... precious in the moments while I hold you, but in an instant, dark like an enemy. Faith and hope lie still under a veil, waiting to be awakened, while destiny unraveled, and slowly flew into the light..." Luke

Chapter One-
Christmas Joys

Saturday, December 29, 1973

Watching as two sparrows on the ground squabbled over a small twig, Jessie sat quietly waiting in the truck for her dad to come out. Her palms were sweaty, and she could barely contain her excitement, anxious to get going. She held tightly to her overnight bag, which was packed nearly a week ago, not wanting to let go of it, for fear she might wake up, and find herself only dreaming. She glanced at the front door of the cabin, taking a deep breath, and watched the steam as she exhaled, float up and dissipate. The morning air was crisp, and the melting snow had turned the entire driveway to mud. The patchy snow in the grass gleamed with sunlit sparkles, like crystal fairies scurrying about. Jessie spent many hours imagining she was a little fairy, with translucent, shiny wings, flying through the wild flowers in the meadow on some magical adventure, free from anything that remotely resembled unhappiness or discomfort. She was too anxious just now though, to delve into any fantasy. She had far too many other things on her mind and there was no room at present, to fill it with such thoughts. The last few weeks she spent writing in her journal, remembering the events of her last visit. The warmth she felt in her Aunt's house at Thanksgiving, lying on Ricky's bed talking, and Luke, taking her to the mall. He kept her white dress and she wondered if he still had it.

Come on Dad, please come out, she thought, and whispered restlessly, "Maybe he changed his mind."

Her border collie wandered over from behind the cabin and sat by the truck door, looking up at her. His whine interrupted her worries.

"I'll be back in a week, Luke. You look after those chickens, and if you see Woosypiti or Lillibelle, tell them I'm at my Aunties." She put her hand out to him and he licked it. Hank, looking rather scruffy, meandered his way out of the front door, tucking in his shirt. Jessie sighed with relief, and Luke ran under the porch, growling. A blue jay up in the tall pine next to the chicken coop began cawing loudly and Hank looked up at it. He grumbled something and climbed in the truck. The cranky old engine didn't turn the first time.

"Fuckin' piece of shit," he muttered, pumping on the gas pedal, and turned the key again.

"Please start," Jessie whispered. The engine caught the second time, sputtering with the strong smell of gasoline, and Hank slammed it into gear, skidding out of the muddy driveway. Jessie felt she would explode any second, as Hank drove down through the canyon. She was consumed with restless anxiety, hoping her dad would not see her excitement. She knew any little thing could set him off, and he'd take her back home. The drive had never felt so long, or bumpy. Every now and then, the truck would slide in the mud, and she'd glance over at Hank for a moment, with pangs of fear that the truck would go sliding off the road, down the ravine, and crash into the trees. He was a reckless driver and she couldn't help but feel it was on purpose, just to frighten her. Usually, he would yell or say some sarcastic remark if she acted frightened, but not today. Today was long awaited, and she would not let his meanness ruin her day.

She tried not to fidget as she watched the thick pines go by, catching a glimpse of sun rays now and again through the trees. Nearly recognizing each tree by heart, her anticipation grew as she sighted the end of the tree line off the mountain, and the first little house in the valley beyond, presented itself. The scents of cow manure and sagebrush replaced the smell of gasoline, and she felt her heart up in her throat as they entered the small town of Smith Valley. She knew it would not be much longer until they reached Mining.

Hank hadn't said two words to Jessie, but that was okay with her. When they arrived at last to the courthouse, he stopped at the curb. Jessie's eyes lit up when she saw her Aunt, waiting by the station wagon, and her anxiety turned to pleasant enthusiasm.

"I left you some sugar cookies in the jar, Daddy," Jessie said, half smiling with her blue eyes gazing down.

He pointed his finger at her and snapped, "You behave!"

"I will Daddy. Thank…" she replied, getting out of the truck with her overnight bag in tow. She'd barely shut the door when he drove away, "you."

My Lord, Debbie thought, as she watched Hank drive away. She reached out as Jessie ran to her, and they exchanged tight hugs. "Merry Christmas, Jessie!"

"Auntie, I'm so glad to see you! Merry Christmas to you!" Jessie said, holding tightly to her Aunt.

"My sweet Jessie," Debbie said in near tears and kissed her forehead. "I'm so glad to see you, too."

"It seems like forever since I saw you, Auntie!" Jessie said, clinging to Debbie as they walked to the car. "I didn't think we'd *ever* get here."

"It has been a long wait hasn't it, sweetheart? We're so happy to have you come home." Debbie smiled and opened the car door for Jessie. "The kids can't wait for you to get home!"

Jessie was in awe at the colored lights on the house when they pulled at last, into the driveway of her Aunt's lovely, warm, home. Jessie's eyes lit up with wonder. "How beautiful, Auntie."

"Wait till you see them at night. Uncle Harry put more up since you were here last!" Debbie happily shifted into park.

Jessie glanced over at the Miller's house as she got out of the car. She was saddened that there seemed to be no one home, until Aimee and Eli ran down the stairs to greet her. They'd been waiting at the window, more excited to see Jessie than ever. Not only because they missed her, but they couldn't wait to open their presents another second!

Jessie set her overnight bag on the sofa as George and Gracie jumped, whined, and wiggled, trying to climb up her legs. "You silly dogs," she said, bending down to pet the little Chihuahuas. She tried to take in all the lovely decorations, but Aimee and Eli scurried her out to the family-room, barely letting her catch her breath.

Maddy was sitting quietly on the hearth, and Jessie felt instantly uncomfortable. However, the sight of a million presents under the tree quickly distracted her attention. She'd never seen so many presents in her life! She wondered about Santa coming, but didn't dare ask. The room was so warm, and the sound of Bing Crosby's *Christmas* was softly playing on the stereo. The smell of chocolate and gingerbread, and wonderful food cooking, filled the house and Jessie's tummy suddenly felt hungry.

"Hey!" Uncle Harry laughed, sitting in his favorite spot. He held out his hand, and Jessie ran to hug him. "How's my girl?"

"Hi Uncle, Merry Christmas." She smiled giddily, as Uncle Harry squeezed her tight.

"You have presents from the Millers, Jess," Eli interrupted, eager to get opening presents.

"Me?" Jessie asked, going over to look at the cornucopia of gifts spilling out from under the tree.

"They all bought you presents, even Mike," Maddy said with a gloomy look on her face, envious of the fact. She was secretly excited about Jessie's coming, but she had her own motives behind that. Maddy's behavior was of no consequence to Jessie though, because hanging on the mantle behind Maddy were furry, red, stockings, filled with delightful surprises. Jessie saw her name on one of them and she pictured Santa coming down that chimney. Her imagination went wild as she anticipated what kind of treasures could be hiding in them. She felt as though the room was filled with magic, and presently, was not concerned with Maddy's typical negativity. Aimee took Jessie's hand, delighted to have her cousin back home, and began to go over the itinerary she had planned for the week.

Eli continued to aggravate his mother, who was in the kitchen fixing up a tray of homemade fudge and cookies to bring out. "Can we open presents now?" he asked quite impatiently and followed her out to the family room.

"Let Jessie get settled, Son," Uncle Harry said, folding up his newspaper.

At once, Jessie was embarrassed. She felt awful, looking at all the faces in the room. "I couldn't buy nothing for any of you."

"We don't expect you to, sweetheart," Uncle Harry said, putting his glasses in his pocket.

"Of course, we don't," Aunt Debbie replied, setting the tray down on the coffee table. Eli was about to have a cow, stammering and wiggling as if the world would come to an end any second. "Eli, please, calm down!" she scolded.

"We know you can't buy presents, Jessie," Aimee said, sitting next to the presents. "We don't care."

"I did draw each of you a picture though," Jessie said, just remembering, and hurried out to the living room to get the pictures from her overnight bag, and a plastic bag of sugar cookies. She eagerly handed everyone their drawings which she had rolled up and tied each one with a string. Maddy smirked as Jessie handed her the picture she made for her, but Jessie ignored it. Lastly, she handed Debbie her drawing and the bag of cookies. "I made these," she said rapidly and under her breath.

"How thoughtful, sweetheart, thank you," Debbie said unrolling her drawing of a rose. "Jessie, this is beautiful."

"Mom, can we open presents now?" Eli interrupted.

"Eli!" Debbie snapped. "Jessie just handed you a gift!"

"Oh, sorry," Eli answered. "Thanks, Jessie."

"I love my drawing, Jessie." Aimee smiled. "I'll hang this up in my room."

"I know you like horses," Jessie said. "I drew him in the meadow by my house."

"Really?" Aimee asked. "Do you have horses where you live?"

"No, but sometimes I pretend there's unicorns in the meadow."

"I'm gonna hang mine up in my room, too," Eli said. "It's real good."

"I thought it would match your dolphins," Jessie answered.

Debbie was ready to cry any second. "These drawings represent Jessie's heart and her thoughtfulness," she sniffed. "They carry a special meaning for each of you, and I hope you all appreciate the love Jessie put into these drawings."

"We do, Momma," Aimee said, about to cry herself.

Jessie felt her mouth quiver. "Well, I dis tried to think of things you like."

Maddy wondered what the special meaning of two deer in the snow meant but decided it best not to say anything.

"I can't think of a lovelier subject, Jessie," Uncle Harry said. He handed Debbie his drawing.

Debbie looked at Harry's drawing. "Why, Jessie, you drew a picture of *me* for Uncle Harry?"

"Yes, Auntie, I know Uncle likes you," Jessie giggled.

Uncle Harry laughed. "I like her a lot."

"Hand me all your drawings," Debbie said, wiping her cheek. "I'm going to take these next week and get them all framed, Jessie. They're just so beautiful...Okay, Eli," Debbie sniffed her nose. "Ready to play Santa?"

"Yes!" Eli and Aimee both shouted, beaming with joy. "Jessie, come sit next to me," Aimee said, patting the floor.

Eli quickly began passing out everyone's gifts. Jessie had never seen such a delightful mess in her life! Reluctant and embarrassed to open her own presents, she sat for a minute, watching how thrilling it was to see everyone tear into theirs.

"Aren't you gonna open your presents, Jess?" Eli asked, setting a large present in front of her. It was heavy, and he could barely carry it.

Jessie gaped at the size of the gift and looked at the tag with her name on it. "Oh," Jessie gulped, "that's for me?"

"Go ahead, honey," Aunt Debbie urged her.

Cautiously, Jessie began to peel the shiny paper from the huge box set before her, finding inside the very first Christmas gift she would remember in her life was a record player from her Aunt and Uncle. It was a real *Magnavox* with movable speakers! Jessie was overwhelmed with feelings of guilty happiness.

"Oh my," she whispered. "Auntie, this is too wonderful."

"Do you like it?" Debbie asked, smiling at Jessie's delight.

Jessie nodded in disbelief that she could receive such a gift.

"Well, open up some more!" Debbie chuckled.

Jessie felt uncomfortable at first and was hesitant to open her next gift, but when she saw how everyone else was digging into theirs, she soon felt at ease and couldn't wait to open the next one.

Each of the kids bought her a record, even Ricky, who bought her the album, *Brothers and Sisters* by the Allman Brothers with the song, "Jessica" on it. Aimee surprised Jessie with two little troll dolls, one with green hair and one with white. Eli gave her a transistor radio. Jessie realized immediately that Aimee and Eli must have remembered her admiration of the dolls and radio when they first met. From her Aunt and Uncle, she received an artist kit, pink flannel pajamas, a pink sweat jacket, two beautiful sweaters, and a red velvet gown. It was a long, V-neck gown with silk straps. They bought Maddy a green one, very similar, and Aimee a purple one. Mr. and Mrs. Miller bought the girls each a tiny diamond necklace with a different diamond shape on each one. Jessie's diamond was a small tear drop.

"Wow! All right!" Jessie heard Eli shout, and looked over at him. He was in ecstasies over his new *Raleigh Chopper* bicycle that Debbie pulled out from behind the wet bar. Uncle Harry went over to help him examine it. Maddy had forgotten her malcontent, caught up in the exhilaration of the morning and was quite pleased with her own gifts.

"Oh, Mom, I love it!" She grinned from ear to hear, wrapping her new, beige, wool jacket around her. "It's exactly the one I wanted!" Grateful exuberance passed from her lips and she went over to her mom and gave her a hug.

Jessie saved Luke's gifts for last. She didn't feel at all strange about him buying her presents. She sensed it was his pleasure, and that made her heart feel warm. She knew right away the beautiful frame was to hold her mother's picture. Inside the box of *See's* candy, he wrote her a note that said: 'the best is yet to come'. She sprayed a wisp of the perfume in the air, picturing him at the mall, buying it. When she was finished, she looked at the pile of gifts next to her and felt like a real part of the family. Just being at Auntie's house was almost like being in heaven, and a strange sense of security came over her. A feeling none of her cousins would understand.

Seeing that Jessie was finished opening gifts, Maddy reached behind the back of the tree and took out a small, brown, teddy bear with a green ribbon on it. She handed it to Jessie. "Here, Jess," she said, seemingly reluctant to give it to her.

"Whad'ya do that for?" Aimee noticed.

Jessie took the bear. It had a tag that read: 'A cute little bear for a cute little girl, from Mike.' Jessie's heart skipped a beat and she felt a wave of something go over her.

"Be quiet," Maddy smirked at Aimee, who returned her remark with an unpleasant face. Maddy had been quite jealous of the gift and was tempted when she first saw it, to hide it and never let Jessie see it, but she knew they would notice it missing, and didn't want Mike to ever find out she would do such a thing. Maddy wanted to be nice to Jessie, remembering the fun they had together last visit, but Jessie was so damn beautiful, and Mike seemed to really like her. She just couldn't help feeling jealous and angry.

Jessie sat quietly, contemplating each gift from each person and what they meant to her. She didn't know why, but she began to feel frightened and uneasy. She could feel her body trembling a bit, but she didn't want anyone to notice. She remembered having similar feelings the last time she came to visit. She was not used to so much going on. She was used to her routine and felt off balance. At home, she did everything at the same time, which gave her a sense of comfort, but here, there was no routine, and although she loved it immensely, the sensation was frightening. She almost wanted to scream and run away. Aunt Debbie noticed Jessie's fretful face, and the sweat dripping down the sides of her head.

"Are you feeling okay, sweetie?" Debbie asked, going over to sit by her.

Jessie nodded, looking up at her Aunt, not understanding it herself.

"Are you sure?" Debbie asked, wiping Jessie's face. "You look pale."

"I'm okay."

"You're not used to all of this excitement. We should have let you get settled first. Maybe you can rest for a while."

"No, I'm okay, Auntie."

"You still have one more gift to open." Debbie pointed to a big box in the corner by the hearth. "Do you want to wait awhile?"

"No, I'm okay."

Jessie couldn't believe her last gift and almost fainted when she opened it. Pete and Lisa went all out, and bought her a mahogany, *Gibson SG* electric guitar with an amplifier speaker. Pete had written on the tag: 'The same one used by Toni Iommi.' Overwhelmed after opening so many wonderful presents, Jessie could no longer hold back her tears and began to cry.

"Mom, why is Jessie crying?" Aimee asked.

"I think those are happy tears, Scoob," Uncle Harry said, smiling.

Jessie nodded. "Thank you, Aunt Harry and Uncle Debbie, for all these wonderful gifts." She sniffed, half crying and half laughing at her blunder.

"Don't cry, sweetheart," Debbie chuckled, wiping a tear from her own cheek. "We love you."

"Yes, we do," Uncle Harry said, getting up and giving her a kiss on the cheek. "You're one of us, darlin' girl. You always were and always will be."

Jessie quietly contemplated the moment. She wanted to fit in. She wanted to belong. She never wanted to go home again.

She was amazed at how quickly everyone opened all those presents. Wrapping paper and ribbons covered the floor. She felt as if she was in a story book, and the excitement was almost unbearable.

"Come on, Jess!" Eli said, embracing his gift. "Let's go outside and ride my new bike!"

"After breakfast, Eli," Debbie said. "We have to clean up this mess!"

"Aw, man," Eli said, frowning.

Jessie immediately began picking up the wrapping paper. "Where are the Millers?" she asked Maddy, sniffing her runny nose.

"They're in Reno, visiting their grandma, I guess," Maddy answered, unsympathetic to Jessie's tears.

"They'll be back tonight," Aimee said, helping Jessie. "We're all going out to dinner. That's why Mom bought us all dresses."

"Oh no," Jessie whispered to Maddy.

"I know," Maddy agreed, feeling the same way. "Mom!" She shouted into the kitchen. "Do we really have to have dinner with the Miller's tonight?"

Debbie came from the kitchen, wiping her hands on her apron. "Maddy, you know we've been planning this for weeks. It's not just the Millers, it's everyone. Can you please just help out, and enjoy the day?

Maddy scowled, sighing, and whizzed past her mother, carrying a handful of gifts down the hall to her room.

"Jessie," Debbie said, going over to her and took her hand. She seemed apprehensive.

"What is it, Auntie?"

"Mr. and Mrs. Miller didn't tell Ricky you were coming here this week. He went with his Grandma to see the Grand Canyon. They felt if they told him you were coming, he wouldn't want to go. They felt it was important for his Grandmother to take him."

"Oh." Jessie's heart sank with disappointment. She was so looking forward to seeing him.

Debbie stroked Jessie's cheek and offered a gentle smile. "I'm sorry, Sweetie.

How about some eggnog? Are you hungry? I've made a delicious ham for breakfast *and* pumpkin pie."

Jessie nodded. "I love your pumpkin pie."

"Let's see about this guitar," Uncle Harry said to Jessie, picking it up, and he plugged it into the amp. He plucked a string and it made a very loud twang, startling him. Jessie laughed.

She felt a bit more at ease after breakfast, as there was lovely family conversation about Christmas, presents, family, and love. Aimee helped Jessie put her things away. Aimee was so sweet and pleasant. Jessie was glad to be with her. She lay on her bottom bunk, with all her presents and her teddy bear, and took a small nap. She was quite exhausted.

~

They had reservations to be at the restaurant by six. The afternoon was spent in commotion with the girls, all crammed in and out of the bathroom, getting ready. Maddy reluctantly came down the hall and stopped in front of the bathroom door, wearing her new gown. "Mom, I am *not* going to wear this in front of the Miller's."

"Why not?" Debbie asked, putting a curl in Aimee's short, blond hair. "You look beautiful."

Maddy looked down at herself. "Because, it's too embarrassing."

"Why are you embarrassed, Maddy?" Jessie asked, wearing her own new gown, watching her Aunt curl Aimee's hair.

"She doesn't want Mike to see her," Aimee sneered.

"Shut up, Aimee," Maddy snapped.

"All right you two," Debbie said.

"Of course, Mike has to see you looking so pretty, Maddy," Jessie said. Her eyes were as blue and serious as could be. "Don't you think? Don't you want him to see you pretty?"

"She's right, Maddy," Debbie said, accidentally spraying Aimee's eye with hair spray.

Maddy thought for a second. If she couldn't be brave enough to do this, she would never be able to do anything, plus, she realized she was being immature, and, seeing how gorgeous, of course, Jessie looked in her gown, she *had* to wear hers. After all, Jessie did promise not to see Mike anymore. Maybe Jessie would keep her promise and stay away from him. "You're right, Jessie," Maddy sighed.

Debbie helped Maddy put her hair up in a French roll and put a thin line of eye liner across her lids. "There." Debbie smiled at Maddy. "You look just like Audrey Hepburn." Maddy turned her head, looking in the mirror and walked down the hall.

Who is Aubrey Hefburn?" Jessie asked.

"She's a beautiful actress," Debbie answered. "Let's see about your hair now, Jessie."

Jessie's hair was too long and thick to put in a French roll, so Debbie put the top half of it up in a big barrette, puffed up a bit, with some strands of curls coming down the sides. "I think your hair is getting lighter, Jessie. It's almost white!"

"It is, but I don't know why." Jessie said, watching Debbie in the mirror.

"I don't either. Usually, hair gets darker as you get older," Debbie said, putting the last curl in it. Then she showed Jessie how to apply eyeliner, some mascara, and blue eye shadow. "You're so beautiful, Jessie, just like your mom. That shadow really brings out your blue eyes."

Jessie's eyes stood out like brilliant, blue, crystals. The make-up gave her an elegant, more sophisticated look, and Jessie stood at the mirror, examining the difference.

Maddy had gone to her room to put her hose on. She tried not to show her envy but was in total fear of what inevitably would take place once Mike saw Jessie. "This is going to be a nightmare," she sighed. Maddy had no clue she was a beautiful girl. She'd had a crush on Mike for as long as she could remember, but his constant, arrogant, rejection toward her had taken quite a toll on her esteem. And now, with Jessie there, she felt utterly hopeless.

Jessie and Aimee helped each other put the necklaces on from Mr. and Mrs. Miller, and Jessie eagerly shared a wisp of her perfume with Maddy and Aimee. Maddy watched Jessie, who always seemed so positive about herself, and longed to feel that way about her own self.

~

Pulling up to the restaurant, Maddy was suffering horrible anxiety, terrified of being dressed like that in front of the Millers, not feeling equally as beautiful as Jessie. She noticed though, that Jessie seemed a little uncomfortable, too.

"Sometimes, I don't know what my mother is thinking," she said to Jessie as they walked into the big lobby of the restaurant. "Aren't you nervous?"

"Yeth, I'm afraid to see Luke *and* Mike. They're going to stare at us like they did at the buffet last time and I fainted."

Maddy fidgeted with her gown. "I can't believe she made me dress like this."

"She's probly just proud of you, Maddy," Jessie said. "You look tho pretty."

Maddy considered the notion of her mom being proud of her, and how dumb, little Jessie thought of it, but she didn't. "Thanks, you look pretty, too."

They could see through the large, pine archway that the Millers were already there. Luke and Mike were both wearing slacks and dress shirts, which wasn't their usual attire.

"Shit," Maddy whispered to Jessie. "They're both so handsome." She and Jessie looked at each other and took a deep breath. They followed their parents into the dining room.

"God damn," Mike uttered under his breath. He felt his body go flush.

Maddy felt relief at first, that Jessie was distracting their attention, but then couldn't stand the way Mike was looking at Jessie and hadn't even noticed her.

"Wow," Luke whispered to Jessie, pulling out her chair. "My God, you're beautiful, Jessie. Is there a better word than beautiful?"

Jessie whispered to him, "Thank you for the presents, Luke. You look tho handsome, too."

He longed to kiss her. "I have to stand back from you tonight, darlin'. Otherwise, I don't think I'll be able to keep my hands off you." His eyes twinkled as she shyly smiled.

Mike smiled his deadly smile and winked at her. Her eyes kept gazing over at him, but she had to breathe in and look away. He was so big and frightening. She thought to tell him thank-you for the teddy bear, but she didn't know how to break through the 'intimidation barrier'.

"Oh, look at these beautiful girls!" Mrs. Miller exclaimed, kissing each of them.

"Thank you, for the necklace, Meg," Jessie said, as Meg bent down to cup her face in her hand.

"You're welcome, darlin'. How elegant you look."

Jessie looked around the room and felt her heart melting. She never imagined in all her life that she would be sitting in a fancy restaurant at Christmas, surrounded by family and friends. Time seemed to stop momentarily, and she thought maybe she was dreaming. She turned at hearing a familiar, cheerful voice, and saw Pete and Lisa come in with Chad. Pete was always so jolly and greeted everyone as if they were a long-lost friend. When he bent down to kiss Jessie hello, she said, "Thank you so much for the guitar, Pete."

"Well, you're very welcome. You're going to need it now, aren't you?" he said, grinning. "You look lovely!"

"Thank you, Pete. You're lovely, too."

Chad took her hand and Jessie smiled coyly as he kissed it. "You're very beautiful, Jessie." He turned to Eli, who was sitting next to her. "Would you mind if I sit next to Jessie? I'd like to speak with her."

"I guess," Eli answered. He was reluctant to move from his spot.

Luke felt his face turn hot. He had a strong desire to punch Chad in the mouth just then, fighting off the urge to tell him to back the fuck away from his girlfriend. He realized, though, how inappropriate and illogical that would be. Luke took the chair across from Jessie, listening to their conversation, but it didn't make sense to him.

Chad began to explain to Jessie about Mr. Townsend, a friend who agreed to represent her as an agent. "Normally," Chad said, "the agent has to hear how well you play, but because he was such a good friend, he was willing to look for a situation for you, sight unseen."

Jessie nodded, not quite comprehending at first what he was telling her, but then she realized what he was talking about. She was a bit surprised and not quite believing it.

"Of course, when I explained to him how beautiful and talented you are," Chad continued, "he was easy to persuade." He smiled and tapped her forehead with his.

"Thank you, Chad," she said quietly, looking at Luke. She could see Luke was upset.

"It was my pleasure, Jessie.

"What should I get?" Jessie whispered to Luke, looking up from her menu.

"Get the steak, of course, Jessie," Chad interrupted, pointing to the T-bone on the menu.

Luke glared at him and Jessie became uneasy about him, hoping Chad would stop talking to her.

After what seemed like an eternity, everyone was finally served and eating. Jessie was happy to be surrounded by all the people she loved, and in spite of Luke, enjoyed everyone talking and laughing, and eating such good food together.

As everyone was finishing their meal, Pete stood up and raised his wine glass. "A toast to you wonderful people here tonight. Happy Holidays!" Jessie looked curiously at everyone lifting their glasses. "It's such a treat having dinner with all of you," Pete said. "And with that, I have an announcement to make. Most of you, I know, but this year I've had the pleasure of meeting a delightfully talented and beautiful, young lady." Pete turned toward Jessie. Jessie suddenly felt a heat wave of embarrassment and wanted to hide under the table. Pete continued, "As all of you know, Jessie is quite a musician, and with Chad's help in L.A., we've found an agent to represent her."

They all were surprised and began clapping. Jessie felt herself turn as red as her dress and worried now, about her agreement and was it for real? Luke's face seemed to go pale, and a fretful scowl came over his brow.

"Also," Pete said, interrupting the excited chatter. "With any luck, and if she agrees, Jessie may be performing in a live concert in February. The Mining County Annual Rock Fest! She has an audition on the first, with a band that needs a guitarist. I have no doubts that they'll love her."

Everyone, except for Luke and Maddy, clapped again. Chad put his hand on Jessie's shoulder. "Congratulations, Jessie, and best of luck."

Mike leaned over the table. "That's far out, Jessie. I went to that concert last year; it's killer. They always have a special guest band play. Last year it was Sweet Destruction." Mike winked at her and smiled. Jessie bit her bottom lip and shyly smiled back, while Maddy felt herself turn green.

After all the commotion died down and everyone was talking to each other, Luke got up and took Jessie's hand. "Can I talk to you for a minute?"

Jessie went with Luke and he walked her out to the lobby. He took her shoulders. "I want you to sit by me."

"Okay. What's wrong, Luke?"

"I just don't like that guy. I don't want you to sit by him. I love you."

Jessie could see in Luke's dark eyes that he was worried about something. "I love you too, Luke."

Her smile and sweet voice melted Luke's heart, and he felt ashamed at being jealous, but still, he couldn't contain it.

"I'm happy for you, Jessie, by the way. If that's what you want."

Luke wasn't happy at all. He suddenly felt the whole world coming between him and Jessie. He wanted to be involved in her life. He wanted to be a major part of her world. He wanted to be selfish and take her away, but he couldn't stand the troubled look on her little face. His eyes softened as he recovered his attitude and gently stroked her chin.

"I'm sorry, baby. I am happy for you." He paused, his eyes searching hers. "You're somethin' else, darlin'," he said and smiled. "Come on, let's go on back."

Jessie nodded, and they walked back to the table. Pete was taking pictures of everyone. Chad played lineman for UCLA, which gave Mike and him something in common to discuss. Jessie was content to sit next to Luke for the remainder of the evening. He whispered little sweet nothings to her and rubbed her leg with his foot. Luke's jealous display did not go completely unnoticed. Mike thought it funny that Luke got so jealous, even though he was becoming increasingly jealous of Luke. Debbie, however, was quite puzzled and decided it might be time to have a talk with Luke, and planned to do so, tomorrow. Maddy was relieved that Jessie sat next to Luke and not Mike. She tried not to stare at Mike, but couldn't help herself, seething with disappointment that he never once looked at her. Even Luke told her she looked nice, but Mike never said a word. Tired of Jessie always being the center of attention, Maddy couldn't wait for this horrible evening to end. She wanted to go home and get out of that gown, which obviously made no difference.

As everyone said their good-byes, Jessie found the courage and walked over to Mike, looking way up at him. Her little lips curled as she whispered, "Thank you, for the teddy bear, Mikey."

"You're welcome, bunny." He winked and kissed her cheek.

She lay in her soft, warm, bed that night, looking up at the bottom of Aimee's bunk, smiling. Though she was utterly exhausted, she could not imagine anything as pleasant as spending her first Christmas with her real family.

Sunday, December 30, 1973

Hank had gotten the bid for a custom remodel on a home over in Nepal. It was owned by a recently widowed woman whose name was Nancy. She reminded him a bit of his departed wife, Jessica. She wasn't as beautiful, but she was quiet like Jessica. Her husband's death left her grievous and she felt the remodel might lighten her spirits. Hank asked her to dinner one night and they began dating. Nancy found drinking with Hank seemed to ease her pain.
Hank took to staying over at her house, never mentioning that he had a daughter, nearly forgetting himself.

♫

After quietly throwing up in the bathroom that morning, Jessie ran to her new guitar in the family room and could be heard playing all over the neighborhood, for a minute. Until Uncle Harry asked her to turn it down. She only wanted to hear how loud it was. It took a bit of getting used to, hearing herself play the new guitar, but she quickly got the hang of it, and couldn't believe how awesome it sounded when she played bits of her favorite songs. She was excited, but at the same time feeling anxiety about the audition and possibly playing at the Rock Fest.

She was scheduled to audition as the lead guitarist for a band called, UnSed. They were a cover band playing mostly Led Zeppelin songs. Their guitarist had found a more suitable situation and they needed a replacement. Jessie's agent, Mr. Townsend, arranged for her to audition for them this Monday, New Year's

Day. She knew Jimmy Page inside and out and wasn't worried about that. She was worried about being on stage, and her dad. Debbie was excited too, though worried about getting Jessie's hopes up. She had an appointment with her lawyer, Mr. Burke, to meet with Jessie's father. She knew that was going to be a fight and could even make him even more resistant to allowing Jessie to visit. It was a big risk, but Jessie's future was important to her, and now she had help.

~

Maddy had been scheming with Jenny and wanted to keep her promise to Mike. Any attention from him was better than none, and this seemed the only way to impress him. That morning when the family was all sitting at the table for breakfast, she interrupted her parents who were talking.

"Mom, can me and Jessie go to the movies and then stay the night at Jenny's?"

Jessie looked up from her plate, surprised at not having been told anything about it. Maddy looked back at Jessie, waiting for her mom to answer. Usually, she didn't have a problem asking to stay the night with Jenny, but this time she felt guilty at her deception.

"I wanted to hang out with Jessie tonight, Momma," Aimee said, disappointed.

"Me too!" said Eli.

"You can tomorrow, Aimee," Maddy argued. "I already planned it with Jenny."

"Well I have plans, too!" Aimee snapped.

"Hold on, girls," Debbie said. "You're putting Jessie in an awkward situation. Jessie, what would you like to do?"

"Well," Jessie stuttered. "Um, I don't know." She looked at Aimee and Maddy who both had anxious faces. She decided it would be better not to make Maddy mad at her. "Well, I can go with Maddy today, and then Aimee tomorrow?"

"Isn't it your night to wash dishes?" Debbie asked Maddy.

"Aimee said she'd do them if I let her borrow my purple sweater."

"That doesn't sound like much of a bargain. Are you happy with that, Aimee?"

"Yeah, I guess," Aimee answered, getting a bit of pancake on her fork. Debbie turned to Maddy.

"Okay." Maddy rolled her eyes. "I'll do her dishes all next week."

"Far-out!" Aimee said.

"I'll do dishes, Auntie!" Jessie gladly offered.

"No, Maddy will do them," Debbie said. "You just have fun at the movies."

Debbie agreed and Maddy was relieved. She wanted to oblige Mike more than anything in the world and that was her only motive. Jessie's interests were insignificant.

"Thanks, Maddy," Jessie said to her. She'd been feeling down about Ricky being gone, and this was a happy surprise. She got up and took her plate to the sink and rinsed it off.

Maddy took Jessie's hand and walked her down the hall to her bedroom. She closed the door, speaking quietly.

"We're not really going to the movies, Jessie. Jenny's parents are out of town and we're planning another poker party," Maddy said, grinning. "You do wanna go, don't you?"

"Yes, Maddy." Jessie nodded. "I do." Her first thought was to ask Maddy if Luke could come, but, maybe later she would ask her.

"We're going to have so much fun." Maddy smiled. "You go on now," Maddy said, practically pushing Jessie out the door. "I have some things to do."

"Okay," Jessie squeaked looking back, curious at Maddy's mysteries.

Maddy shut the door. Hesitantly, she walked to her phone. She knew Mike's work number by heart and had called it one night just to hear his voice, but quickly hung up. Somehow, she also knew his work schedule by heart. She whispered to herself, "You can do this, you can do this." She took a deep breath and nervously dialed the number. Mike answered.

"Bill's Chevron, this is Mike."

Maddy gasped. She wasn't expecting to hear his voice so soon and couldn't speak right away.

"Hello!" he barked sarcastically, thinking it was just another chick playing games.

"Mike?"

"Yeah, who are you?" Mike said, curtly.

"It's Maddy."

"Maddy! What's goin' on?"

"Uh, tonight at Jenny's house; Jessie will be there."

"You're far-out, Maddy. What time?"

Maddy was so turned on by his deep, sexy voice; she could hardly pay attention to what he was asking her. *Far-out?* Her mind was spinning; she could barely breathe, let alone speak. *Oh, I hate you, why do I love you so much…* "Um, six-thirty…and-and Jenny said to bring Kevin." *Did I actually speak?*

"I thought she was through with him?"

"Well, Tommy broke up with her."

"Humph," Mike grunted. "Well, thanks a lot, Maddy."

"Mike! She--she doesn't know you're gonna be there."

"A'right; thanks, I owe you one." Mike hung up looking at his watch, contemplating the hours till then.

Maddy hung up disappointed and regretting her plot. Oh, the pangs of a young girl in love. It was ridiculous trying to impress Mike by setting Jessie up with the one man in the world she wanted Jessie the farthest away from and liking Mike so much was utterly miserable. All he cared about was getting it on with Jessie. He didn't even say good-bye.

Chapter Two – Children Behave

Ricky was gone, and Jessie worried she might never see him again. The bleakness of her past prevented her from imagining any future. The dark shadow of her world was like a wall that blinded her to anything beyond. Time for Jessie was only measured in the present moments that slipped quickly by. After breakfast, she spent the day moping around the house. Without Ricky there, she felt different. She stayed in Aimee's room with her for a bit, talking and playing her albums. Eli tried to show her how to ride his bike, but that didn't turn out well. Jessie didn't have the coordination for such things. Then she helped her aunt clean. That was something she was used to. She cleaned the bathrooms and insisted on helping Debbie clean out the refrigerator. Her mind kept going around in circles. She missed Ricky, but she couldn't stop thinking about Luke, either, and how upset he seemed. Depression was taking hold. She didn't know she could feel depressed at her Auntie's house like she did at home, and it disappointed her.

"Is something wrong, sweetheart?" Debbie asked.

"I miss Ricky," Jessie sighed, wiping a shelf of the fridge.

"I'm sorry, honey, but I'm here," Debbie said with a gentle smile.

"Yes." Jessie nodded. "Auntie, would you sit with me for a minute?"

"Of course." Debbie took Jessie over to the front-room sofa. Jessie sat next to her and lay her head down on Debbie's shoulder. Debbie stroked Jessie's face. "Do you really miss Ricky that much?"

"Yeah, I don't know what it is. I dis feel sad."

"Well, you know, you sort of always get like this when you come here. I think you focus too much on having to go back home and don't allow yourself to enjoy your time here."

Jessie nodded. "I guess tho."

"I know you said Ricky's not your boyfriend, but you seem pretty attached to him."

"Auntie, I think he's my best friend in the whole world." Jessie sat up, looking at her aunt. "I never known anyone that likes me tho much. *Well, 'cept Luke,* she thought. But, I can talk to Ricky real easy. Oh, I love being here with you, and Aimee, and Eli, they're my cousins, but I wish I could see Ricky, too, while I'm here."

"I understand and I'm sorry he's not here, honey, but you'll see him again." Debbie stroked Jessie's face. "I know it's hard on you, because you're so far away and alone all the time. We'll just have to keep you so busy you don't have time to feel sad. Tomorrow we'll all go out shopping and have a family day. How does that sound?"

"Good...Auntie, everything here seems, well, wild, confusing, like I never know what will happen, but I don't want to leave you, either. I love being here with you, and I like sitting here with you like this." Jessie laid her head back down on Debbie's shoulder.

Debbie stroked her face, again. "I love you so much, Jessie. I know it's upsetting for you, because you don't want to leave, and you're used to doing the same things every day. You have a routine and no one to upset it. I realize you're not used to being around so many people, but you'll have to get used to it. We're doing everything we can to keep you, and we want to keep you." Debbie sat up to look at Jessie. "Jessie, we're going to give you your own room."

"You are?" Jessie asked, looking up at her aunt.

"Yes. Uncle Harry and I are going to remodel the basement and put our bedroom down there, and that way you can have ours. It will be your own room. Won't you like that?"

Jessie's eyes lit up. "My own room? Here? Yes, I would!" She paused a moment and then with a serious face she asked, "Auntie?"

"What, sweetheart?"

"Can it be pretty like Aimee's and Maddy's?"

"Certainly. You can fix it however you like." Debbie smiled.

"Auntie?"

"Yes?"

"Can I call you Momma?"

Debbie took Jessie's face in her hands and kissed her forehead. "Oh, my Jessie," she sighed, "Of course you can. I'm so happy you're back in our lives. I want to be your Mom. I want you to feel happy and comfortable here with us. I want you to feel you're just as much my child as if you always were."

Jessie nodded as Maddy came out of the hallway from her room. "What's wrong?" Maddy asked.

"Nothing, Jessie just needed a little cheering up, that's all," Debbie answered, wiping her wet cheek.

"Well, come on, Jess." Maddy motioned to her. "It's time to get ready."

"There now, see?" Debbie said, stroking Jessie's hair. "You'll have fun at the movies."

"Thank you, Aunt--Momma," she said and went with Maddy into the bathroom. "Would Auntie really be mad if we're not really going to the movies?" she asked Maddy.

"Shhh, shut up, Jessie. What do you think?" Maddy answered, turning to the mirror to brush her hair.

"I don't want her mad at me."

"Cheer up, Jess. It'll be fun. It's just going to be us girls tonight. We decided to just hang out without any guy problems." Maddy felt bad deceiving Jessie like that, but she'd made a promise to Mike, and that was more important.

Jessie sighed, happy to go out with the girls and have fun. After all, she didn't get to hang out with Maddy and Jenny very often, and Maddy seemed to be being nice now. She liked hearing them talk about boys. It helped her feel more normal about herself, and she liked the independence she felt when she was with them.

Ready and waiting, Jessie sat on the sofa, watching TV with Eli, wondering why Maddy was taking so long to get ready.

Finally, Maddy came down the hall carrying her back pack. "You ready?"

Jessie nodded as she grabbed her overnight bag.

"Bye, Mom!" Maddy hollered.

"Bye, Momma!" Jessie also yelled and Maddy looked at her funny.

"Good night, girls. Have fun," Debbie said coming from the kitchen, "And be careful!"

As the girls drove off, Debbie heard Luke's Cuda pull up to his house. She thought now might be a good time to have that talk with him. She ran outside and hollered over to him as he was getting out of the car.

"Hi, Luke! I wonder if I might speak to you a moment?"

Shit, Luke thought. He'd tossed and turned all night, regretting his lack of discrepancy the night before, and now he was anticipating the repercussion. He took a deep breath. "Hey, Debbie," he said, walking toward her. "How are you?"

"Do you have a few minutes? I'd like to speak to you about Jessie."

Fuck. Luke cleared his throat. "Sure."

"Well, Jessie says you've been taking her to lunch. She tells me you're just friends and that you help her not feel so isolated."

Luke cleared his throat again. "Yes, ma'am, I have. I been kinda worried about her, all alone."

"I can understand that. I worry about her too." Debbie said, sensing that Luke was uncomfortable, but she had questions. "Luke, I'm gonna get right to the point. Last night, at dinner, I noticed you seemed a bit uneasy about the attention she was getting from Chad. Is there anything going on that I need to know about? I mean, with you and Jessie?"

"Well, no ma'am. Not really. It's pretty much like Jessie says, we're just friends." Luke desperately wished he could tell the truth and get it out in the open, but as yet, there wasn't any real truth. "I do like Jessie, ma'am, but she's well, kind of with Ricky. And, I just really care about her and…I'm, well, thank you for askin'."

"Luke." Debbie smiled. "I like you, Luke, I think you're a fine young man, and I'm glad that you care about Jessie. She needs good friends in her life."

"Yes ma'am. I think so, too."

The look in Luke's eyes and his awkward behavior, told Debbie what she wanted to know, and she intended to keep a close watch on the situation. "I just need to know what's going on with her. I love her terribly."

Luke forced a smile. "Sure, I know that, Debbie." He wanted to say more, but there was nothing to tell Debbie, because he really didn't know himself where he stood.

~

What the hell are you doing, Madison? Maddy asked herself as they pulled up to Jenny's condo and got out of the car. She was having serious regrets, dreading what inevitably was sure to take place. Not only was she deceiving Jessie, she was betraying herself. But the wheels were set in motion and there was no turning back, now. She took in a deep breath, looking at Jessie and knocked on the door.

"Come in girls!" Jenny grinned, opening the door. "Welcome, *hiccup*, to the pajama party!" She stumbled, almost falling over and grabbed the door. "Well, go get your pajamas on!"

"Drunk ass," Maddy chuckled, walking through the door.

"Pajama Party? What's a Pajama Party?" Jessie asked, setting her bag on the sofa with Maddy's. Jessie wondered what was wrong with Jenny but was at once distracted by a big lighted tree in the corner of the living-room.

"It's a, *hiccup*, party where the girls all come in their pajamas," Jenny giggled.

"And then what do we do?" Jessie asked.

"We gossip!" Jenny and Maddy both answered, laughing.

"Come on, Jess, let's go change," Maddy said.

"Gothiping is bad," Jessie announced, following Maddy into the downstairs bedroom.

"Come on, Jessie," Maddy replied. "Don't be a party pooper. What fun is girls' night if we can't gossip? How else are you gonna know about things if we don't talk about what's happening?"

"Oh," she said, unsure.

Jenny poured the girls each a large tumbler of Gallo, which she obviously had already started on, while the girls changed into their new pajamas. Jessie brought her teddy bear from Mike. She put her new pink sweat jacket on over her P.J.'s and put the teddy bear inside her jacket.

"What'd you bring that for?" Maddy asked, jealous about it.

"Well, I never had no teddy bear, well, I like him."

Resentful and not appreciating Jessie's lack of ever having anything she said, "Oh, well, aren't you kinda old for that, now?"

"Old? I'm not old," Jessie said, following disgruntled Maddy out to the dining table.

"Do you think he'll really show up?" Maddy whispered to Jenny.

"Who?" Jenny asked.

Maddy clicked her tongue. "Who do you think?"

"Mike?" Jenny blurted out loudly.

"Shhh, shut up!"

"What do *you* think, Maddy?" Jenny whispered, looking over at Jessie. "Why? Do you want me to call him, and tell him to forget it, now?"

Maddy shook her head and sat down at the table.

Jenny handed Jessie her glass of wine. "Is that the, *hiccup*, bear you got from Mike?"

"Mm hmm, isn't he the cutest bear?" Jessie took a sip, barely able to hold the huge glass and shook her head. The wine was sour in her cheeks.

"Oh, Maddy, guess what?" Jenny asked excitedly, grabbing Maddy's arm. "My parents are buying another condo in South Shore and they're going to let me live here by myself, when I turn eighteen!"

"What? Really?"

"Psyche," Jenny laughed.

"Jenny?"

"No, really, I was thinking like, maybe you could come live here with me and we could like drive to UNR together. Wouldn't that be bitchin'?"

"Shit, are you serious! That would be totally cool!" Maddy said and they both grabbed each other's arms and started jumping up and down. "I would *so* love that!" Maddy giggled. Jenny lost her balance and fell on the floor. Maddy put her hand to her mouth, laughing. "You're such a spaz, drunk ass."

Jessie smiled, watching them. She couldn't imagine anything so wonderful herself, and wished she were almost eighteen.

"Oh, you gotta, *hiccup*, hear my new album," Jenny said, picking herself up off the floor. "I got Elton John's *Tumbleweed Connection*."

Maddy asked helping her up, "Does it have that one song I like on it?"

"Come Down in Time," Jenny said, stumbling to the stereo.

The girls sat at the table with their glasses of wine, singing to the album. Jenny dealt out the cards and they began to play.

Maddy gulped down her wine, in a hurry to catch up with Jenny. "Come on, Jess, drink it down."

"It's thour," Jessie said, taking another taste.

"Just drink it fast, it won't be sour anymore."

Jessie gulped down half of her glass and shook her head. "Eww," she said quivering, and wiped her mouth. "That's kind of nasty."

Jenny laughed and poured them another pint, spilling half of it. "Did you see Taylor on Friday?"

"She looked ridiculous," Maddy smirked. "I'm surprised they didn't send her home, wearing that halter top."

Jessie didn't drink this glass so fast. It was making her sleepy, and she wanted to hear about Taylor, a person who was suddenly intriguingly, fascinating. Maddy snickered at Jenny, as she tried to put the bottle of wine back in the fridge.

"You should see Taylor, Jessie," Jenny said, almost dropping the bottle before she set it on the shelf.

"She is like, *thee* most ridiculous girl at school," Maddy said, giggling. "The guys are always cutting her down and she doesn't even get it. She dresses like *hiccup*, this big tramp and always chases after Mike, even after he's rude to her. Jessie was captivated, listening.

Taylor is like, madly in love with Mike, but he can't stand her," Jenny said.

"That!" Maddy exclaimed, tipping her glass, "is one girl, I would never be jealous of."

"For sure, you should see her stupid *hiccup*, face, Jessie," Jenny said, stumbling back to her chair. "She's all like, making weird flirty faces at him and *hiccup*; he always tells her to get the fuck, *hiccup*, away from him. But she's like, sooo dumb, she just keeps going back for more. She thinks she's like, so sexy, but she's so gross."

"You'd think she'd get it one day," Maddy hiccupped and slurred as she spoke. Suddenly Jessie felt sorry for Taylor and how they were talking that way about her.

"Do you know, Jessie?" Maddy toppled, anxious to discuss Mike, no matter the content. As long as his name passed her lips she was satisfied. "Just about every girl in school has like, this big crush on Mike. You should see the bathroom walls."

"And you too, Maddy?" Jessie asked, sadly.

Maddy stopped laughing and looked at Jessie.

"Don't you feel sorry for Taylor?" Jessie asked, puzzled.

"Sorry?" Jenny hiccupped, "No. Luke, too. Nobody can believe he broke up with Sissy. They've been together like, forever; it's kind of a bummer."

"I know," Maddy said. "I wonder if he likes someone else, and who the lucky girl is."

"We saw them at the mall in Reno," Jessie naively announced. "Taylor has a lot of make-up."

Maddy looked over at Jenny and the two of them stopped smiling. "You've seen Taylor, Jessie?" Maddy asked bewildered, "When? Who did you go to the mall with in Reno?"

"With Luke," Jessie innocently answered.

"What?!" Maddy snapped. "Luke? Luke Miller?"

Jessie nodded, smiling. "And we saw Sissy, too."

"You and Luke went to the mall together, and Sissy and Taylor were there?" Jenny asked.

"Mm hmm," Jessie muttered innocently, gulping a big swallow of wine and shaking her head. Maddy sat looking at Jessie, with a confused look on her face.

"Really, Jessie? And Sissy saw you? Did she say anything? How did she act?" Jenny asked.

"Mm hm, nothing, she didn't thay nothing." Jessie was somewhat excited to have her own bit of news to talk about, and the girls seemed so interested. "Taylor asked Luke how Mike was, though."

"Of course, she did, she's so stupid," Jenny smirked.

"Jessie, you went to the mall with Luke?" Maddy asked again, with a painful look on her face, still not believing she'd really heard that.

"Yes, is that why Mike doesn't like her? Because she's stupid?"

"That's only half of it!" Jenny laughed.

"When did you go to the mall with Luke, Jessie?" Maddy asked again, still not comprehending.

"Well, he picks me up for lunch at school thometimes."

"Like really?" Jenny asked, and she and Maddy both looked at each other.

"Since when, Jessie?" Maddy didn't believe her.

"Are you going out with Luke, Jessie?" Jenny asked. "I mean, is he like, your boyfriend?"

"No, he's dis my friend. Since I met him, Maddy."

"That must be why he broke up with Sissy. Everyone at school is like, totally shocked," Jenny said to Maddy, who was too stunned to speak, and it suddenly dawned on her about Luke being so weird with Jessie at dinner.

"It is." Jessie smiled, biting her finger. "He told me that's why, because of me."

"Jessie, do you have any idea how popular Luke and Mike are, and how impossible it is to go out with either one of them?" Maddy snapped.

"I'm not sure how you mean? Is that 'portant?"

Jenny and Maddy looked at each other. Maddy couldn't help but be jealous of Jessie just then, but was intrigued by her, too. They were both intrigued by how every damn one of those Miller boys wanted her, and Jessie seemed so dumb about it. The Miller Boys!

"Have you had sex with Luke?" Maddy asked under a scowling, worried brow. Jessie wasn't sure if she should answer that, but they were both staring at her with eager eyes, and she nodded.

"For heaven sake," Jenny said in disbelief. "Like, when? Where?"

"Well, once we went to Lake Tahoe to a cabin," Jessie said, brushing the hair from her forehead. "But he only kissed me." She wasn't sure why this all seemed so important.

"Our cabin?" Maddy asked.

"Yeah, then once at a big place in Reno, then to a Motel in Smith Valley, and thometimes, in the car."

"I don't believe it! I don't believe you, Jessie!" Maddy snapped. She could feel her face red with anger. "I thought you said he wasn't your boyfriend?"

"He's not my boyfriend." Jessie frowned. "I wanted to ask you if Luke could come here tonight, but I guess then we couldn't have a girls' night."

"Ooh no," Maddy answered adamantly, shaking her head. "Not tonight. Why are you having sex with him if he's not your boyfriend, Jessie? What about Ricky?"

Jessie's eyes turned grievously intense. "Luke loves me."

"My God, Jessie." Maddy felt like her heart was broken and all she could do was look at Jessie. "I don't understand, Jessie."

Jessie was getting flustered now and was totally confused by this questioning. She had no idea how to answer.

"We...ell," she stuttered. "I 'on't know. He asked me to be, but, anyway, I don't want no boyfriend. They dis break up with you and make you cry."

"God, Jessie." Maddy shook her head. "Don't you know you just don't go around having sex with guys, unless they're like, your boyfriend?"

"Why?" Jessie asked, confused. "Am I going to be in trouble now, Maddy?"

"Because Jessie. You just don't. Someone's gonna get hurt. Even I haven't had sex yet. What if you get pregnant?"

"Oh," Jessie gulped, and a surge of anxiety past through her body. She felt she'd said too much now, and had no intention of saying anymore, especially about the pregnant part. She was trying not to remember about that, and her logic about such things was not adequate enough to contemplate or practice any common sense. She knew when she felt uncomfortable, but she didn't always know why.

Maddy was quite disgusted now and wished she hadn't invited Mike. She knew that was exactly what Mike was planning. *Disgusting pig,* she thought, and she could see how ignorant Jessie was about the whole thing. She felt so jealous and cheated. She lived next door to those boys all her life, and hoped one day they might at least, treat her like a human being, and now, along comes Jessie, and only after a brief encounter, they were all over her. It was so unfair. She looked at Jessie though, and for a moment, felt sorry for her. Like maybe, they were taking advantage of her ignorance. Maybe, she was, too.

"Are you going to tell on me to Momma now, Maddy?" Jessie asked. Her face was quite distressed.

Maddy forced half a smile. "I guess not, Jess. I guess we have to keep our secrets confidential if we're going to hang out together. But you have to do the same for me."

"I will, Maddy. Thank you, Maddy, for not telling on her to me."

"Hey, let's have some more wine," Jenny interrupted. "And talk about something else?"

"I don't want no more," Jessie said, just as Matt, April, and Jake came in the door.

"The Poker god has arrived!" Matt said loudly, as he walked into the kitchen carrying a case of beer.

Jenny ran over to April and they hugged each other, all googly. "Your hair looks great!" Jenny said, seeing that April had gotten a permanent wave.

"Thanks," April replied, "I just had it done last week."

Jessie, now oblivious to the fact that it was supposed to be 'girls' night', was glad to see more people, and relieved about the interruption. She liked Matt and April, and she could see Maddy was happy to see Jake there. He sat next to Maddy and gave her a kiss.

"I see you girls have already started to party," Matt said, putting the beer away in the fridge. "Here babe," he said to April, handing her one.

"While we were like, *hiccup* waiting on the beer, we had a little, *hiccup*, wine," Jenny giggled.

"I think more than a little," April chuckled and set her purse down on the counter, opening her beer.

"You girls ready to lose at poker tonight? Matt asked, handing the girls all a beer. "Jake, a beer?"

"Does a bear shit in the woods?" Jake answered.

"Well, come get it. I'm not your serving wench."

"We're not going to lose at poker, Matt," Jessie said, quite seriously.

"Well, we shall see, little one. We shall see." Matt sat down at the table and picked up the deck of cards.

~

Mike, the cocky, Joe-jock stud, and heart-throb of nearly every girl at Mining High, didn't remember ever feeling as nervous or anxious. All he could think about all day was Jessie, and finally getting to see her. He couldn't wait to get home and take a shower. Kevin called him to see if he was ready.

"I'm takin' my own car, man. Just meet me over there," Mike told him.

"She really broke up with Tom and asked me to come, huh?"

"That's what she said."

"Right on!" Kevin exclaimed. "I *love* that girl in bed."

"Keep your shit to yourself," Mike snorted, not wanting to get any visualization. "I'm not goin' in till you get there, so don't fuck around."

"Why not?"

"Why do you think, shithead? They're your dorky ass friends, not mine. I'm only goin' for one reason."

"Yeah, that would be a hot little blonde, with big ole tits."

They both managed to get to Jenny's at the same time. Kevin charged through the door, with Mike following him.

"Aw, more of my minion," Matt spoke out in a funny voice.

"What's a fricken minion?" Kevin asked. He went over to Jenny, who giggled, and eagerly accepted his kiss.

"It's a thbordinate," Jessie answered, kneeling on her chair, in her new pink pajamas and stocking feet.

Mike chuckled and immediately pulled out the chair next to Jessie. He took his jacket off and hung it on the back of the chair. Massively, huge muscles bulged out of the sleeves of his light blue T-shirt, and his alluring hazel eyes were smiling as he sat down, looking at Jessie.

Maddy watched him, feeling pangs of jealousy, but there wasn't a thing she could do about it. This whole set up was her fault, and now she was there with Jake, so she'd just have to try to endure it. And Jenny was so fickle, giggling and slobbering all over Kevin.

"Hi, Mikey." Jessie smiled, slightly intoxicated. She was leaned over the table holding her cards. "Did you come to play cards at the Pajama party?" she asked, raising her brow.

"I did." Mike moved his chair in closer to Jessie. "You haven't been drinking, have you, little bunny girl?"

Jessie hiccupped, nodding. Her eyelids were falling, her hair was all messy and she was toppling a little in her chair.

Damn, you're beautiful, he thought, unable to take his eyes off her. "Bad girl," Mike said, smiling. "You serving alcohol to minors, Matt?"

"You betcha. Hand me all your cards," Matt answered, gathering the cards being tossed to him.

"I'm not nervous of you now, Mikey." Jessie set her cards down in front of her and sat down on her feet, watching curiously at Mike.

"Nervous? What are you nervous about, Bunny?" He picked up Jessie's cards tossing them to Matt and took a cigarette out, lighting it. Kevin handed him a beer and Mike offered the cigarette to Jessie.

"Ick," she said, holding her hand up. "They make me thick." She put her lips out and closed her eyes. "Why do you keep calling me that?" she asked, wobbling.

Mike contemplated her lips, her hair, her face. *My heart is pounding. Where did you come from?* He leaned toward Jessie.

"Because you're a cool chick, and bunnies are soft, like you." Mike smiled, stroking her arm.

Maddy watched, regretfully, and couldn't believe how Mike was talking to Jessie. She would never have imagined him being remotely sweet in any possible way. Neither did he.

"That's why I'm nervous of you, when you do that," Jessie said, pulling away from his hand.

"You mean touch you?" Mike smiled.

"Yeth."

"What's that in your jacket, Jessie?"

"My bear." She took it out of her jacket and rubbed it on her face looking at Mike and then closed her eyes.

"That's a lucky little bear," he said, leaning his head on his arm.

"You gave it to me." She was about ready to fall over.

"Yeah, you probably shouldn't drink anymore, little girl. You look sleepy."

"Okay," she answered, putting the bear back in her jacket, and took a drink of her beer. "I'm not a bad girl, Mikey."

"Well, don't drink, bunny."

"Maddy says wine's not sour if you drink it fast."

"She did, huh?" Mike said, stroking Jessie's hand. "It's not sour, if you don't drink. You shouldn't be drinking, Jessie."

"Well, you're drinking."

"Yeah, but you're preg…uh, you're a baby."

"I'm not a baby." Jessie pulled her hand away.

"Yeah, ya are."

"I'm mad at you!" Jessie snapped, frowning.

Mike chuckled, "Why, cuz I don't want you to drink?"

"Because, you said I'm a baby!"

"Gimme that beer." Mike grinned, attempting to take it.

"No. Go away."

"Aright, suit yourself, get drunk." Mike picked up his hand of cards.

"Um, Mikey, Maddy thays you got a car. A theventy Chevelle?"

"I did. You wanna see it, it's pretty decent."

"After the game." Jessie hiccupped, looking at her new hand of cards. "This is a bunch of *crap,*" she said, frowning. "Why did you get a Chevelle?" she asked, trying to arrange her cards, and keep her eyes open.

"For you, let me see," Mike said, trying to look at her hand.

"No, get away." She frowned, holding her cards against her chest. "Cheater."

"Cheater?" Mike laughed at her small, but deadly voice.

"Kevin, tell Mikey to not look at my cards."

"You want me to smack the fuck out of him, honey? Kevin answered, arranging his own cards.

Jessie grinned, toppling back and forth in her chair, and snorted, "Yeah."

"Maybe he'll let us all smack the fuck out of him, Jessie," Matt said. "I'm not used to seeing him without a black eye."

"You're a funny fucker," Mike smirked, holding his cards in his lap, looking at Jessie.

"What are you gonna do, chuckle fuck?" Matt asked Jake.

"I'm gonna fold, you fat fucker, because of this bogus hand you dealt me," Jake answered.

"Ooh, foul language and name calling," Matt said. "Why don't you go put your bikini on and make some snow angels out in the snow, or go downtown and solicit some male sex?"

"Ha-ha, real funny, dream on," Jake answered, while the girls were all cracking up.

Jessie laid her head down on her arm looking at Mike. "You guys are funny."

Mike grinned. "It's your turn Jessie, aren't you gonna play?"

"Play what?"

"Cards."

"Oh-I-I." She sat up looking at her hand. "They won't be still."

"Let me help you, baby." Mike coddled her, reaching for her cards with his cigarette hanging out of his mouth.

"Stop that!" Jessie said and slapped his hand away. She laid down a small straight, flicking the cards with her finger.

"Son-of-a-bitch," Jake whined.

"Jesus, you're the little cheater, Jessie," Mike said. "I thought you said you had a hand full of crap?"

Jessie leaned over at Mike, smiling, trying to keep her eyes open. "That's because, I was using my poker face like Matt says when you have a good hand."

"Oh really?" Mike grinned. "So now we know when you have a good hand, because you start lying."

"Lying?" Jessie asked. "I didn't lie."

"What do you call it then, bunny?"

"Um, Mikey, what color is your car?"

Mike laughed taking a drag of his cigarette, looking at his hand. "Aright, bunny, it's blue."

"I think we better catch up with these girls," Kevin said, chugging down his beer and getting up to get another one. "Anybody else while I'm up?" He threw a joint to Mike. "Here, light that."

"Yeah, bring us all another brewsky," Matt replied.

"Mikey, what is that cigarette you are smoking?" Jessie asked. "It smells funny."

"It's mary ju wanna." Kevin answered. "Pass it here."

"It's pot, bunny," Mike said, trying to hold in his hit and handed it to Kevin.

Jessie sat up to look at Mike. "Pot? Pot is a drug, isn't it?"

"Yeah," Mike coughed.

"Aren't you afraid of doing a drug?"

Kevin laughed, "You know that retarded kid, Eric, Mike?" he asked. "Bogie gave him a hit of acid and he spazzed out in P. E. last Friday. Coach was givin' him a bunch of shit at first and all the guys were laughing, then Gary burned him and told Coach what happened. He was fuckin' pissed."

"That's not cool, man," Matt spoke up.

"It was funny as shit," Kevin chuckled. "Gary told Bogie he was gonna beat the fuck out of him."

"It ain't funny, dumb fuck. Bogie's a fuckin' loser," Mike said, looking at Jessie. "What if someone did that to Jessie? How fuckin' funny would it be then?"

They were all a bit shocked at Mike's instant anger. Even Mike was surprised.

"What would they do to me, Mikey?" Jessie asked.

"Give you drugs, Jessie. Don't take anything from anyone."

"I don't take drugs, Mikey."

"Well, you might not know it's a drug."

"Because I am retarded?" Jessie asked, quite seriously.

"What? No, Jessie," Mike said. "Because, they might put it on something and you wouldn't know it."

"Why?" Jessie asked.

"Some drugs are invisible, Jessie," Matt said. "They could put it on anything and you wouldn't know it."

Mike looked sternly at Jessie. "Don't take anything from anyone."

"What the fuck's the matter with you?" Kevin asked Mike, curious at Mike's sudden, unusual behavior. "Are you gonna give us all a lecture about drugs now, Mike?" Kevin grinned.

"No dumb fuck. Didn't you hear anything I just said?"

"All right, man. Let's just fuckin' drop it. Sorry I said anything," Kevin said, looking at his hand of cards, feeling a bit embarrassed that he brought it up.

Mike normally wouldn't have thought much about what Kevin had just told him, but knowing Jessie now, made him feel strangely concerned about Eric *and* Jessie.

"Let's go talk out in the living room," April said to Jenny and Maddy, no longer interested in playing cards, or Mike and Kevin arguing.

"Why don't you have a Pepsi, bunny?" Mike said, seeing Jessie falling asleep.

"I want beer, not *Pepsi*." Jessie pouted, putting her head up. She yawned a big yawn and put her head back down on her arm and closed her eyes. "Can I have a thigarette now, Mikey?"

"Ooh Mikey, can I have a thigarette, too?" Kevin mimicked Jessie and lay down his cards.

Mike gave Kevin a look. "You really wanna go down this road, son?"

Kevin cleared his throat, rubbing his nose. "Sorry, Jessie."

Matt heckled, "Way to back down, jack ...off."

"I can't play no more," Jessie said, handing Mike her cards. "Here Mikey, you help me."

"Don't drink anymore, baby."

"Okay." She closed her eyes.

Mike picked Jessie up and laid her down on the sofa.

"We're sleepy," Jessie said. She took out her bear and held it against her face.

"I know ya are." Mike pulled the blanket over her. He stroked her cheek and went back to the table.

~

It was one in the morning when Mike took his boots off and lay down behind Jessie on the sofa.

"I'm cold," Mikey."

Mike wrapped his arms around her and whispered in her ear, "Wanna go upstairs and git under the covers, bunny?"

"Yeah."

Mike let her body fall into the middle of the sofa as he laid over her and gently kissed her lips.

"No, don't," she said, with her eyes still closed.

Mike kissed her again. "What do you mean, don't?"

"Don't kith me."

"I wanna kiss you, Jessie. I dig kissing you. I been missing you, thinking about you." He kissed her again.

Jessie looked up at Mike and he stared back at her.

"Let's go upstairs baby, and git warm."

"I can't."

"Why? I thought you said yes," he whispered, kissing her neck. "I miss you, Jessie."

"Don't mith me, Mikey."

"I can't help it. I miss you. You're so beautiful," he said kissing her lips again. "Beautiful and sweet, I wont you, baby."

"No."

"Please don't tell me no, Jessie. I came here just to see you."

"You did see me, already. You're trying to make me want you," Jessie said, trying to keep her eyes open. "You're not my boyfriend."

"Jessie, stop saying that to me," Mike said, kissing her neck, her face, her chest. "I want you to want me, Jessie. Don't make me beg. Let's go upstairs." Mike unzipped her jacket and kissed her breasts through her top. "Come own, baby. Let me make love to you."

Jessie began to breathe heavy. "But Mikey…"

"I want you, Jessie."

"Mikey, no. Everybody wants me, now. Maddy thez I can't have thex no more."

"Fuck her." Mike said and lay his head down on her chest for a minute. He moved up to her mouth and kissed her again, pulling softly on her lips. "Baby," he whispered. "Pretty baby, I'm not wantin' sex. I wanna make love to you." He moved his head back down to her chest.

"Mikey," she panted. "Do you have my…oh, my name in your book?"

"What book?" he asked, unable to release his mouth from her.

"The black book…oh, you have with all…oh, all the girls' names in it."

"I don't have a book like that." He slid his hand up under her top and caressed her breasts, kissing her lips. "You're so soft, baby." Jessie was panting and couldn't stop rocking her chest. "You're so beautiful," he whispered, "little tittie girl."

"Mikey…"

Mike picked Jessie up and took her upstairs, laying her on the bed. He shut the door, locking it, and laid down over Jessie. Slowly, he kissed her again and again, as each kiss provoked in him a wanting he never thought possible. "I haven't been able to stop thinking about you, sweet young thing."

Jessie felt helpless, with unfamiliar emotions, with no understanding of these new sensations that were awakening in her. She didn't realize the depth of being close to someone, someone who wanted to be close with her. She never knew it was possible that someone might love her or think she was important. She didn't know how to fight off the ecstasy of the moment. She was over-powered and flattered by Mike wanting her, unable to contemplate or determine his sincerity. But something else was stirring in her; a darkness from the past. Not a memory, but a sense of fear that she didn't understand.

"Mikey," she whispered, holding on to his upper arms and squeezing the muscles. "I'm not afraid of you."

Mike stopped to look at her. "I don't want you to be afraid of me, Jessie."

"I won't be scared of you."

"I don't want you to be scared of me. Why? Are you scared?"

"I'm not scared of you," Jessie answered defiantly. "I won't be scared of nobody. You could bite me and pinch me, and I won't *ever* be scared."

"Jessie, what are you talkin' about? I won't ever do that to you…why? Did someone do that to you?"

"You might," Jessie said, looking into his eyes.

"Baby, I won't ever hurt you. Don't be afraid of me, Jessie."

Mike pushed himself up on his arms and began to undress her. His youthful desire took over any sensibility he might have contemplated, having only one thing on his mind. She was beautiful, and he felt extremely intimidated by her. Making love to Jessie was the sweetest…pleasure…Mike had…ever…known.

~

Mike stroked Jessie's little hand as she slept, watching her face as she breathed, wondering about her mysteries. Her eyes opened, and she smiled.

"Talk to me, Jessie."

Her face peeked out from under her hair. "Talk to you 'bout what?"

He smoothed the hair away from her face. "Why did you think I would hurt you?"

"Because, I think I'm bad," she said, staring at him.

He caressed her face, stroking her hair, "Bad? Why? Why would I hurt you for making love? Making love isn't bad, it feels good. Don't you like it?"

"Well, I'm not s'pose to do that."

"Jesus, Jessie," Mike said, rubbing his forehead. "Jessie, everyone does that, that doesn't mean you're bad. Why do you think you're bad, because something feels good?"

"Because…because I'm stupid." Jessie squinted, glaring seriously at Mike.

"You're not stupid, Jessie." Mike took her face in his hands. "You're brilliant."

"Well, I'm retarded," she said, frowning.

"What? Why do you say that? Who told you that, anyway?"

"No one, I dis know. People…I read about people like me. I know I'm like that. I don't think good. Maddy thinks I'm stupid."

Mike brushed Jessie's face with gently sweeping lips. "I don't care what Maddy thinks, and you shouldn't either. You're not stupid, baby. You're beautiful. You're brilliant and beautiful. You play violin so pretty, you're so talented. Don't say you're retarded. It's not bad to feel good, and you don't have to be hurt, Jessie. Who else hurt you?"

"Nobody."

"Why d'you think I would?"

"Well, you have glasses."

"Glasses? What does that have to do with anything?"

Jessie eyes had a strange, almost eerie look on her face.

"What'd that fucker do to you, Jessie?"

"Who?"

"The *he* you're not telling me about, when I asked…"

Jessie rolled over, looking at the wall. "Don't talk to me no more."

Mike leaned over Jessie, stroking her face. "I'm sorry," he said, wanting to be inside her head.

Jessie turned to look at him. "Um, Mikey, do you have a girlfriend?"

Mike shook his head. "No," he muttered. He was distracted; feeling almost guilty, if that were possible for Mike. He didn't know much about her background, but he remembered once she'd started to tell him about someone that hurt her as a child, and it must have twisted something up in her head. Something happened to her and she was trying to make sense of it in a peculiar way. Her sweet innocence was so endearing to him. He caressed her face until she closed her eyes and laid his head on her chest.

Monday, December 31, 1973

Mike woke up to the most beautiful, little angel ever created. Her face was as pure and sweet as ever he had seen, but it held a sadness that drew him in. Her long, flowing, hair was spread out, cascading over her little body, like a blanket of silver. Her tiny hands framed her precious, little bunny face, and her big, pouty, lips were begging to be kissed. She was so unreal, so perfect, like some wild little creature. He was bewildered, as if under a spell. He held her hand in his, amazed at how his hand completely enveloped hers. Her breath was so soft. He couldn't resist kissing her lips. Jessie halfway opened her eyes and smiled at him. Her eyes were strange, and somewhat frightening, but altogether captivating and full of mystery. He was so in awe of her. He pulled her tightly to him. She rolled over and put her arms up around his neck, rubbing her breasts across his stomach as she kissed his chest. She said something to him in some different language with her soft, sweet voice. He didn't know what it was, but it was wild.

"What did you just say to me?" he asked.

"Je veux que vous, vous êtes Mon grand garcon sexy." She smiled with her eyes half open.

"What does that mean?" he whispered, smiling.

"I want you. You're my big thexy boy."

"Where'd you learn to talk like that?" Mike grinned, rubbing her back. "You speak French, baby?"

"Oui."

"Do you lisp in French, cute little girl?

"I don't lisp." She quickly pouted, frowning.

"Yes, you do." Mike smiled and tickled her neck with his lips. "Damn, I don't know how you could ever think you're retarded." Mike kissed her forehead. "Little kitten."

"Meow, meow," Jessie purred.

Mike pulled her over on top of him and held her tight against his chest, his eyes searching hers, as he stroked the silky strands of her silver flowing hair. "Mmm, baby, you feel so good. You got it, baby…You got it all over me. You know that, don't you?"

Jessie closed her eyes, laying her head down on his shoulder.

"The first time I saw you, I was sprung. You and your pink nail polish. I haven't stopped thinking about you since that day." He stroked his hand down her back, caressing her hair against her body. "I was hot for you the minute you asked me if I liked your damn pink nail polish. I never saw anything so beautiful in my life. The way you walk in those tight ass jeans, and your cowboy boots. I never saw anything as sexy in a pair of jeans. The way you caught that football, and looked up at me when I tackled you, your beautiful face that intimidates the fuck out of me, that first kiss that still blows my mind. I can't forget those things, Jessie. I see your face a hundred times a day in my head. I'm so hot for you, little girl," Mike said, hugging her and smoothing his hands all over her body.

She couldn't say anything. She was confused by most of it, though she knew it meant he liked her. She rolled over next to him on her side, rubbing her bottom against him, holding her hair up over her head. He looked down at her body.

"Yeah, you know you're fuckin' beautiful, don't you?" He caressed her, studying her curves. She put her arm up around his neck. "Jessie, the French girl," he whispered, caressing her underarms.

"I am French, Mikey. My Grampa was a French, from Weeziana."

"Mmm."

Jessie put her finger in his mouth. "Mikey, did you say you got a Chevelle, for me?"

"I did. You haven't come outside to see it yet."

"For me?"

"Yeah, for you, bunny. It's a bad-ass car, just like you."

Jessie pulled her Teddy bear out from under her and held him up in the air, swinging his arms. She giggled, with a little piggy snort.

"What made you think I have a black book with girl's names in it?" Mike smiled, pushing her lip up with his finger.

"Maddy says guys have books they write girls names in." She laid teddy on her chest.

"Maddy," Mike scowled. "That girl don't know shit about me. Well, I don't, and if I did, your name would be the only name in it...Jessie, how can I see you more than never? Why are you still wearing my chain?"

"Quiet, Mikey," she whispered. "Don't talk about that...does it have baby moons?" She lifted her brow.

"No, Cragars," Mike answered, kissing her neck, "I wanna talk about it...Jessie."

"No, I have to go to sleep, now." Jessie yawned, closing her eyes.

Mike sighed, "You're impossible, Jessie."

~

Mike woke again to the room lighted by the morning sun, holding Jessie as tight against him as he could. He couldn't comprehend how anyone could be so beautiful, looking at her and feeling intimidated by her looks. He leaned over, kissing her little mouth with her thumb in it. He felt dizzy staring down at how adorable she was. She always gave him some new surprise. Her little Teddy bear was squashed down between her breasts, but she was so adorable with that stupid little bear. He felt relieved she didn't have to rush off this time. He snuggled up to her, slipping his finger under the chain around her waist, caressing her belly. Jessie stretched her body and opened her eyes halfway, noticing Mike staring at her. She rolled over toward him.

"Why are you looking at me?" she asked, feeling shy.

"I'm not allowed to look at you?" he said getting up on his arm. "You're still wearing my chain?"

"Well, you're dis staring at me."

"Okay, so I won't look at you, fuck," he said, lying down.

"Because you gave it to me," she sighed, cuddling up to his chest. "I don't have to leave, Mikey."

Mike took her hand and put it up to his mouth and sucked on her thumb. "You always suck your thumb?"

She blushed at her embarrassment and pulled her thumb out of his mouth. "I don't thuck my thumb, and you don't know that!"

"Pff, oh, really?" He chuckled, grinning down at her little frown. "And you don't lisp, either."

She stretched her legs out of the blanket. "No!"

"Your little toes are pink. How come your fingernails aren't painted?" he asked, rubbing her fingers.

"Because...I got in trouble at school, I couldn't get it all off and we're not allowed to wear polish, and I had to do detention."

That's bullshit. Don't you have polish remover?"

"Mm mmm."

Mike leaned his head on his arm. "How long can you hang out with me, Jessie?"

"I don't know. I have to ask Maddy. They said they wanted to go to the mall and go ice-skating."

"You know how to skate?"

"No, I never have." She ran her finger over his chest, looking at it.

"I'll teach you how." Mike's deep voice echoed through his chest.

"You know how?"

"Yeah, we go all the time. Well, we use to. They put that new mall up around the big pond."

"I know. My daddy's company did. Nelson's Construction."

"Really? Your dad owns Nelson's? I bet he got a bank load of money on that deal. It's pretty nice. Your dad built that mall and you've never been there?

"Mm mmm."

"I'll take you there, baby," Mike said, running his finger under the chain around her waist. "You can ride in my car with me. We can eat breakfast. They have a coffee shop, or somethin' there."

Hearing breakfast, Jessie jumped out of bed and ran into the bathroom. She threw up in the toilet, coughing.

"Guess that means you don't want breakfast, does it, bunny?"

Jessie gagged again. She sat on the toilet to go pee, and then rinsed out her mouth.

Mike held the blanket up as she climbed back in bed. "Little naked girl. You been having a lot of morning sickness?" he asked, pulling her close.

"Every day." She closed her eyes and pulled the blankets up over her head, cuddling up to his chest.

"I'm sorry. That's no fun."

"How do *you* know I'm pregnant?"

"Luke."

"He told you?" she said, pulling her head out of the blanket, looking at him.

"Well, yeah, I gotta help take care of you, don't I?" Mike paused, "It could be mine."

"Even if you use a rubber?"

"Well, they don't always work. I'm sorry you're pregnant, Jessie. We're pretty stupid all wantin' you like this. I know we must be making things hard on you," Mike said stroking her cheek. "If you weren't so damn irresistible. It's pretty sick, isn't it? It's gonna hafta be up to you, to choose one of us, if that's what you want."

"Choose? What do you mean, choose?"

"Well, we can't all be your boyfriend, Jessie. You're gonna hafta pick one of us, or none of us."

"But none of you are my boyfriend. Why do I have to pick?"

"Jessie, are you really that ignorant? Someone's gonna get hurt."

"Why? Who will be hurt?"

"Who do you think, bunny? The one who doesn't get picked.

"Does it mean, if you have thex, you have to be my boyfriend, like Maddy says?"

"Well, I guess not. But I'd like to be," Mike said, resting his chin on her head.

"I don't want to talk about this no more." She hid her face under the blankets. He rolled over putting his face down in hers.

"Mikey, you make my pee-pee feel good. Why does that feel tho good?"

He grinned. "I don't know, but it does, doesn't it?"

"Do you feel like I feel when that happens?" she asked, pulling the blanket down.

"Yeah."

"And you're not bad?"

"No, baby."

"Or me?"

Mike shook his head, smiling at her.

"Good things are always like that, aren't they, Mikey? They come fast and go away fast. Like cuming, or Christmas, or a good song, or being with you." Jessie stroked his face. "Or people you love."

"Yeah, but you get to do it again." Mike lay next to her, resting his head on his arm, looking down at her. He picked up Teddy and said, "Teddy and I have decided to give these two names." He rolled over her and gently held her breasts up, admiring them.

"Why did you dethide that?"

"Well, cuz Teddy likes these two so much, they need a name. This one is gorgeous," Mike said pulling on her right nipple with his lips. "So, her name is Gigi. And this one is beautiful," he said pulling on the other one. "So, her name is Beebe."

"When did Teddy tell you that?" Jessie asked skeptical, looking down at Mike's smile.

"This morning, when you were asleep, and he was suffocating between them."

"That's silly, Mikey," Jessie snorted. "Teddy doesn't talk."

Mike laughed. "Yeah." His eyes were beaming with adoration for her.

"Are you laughing at me?" She pouted.

"No baby. You're cute," he said smoothing his hand down her body. "I love your little pussy."

"What?"

"You never heard pussy, before?" he asked, raising his brow.

"Well, it's what my dad always calls Carl, and what you call Kevin."

Mike laughed. "Baby, this," he said, gently squeezing her.

"Why?"

"Because, it's soft and furry, like a kitten."

"Oh? Then why is Kevin and Carl soft and furry?"

Mike laughed, again. "Jessie, come on. When a guy says that to another guy, he's calling him a little, scared-ass bitch. I mean, the guy is scared, like a little girl."

"Men get scared?"

"Some."

"Do you get scared?"

"No."

"Is that because you have big muthles?" she asked, rubbing his chest and arms.

"I have muscles cuz I'm built that way, and I lift weights."

"And, if I lift weights and have muthles, then I won't be scared. I won't be a pussy."

"Jesus, Jessie." Mike laughed. "You're so dumb. Do I have to explain everything to you?"

"That's because I am *dumb!*" she frowned, not thinking Mike was funny at all.

"Baby, what did I tell you last night? You're not dumb. I'm just playin' with you. Don't say that."

"Yeth I am. That's why people don't like me. That's why the girls at school don't like me and call me names, and you call me names, because I am dumb!"

"I never call you names and that's not why they don't like you. They don't like you because you're so beautiful and they're jealous. They don't like you because you're so smart and they're ignorant cunts."

"What does that mean?"

"Never mind. What names could they possibly call *you*?" he said, smiling.

Jessie frowned, and her eyes began to water. She didn't want to answer that.

"Tell me, I'll go beat 'em up," Mike said, laying over her, holding her face.

"They call me...they call me, *piss-ant*."

Mike chuckled, "Piss-ant?"

"You're laughing at me." Jessie began to cry.

Mike took her face in his hands. "I'm sorry, baby, you're so cute. Want me to go to your school and beat 'em all up?" Mike smiled, caressing her face. "I'd be your little boyfriend if I went to school with you and tell 'em all to fuck off."

"We don't have no boys at school," Jessie sniffed. "If you went to school with me," Jessie said, pondering. "They always lisp and call me *Jethie Nelthon.*" Jessie sarcastically cocked her head.

Mike took his finger tracing her mouth and pushed her top lip up. "Your mouth is so sexy. You make such cute little faces with it; you talk so cute with it. I wanna put my lips all over it."

"You're tho handsome, Mikey." She traced his lips with her finger. "Maddy and Jenny say all the girls at school are in love with you. How come you're not a boyfriend to any of them? Don't you like any of them?"

"No."

"You don't like no girls?"

"I like girls. I like you, don't I?"

"Maybe if you weren't tho handsome they wouldn't like you no more."

"And maybe if you weren't so beautiful everyone would leave you alone?"

"Maybe."

"I don't think so, Jessie. You're beautiful from the inside out."

"Maybe you don't think about them right. Maybe you don't think about them like friends, just thex."

"You're right. I don't need *girl*friends. They wanna hang all over you, make you call them all the time, play head games, and talk about stupid shit. I'd fuck most of them if they didn't come with all the bullshit."

"And we are talking about stupid shit?"

"No. Yeah, you make me talk like an idiot." Mike smiled at her.

"You might one day, Mikey. Maddy loves you."

"I know that," he answered, not wanting to hear it.

"She can't help it, Mikey. You *are* thuper handsome and strong. She gets sad when you ignore her. Don't you want to fuck her?"

"What?" Mike chuckled, surprised. "*No*. Don't talk like that."

"Well, you do."

"She's not my type, and why should I have to pay attention to her? And why do you want me to like other girls? Are you trying to get rid of me?"

"I want you happy."

"I am happy. I'm the happiest fuckin' guy in the world right now. Why don't you think I'm happy?"

"Because, you don't have no girlfriend?"

"Having a girlfriend doesn't always make a guy happy, Jessie. Why don't you want a boyfriend?"

"Because, he will make me cry."

Mike looked down at Jessie's little face, wondering if he would make her cry.

"I think you're cranky, now," she said.

"I'm not cranky. I will be though, if you don't shut up about this." Mike began kissing her neck.

"Thee how mean you are?"

"I'm not mean, baby, I'm horny," Mike said as he laid over her. "Horny for you."

"What does horny mean to you?" Jessie whispered, as he began to make love to her.

"It means you want someone real bad, like I want you right now." He wrapped his hands around the top of her silky head.

"Mikey, I love you plugged in me. I love how good it feels in me, like you put something in me that turns me magic." Jessie closed her eyes and held onto his arms. She put her legs up around him.

Mike smiled down at her, and her funny little words. "Me too, Jessie."

~

"I'm sick," Jake whined at Maddy, leaning over the dining-room table. "My head is pounding."

"Quit your belly aching. If you're gonna play, you're gonna pay," Kevin said, sipping on a cup of black coffee. "Are we gonna go out to the pond, Jen?"

"My head hurts a little too," Maddy said, pouring herself a cup of coffee. "Want some aspirin?"

Jake nodded and Maddy took some aspirin out of the cabinet.

"Call your mom and see if you and Jessie can go skating, Maddy." Jenny said.

"I'm worried she'll say no. She wanted us to go shopping with her and Aimee."

"She won't say no, tell her Jessie really wants to go. You know your mom's a sucker when it comes to Jessie."

"Yeah, I know. Well, you guys be quiet," Maddy said, and dialed the phone... "Mom, we wanna go ice skating today, is that all right?"

"Madison, Aimee's planning on spending the day with Jessie. You know that. We're going shopping today."

"Can't we go tomorrow, Mom? Jenny's cousin, April, and her friend, Matt will take us. Jessie's never been skating before and she really wants to go."

"Let me talk to Jessie."

"She's in the bathroom, Mom."

"Well," Debbie sighed, "all right, but I want you two home by three o'clock, today. And call to check in."

"We will, Mom. Thanks!"

"I told you." Jenny grinned.

Maddy nodded as Mike and Jessie came walking downstairs holding hands, and after taking a long shower.

"Thanks for using all the hot water, *A-hole,*" Kevin said to Mike. Jenny was sitting on his lap, and they were being disgusting.

"Go upstairs and do that shit, man," Mike said.

"Yeah, you guys are fuckin' gross," Jake replied, leaning his chest against the table.

"You never minded it before." Kevin grinned at Mike.

"Yeah, well, shit for brains, not here, okay? You got little underage girls here. They might run off and tell their mama." He sat down next to Jessie at the bar, smiling at Maddy who was standing by the coffee pot in the kitchen.

Maddy gave Mike a hurtful look. "Jessie, Momma says we can go skating. Do you wanna go?"

Jessie's face became all aglow. "Really? Now you can teach me, Mikey!"

He smiled and winked at Jessie squeezing her hand. "Any more coffee?" he asked Maddy, lighting a cigarette.

"A little bit. I have to make some more."

"Thanks for drinking all the fuckin' coffee, *A-hole,*" Mike said to Kevin.

Maddy handed him a cup of what was left. "Thanks," Mike said, looking at Maddy a little different than usual. "You don't need to make anymore. We'll get some later."

Maddy smiled.

Mike took Jessie outside to see his car. It was a dark, metallic-blue, 1970 *Chevelle Super Sport* with the two black racing stripes. It had a black leather interior and a cut-out bench seat for the gearshift.

Jessie ran her hand across the driver's door. "It's beautiful, Mikey. It does have Cragars."

"I like Cragars. I like the seat. You can sit next to me." Mike grinned. "I got a lot of work to do on it. It needs new headers and gaskets and stuff, but I did get a new eight-track put in."

"Can you play any music?"

"Yep, anything you want."

"I love it, Mikey."

"Sit down in there," Mike said, opening the door. "Someday, I'll teach you to drive it."

"Oh?" Jessie asked, climbing in. "I don't think tho. I can't see out the window. You better dis drive."

Mike drove Jessie in his *Chevelle* to the skate pond, while everyone else squeezed into Kevin's blazer. Jessie took her overnight bag and read her Science homework chapter on the way.

"Mikey," she said, looking up from her book. "Do I talk about stupid shit?"

He frowned, glancing at her. "No."

She leaned her head on the window, looking at him. "I don't want you to call me all the time."

"I know, baby, you're a good girl, but I wouldn't care if you did. Conversation with you is sweet, you're sweet. You're natural and not fake. What's that you're studying, little Einstein?"

"Perturbation."

"Pertur, What?"

Jessie put her book down, looking out at the snow along the roadside and explained as she memorized: "The orbits of the planets are governed primarily by Kepler's laws of planetary motion. Those laws are overthimplified to the extent that each planet is considered to be controlled only by the gravitational attraction of the thun. In reality, the orbit of each planet is influenced by the other planets to a thmall degree, as well as by the thun. The influences of the other planets are called perturbations and must be taken into account when calculating planetary orbits."

Mike laughed. "Did you just memorize all that?"

"Of course."

"Oh, okay," he said, chuckling. "So, you're the sun and we're all orbiting around you, controlled by your gravitational attraction. But none of us can keep away from you, so we're all perpetrators."

Jessie looked curiously at Mike. "Not exactly, you can't live without each other, either. It's not perpetrator anyway, that's a bad person who commits a crime. That's a bad guy, Mikey."

"Well, you are underage. Guess we're perpetrating you. I am eighteen now, you know. I could go to jail for fucking you."

Jessie's eyes nearly exploded in their sockets looking at him. "Mikey, I don't want you to go to jail!"

"Well, I'm not gonna stop fucking you. You want me to stop fucking you?"

"No." She shook her head, pouting at him.

"You're too fuckin' cute." He smiled at her. "I'm not gonna go to jail, bunny. Not unless you plan on telling the cops on me."

"I won't never tell the cops, Mikey, I promise. Mikey, when did you turn eighteen?"

"November second."

"I missed your birthday."

"Yeah. I went out with Kevin and Gary and got drunk. What's your worst subject in school, bunny?"

"Um, English. I can't learn it. It doesn't stick in my head like science or history. I know math good."

Mike smiled. "Apparently, you don't know English too good. You wanna see how fast this Rod can go?" Mike asked, stepping down on the throttle.

"Fast like Luke's?"

"I'd kick his ass…"

They pulled into the parking lot of the outdoor mall, close to the skate pond. It was located seventeen miles west of downtown Mining, in a green valley surrounded by pine trees. The area was under new development with high end residential homes. The shops were designed to fit into the environment and looked like mountain cabins, with wood siding, green metal roofs, and river rock foundations. Existing Jeffrey pines were left standing strategically to embellish the theme of the mall. The pond was surrounded by a pine-rail fence that was decorated in garland for the holidays. There were outdoor picnic tables and a small coffee stand and ticket booth next to the pond.

The air was cold, but the sky was cloudless and blue, and the sun shone bright. Patches of snow remained melting in the meadow on the other side of the pond, which overlooked the pine covered hills. There were big piles of black snow around the parking lot where the front-end loader had cleared it off. Kevin pulled up in his blazer, and parked next to them.

They all had breakfast at the Black Bear Coffee Shop, and then Mike walked Jessie to the drug store.

"Aren't we going to skate, Mikey?" Jessie asked, trying to keep up with his long legs.

"I need to get something first." Mike said and dragged Jessie by the hand around the drug store for a while, until he found what he was looking for. He took a bottle of nail polish remover off the shelf handing it to her.

"Here, bunny, now you can wear your pretty, pink polish. Do you want some more polish, too?"

Jessie shook her head examining the polish remover and then up at him. "Thank you."

"There's something else I wanna get you."

"Why?"

"Because, you're cute. Be quiet and don't give me any crap." Mike put his finger on Jessie's mouth just as she was about to talk. After he paid for the item, he walked her to the Mountain Clothing Store. Directly, he pulled her over to a coat rack and took up a white fleece jacket with light blue snowflakes embroidered on the front. He took her plain, blue jacket off her and wrapped her in the white one. "Yep, you're cute. Do you like it?"

"Yeah, but I don't want you buying me stuff, Mikey."

"Well, get used to it. I was gonna buy it for you before, but I didn't know if it would fit."

"It's very soft... I like it." Jessie smiled, running her hand over the fleece. She didn't seem to have much say in the matter. He grinned, taking it off her and walked over to the counter to pay for it. Jessie noticed on the shelf in front of the store window, some teddy bears like the one Mike gave her. There was a whole assortment of Teddy bear clothing next to the bears, when she spotted a little fleece jacket, just like hers.

"Look Mikey," she snorted her piggy snort, holding one of the little jackets up. He took it from her and gave it to the lady at the counter, getting out his wallet.

"Well, I have to get teddy out of my bag now."

"What's he doing in there? Isn't he going skating with us?" He put his wallet back in his pocket.

"Yeth, I forgot him for a minute."

"Well let's go get 'im."

They walked out to Mike's car and Jessie took out her bear and dressed him in his new jacket, while Mike smoked a cigarette. Though it was very childish,

Mike felt like he'd given her something she really appreciated.

She put the bear down inside her coat. "Okay, we can go now."

The cold air turned their breath to steam. They walked to the ticket booth to rent their skates and went over to a table by the pond. Mike quietly helped Jessie put her skates on while she watched everyone skating. The ticket booth was playing holiday music over the loud speakers. When they got onto the ice, Mike held on to her as she tried to get her balance.

I don't think if I can do this, Mikey," she said, squeezing his arms.

"Sure, you can, you haven't really tried yet, bunny." He got in front of her and pulled on her arms, while he skated backwards. "Come own, baby, push your feet along."

"I am," she answered, trying not to fall. Her legs kept spreading apart.

"Keep your legs together!" he laughed. Jessie started to fall, and Mike took her over by the rail. "Here, you stay here and hold the rail, and watch me."

Mike left her by the fence while he skated effortlessly around the pond. Burl Ives, "Rudolph the Red Nosed Reindeer" was playing over the speakers. Jessie was intrigued looking out at everyone skating. She felt as though she were in a Christmas storybook. Mike held out his arms as he came back around to her. He stopped at the rail, putting both hands on either side of her and kissed her.

"That's how, baby." He picked her up and she wrapped her legs around him, holding on to his neck. Her eighty-five-pound body felt like a pillow compared to his large frame, as he skated around the pond, carrying her.

"I like it better when you carry me, Mikey. Tho does Teddy."

He set her back down. "Let's try it, again." He held her hand as she pushed her feet along the ice.

"Don't let go," she said, holding his arms.

"I'm not, baby. You're getting it."

Maddy and Jake skated past them. Maddy yelled out, "Come on Jessie, you can do it!"

Jessie could see everyone was having a great time. Matt and April were going around the pond so fast she could barely keep track of them. Kevin wouldn't stop grabbing at Jenny, and they were just fooling around in the middle of the pond, being gross.

Mike and Jessie went a little way, but she lost her balance, and started to fall again. Mike laughed and grabbed her before she fell. He picked her up, skating around the pond with her arms wrapped around his neck. He liked the idea of showing Jessie off, proud to be seen with her.

"Let it Snow" was playing on the speakers above, and when they sang the part, *Oh the weather outside is frightful,* Jessie sang along, except on the next line, she whispered in Mike's ear, giggling, "*And your dick is tho delightful.*"

"Silly girl, where'd you learn that?" Mike grinned.

"Um, I heard a girl at school one time singing that, but now I know what she meant."

"Your little pee is delightful." He smiled, rubbing his nose on hers. "You love your little pee-pee too, don't you?"

"Because she feels good," Jessie giggled. "Don't you love your dick, Mikey?"

"Yeah, you bet."

He was obviously a very good skater, and Jessie could see he wanted to skate. "Mikey, put me over by the fence, so you can skate. Me and Teddy will watch you, now."

"Aright, bunny." He left Jessie at the rail and took off as fast as he could toward Kevin. He grabbed Kevin's arm, accidentally throwing him toward some people that were in the way. Kevin missed them but fell on his butt. Jenny skated over to him laughing, and he pulled her down on the ice. Then Mike went faster to catch up to Maddy. He took her around the waist and twirled in a circle with her.

"Thanks, Maddy." He smiled at her and let go, taking off again.

Maddy was in shock and almost peed her pants, and so were Taylor, Sissy, and her new boyfriend, Victor. They had just come up by the rail, watching. Victor, a fullback on the varsity team with Luke last year, was built stocky, with short black hair and blue eyes.

Taylor walked up behind Jessie, who was leaning on the other side of the rail, watching Mike. "So!" Taylor snapped, frightening Jessie. "You're going out with *Mike now,* too?"

 Her face was scary to Jessie and reminded her just then of Tammie. Jessie moved down a bit, holding on to the rail. Mike came skating over to Jessie and put his arms around her. He gave Taylor a dirty look.

"Hi Mike," Sissy said. Taylor stuck her nose in the air, looking away.

"Hey," he answered, a bit out of breath. He shook hands with Victor. "Hey, Vick."

"How's it going Mike?"

"Aright."

"How's the team this year?"

"It sucks; Andy's a fuckin' loser."

Victor chuckled, "Luke *is* pretty tough to replace. Coach still fucking with you?"

"Naw, he's backed off.

"Nepal has a pretty good defense this year."

"Yeah."

"You wrestling again this year?"

Mike nodded. "Hey, we'll see you around, man." Mike took Jessie by the hand. "Come own, baby," he said, ignoring Taylor and the dirty look on her face. He picked Jessie up and she wrapped her legs around him.

"That's unusual," Victor said, watching them skate away. "Seeing Mike with a girl that way."

"She's the little tramp Luke was with at the mall," Taylor said, glaring out across the pond.

"Humph," Victor grunted. "Well, Mike's scene is usually diggin' on tramps, but she don't look like no tramp."

"I heard she's retarded," Sissy smirked. She quietly reveled in the idea that Luke was apparently being thwarted, feeling a bit vindicated. She and Victor went out on the ice, while Taylor sat at a table, took her compact out of her purse, and put some more lipstick on.

"Hi Taylor!" Maddy and Jenny both yelled, waving and laughing as they skated past her. Taylor put her nose in the air.

"You want some hot chocolate, bunny?" Mike asked Jessie, as he skated toward the coffee stand. "You didn't eat much breakfast."

"Yes, please, Mikey."

After getting their drinks, they walked to a table and Mike straddled the bench, leaning back on the pine rail.

"Come 'ere," he said, pulling Jessie close against his chest. He took out a cigarette and lit it, then he kissed her neck. "Are you having fun, baby?"

"MM hmm." She was shivering cold, trying to warm her hands and face from the heat of the Styrofoam cup, as she sipped her cocoa. "Tho is Teddy." She took the bear and straightened his jacket, then rubbed the bear on her face and put it back inside her jacket. Her jaw trembled, from the icy air. "It's beautiful here, like a book. Thank you, Mikey, for taking me here."

"You're not cold are you, bunny?"

"I'm okay." She shivered. "This jacket is *warm*. Thank you."

He wrapped his big arms around her and leaned down, rubbing his face against hers.

"You're freezing, little bunny. Let me warm you up. So, you never been here before?"

"I hardly been to any place, 'cept with my Auntie to the mall in Reno, and when Luke took me one day to the mall, where we saw Santa, even.

"Santa?" Mike chuckled.

"Yep, but Luke said it's not really Santa."

"No place? You don't go into town to buy clothes, or groceries?"

"No, Mrs. Hastings always buys groceries for us, and Daddy brings them home. One day, when I'm big, I'm going to have my own house and go to the store by myself and buy thome chocolate."

"Chocolate?" Mike smiled, talking in her ear. He found it hard to believe that Jessie had never been to the store. He couldn't imagine, in America, 1973 that someone was kept so sheltered with so many places and things to see. *What kind of idiot was this guy, anyway, not even taking his daughter to the store?*

"Mm hmm." Jessie nodded, taking another sip.

"Your dad don't buy you any chocolate, Jessie?"

"No, he didn't buy me nothing."

"What about your clothes, he doesn't buy you clothes?"

"One time he did, before I came to see my Auntie."

"Well, then where do you get your clothes?"

"I always got my clothes from church, when Miss Jennings would take me to the basement. Auntie bought me clothes, and Luke. She said I could call her Momma, now."

"Even your panties? What did you wear, used panties from church?"

Jessie didn't answer. It would be too embarrassing, and now she didn't like him asking her anything.

"Turn around, Jessie," Mike said. Jessie turned and faced him. He looked in her eyes. "Why doesn't your dad take you anywhere? Don't you ask him?"

No. I can't...I don't know." She raised her brow. "Well, I don't think he likes me. He gets angry and he thays that people are nosey about me and I'm better to stay at home."

"He must be a real asshole. Do you like staying at home?" Mike asked, already knowing the answer.

"No, of course I don't. I hate my home. There's no one there. It's far away and there's nobody there."

"He never told you about your Aunt?"

Jessie shook her head, looking out across the pond. Her face was sad. Mike couldn't imagine being so alone for so long. It was no wonder that Jessie was so innocent and ignorant. He put his hands on her face and rubbed her cheek with his thumb. He bent down, kissing her lips.

"Your face is so pretty. Your blue eyes are so beautiful in the morning sun."

Taylor was watching them. She felt deeply hurt and disgusted. She'd never been so jealous of anyone in her life. Mike was completely enraptured with

Jessie. She went out on the ice and joined Sissy and Victor. Jessie watched her.

"Maddy and Jenny say Taylor loves you and you're mean to her."

"Maddy and Jenny…those girls sure talk about me a lot, don't they?"

"Yeah, because you're 'portant. Mikey, why are you mean to Taylor?"

He tossed his cigarette, blowing out a puff of smoke. "I can't stand that girl. I have to be mean to her, or she won't leave me alone."

"Is she not pretty?"

Mike looked momentarily out at the skate pond and then back at Jessie. "She's probably beautiful, under all that make-up, but pretty is as pretty does, and she don't do pretty."

"Because she is stupid?"

"No, because she's annoying, and she doesn't get that I don't like her."

Jessie looked at Mike. "She's scary. I'm afraid of her."

"Scary?" Mike chuckled. "She is kinda scary. You wanna go to the Safeway store, peanut? I'll buy you some chocolate?"

"Okay," Jessie squeaked, smiling.

An elderly couple stopped at the table in front of them. They seemed to be in distress and were speaking to each other in Spanish.

"*Disculpe me*," Jessie interrupted them. She sat up as she could hear they needed help. "*Puede ayudar con algo?*"

"*Me puede, decir cual carretera puedo tomar para ilegar a Reno*," the woman spoke to Jessie.

Jessie looked at Mike. "They need directions to the road that goes to Reno."

Mike was stunned momentarily, completely impressed. He looked at the couple. "Take this main street out here, and follow it to Blue Lupine Drive," Mike said, pointing, as Jessie translated. "Turn right and follow that to Farm District Road. That turns into Highway 50 to Reno."

The woman took Jessie's hand with a grateful smile and thanked her. They both nodded and smiled, waving as they left. Jessie felt pleased that she was able to help them.

"Speak any other languages, Jessie?" Mike asked.

"*No, monsieur, only Françoise.*"

"Mm." He smiled, squeezing her. "If you ever talk about being stupid again, I'll smack the shit out of you; my little French baby."

"*Ou la la*," Jessie answered, smiling.

"You wanna try and skate again?"

"*Oui.*"

He grinned and winked at her. "At least I can do *something* you can't."

Maddy and Jenny, and Matt and April came over to the

table and sat down. Kevin and Jake came over, carrying trays of coffee and cocoa.

"We're thinking of going to the movies, if Mom lets us. You wanna go, Jessie?" Maddy asked.

"Go to the movie theatre?" Jessie asked, excitedly. "Mikey, I want to go!"

"Aright, baby," Mike said, man of little words that he was.

"What is the movie? Jessie asked.

"I wanna see *Serpico*," Jake said.

"Yeah, so do I," Kevin agreed.

"The girls don't want to see that," Matt said.

"I suppose they wanna watch some girl movie," Kevin said to Jenny, grabbing at her.

"No, we wanna like, make out," Jenny giggled.

Mike was realizing how stupid everyone sounded, as if going to the movies was just something you took for granted, and how spoiled the rest of the world must seem to Jessie.

"What do you wanna see, Mike?" Jake asked.

"I don't give a fuck. I won't be watching it, anyway. Let the girls pick."

"How come you're not going to watch the movie, Mike?" Jessie asked, puzzled.

"Did you call me Mike?" He scowled his eyebrow at her and smiled.

"Don't you want to go to the movies?" Jessie asked.

"Yeah, I wanna watch Jessie at the movies," Mike answered, hugging her. "Let Jessie pick, she's obviously the only one who wants to see the fuckin' thing."

"I wanna watch the movie," Jake whined.

"You're a fuckin' pussy," Matt laughed.

Jessie turned around to Mike and whispered in his ear. "Is Jake afraid of the movie?" She looked up at him with serious eyes.

"Why?" Mike chuckled, taking a drink of his coffee.

"Because Matt said he's a puthy about theeing the movie."

Mike choked, overcome by amusement. "Shit, Jessie," he laughed, looking down at the coffee he spit out on his leg.

Jessie looked at Mike, smiling but confused. She wasn't sure why he was laughing.

"I wanna see *Serpico,* too," Maddy said."

"Yeah me too, Al Pacino is like, sooo sexy," Jenny giggled.

"Jesus," Kevin said, grabbing at her again.

"Don't say that." Jessie scowled at Kevin.

Maddy realized how much she was enjoying herself, in spite of Mike and Jessie, and didn't want her adventure to end. "I better call Momma." Maddy took Jessie's hand. "Come with me, Jess."

They went to the phone booth by the ticket stand. Maddy begged Debbie to let them stay and watch the movie and asked if they could stay the night again at Jenny's. Debbie was hesitant and asked to speak with Jessie. Maddy handed her the phone. "Here Jess. Mom wants to talk to you."

"Hi, Momma," Jessie answered.

"Are you having fun, Sweetie?"

"Yeth! I'm having a terrific time, Momma! I'm learning how to skate, and we want to go see Therpico at the movie theater!"

"I'm glad you're enjoying yourself, sweetheart, but remember you said you'd spend the day with Aimee?"

"Oh. Oh, I forgot Momma. Okay, we have to come home, then," Jessie said, cheerfully.

Maddy took Jessie's arm. She looked like she was about to cry.

"Is that what you want to do, Jessie?" Debbie asked.

"Oh, um, well," Jessie stuttered, seeing the unhappiness in Maddy's face. "Well, Maddy is having fun, too, and well, I do want to see the movie." Jessie bit her lip, looking at Maddy, whose faced changed back to hopefulness.

"Well, all right," Debbie said. "As long as you're having a good time. But I want you home by nine o'clock in the morning, so we can go shopping, and put Maddy back on the phone, please, sweetheart."

"Yes, Momma! Thank you, Momma! Good-bye…She wants to talk to you now, Maddy," Jessie said, handing Maddy the phone.

When they returned to the table, Maddy was delighted to tell Jake, "We get to stay at Jenny's again."

"Your mom doesn't have any plans for tonight?" Jenny asked her.

"No. We celebrate by shopping all day."

Jessie sat back down between Mike's legs, putting her feet up on the bench.

"You get to stay the night again, Jessie?" Mike whispered, kissing her neck.

She nodded and took another drink of her cocoa.

He squeezed his arms around her. "Two nights in a row with a bunny rabbit," he whispered in her ear, tickling her neck with his mouth. Jessie shrugged, giggling.

"Jake and I have a shitload of fireworks in my car," Matt said. "You guys gonna stay up to light 'em off?"

"Right on'," Jenny answered.

"Yeah, all right," Kevin said. "Mike and me were gonna go downtown, but that sounds all right."

"Fireworks? Jessie asked Matt.

"For New Years, Jessie," he answered.

Jessie looked at Mike, puzzled.

"You'll see baby." Mike smiled, "If you can stay awake that long." He tickled her side and she giggled.

They all went with Mike and Jessie to the *Safeway* store, so they could buy their own junk food to sneak into the theater. Mike walked Jessie around the store and she awed at everything, fascinated by the variety of foods there. Mike couldn't get over how someone could be fifteen-years-old in 1973 and had never seen the inside of a grocery store.

"Can I have one of those?" Jessie asked Mike, pointing to a big, red juicy apple in the produce section.

"Yeah." Mike smiled picking out two big ones. "I wont one, too."

Jessie couldn't decide what kind of chocolate to get, there was simply too much to choose from. "What kinds do you like, Mikey?"

"I don't really like chocolate that much, bunny. I like *Reese's Peanut butter cups*, though. Do you wanna try one?"

"Eww, no. I eat peanut butter samwich almost every day."

"Yeah, I guess that gets pretty boring, peanut." Mike picked out a *Three Musketeer's* bar for her.

Mike took Jessie up to a top corner row where there were only two seats.

"Aren't we going to sit with everyone, Mikey?"

"No." He put her on his lap and when the lights went out, he was desperately trying to seduce her, but she was totally engrossed in the film.

"Mikey, you can't fuck me right here," she whispered, leaning her head back on his shoulder.

He laughed at her sudden, serious use of the "F" word, almost even offended. "Wanna bet?" he asked, with his hands up her sweater.

"We can have thex later. I want to watch the movie, Mikey." Jessie squirmed.

He kissed her neck. "Mm, you're gonna make me sad, Jessie."

"Stop it, Mikey, please." She put her hand on top of his, pulling them out of her sweater. "I want to watch the movie and you're making me...horny."

"That means you're ready for me, baby," he whispered, smoothing his hand across her breasts.

"Mikey, please stop it and watch the movie."

"Okay, bunny," he sighed, putting his arms around her. "Why do you say fuck, anyway?"

"Isn't that what you thay, Mikey?"

Mike didn't answer. He thought about that, and what kind of an influence he'd been on her. He was realizing she was like a baby, learning about the world for the first time.

~

Jessie was a bit frightened by the movie. When they returned to Jenny's house, she sat with Mike on the couch and they watched *Rowan and Martin's Laugh-In*. Jessie felt better, watching a funny show on television, being in a warm, comfortable room full of friends. It was nothing like the dull lit, cold, empty living-room at her home. Sitting cuddled up next to Mike, she started to feel some little pings in her belly, and some mild cramping. It was just little infrequent annoyances, so she ignored it.

She began to fall asleep, when someone lit off some premature fireworks and it startled her. She sat up and her eyes were frightened. "Mikey, someone's shooting a gun."

"It's just the fireworks, babe," he said, caressing her hand.

"Oh, it sounded like my daddy shooting guns in the trees." She lay down resting her head in Mike's lap and he caressed her face.

"Stay awake, Jessie," Maddy said, seeing she could barely keep her eyes open. "We're gonna watch the New Year's celebration at Times Square."

"I'll wake her up," Mike said. "Just let her sleep." Mike was thinking about the night before. He couldn't get it out of his head, or how adorable she was all day, bewildered by the strong affection he was beginning to feel for her. He lay down next to Jessie and let her sleep.

At eleven forty-five, he woke her up with little kisses on her face. Everyone was watching the *Celebration at Times Square*. Matt had gotten all his fireworks out of the car and set them up on the walkway outside the front door.

As midnight approached, many of the tenants living at the condos were standing outside. They counted down to midnight and lit the fireworks in the parking lot, while the entire complex was screaming and yelling with excitement. Mike held Jessie with his arms around her, enjoying her excitement at her first New Year's celebration. Mike whispered in Jessie's ear. "I wanna make love to you, Jessie."

Jessie felt herself strangely attached to Mike, too. Not like how she loved Ricky or Luke. It was different. He was different. He was quiet. She found his silence somewhat familiar, even his cussing and intimidation felt familiar. It made him strong and she felt oddly safe with him. She answered Mike by putting her arms around his neck and reached up to kiss him. "Mikey," she whispered to him, softly rubbing her nose on his chest.

Mike picked Jessie up and carried her upstairs. He endeavored to make soft, passionate love to her, embracing everything about her that he admired, her softness, her innocence and childlike ways, her brilliance, her ever-evolving mysteries and talents. The way he couldn't wait to be around her, as if it was the greatest privilege in the world. He cherished her smile and quiet, funny, little personality. She had power over him and that turned him on. She was like no other girl he'd known. The most beautiful girl he'd ever seen. Her looks were surreal, unearthly. Her eyes were magical; her lips were like Love Potion Number Nine. The touch of her skin or the sight of her face kept his mind spinning and his heart racing. He lay over her, holding her face, unable to break the magnetic power her eyes had, drawing his eyes to hers. She was so soft and tiny under him, and the way she whispered his name over and over, in her little voice. Mike was terrified. Life would never be the same again.

~

"Mikey," Jessie whispered looking up at him. "I like being with you. You feel like magic."

"Magic?" he asked, staring into her eyes, holding his arms around her little head.

"When you're in me, it feels like magic. Like there's nothing else in the world 'cept you and me, and nobody can get me when you're on top of me."

"Jessie, you're not going steady with Ricky?"

Jessie shook her head.

"With Luke?"

"No, I'm not going steady with no one, I told you already."

"Why?"

"Because, I don't want to cry."

"Well, that's always been my philosophy, too, but, I think if you really like someone, it's okay."

"No, that would be worse," Jessie answered, worried about what Mike was asking her.

"Don't you like Ricky?"

"I love Ricky. He's my best friend in the world."

"Well, what about Luke?"

"I love Luke. Luke takes care of me and loves me tho much."

"I don't understand, Jessie. If you love Ricky and you love Luke, why did you make love with me?"

Jessie was not sure what Mike was asking her. "Because I like to. It feels nice when people love me."

"I get that, but don't you think Ricky would be hurt if he knew you were sleeping with Luke, or me?"

"He's not my boyfriend," Jessie answered, puzzled.

"Well, Jessie, it doesn't matter if he's your boyfriend or not, he loves you."

"I love him, too. Why do we always have to talk about this?"

"Well, can't you see what you're doing to him? We have to talk about it, because it's always gonna be a problem."

"What did I do to him? I love him."

"You really don't understand, do you?" Mike asked, looking in her eyes. "You didn't do anything. You just did what felt good."

"Did I do a bad thing?"

"No, Jessie. I guess you just have to realize you can't have sex with everyone that wants you. You'll fall in love with every mother fucker in the world."

"I don't know what you mean. Ricky wanted me and he told me he wanted me and he made me feel tho good, and I liked him, and he talks to me and likes me." Jessie had tears welling up in her eyes. "Luke wanted me, and he touched me, and was tho nice to me and he kissed me tho soft, and he loves me."

Mike wasn't sure how to explain it to her and wasn't sure if he understood it himself. "Well, I can't have Luke trying to beat the fuck out of my face all the time, because *I* want to be with you."

"What do you mean, Mikey…Luke hits you in the face?"

"Fuck, yeah. He doesn't want me to be with you. I don't want you to be with him."

"Is Luke going to hit Ricky in the face too, Mikey?"

"I don't think so." Mike smiled.

"Why do you always laugh when I'm afraid? Why isn't he going to hit Ricky?"

"I don't mean to, baby. You just say things sometimes that I'm not ready for. Because, well, Ricky's just a kid. He doesn't know about Luke or me."

"I don't like what you're saying to me." Jessie pouted.

"No, I guess not, Jessie. But I'm not gonna stop wanting you, either."

"I think you're telling me something…I think you're telling me that I can't love nobody, or something will happen, and Luke will be mad, and Ricky won't like me no more."

"What I'm telling you, Jessie, is that we all want you, and that's gonna be a problem. Luke wants you to himself. Ricky wants you to himself, and so do I."

"You have me to yourself right now, Mikey."

"All the time, Jessie, and no one else."

"You mean like married, all the time? Like my Auntie and Uncle are married all the time?"

"Well, yeah."

"Oh no, Mikey, I can't do that right now. I'm still a baby."

"Well, you can't be a baby anymore if you're old enough to have sex. And you can't have sex with everyone that wants you."

"You do."

"What do you mean, I do?"

"Ricky says you have sex with all the girls."

"But I don't love them afterward or see them again."

"Then why don't you want me to? Why do you want to see me again?"

"For the same reason Luke wants to see you again, and Ricky wants to see you again, because…I love you."

"You love me? You love me, Mikey? …But I didn't tell you to."

"You didn't have to."

"You're the one that kept wanting me, 'member?"

Mike gently wiped the sudden tears from her cheek. "Of course, I do. That's what I'm talking about. Guys are gonna beg the fuck outta you. You can't have sex with everyone that wants you. You have to learn to say no."

"I did thay no." Jessie's voice trembled.

"Yeah, you did, didn't you?" Mike took a deep breath, holding Jessie's head, caressing her face. "I don't know what we're gonna do, Jessie. I guess that's why your old man keeps you away from people, we're all fuckin' animals."

"Should I go home now, and tell you no, now?"

"I hope not, Jessie. I guess that's gonna be up to you."

"But I'm not going to." Jessie pouted and rolled over on her side. "I'm not ever going to. I don't want to be big."

"I thought you wanted to grow up and have your own home and go to the store by yourself."

Jessie rolled over and looked at Mike, wiping the hair from her eyes. "But I don't want to tell you no."

"I don't want you to tell me no, either." Mike pulled her over to him, kissing her face. "That's the problem with having sex…sometimes, you fall in love and then…you're fucked."

Chapter Three - New Year's Consequences

Tuesday, January 1, 1974

Luke lay in bed, tormented. The nightmare he woke up from left his heart racing and his mind full of anxiety. Hank had disappeared with Jessie and no one knew where she was. Luke got up and went to the kitchen to get some water. He sat at the bar and lit a cigarette, contemplating the reality of that possibility, and the dilemma they were all in.

Mike woke up uneasy, too. The room was dark. He reached for Jessie but turned to find her gone. He lay there for a moment and rubbed his eye, wondering if she left, or if she was just in the bathroom. He sat up to pull his jeans on when he heard a small, muffled sound. It grew louder when he realized it was Jessie, moaning and panting in the bathroom. "Jessie," he called, quickly pulling up his jeans.

Suddenly, she screamed out an ear-piercing scream. He ran to the bathroom and switched the light on. He found her curled up in agony on the floor. She was lying on a towel soaked in blood. The toilet water was dark red with blood-blood smeared on the seat, all over Jessie's body. Her eyes were red, wet with tears, and she screamed again. "I'm in the trees, Mikey, come get me…Don't touch me…oh, the trees."

"Shit! Jesus!" Frantically, he bent over her. "Jessie," he said trembling.

"What are you talking about, oh baby, shit…"

"Don't touch me! It hurts!" Jessie screamed again, squeezing her arms around her head. Maddy came running into the bathroom with everyone else in the house following, and they quickly filled the doorway.

"What's wrong?" Maddy shouted. "My God! I have to call my mom!"

"No!" Mike yelled. "Don't, *dammit*! I'll call my mom."

Jenny felt Jessie's forehead. "She's burning up with fever." She unrolled and big wad of toilet paper and began to wipe up the floor. Maddy wet a wash cloth with cold water and put it on Jessie's forehead.

Mike ran down stairs and phoned his mom. Luke picked up the receiver at the bar and heard Meg answer. He was about to hang up when he heard Mike in a panic.

"Hey, Mom," Mike said, short of breath.

"Michael, what's the matter? It's two o'clock in the morning, where are you?"

"I'm okay, Momma, I'm with Jessie."

"Jessie? What are you doing with Jessie?" Meg asked, and Luke thought it. He didn't speak, waiting to hear the answer.

"Not right now, Mom, she's in a lot of pain. She's bleeding everywhere and screaming. I don't know what to do!"

"Where is she bleeding at? What happened, Michael?" Meg snapped. She could hear Jessie's screams in the background. "Michael, what's going on?"

"I don't know Ma, she's laying in the bathroom, bleeding everywhere!"

"Well, take her to the damn hospital, Michael! She's in pain! I'll meet you there."

Luke hung up and ran to his room, quickly getting dressed.

"Mom," Mike said, "please don't call Debbie, and Mom, don't tell Dad."

"I won't. Damn-it Michael, take her to the hospital!"

Mike ran back upstairs, "I'm taking her to the hospital!" he shouted, quickly getting dressed. Jessie wouldn't stop screaming.

"I'll go start the blazer," Kevin yelled.

"Jesus, Jessie," Mike said, quickly pulling his shirt over his head. Her screaming was agonizing, and he felt helpless.

Maddy tried to get Jessie dressed, but touching or moving her only made her scream louder. Maddy put a towel around her and Mike wrapped her in a blanket.

On the way to the hospital Jessie kept whispering, "Come get me, Mikey, I'm in the trees."

"What does she keep saying?" Maddy asked Mike.

"She's in pain, I don't know."

~

Luke was seething with rage, as he drove Meg to the hospital. He couldn't speak. Meg kept huffing and sighing, "Debbie is going to be so upset. I don't know what's going on, Luke. I wish you'd say something."

"Mom, I'm angry. I can't talk right now. I just wanna git there, please. You'll find out when we get there. If I talk, I'll just...I'll just say somethin' you don't wanna hear."

~

The receptionist at the desk wanted to ask a hundred questions, but Jessie was screaming so loudly.

"She's going to have to stop that screaming," the woman said, rather curtly. "She's going to upset the people in the waiting room."

"Jessie's retarded, lady!" Maddy snapped at her. "She's not going to stop screaming."

The woman and Mike both gave Maddy a strange look. Maddy had never thought to call Jessie that, but the woman had made her mad and she wanted Jessie to be seen right away. The triage nurse came out hearing that and hurried to take Jessie to a room.

"She's pregnant," Mike told the nurse.

Maddy glared at Mike. "Pregnant?"

"Yes, Maddy. Don't tell anyone, damn-it!"

"Well, it's kinda late, now, Mike." *Shit, Luke and Meg*, she thought as she saw them both race into the waiting room.

Where is she? What's wrong?" Luke snapped at Mike, who was standing against the wall.

Mike walked away from him. "She's in there. I don't know. She just started screaming and bleeding all over the fuckin' place."

Luke was beside himself with rage, wanting to punch Mike in the face. He couldn't look at him. He walked over by the emergency door, looking out. Meg tried to ask Luke what was going on, but he snapped at her. "Later, Mom, please. I can't talk right, now. Later."

After a short wait, the doctor came out. He didn't expect to see so many anxious faces, all standing up and gathering around him. "I'm Dr. Martin. Are you Jessie's family?"

"Yes, how is she?" Meg asked, anxiously.

"Jessie's had a miscarriage," he said to Meg, seeing she was the only adult.

"She sees Dr. Russell, in Smith Valley," Luke spoke up. "He didn't think she'd keep it."

Meg looked at Luke, surprised.

"So, you know about her condition, then? Are you the father?" Dr. Martin asked.

Luke nodded. "Yeah."

No one commented, but they all had their own thoughts about it.

"She's somewhat delusional," Dr. Martin said. "I'm more concerned with her mental state than her actual physical condition, which isn't nearly as bad as her behavior about it."

"She kept saying weird things," Maddy said.

"What things?" Luke asked.

"I don't know, something about trees." Maddy answered.

"Hmm, like I said, she's a bit delusional," the doctor said. "Could be from shock or the Demerol."

"Will you keep her here?" Meg asked.

"No. Her bleeding has stopped, and her vitals are good. I don't think we'll need to keep her. Just follow up with Dr. Russell."

"Well, can we see her?" Luke asked, trying to avoid any further conversation.

"Yes, you can go in, only two at a time, though. She's pretty sedated right now."

Luke went into the room and put his hand on Jessie's forehead. "Hey, baby."

"Luke, our baby is dead," Jessie said, in a daze. She had big tears running down her face.

"I know, darlin'."

"Our baby is dead, Luke. We should have gone to the clinic place, Luke. 'Member my dream I told you? I had the baby and I was screaming? I want my baby," Jessie cried. "I want my baby."

"I'm sorry, darlin'. You're okay now, Jessie." Luke squeezed her hand, caressing her head.

Meg came in and kissed her forehead. "I'm sorry, Jessie," she said, feeling responsible for whatever was going on with Luke and Mike. Jessie couldn't keep her eyes open.

Mike couldn't go in. He turned to Maddy. "She needs her clothes, Maddy. Can you take her to get them?" he asked Kevin.

"Yeah, sure."

"I don't know if I should leave," Maddy said, "I'm worried."

"She'll be all right," Mike said. "She'll want them."

Maddy nodded, looking anxiously at the door.

"Maddy," Mike said, taking her arm. "Please don't tell your mom. It's not that she shouldn't know. It's just that…it might mess up her custody case, you know?"

"Yeah, I know." Maddy felt just as guilty as Mike and Luke. She felt responsible for putting Jessie in that situation.

A woman came in Jessie's room, wanting information for billing.

"Send the bill to my house," Meg told her. She gave the woman her name and address.

"I'll pay it, Mom," Luke said, looking up at her.

Meg gave him an angry look. "I wish you boys would tell me what's going on," Meg snapped, signing the form.

"We'll pay it, Mom. There's no way to tell you, Ma, about what's going on." Luke looked at Jessie. He took her hand and kissed it, rubbing her forehead.

"It's too ridiculous."

Meg went back out to the waiting room, to find Mike, pacing.

"We're both in love with her Ma, that's all." Mike rubbed his bloody arm, unable to look at her.

"I don't understand, Michael. She's only fifteen! What are you thinking? What about Ricky? Is he having sex with her, too?" she asked, terrified of the answer.

"Yeah, Ma, he is." Mike didn't know how to protect her from all this sudden information.

"Debbie is going to lose her mind!" Meg rubbed her cheek, turning away.

"She can't find out, Mom."

"Well, what did you boys plan on doing, anyway, Mike?"

"Luke was gonna take her to get an abortion. We were both gonna pay for it."

Meg huffed. "Is that how you show you're responsible, Michael?"

"No," he said, walking around in circles. "It just happened, Ma. It just happened."

"I can't believe Luke, either. What about Sissy?"

"I guess he broke up with her. Ricky doesn't know about her being pregnant, Mom." Mike took her arm. "We didn't think he should know."

"You don't think he should feel responsible, too?"

"Yeah, we just don't want him to know-to know..." Mike looked down, unable to finish his sentence.

"To know you two are both having sex with his girlfriend."

"She's not his girlfriend, Mom. She's not anyone's girlfriend."

Meg's disappointed face was skeptical, looking at him.

"Don't think about her like that, Mom. Jessie's a good girl. She told me no. I just wouldn't take no for an answer." Mike's eyes began to tear. "It's just that...she's so beautiful. She's so damn perfect." Mike sat in a chair, holding his head in his hands. Meg sat beside him and took his arm.

"Please don't think bad of Jessie, Momma." He rubbed his hands on his jeans.

"I don't know what to think, Michael. I just can't tell you how disappointed I am in you boys. Oh, poor Debbie," Meg sighed, looking out across the room. She found herself in an unfamiliar, awkward position. Debbie had been her friend for years. She never imagined her boys might come between that friendship, or that the boys would be fighting over the same girl… Debbie's girl.

The wait was quiet and uncomfortable. Shortly, Maddy and Kevin came back with Jessie's clothes. Maddy wanted to speak. She wanted to tell Mrs. Miller she was sorry, but the words wouldn't come.

Luke came out of Jessie's room and told Meg, "They're gonna let her go home as soon as she wakes up."

"We have to be home by nine," Maddy said. "We promised Mom. She's been waiting to take us shopping."

"I think you'll make it home by nine," Meg said, looking at her watch. "I don't know if she'll feel well enough to go shopping, though." Meg looked angrily up at Luke.

"I don't know what to tell her," Maddy replied. "Mom will want to know what's wrong."

"I don't know, either, Maddy," Meg said. "I think for now, we'll have to leave it up to Jessie, and what she wants to do."

"No," Luke said. "That's not necessary. I'll deal with it."

"It's my fault, Mrs. Miller," Maddy said to Meg. "I should have never taken her to Jenny's."

"It's not your fault, Maddy," Mike said, stretching out in the chair.

"Let's not get into whose fault it is," Meg said. "Right now, we need to get her home. Mike, you'll have to get her back to Jenny's."

"And keep your fuckin' hands off her!" Luke snapped, going back into the room with Jessie. He sat in the chair next to her, laying his head on the bed, and took her hand. A nurse came in to check Jessie's temperature and blood pressure, and it woke her up. Jessie ran her fingers through Luke's hair.

"Luke," Jessie whispered softly. Her mouth was dry.

"Hi, baby," he answered, putting his head up. "How you feeling?"

"I don't know," she said, trying to open her eyes. "I'm thirsty."

"I'm so sorry, baby." Luke stood up and kissed her cheek.

"I mith you, Luke." She closed her eyes.

"I miss you so much, Jessie," he said, laying his face on hers.

"Can I go home, now?"

"Yes," the nurse answered, taking out Jessie's I.V. "Soon as you wake up, and we get all this stuff off you. I'll get you some water." She smiled, admiring at what a handsome couple they seemed to be, and went to get Jessie some water.

"Jessie," Luke whispered. "You have to go back to Jenny's with Maddy. I know this sounds terrible, darlin', but you can't let your Aunt know what's happened. It will be bad for her custody case, and she'll probably never let you see me again, and I wanna see you again, baby."

Jessie nodded. "I don't want Momma to know. She'll be mad at me, and thend me home. Oh," she gasped, rubbing her stomach.

The nurse came over and handed Jessie a small paper cup of water. "We'll give you some pain medication to take. It will probably make you sleepy though."

"Momma will always love you, Jessie," Luke said. "I have to leave you now, darlin'. I gotta take my mom home."

"No, Luke." Jessie pouted.

"I got to, Babe. I'll see you as soon as I can, later today. Okay?"

Jessie closed her eyes, nodding. Luke kissed her cheek and walked out of the room. He went over to Meg, who was uncomfortably, trying to lie back in a chair.

"Come on, Ma. Let's go," he said, rubbing her shoulder. He couldn't stand leaving Jessie there, and especially with Mike. "Take care of her Maddy, she's awake now."

Maddy went into Jessie's room and helped her get dressed. Jessie signed a discharge form, and they wheel chaired her out to the Blazer. Mike picked her up and sat holding her in the front seat.

It was six-thirty when they got back to Jenny's. Mike lay on the couch with Jessie, holding her tight. He was glad it was over and she wasn't screaming in pain anymore. He fell asleep and began to dream…

He was in a room, somewhere. There were people in the room. He couldn't see what they looked like, they were only shadows, but there was a vivid, little girl. She was about three or four years old. She was precious and innocent, with long blonde hair, but she was naked. There was a butcher knife, lying on a table and the child picked it up. An old woman in the room was telling the little girl to give her the knife. A man came up to the little girl, screaming at her, "You're not supposed to play with knives!" He grabbed the knife from her and spanked her. The child's eyes were terrified with big tears falling. The old woman was trying to rescue her. The child screamed, and Mike woke up. His heart was racing.*

Maddy leaned over the couch to wake Jessie up. "We gotta get ready to go now, it's eight-twenty."

Mike was still shaken by the dream. He looked down at Jessie's little face and realized she was the little girl in the dream.

"Sweet baby," he whispered, kissing her face. "Wake up, bunny, you gotta go."

Jessie stretched, halfway opening her eyes. She shook her head. "No. I want to stay here with you, Mikey." She rolled toward him and pushed herself into his chest as close as she could. "I want to stay here with you."

"We can't do this right now, Jessie. I want you to stay with me too, but you can't right now."

"Mikey," she whined.

"Come, on babe. Get up. I'll see you in a little while."

"How do you know that, Mikey? How do you know you'll ever see me again? I want you," she whispered, putting her face up to his.

"I wont you too, baby, but you gotta go right now." He got up and sat at the end of the couch, realizing she was going to do this all morning if he didn't make her get up. He started to put his boots on. Jessie lay there looking angry at him. He went to her, bending over her face.

"*Get up,*" he growled in a deep voice.

"Get away from me!" She pouted and pushed him.

"You are a brat; you know that? Okay then, see ya later," he said, getting up.

"No!" She held her arms up to him, pouting. "Kiss me."

He bent down over her, again. "Kiss you? I thought you wanted me to go away."

"No." She pouted and closed her eyes, sticking her lips out.

Mike kissed Jessie and she wrapped her arms around his neck as tight as she could.

"You have your big audition tonight, remember?" He smiled.

She nodded.

"Are you nervous?"

"No."

"You're not nervous?"

"Not really."

"Do you know what you're gonna play?"

"Whatever they want, I guess."

"Well come on, little bunny girl, get up," Mike said, pulling her up to sit.

"Oh," Jessie groaned, holding her stomach.

"Still pretty sore, huh? "I'm sorry, baby. Sure hope you feel better by tonight."

She held his arm to stand up. "Where's my teddy?" she asked, looking around.

"He's still in the bed upstairs. I'll go get him."

Jenny had cleaned up the bathroom and straightened up the guest bedroom. Teddy was lying on the bed.

"Sure," Mike said to it. "You just sleep through it all and leave me with all the trouble. Then you get the girl."

Jessie didn't say good-bye to Mike. She just left out the door and got in the car. Mike was kind of hurt by that, but that was how Jessie was. Maddy lectured Jessie the entire drive home, while Jessie quietly, ignored her.

Shopping was awful. Debbie was disappointed that Jessie wasn't feeling well enough to enjoy herself.

"I'm sorry I'm ruining all your fun," Jessie said to her Aunt. "But you don't need to buy me anything else, Momma. You already done so much for me."

"Don't be silly, Jessie, you can't help it if you don't feel well. Maybe we could just go sit at *Woolworth's* for a bit and rest."

Aimee thought that was a great idea. She loved to eat, and especially French-fries. As they sat in their booth, Debbie looked across the table at Jessie and Maddy.

"Look at you two sour pusses," Debbie said, noticing the unsettled looks on their faces. "What's the matter with you two, anyway?"

"They're just boy crazy," Aimee sneered, grinning.

"Boy crazy?" Debbie asked. "Is that what this is?"

"Yes, Momma," Maddy answered. "I should be old enough to have a boyfriend, now."

Debbie could see she was serious. "Is there something you need to tell me, Maddy?"

Maddy didn't answer. Jessie felt strange and didn't want to say anything, either.

"I'll have to talk it over with your dad," Debbie replied. "Is there someone you have in mind?"

"Well, actually, there is," Maddy answered, her spirits lifted a little.

"Really?" Debbie asked, smiling. "And who is this young man, sweetheart?"

"His name is Jake. He's a friend of Jenny's."

"And apparently, you hung out with him all weekend." Debbie scowled. "Well, we'll have to meet him, Maddy, *after* I discuss this with your father."

Jessie felt sick and sad about her lost baby. She wasn't quite sure why it was so important for Aunt Debbie to discuss it with Uncle Harry, and why it seemed so bad for Maddy to have a boyfriend. Aimee wanted to look at one more store, after they left *Woolworth's.*

"Okay," Debbie said. "But I think Jessie needs to get home and rest. Cramps are certainly no fun. She has her audition tonight and she needs to rest."

Jessie couldn't have agreed more. Once home, she spent the rest of the day, lying on the couch, watching television. Debbie gave her some aspirin and a heating pad, and she slept for three hours.

~

"This paint is the wrong color," Mrs. Mathews snarled at Luke. She slammed her quart of paint down on the counter. She was always a difficult customer anyway, but today Luke's patience was thin.

"This is the second quart I've had to buy, young man. It's supposed to look like this." She shoved her sample at Luke. Her snooty, withered face reminded him just then of Myra Gulch. "Good help is just hard to find these days. Why, when Earl ran this place..." She carried on without taking a breath.

"Yes, ma'am." Luke tried to be polite but all he could think about was Jessie. "We won't charge you, ma'am." He took her quart and stuffed it under the counter, grabbing a new base paint.

"I hope I don't have to bring this one back," Mrs. Mathews snarled, clutching her purse.

Yes, ma'am." Luke put her new quart on the counter and opened it. He placed a dab on the lid and blew on it. He held the sample next to the dry dab. "Looks real close to me, ma'am."

Mrs. Mathews looked down her nose at the paint. "I don't want close, I want exact." She put her head closer. "Well, put the lid on it," she growled.

Finally, rid of her, Luke took off his paint apron and went over to John who was stocking a shelf with packaged nails. "I'm gonna take off, John. I got somethin' to do."

"You sure are missing a lot of work, Lucas boy."

Luke nodded, anxiously looking at his watch.

Hope she's worth it. You really broke up with Sissy, eh?" John said, dropping a box of nails.

Luke bent down picking it up and looked at John. "I'd die for her."

~

Maddy was not expecting Luke to be standing on the porch when she opened the door to answer the bell. "Hi, Luke," she said, surprised.

"Hey Maddy, I came to see..."

"Hi, Luke," Debbie said, coming out of the kitchen.

"Hey, Debbie, I came to see Jessie for a minute, if that's okay?"

Debbie was a bit puzzled. "Well, she's sleeping right now."

"I'm awake, Momma," Jessie said, rubbing her eye.

Without waiting for Debbie's answer, Luke went over to the couch and sat next to Jessie. "Hi, Jessie," he said gazing at her, wanting to touch her.

"Maddy," Debbie called. "Come in the kitchen, please."

"Hi, Luke," Jessie smiled, slowly sitting up. Luke took her hand and rubbed it on his cheek and then kissed it. He started to put a tiny silver bracelet around her wrist.

"Luke!" Jessie whispered, pulling her hand back. "What are you doing?"

"Shhh, just be still. I made an appointment for you to get on the pill, next week."

"Luke, please don't give me this."

"It's too late, it's yours. Where'd you get this bruise?" he asked, looking at her wrist.

She pulled her hand away, looking at it. "I don't know, from skating."

"Well, it's for Tuesday the eighth, at two. I'll pick you up. You'll have to let the school know." Luke longed to kiss her. "How are you, baby?" he whispered, close to her ear.

"I'm better, but I'm sad, Luke. I'm sad about the baby. I wanted my baby."

Luke was heartbroken at the sorrow in her eyes. "I'm sorry, darlin'. I'm sad too," he whispered, taking her hand. "I wish things were different, it just wasn't the right time. I love you, Jessie."

"I love you, too, Luke. Auntie knows you been seeing me at school, now.

"I know."

"Mother told her."

"What does she say about it, Jessie?" Luke asked, anxiously.

"She asked me if you were my boyfriend. I told her you're my friend. She told me if I think I might have to have thex with someone, please let her know so she can get me on the pill, but she doesn't really want me to have thex." Jessie smiled. "She also said if it makes me feel better, she was happy that you come to see me."

"I know. I talked to her, too. Did you know?"

Jessie nodded.

"Well, what do you think?" Luke asked, feeling hopeful.

"Think about what?" Jessie said, never on the same page as Luke.

"About being my girlfriend?"

Jessie laid her head back down. Luke was desperate for an answer he knew was impossible for Jessie to give.

"Luke, why did you hit Mikey in the face?" Jessie pouted.

"Because, Jessie. I love you. I don't want Mike to see you."

"If you hit him in the face, will he stop?"

"No. Only you can tell him to stop."

"Luke," she said sadly, looking at the television. "Please don't hit Mikey in the face."

Luke exhaled a deep breath. "I'm sorry I asked you that. I don't mean to push you. Do you think someday, you might think about it, Jessie?"

Jessie closed her eyes. "Can't we dis be together, when we're together? You know I love you, Luke."

He was not happy at all with that answer and wanted to yell at her for being with Mike, but he couldn't. He didn't have any more right to be with her than

Mike did. He felt desperately threatened by Mike, now, and couldn't wait for next week, so he could have her all to himself, again. It was a twisted nightmare.

"I'll keep it," Jessie said, smiling. "Thank you." She kissed the bracelet. "Luke, can we go to the cabin again, someday?" she said, sitting back up. "I like to pretend we live there."

"Anytime you want, Babe."

"I have my audition tonight."

"I know." He felt threatened about that too, and thought, *I wish you'd just marry me, you're so impossible.*

Jessie did want to marry Luke, and live in a nice house, and have babies, and live happily ever after. When she was with Ricky, she wanted to go steady with him, play football, and talk. When she was with Mike, she wanted to hide in him forever. Jessie also wanted a new life. She wanted to grow up, move away, and pretend she'd never met any of them. She wanted to go to college, play guitar, meet Ozzy, be independent, and never have to go to her home or see her dad ever again. The choices were debilitating, and it was easier not to think.

Debbie took Maddy by the shoulders and looked sternly in her eyes. "Was Luke with you girls this weekend?"

"No, Mom." Maddy's eyes were suspicious.

"You're not lying to me are you, Maddy?"

"No, Momma."

Debbie let go of Maddy's shoulders and sighed. "I think Luke's in love with Jessie."

"I think so, too, Mom."

"Well," Debbie sighed. "We'll talk about this later."

Debbie had been thinking a lot about Jessie with Luke. She always hoped Luke and Maddy would get together someday, but Maddy, obviously, always liked Mike. She didn't feel that would ever happen as far as Mike was concerned, which was fine with her. But now, seeing Luke's marked preference, she believed Luke would be good for Jessie. Jessie was young, but she didn't want her to get stuck with someone like Hank. With Luke, maybe her fate would be a happy one. Time seemed to be of the essence for Jessie. Maybe it felt imperative to get Jessie in a safe place as soon as possible, preventing her from any painful, unnecessary relationships, and further abuse from her father. Her custody battle felt impossible and though the possibility or prospect of marriage to one so young was wrong, maybe it was better than the situation Jessie was in now. It was a lot to think about, but it seemed a necessary option to consider.

"Luke," Debbie said, coming out of the kitchen. "Would you like to stay for dinner? We're having pot roast?"

Luke looked at Jessie and she nodded, raising her eyebrows.

"I love your pot roast, Debbie," he answered, knowing that at least Debbie approved of him being Jessie's friend. He stayed until it was time for them to go to the audition.

Chapter Four –
Sprouting Wings

J essie stood looking out the front room window, watching Luke go into his house. She was tired and weak, but she felt good about the audition. She felt good about doing something on her own, something she was good at. She realized she'd been getting lazy about her lisp and decided she would try hard not to do it. This was no time to be a baby!

"Don't you want to put something else on, Sweetie?" Debbie said.

"Like what, Momma?" Jessie asked, wearing her jeans and cowboy boots.

"Well, something a little dressier."

Jessie unconsciously fidgeted with her new bracelet. "To play in a rock band?"

"Oh. Well, I guess you're right. You have to look like a 'rocker' I suppose...I see you're wearing a bracelet. Did Luke give it to you, today?"

"Yes, Momma," Jessie answered, pulling her sleeve down over it.

"It's pretty. Why did he give it to you, sweetheart?"

"I don't know, Momma." Jessie was uneasy about it and Debbie didn't want to pry, but her curiosity was overwhelming.

"He likes you, doesn't he?"

Jessie nodded, looking as though she were in trouble.

Debbie stroked Jessie's hair. "But you're confused about Ricky, is that it?"

Jessie bit her lip and nodded.

"Well, sweetheart, you have your whole life ahead of you. They're both nice boys, but you don't have to make any decisions, you're still too young to be worried about boys."

Jessie looked back out the window, and Debbie could see she was torn, but that it was not something she could decide for Jessie. Jessie needed guidance, and she would just have to be there for her.

♫

Pete met the family just inside the door of the Community Center. He shook hands with Harry who carried Jessie's new Gibson. Jessie had Grandma's old six-string slung across her shoulder. Eli was as eager to meet the band as Jessie was.

"I brought my Gibson too, Jessie," Pete told her. "I think you'll need to play this one, it's not tuned down like yours. Jessie, there's four other people auditioning. I didn't realize there were going to be this many, so we might be here awhile. I'm sorry."

"That's okay, Pete," Jessie said. She felt strangely calm.

"We've got three things in our favor though," Pete said to them.

"What's that?" Debbie asked.

Pete took Jessie's hand. "You're good, you're a girl, and you're adorable. They won't be able to resist you."

Jessie smiled and went with Pete and her family to sit in the folding chairs. The band members were all in their early twenties. Their lead singer, Mark, had long, straight blond hair, and sideburns. The bass player, Alex, had long wavy brown hair. On keyboards was Jeff. He had shorter blond hair, with a mustache. The drummer, Chris, was a tall, skinny red head.

The family watched, listening to the first three guys audition. Jessie paid attention to every detail. The first two to audition were pretty bad, actually. The third guy was good. His timing was off at first, and they had to start *Rock and Roll* and *Black Dog* twice. He could play *Stairway*, but there wasn't a guitarist who hadn't played that a million times. Jessie felt she was better, not in an arrogant way, but she had an ear for the sound, the timing and the rhythm and she could hear it, when he was off.

Mark called, Jessie Nelson. When Pete and Jessie walked up to the band, with her two guitars in hand, they were all a little bewildered. The bass player, Alex, said to Pete, "You're not serious, are you? How old is she, twelve?"

"We thought you were a guy," Mark said, smiling. "Your name *is* Jessie." He held his hand out helping her and took her Gibson case and set it down while

Pete took his Gibson out of its case and set it next to Jessie's.

"Come on, man, get real," Alex complained.

"Be cool, man. Give her a chance," Mark said to Alex. "My name is Mark, it's nice to meet you, Jessie," Mark said, taking her hand. "Can you play *Stairway* for us, Jessie?"

Jessie nodded and sat with Grandma's guitar, fine tuning it for a minute. She started right off, having her own little twist to the song. Mark was impressed. As they all listened, it was like listening to Jimmy himself. Halfway through the song, Mark waved for her to stop.

"Let's do *Whole Lotta Love,*" Mark said. He could tell she might be a little better and wanted to hear her play. He helped her plug Pete's Gibson into the amp and adjusted the volume. When Jessie began to play, Eli realized he knew the song, and was ecstatic at seeing his little cousin, playing like a real musician. Aunt Debbie sat with goose bumps, listening, as did everyone. Jessie played the entire song, without skipping a
beat. No one was more impressed than Mark.

"*Heartbreaker,*" Mark said next. When Jessie got to the lead guitar solo, Mark got chills. She was better than their previous guitarist.

"Damn, you're good," Mark said, when they finished. "What else can you play?"

"Whatever you can think of," Jessie said, shrugging.

Mark smiled. "Okay. Play what you like." He wanted to hear what she was really like. What she really had in her.

Jessie picked up her new Gibson, plugged it in to one of the bass amplifiers, and started to play *Wheels of Confusion.* It wasn't one they played, but Chris picked up on it. He was a huge Black Sabbath fan, himself.

"A Black Sabbath fan, eh?" he asked, smiling at Jessie. The band was turned on and Mark could see that Jessie was a natural. They were all amazed at the big talent, coming from such a small, little girl. Even Pete didn't realize how good she was.

"Do you know S-*Supernaut*?" Jessie asked Chris. She soundly pronounced the "S" in *Supernaut.*

"Yeah," he answered, nodding. He played a piece for her.

"Do you play any other instruments, Jessie?" Mark asked.

"The violin and piano."

"I think we just auditioned for you, Jessie," Mark said, taking her hand. "It was a real pleasure having you come here tonight and play. You're really awesome."

"Thank you," Jessie said. "I really liked it."

"Well, what do you guys think? I like her," he asked the band, and they all agreed. "Welcome to the band, Jessie," Mark said smiling, and took Jessie's hand. Pete came up and congratulated Jessie with a big hug, then introduced himself to Mark. Jessie began to put her guitar away when Chris and Jeff came over and told her how amazing she was and asked her about her guitars. Alex was a little hesitant. He didn't want to play with a chick and certainly not one as good as she was. But, he did go over to her. "Hey, you're real good," he said.

"Thanks," she said, as Pete helped put the guitars away.

Mark told the last guy waiting to audition, "Thanks for coming, but I think we'd like to keep Jessie. If it doesn't work out, we'll call you back in."

"Hey, no problem, man," he replied. "She's better than I am."

Mark spoke some more with Pete about their schedule. Pete advised him there were a few issues they were trying to straighten out. That they were in the process of negotiations between Debbie's lawyer and Jessie's dad. "He's gonna be a little difficult, but we didn't want her to miss this audition," Pete told Mark. "He doesn't allow Jessie to do a lot of stuff. But we're sure we'll get this thing going."

"Mm, that's a bummer," Mark replied. "Offer him money, man. That works every time. We sure want to keep her. We have to start practicing right away. We might have to change our sets. I like this Black Sabbath stuff."

The audition was exciting, but Jessie was tired, and her cramps were still nagging at her. She and Aimee fell asleep on the way home. Elijah and Maddy went on and on about how good Jessie was, and couldn't wait to see her perform at the Rock Fest. Even Uncle Harry was beaming with pride. Debbie was especially impressed, but worried about Hank and what he was going to think about it.

Chapter Five - Round Two

I t was ten-thirty when they pulled into their driveway. Elijah carried Jessie's guitars as she walked slowly to the stairs, holding her stomach. She glanced across the street and saw Mike, waiting in the window. She stayed looking for a moment, but then went into the house.

Mike was worried about her and wanted to see that she was okay. He was beginning to feel that maybe he was getting his come-up-ins with Jessie. Maybe karma was catching up to him for being such an ass with girls. Jessie seemed to be doing the same thing to him with Luke, that he'd been doing with Deborah, although he understood with Jessie, it was not so intentional. He was thinking maybe he ought to just leave Jessie alone, but, hmm, that was gonna be tough. He couldn't stop thinking of her and what he'd been discovering about her over the last few days. Her apparent fears and lack of relational sensitivity were heavy on his mind. He thought maybe she needed some psychological help with whatever she could have possibly suffered as a child, and with what the tree thing was all about. Whatever it was, he wanted to know more about it. He sat up late, reading his mother's medical journal.

Luke came out of his room to use the bathroom and when he came out he found Mike still up, reading.

"It's two o'clock in the morning. What are you doing with Mom's medical book?"

"Education, son." Mike took a cigarette out of his pack on the end table and lit it. "Trying to figure out why Jessie's so kinky." Mike knew he shouldn't have said that the second it came out of his mouth, but it was too late now, and maybe he did want to say it.

"What! Luke snapped, glaring at Mike. "What the fuck are you talking about?"

"Jessie's into pain, man. Don't you fuckin' know that?" Mike instantly felt vindictive toward Luke and mostly just wanted to get a rise out of him. He set the book down, too irritated to read it now.

"That's bullshit!" Luke pointed his finger at Mike, remembering the bruise on her wrist. "Stay the fuck away from her!"

"She doesn't belong to you, Luke," Mike said, getting up from the recliner. "I don't know what you broke up with Sissy for."

Luke flew into Mike and grabbed him by the back of the head, slamming his knee into Mike's stomach. He went to swing at him, when Mike grabbed his arm and body slammed him down on the floor with a loud thud. He smashed his face into the carpet, pinning both of his arms back.

"Get off me, mother fucker!" Luke grunted, trying to pull himself over Mike. The thumping noises and loud grunting woke up their parents.

Mike had Luke pinned to the floor, grunting in his ear, "She's not yours, man, and as long as she's fuckin' me, I'm not gonna stay away from her!"

"I will fuckin' kill you, if you hurt her, fuckin' asshole!" Luke yelled, struggling to free his arms, and trying to wrap his leg around Mike's. He threw his head back and hit Mike in the chin. Mike groaned for a second, pushing down on Luke with his body.

"I'm not gonna hurt Jessie," Mike grunted, trying to keep Luke pinned. Luke was trying to get his leg over Mike's.

Meg and Tom came running down the hall. "Boys!" Meg yelled. "Stop it! Stop it right now!"

"What's all this about?" Tom said, grabbing Mike's arm. "Get off your brother, Michael!"

Mike pulled his arm away from Tom and let go of Luke, pushing down on him. He got up and walked into the kitchen, rubbing his chin. Luke stood up, seeing his mother's distress. His face was red, and he pulled his shirt down. "It's okay, Ma," Luke said, catching his breath. "Mike's just being a *fuckin' prick* as usual." His lip was bleeding and he wiped his hand across it.

"What are you boys fighting about?" Meg snapped, wrapping her robe tightly around her stomach.

Mike came back out to the living room. "Go to bed, Ma, it's nothing."

"Michael!" Tom snapped, glaring at Mike, as usual. "Watch your tone with your mother."

Mike took the cigarette he left burning in the ashtray and walked past his dad to go to his bedroom. Luke looked at his mother. He bitterly hated Mike at that moment. Jessie was too good for his twisted, sorry ass.

Tom went back to bed, but Meg insisted that Luke tell her what was going on. She went to the kitchen sink and wet a washcloth.

"I can't talk about it right now, Mom," Luke said, sitting at the bar. He lit a cigarette. His mind was racing with guilt and anxiety. This whole thing was getting way out of control. His world seemed to be falling apart, but he couldn't blame Jessie. She didn't throw herself at him. She didn't ask him to get involved with her. She didn't ask for any of this. He could only blame himself, but he wasn't ready to give her up, especially not to Mike. He was too in love with her. She was worth anything he had to go through.

"It's over Jessie, isn't it?" Meg asked, wiping his mouth with the washcloth.

"I broke up with Sissy, you know," Luke said, trying to pull away.

"Why? You two have been together so long."

"Too long. I just don't love her anymore, that's all. Quit, Mom," he said, and pushed Meg's hand away. He took the washcloth and wiped his mouth.

"I'm sorry, honey." Meg stroked his face. "I wish I could help you. I can see what a mess you seem to be in. I don't get it, Luke. You were doing so good. I don't understand how you and Mike managed to get involved with her. I know she's a beautiful girl, and darn captivating, but I'm quite sure Ricky thinks Jessie's his girlfriend."

"I don't know, Momma. I don't know how to explain it, when it doesn't make sense to me, either. I'm torn, Mom. It's my own fault. You're right, she captivated the hell out of me and I wasn't thinking. Go on to bed now, Mom," Luke said, giving her a kiss. "I'm all right."

"Is that why you've been missing so much work, Son, because of Jessie?"

Luke looked at her, taking a drag of his cigarette. He leaned his head on his arm, rubbing his forehead. "Don't worry about it, Mom. There's nothing to talk about right now. I don't even know what's going on."

Meg could see neither of the boys could talk about it. She went to bed, in deep distress.

Luke sat at the bar, wondering about what Mike said about Jessie, being into pain, and if she was, why didn't she say anything to him about it? Mike was lying, just trying to piss him off. He detested Mike right then, feeling humiliated and angry. Unfortunately, he understood that Mike was probably just as captivated. He longed to run away with Jessie, but that would only cause more problems for her and Debbie. Jessie hadn't committed herself to him, anyway. He was starting to understand what real pain was, and it scared the hell out of him.

~

Jessie's night was long and difficult, with many troubling things on her mind. Losing the baby was more painful than she could imagine and depression was lying heavy over her like a black fog. Luke was hurting, and she was beginning to understand what everyone was talking about. She never imagined she would hurt him; he was her rescuer, her knight in shining armor. She had so much fun with Mike, skating and shopping, but not only that, he was also growing on her, like a vine, embedding itself inside her soul. The audition gave her extreme feelings of liberation and self-worth, but she worried now, that her dad would keep her from playing. Luke didn't want her to, either. She could tell. She also felt she was letting her Aunt down by not telling her about everything going on in her life, and Aimee seemed a little mad at her. She still had three more days with her family, but then she'd be back home, in hell. She was going to be sixteen in two months, still two more years until she was eighteen. Two more, seemed like eternity years. She didn't think she would survive. She thought about staying home from now on and not seeing anyone, anymore. Her heart was being ripped apart in a million different directions, but then she thought about never seeing any of them again, and that was worse. Tomorrow, she would ask Maddy to take her to the hardware store, so she could visit Luke. She missed him and didn't want him to be sad.

Mike lay in bed, wishing like hell he hadn't said anything to Luke. He knew that's not what Jessie's problem was and he should have kept it to himself, but he'd never had to put a harness on his mouth up to now. He knew why he said it; to piss Luke off. He was totally wound up. This whole thing was turning into a bunch of bullshit! *All this over one tiny little girl.* He never imagined he would allow himself to be caught up in anything so damn annoying and humiliating as fighting over a girl with his brother. But he was involved now, with no intentions of ignoring Jessie's obvious issues. She needed to get some help, a psychiatrist. Maybe he needed one himself. He tried to sleep but couldn't. He was terrified of the feelings he was having for Jessie. He had absolutely zero chance with her. What started out as fun was turning into a nightmare. He no longer saw her as a plaything. She was a beautiful little human being and his arms suddenly felt empty without her. Something was messed up with her, in her head, and that only made her more endearing. She wasn't Luke's, she wasn't Ricky's, and she wasn't his. He didn't have anything to offer her like Luke did. It was apparent she couldn't make decisions, or even take care of herself, and she obviously wasn't going to choose any of them. Shit, how long could that go on? For all he knew, she was right. How did anyone know if they'd ever see her again? Her dad could pack up and move away with her at any time, or never allow her back, or maybe something even worse. He imagined being married to Jessie. That didn't seem so perfect. How would he take care of her? He had no intentions of going to college for anything. No real goal in mind for his future. When he was younger, he wanted to be a firefighter or a cop, but he'd kind of forgotten about that. It wasn't too late. He could still go for that. He'd have to buy her a house, but he'd never saved his money up like Luke did. He couldn't just marry her without some stability in his life, or any means of taking care of her. She deserved the best of everything, not the lonely, empty life she already

had. Even if she never married him, he couldn't live with his parents forever. He was going to have to move out on his own, eventually. What, and live in an apartment with Kevin? That thought was totally depressing. Jessie kept bugging him about getting a girlfriend. What was that all about? How would that ever be possible? He could never find anyone like her again. He felt totally fucked. He'd wasted his whole life being an idiot. At least he was almost finished with high school. Next week, after Christmas vacation, he would find out from the school counselor what he needed to do to be a cop.

~

"I think Luke's in love with Jessie," Debbie said to Harry as she lay down next to him in bed.

"What makes you think that?" Harry asked, looking up from his planner.

"The other night at dinner, he seemed upset that Chad was talking to her. I saw him take her out to the lobby and when they came back, Jessie was sitting next to him. I asked Luke about it the next day."

"And?" Harry asked, setting his glasses and planner down on the nightstand.

"He said that he was concerned about her, but she was kind of with Ricky. Mother Magdalena told me he's been taking to her lunch. And well, I could see it in his eyes. Today he came to visit her, out of the blue, and gave her a bracelet."

"Well, it was bound to happen, babe. She's a looker, and boys will be boys. You know her mom had the same problem."

"I don't know what to do, Harry. She's so young. I've even been having stupid thoughts of wanting her to marry Luke, just so she could get away from Hank, and you know I've always said what a perfect husband he would be."

"And what about Maddy?" Harry asked, grinning.

"I know," Debbie sighed, cuddling up next to him. "She's so jealous of Jessie. I don't know what to do about that, either, Harry. I remember the first day I picked her up, we stopped for ice cream. She told me, 'girls don't like me' and I worried about that happening with Madison. And well, I have dreams for Maddy, too, but Maddy has her whole life ahead of her. I'm not so sure with Jessie. I have this overwhelming feeling that I have to get her safe, right now. I want Jessie to have a happy life from now on. I don't want her to go through with what Jessica went through and meet some jerk that will treat her bad, but, I know it's not my decision to make."

"What about Ricky?" Harry asked. "Seems like they have a thing going between them."

"Well, I think it just puppy love. I hope. You know, Mother told me Jessie was immature for her age. I know she hasn't been exposed to much of the world and she is naive, but except for her speech, Jessie seems to be more mature than Aimee, and maybe even more so than Madison in a lot of ways. She certainly has more responsibilities and respect. I need to get to know her better. I don't want her to go back, Harry," Debbie sobbed as he cuddled her. "She needs us, now, more than ever."

"I know, sweetheart. I don't either. All we can do is our best, and hope and pray about it."

Wednesday, January 2, 1974

Maddy advised her mom that she and Jessie were going to pick up Jenny and then go downtown, when they were finally up and dressed at eleven thirty.

"Well, when do you suppose we can all visit together? Eli, Aimee, and I would like to spend some time with Jessie, too, you know, Maddy."

"We will spend time with you, Momma, I promise," Jessie said.

"Are you feeling better, today?" Debbie asked Jessie.

"Yes, Momma, much better." Jessie adored calling Debbie Momma now. It helped her to feel like she was a daughter.

"So, is it all right, Mom?" Maddy asked.

"Well, Aimee's made plans with Courtney today, so I guess it would be okay, but you girls call and check in." Debbie was actually happy that maybe Maddy might be bonding with Jessie now, and not so jealous of her.

~

"Is Luke around?" Maddy asked the cashier at the hardware store.

"Yeah, somewhere. Luke!" she hollered, looking around.

Luke came down an aisle, wearing his paint apron. When he saw Jessie, his eyes lit up and he almost tripped himself getting to her. He couldn't help himself and hugged her. "Hi, baby," he said, kissing her cheek.

Maddy was still a bit surprised by that and realized that Jessie was sure telling the truth about Luke.

"Maddy brought me to thee you." Jessie squirmed, trying to pull her face out of Luke's arms.

"Oh." Luke cleared his throat, almost forgetting Maddy was there. "Thanks, Maddy. What are you girls up to?" Luke looked at his watch. "It's about lunch time, you wanna go eat?"

"Thanks Luke, but I was hoping to leave Jessie here with you for a while," Maddy told him. "I'm gonna go pick up Jenny so we can go downtown."

"You mean you're gonna leave this cute little girl here with me?" Luke smiled.

"I told Mom we'd be home by dinner," Maddy answered.

"That's all right by me," Luke said, looking at Jessie, holding her. "I'll bring her home."

"Well," Maddy said, "maybe I better pick her up here, like at four. I don't want Mom to wonder why we're not home together."

"Yeah." Luke realized he wasn't being discreet, but sensed Maddy wasn't too ignorant about it.

"Be here at four," Maddy said, walking out of the store.

"Ellen," Luke said to the cashier. "This is Jessie."

"Hi, Jessie, nice to meet you." Ellen smiled. "Luke never stops talking about you."

"Hi," Jessie shyly replied.

Luke took Jessie's hand and began to walk her toward the back of the store. "You got Maddy to bring you here, babe?"

"Yeah, she knows, now. I told her about you." Jessie suddenly noticed Luke's black and blue, fat lip. "What happened, Luke?" She frowned, looking at his mouth.

"It's nothing, babe."

"Did you hit Mikey, again?"

"No, babe, come on, I'll show you around."

"Did Mikey hit you?"

"Jessie, never mind," Luke said, pulling her down the aisle.

Jessie didn't believe Luke and was still frowning, looking at it. "Okay, show me your work, Luke."

"It's just an old hardware store, not too much to see. I think the buildings about a hundred and fifty years old," Luke said. It did smell like an old building. It was part of a row of buildings, built in the 1800's. Its walls were red brick, with wooden planked flooring. There were two front picture windows on either side of a single French door. It was a small store, with one check-out counter, four long aisles of shelves, plus shelves against the walls, with a paint counter toward the back. Three dusty fans twirled overhead, and the ceiling had pipes going across it, with rows of fluorescent tube lights.

"What do you do at your work, Luke?" Jessie asked, just as an old man wearing bib overalls with white hair walked over to them.

"Say there, young man. I need a half-inch galvanized fitted pipe, like this."

He showed Luke a rusty piece of pipe.

"Sure, Mr. Cooper," Luke said. "Come this way." Luke walked him to the plumbing aisle with Jessie following. He quickly picked out the part for Mr. Cooper and handed it to him.

"Pipe under the sink rusted out. I gotta replace it now," the old man said. His hands were somewhat shaky. "What d'ya do to yer mouth, Son?"

"You might think about changing out some of your lead plumbing to plastic PVC piping, Mr. Cooper," Luke advised him, ignoring the question.

"Naw, I'll stick with galvanized."

"Do you need any plumbers tape?"

"No, I got some at home."

"Well, can I help you find anything else, Will?"

"Do you think you'll be getting in that new chargeable drill soon, Luke? I'd sure like to see it."

"Yeah, they should be in next Wednesday."

"Who's your little lady friend, Luke?" Mr. Cooper asked, smiling at Jessie. Luke smiled. "This is Jessie."

"You sure are perdy, little lady." Mr. Cooper took Jessie's hand in his withered, shaky hand. Jessie smiled and blushed at old Mr. Cooper.

"Well, don't work too hard, Will," Luke told him. "Come on, babe," Luke said to Jessie, taking her hand. He led her toward the back of the store. The office went upstairs as it was stationed above the small warehouse. Down the hall past the stairway, was a small break room with a back door that led to the overhead door of the warehouse.

John came out of his office as Luke was taking Jessie toward the break room. "Hey Luke, you leavin'?"

"Yeah. John, this is Jessie."

"Well," John chuckled. "Hello, Jessie, nice to meet you, finally." He had a reddish tint to his skin and cheerful, blue eyes.

Jessie smiled, blushing. Luke quickly walked Jessie back to the break room and pulled her close, wrapping his arms around her. Passionately, he kissed her. "I miss you so much when I can't see you, baby. I hated leaving you yesterday. Are you feeling better?" he asked, stroking her face.

Jessie nodded, looking up at him. "Yes, I'm better now, Luke. This belongs to your parents, Luke?"

"Mm hm, I love you so much, Jessie. I'm so sorry about everything. Let's go somewhere."

"To the cabin?"

"No, that's too far out. I have a nice place in mind."

"Where will we go to, Luke?"

He hung his apron up on the wall inside the break room. "You'll see."

Luke drove Jessie to the Pine Tree Lodge, which was a short twenty-minute drive outside of town. It was a well preserved, old Bed and Breakfast lodge that belonged to some friends of Mr. and Mrs. Miller. A huge porch surrounded the log building. A large cozy sitting room with a big River Rock fireplace all ablaze, greeted its guests as they entered. Deer and Elk trophies hung on the pine-lapped walls, and the stone flooring led to the front desk, a dining hall, and rooms upstairs. There were two guest rooms downstairs. Luke asked the desk clerk, Dan, for a key to one of those rooms. Dan smiled and winked at Luke, handing him the key.

"How's retirement?" Dan asked.

"Terrific. I was glad to see this year end."

"I hear Andy's no good."

"I think he's all right."

"I don't think he's got the respect you had, though. Too bad Mike couldn't have gone out for it."

"Mike couldn't take it," Luke half chuckled. "He'd be telling everyone to fuck off and trying to beat the shit out of everyone by the first week."

"Yeah, you're probably right," Dan laughed.

"Well, thanks, Dan." Luke turned, taking Jessie through the sitting room and into their room.

Jessie looked around as Luke locked the door. She admired the elegance of the room, with its knotty pine walls, soft, white carpeting, and a big stone fireplace, already blazing in the corner between two picture windows. A cozy, white sofa faced the fireplace. The large, pine bed had a lovely white coverlet, with lots of fluffy pillows. "How do you know about all these good places, Luke?"

"I've lived here most of my life, darlin'."

"It's beautiful, Luke."

Luke took Jessie in his arms, kissing her ever so softly.

"We're not here to do anything, I just wanna be alone with you. I just need to hold you in my arms."

Jessie nodded, softly gazing into his eyes. He picked her up and carried her to the sofa, sitting down with her on his lap.

"My sweet, little lady," he said, caressing and kissing her face all over. "My little Jessie girl, I love you."

Jessie sat quietly in Luke's arms, looking up at him. Luke sighed, gazing at her. "Every once in a while, if a person is lucky enough, they meet someone, and the minute they see that person, their heart skips a beat and smiles so warm. You're that person for me, Jessie. Every time I see you, my heart races and I feel so much love for you...you're being so quiet, Jessie. That makes me nervous."

"I'm dis amiring you, that's all," she said, but then frowned. "Have you and Mikey been fighting again?" She touched Luke's mouth.

"Don't worry about it, darlin'." He took her hand and kissed her finger.

"I don't think you're telling me the truth, Luke. Please don't fight with Mikey. Please don't fight with your brother."

Stop seeing Mike, then, he was dying to say, but bit his tongue. He didn't have the right to tell her who she could or couldn't see. "Did you have a nice Christmas?"

"I did. I got so many presents, I couldn't believe it. I never had no presents."

"I'm sorry, baby. I wish I could've been there with you."

"You went to your Grandma's?"

"Yeah."

"I want to see your Grandma."

"You will. How did your audition go?"

"Good. They picked me," she answered, still pouting.

"Of course, they did, you're amazing."

"I know you don't really want me to, Luke. I won't if you don't want me to."

"Jessie, I can't take that away from you, I'm just jealous, that's all. I want you all to myself. I don't want to share you with anyone. I know I can't be that way. I can't force you into a decision. It's just really fuckin' hard. You mean so much to me, baby."

"Is that why you're tho sad?"

"Yeah."

"And that's why you and Mikey are fighting...Luke; I didn't try to be with Mikey. I didn't know he was going to be at Jenny's house. He dis...he dis does the same thing you do. He starts kissing me, and holding me, and I can't stop it. I tell him no, but he kisses me anyway, and he touches me so soft, I can't stop, I want it. I want to be kissed and loved."

"It's called seduction," Luke said, afraid of it. "I know all about it. You're just so easy to seduce cuz you've been ignored and alone all your life, and you're so beautiful, no one can resist you. It's not your fault." Luke leaned back on the couch, holding Jessie's face against his chest. "Jessie, in the hospital, you said, 'our baby is dead'. Do you think it was ours?"

"Yes, Luke."

"Why do you think that, darlin'? You don't think it could have been Ricky's or Mike's?"

"No...I think she was ours."

"I'm sorry, baby. It was that first time. I knew it was wrong, but you needed me, and I needed you. I didn't have any control."

"Luke," Jessie said, closing her eyes. "I'm not tho beautiful. I don't want to be bad. I want to be good, but I don't know what happens."

"Baby, you're not bad. You want to be loved, just like everyone else in the world."

"I am bad, Luke. I'm hurting everyone, and I'm sad about the baby. I'm not very smart, Luke." Jessie looked up at Luke, and her tears began to fall. "I wanted my baby. We should have gone to the clinic place in California, Luke, then baby would be safe. She would be safe. Where would they take her to, Luke?"

"What do you mean, Jessie?"

"Where would she go, Luke?"

"Baby, they weren't going to take her anywhere," Luke swallowed, realizing now, what Jessie was telling him.

Jessie's eyes were full of sorrow and she cocked her head, "You mean, give her a new mommy?"

Luke was quite bewildered, looking into Jessie's eyes. He swallowed again, "Baby, is that what you thought? You-you don't know what an abortion is?"

"No, Luke, what is it?"

Luke could barely look at her painful eyes, and a tear rolled down his cheek.

"Luke, what were they going to do?" Jessie asked intently, "Not give her a new mommy?"

"Baby, they were going to...they were gonna..." Luke couldn't finish, and his eyes were watering.

"They were going to kill her, Luke? Is that what?" Jessie's voice trembled.

"Baby..."

"No!" Jessie gasped. "You mean they were going to kill her? No! I won't do that! I won't ever do that! You wanted to kill my baby, Luke?" Jessie put her head in Luke's chest, crying mournfully, "Why would they do that!"

Luke held Jessie's head against his chest, sobbing, "No, baby, I didn't want to. I wanted to marry you, Jessie, and be her daddy, and help you take care of her. I didn't *want* to do that, baby. I thought you understood, sweetheart, I thought you understood."

Enraged, Jessie unexpectedly bit his chest. She looked up at him, wiping her mouth, with angry eyes.

Luke looked down at her steely, painful, little face. "They couldn't give her another momma, Jessie. Not unless you stayed pregnant with her till she was born. What would your daddy think if you were pregnant? We both know how that would turn out."

"I would hide her, and he wouldn't know!" Jessie snapped.

"Jessie," Luke said, holding her face in his hand. "He would know. You couldn't hide it, baby. You wouldn't have been able to take care of her, not without me. I'm so sorry, darlin'. I…I'm so ignorant. I'm ignorant about you, what you know and what you don't know. It's hard for me to understand the world you come from. I take for granted what most of us have been exposed to and I forget you haven't been exposed to the same things, and I feel like a real piece of shit right now…I almost wanted you to be pregnant, so you'd marry me, so I could take you away, and that was wrong. I know you're sad, I'm sad too. It's over though, and you're okay. I hate seeing you hurt like this. We just can't be having unprotected sex, baby."

"God took her. He took her Luke, and now she's with him, and Momma."

"Yes, Jessie." Luke stroked her face. "She's safe now, and we can be relieved, kind of, that we didn't have to go through with it…we can thank God about that and ask him to forgive us, me, and not ever do that again. Okay, baby? Please don't be sad anymore. She's with him…and you'll see her again, one day."

Jessie nodded up at Luke. "K, Luke, I'm sorry, too, Luke," Jessie said, sniffing her nose.

They both sat quietly, frustrated and sad. Jessie listened to Luke's heart beat and felt him breathing as he gently stroked her face.

"I know it hurts you, Luke. I don't know what to do. I don't want you to be sad and fight with Mikey. It hurts me, too."

"Then stay away from Mike, Jessie. I can't stand you being with Mike. It's tearin' me up. He's no good for you."

"Luke, when I think about it…I-I want to, but I can't stay away from none of you. Ricky would be tho sad, Luke. I can't make him sad. I would miss him; I would miss my Ricky."

"And Mike?"

"I try, I tell him no, but he breathes at me and…dis like I can't stay away from you, when you breathe at me. I love you."

"How do you love all of us?"

"Because you love me."

"This is so damn ridiculous," Luke said, getting up. He went over to the window.

"Maybe I should not come see my Auntie no more," Jessie said, lying on the couch. "I think I should dis stay home." Her face turned to bitter pain. "But I can't stay home…I'd rather be dead! I'd rather be dead, Luke, than not see any of you. I love you. You're all like my family, now." Jessie cried, covering her face with her arms. "I'm not smart enough for this. I'm stupid."

"Don't talk like that, Jessie." Luke went back and knelt by her, wiping her tears. "I'm sorry, it's not your fault, and you're not stupid, baby. I'm trying to understand the world you come from is all, and I know you are, too. Let's not talk about this anymore. There's nothing we can do about it. All we can do is be happy when we're together, like you said. That's all we can do. Please don't cry. I don't like you to cry. Something will work out. It has to." Luke gently kissed her face, stroking her hair.

"Please don't stop seeing me, Luke. Don't stop getting me at school. I need you." Jessie grabbed on to Luke's arms. "You keep me alive."

"I won't, baby," Luke said, sitting back down to hold her. "I can't stop seeing you. Jessie, I'm gonna buy a house, so when we're alone we can go to our own house."

"But you won't live with your Momma no more. Aren't you happy at your house? How will I see you when I go to my Auntie's?"

"I'm not gonna live with my mom forever. We have to grow up, you know?"

"Things would be better if I was grown up. I could do what I want. I would never see my Dad or that…that cabin again. I hate it there. I hate that place. I'm all alone there."

"I know you are, darlin'. When I buy our house, you'll never have to go there again… Jessie?"

"What, Luke?"

"Don't have sex with anymore guys. I think you'd fall in love with anyone that…that breathes at you."

"I won't Luke. I don't want no more guys. I promise."

The two of them lay silently, confused and torn. Luke stroked Jessie's face, wishing somehow, he could convince her that things had to change. He kissed her forehead and exhaled with frustration. "Love shouldn't feel this way, baby," he said. "Love shouldn't be painful…Jessie, I have so many things I want to know about you, things that are bothering me."

"What things, Luke?"

"Remember in the motel room, you told me about Jesus coming to see you, and you asked me if I believed in him?"

"Yeah."

"What was happening then? You said you were afraid. What were you afraid of?"

Jessie looked at Luke, watching his dark eyes. It was impossible for her to answer that. *No one must ever find out about that, ever.* "Um, spiders," she told him.

"Spiders?" Luke asked, stroking Jessie's face. "Jessie, the doctor said you have scars, like you'd been injured. I know you don't want to talk about it, but it really bothers me. It bothers me that you won't say, and that you don't trust me. And mostly it bothers me that I don't know why or what happened."

"I can't tell nobody nothing." Jessie scowled. "I want to talk about nice things now, Luke. Can't we?"

Luke sighed, frustrated. "Jessie, I love you more than anything in the world, and I want you to be happy more than I want anything. I want you to know that you can trust me, and that I would never do or say anything to lose your trust. But if something bad is happening to you, I need to know, Jessie. No one can do anything about it if they don't know."

"You can't portect me, Luke. No one can. Not long as I live where I live, and no one to keep me safe. I can only trust me."

"I can protect you, Jessie. I can take you away and keep you safe with me always, if you'd marry me."

"Luke, you're trying to make me choose, and I can't right now. I can't. I can't hurt Ricky."

Luke stroked the hair off her face. "I get that, baby." He let out a deep breath. "I hope that changes soon, I don't want you to be hurt, ever."

"You know where my favorite place is?"

"Where, baby?"

"It's in my Auntie's kitchen. When we're all there. When everyone is there, and we're all together, eating dinner and happy. Or in the family room, like on Thanksgiving. I never felt so happy than I did that day. When you're all in the yard, playing football and everyone is there, and Maddy and Jenny, and everyone loves me, and I'm not alone.... Luke, hold me. Hold me and kiss me."

Luke held Jessie, knowing her isolation and loneliness was what she suffered from the most. And she was right; she had no protection when she was home. He knew that was why she couldn't speak out, and why she couldn't resist any positive attention. He couldn't feel jealous about that, as much as he wanted to.

"Luke, don't ever stop making love to me," Jessie whispered. She put her arms around his neck. "Please don't stop loving me."

"I won't ever stop loving you, Jessie. I do wanna make love to you, so bad, but we have to wait till you're on the pill, now. I'll just love on you for a while. Want me to make you cum, baby?"

"No, dis love me." Jessie closed her eyes, as little tear drops fell down the sides of her face. "Luke? What is your name? I mean all of your name?"

"Lucas Craig Miller," he answered, stroking her face.

"Lukiss? Like, kissing Lukiss?"

"Yeah." He smiled lovingly.

"What is Ricky's name?"

"Richard Scott Miller."

"Lukiss Craig Miller," Jessie whispered.

Maddy was in her car waiting when Luke pulled up in front of the hardware store. He leaned his arm on the steering wheel and smiled at Jessie.

"It's so damn hard to say good-bye to you, darlin'. You still have a few more days at your Aunties."

Jessie nodded. "I call her Momma, now."

Luke stroked her face. "That's nice, baby. What's your name, Jessie?"

"Jessica Nelthon. I have only two names. I want my middle name, Michelle."

"Jessica Michelle Miller," Luke whispered. "That sounds pretty." He gently smoothed the hair off Jessie's face and kissed her.

"Did you call me Jessica Miller?"

Luke grinned. "Yeah, I'll see you again before then, and on Monday, for sure."

"K," Jessie pouted, not wanting to leave him.

"You're so pretty, little Jessie," Luke said, kissing her hand. "My little biter," he grinned. "Thank you, for keeping my bracelet." Luke went around opening her door and then opened the door for her on Maddy's Volkswagen bug.

"Thanks, Maddy." He kissed Jessie one more time and shut the car door. Jessie watched Luke watching her as he waited, waving good-bye.

"*How the hell!* Maddy suddenly burst out, frightening Jessie and made her jump. "Did you ever manage to get Luke, and Ricky, *and* MIKE, Jessie? I don't understand that! Do they all know about each other?"

Jessie looked at Maddy, as she backed out of the parking spot. "Mikey and Luke do."

"Well, what do they think about that?"

"Luke is thad."

"And no wonder, Jess. What about Mike?"

"I don't know, I guess so."

"Well, doesn't that bother you, that Luke is sad? I thought you weren't gonna see Mike anymore." Maddy knew that was really stupid of her to say, since she's the one the set the whole thing up in the first place.

"Yeth," Jessie said, looking down. "I didn't mean to see Mike, he dis came."

"Well, why don't you just pick one, Jessie?"

Jessie's sorrowful eyes looked up at Maddy. "Could you, Maddy?"

Maddy thought about that for a minute. "No…No, I couldn't pick, either. I know I like Mike, but if Luke or Ricky loved me like they love you," she sighed, "no, I couldn't pick."

"I'm sorry, Maddy, about Mikey. I told him he should be nice to you, because you like him tho much."

"Jessie! Why the hell did you tell him that?"

"Well, he already knows you like him, Maddy."

"He does?"

"Yeah, he told me he does."

"And I suppose he thinks it's disgusting or funny."

"No, he doesn't think that. He says you're dis not his type.

"Well, thanks, thanks a fuckin' lot Jessie. I already know that."

"Are you mad at me, Maddy?"

"Yes!" Maddy took a deep breath and sighed. "No."

"I dis told him he should be nice to you. He might need you to be his friend one day."

"Well, thanks Jessie, for whatever that's worth. You know, he wouldn't like you if you weren't pretty, don't you?"

"Oh." Jessie sadly looked down.

"I'm sorry, Jessie, I shouldn't have said that. There's more to you than looks, but," Maddy heaved, "I wish I looked more like you."

"Well, why don't you dye your hair blond and grow it longer? Then you'll look like me, Maddy."

"Hey, that's a great idea. I wonder if Mom will let me."

"You're almost eighteen. You could do it then."

"Maybe she'll just let me try blond highlights. I could see how that would look."

"Maddy, you are pretty; you should dis be happy about that. There's a lots of boys that will think you're pretty. Jake does."

~

"We're home!" Maddy yelled to anyone who was listening.

"Who cares!" Eli mimicked. He was sitting on the couch watching *Scooby Doo*. Jessie sat next to him, immediately interested in the cartoon. Maddy went to her room.

"Where's Momma?" Jessie asked Eli, barely able to concentrate on her question. Her eyes were glued on *Scooby Doo.*

"She's in the basement with Dad," he answered, just as distracted. The phone rang, and Aimee ran to get it.

"Hello!" Aimee answered, hoping it was Courtney.

"Can I talk to Maddy?"

"Hang on," Aimee said, disappointed. She set the receiver down on the bar. "Maddy! It's for you! It's a boy! And don't be on the phone all day. I'm waiting for Courtney to call!"

"Hang it up, Aimee!" Maddy shouted, getting the phone in her room. "Hello."

"Hey, Maddy, it's Mike."

"Mike! Shit, wait Mike." She covered the receiver with her hand. "Aimee, hang up the phone!"

"Maddy, I want you to have Jessie meet me outside tonight, after everyone goes to bed."

"What for?" Maddy asked, irritated.

"Because, I wanna see her."

"I don't know, Mike. Why don't you just tell her that yourself? Jessie!" Maddy yelled, angry with Mike. *Haven't you caused enough trouble?* She thought. She really wanted to tell him to leave Jessie alone.

"Maddy! Wait!" he said. "I need you to make sure she wakes up. I know how hard she is to wake up.

"Well, what if *I'm* asleep?"

"Do you want me to call you?"

*Of course, I want you to call me, you stupid fucker, s*he thought. "No, you'll wake up the whole house."

"Well, can you just do it for me?" Mike asked. "When's a good time, I mean, when is everyone in bed?"

Maddy exhaled, "Usually at eleven. Do you want to just talk to her? I'll go get her."

"Are you gonna make sure she's awake for me?"

"Yeah, I guess."

"Okay, thanks. Yeah, let me talk to her."

"Jessie!" Maddy yelled again, putting the phone down. Jessie reluctantly had to stop watching cartoons and meandered down to Maddy's room. Maddy sat on her bed and began to paint her toe-nails. Mike couldn't believe how fast his heart was racing.

"Hello," said the smallest, softest little voice in the world.

"Hi, Jessie."

"Who is it?" Jessie asked Maddy.

"It's Mike, baby."

"Mikey?"

"Yeah, what are you doing, little bunny?"

"Watching TV, and we're eating dinner in a minute."

"Your voice is so cute; you sound like a little girl."

"I am a little girl. What do you want?"

"Well, I want you. I missed you today, where were you, peanut?"

"I went with Maddy somewhere."

"You're not gonna tell me where?"

"No."

"Well, how are you feeling, baby?"

"I'm better. I have to eat now, Mikey." Jessie stood, jerking her legs, anxious to get off the phone and go back to her cartoon.

"I'm glad you're better. I been worried about you. Don't you wanna talk to me, sweet little thing?"

"I thought you don't want to talk to no girls on the phone?"

"I do if it's you."

"Oh? Well I have to go eat dinner now."

"Jessie, wait. I wanna talk on the phone with you."

Jessie sighed, "What do you want to tell me, Mikey?"

Mike chuckled. "You're something else, you know that? I just want to hear your sweet little voice."

"But I don't know what to say."

"I don't know, what do you girls talk about on the phone?"

"I never talked on the phone. Maddy, what do girls talk about on the phone?"

"Boys," Maddy answered, eavesdropping.

"Maddy said we talk about boys on the phone."

Mike laughed. Even Maddy chuckled.

"Mikey, are you laughing at me?"

"No, baby, I'm not laughing at you. I wanna kiss you."

"You can't kiss me on the phone." Jessie smiled.

"Yeah, like this." He made a kissing sound over the phone. "Did you catch that kiss, pretty baby?"

"Mm hm."

"Kiss me back."

"Mikey."

"What? Kiss me back."

"Maddy's right here."

"So, kiss me."

Jessie made a little kiss on the phone.

"Is that all? I could hardly feel that."

"You can't feel that," Jessie snorted, grinning.

"Yeah, I can. I feel it good. Kiss me again, baby."

Jealous, but intrigued at the same time, Maddy was allowing herself to feel close to Mike through Jessie. She'd never seen Mike's tender side, and now she could see it by his behavior with Jessie. It made her realize he might be a real person after all. Not the mean asshole he tried to make everyone think he was.

Aimee came down the hall and knocked on Maddy's door. "I'm waiting for Courtney to call me, how much longer are you gonna be?"

"It's her turn to use the phone, Mikey." Jessie said.

"Just a minute!" Maddy yelled to Aimee.

"Well, she can wait a few minutes," Mike answered. "I'm not done talking to you."

Jessie didn't say anything.

"Jessie, I want you to come outside tonight, later. I want you to go out with me."

"I don't think so, that wouldn't be a good girl."

"Jessie, I'm gonna be waiting for you outside. Maddy said she'd wake you up if you're asleep. Please come outside, baby. I need you...to come outside."

"But I might be tired."

"Jessie, don't you wanna see me, baby?"

"Um, I do."

"Well, then, come outside-when Maddy tells you. Please?"

"Okay, Mikey. I have to go now."

"Aright, baby."

Jessie hung up the phone. "Okay, Aimee, you can use the phone!"

Mike jerked his head and held the phone receiver out, looking at it. He wasn't expecting Jessie to hang up like that.

"Jessie, why do you give Mike such a hard time?" Maddy asked.

"Did I?"

"Well yeah. You always make him beg all the time."

Jessie snorted her little piggy snort and grinned, "I know."

Maddy laughed. "Well, you just keep him begging, Jessie. He's earned it."

Chapter Six – Temptation

M ike's outside waiting for you, Jessie," Maddy whispered, leaning over Aimee's bottom bunk bed.

"No," Jessie said, pulling her blankets up and rolling over. "I'm sleepy."

"Come on, Jessie. You told him you would go outside," Maddy said, shaking her shoulder.

"No, it's cold. I don't want Luke sad at me no more."

"Put your jacket on! *He's outside waiting for you!*" Maddy snapped, shaking Jessie's shoulder again. Maddy was anxious, wishing that she was the one going.

Jessie sat up squinting at Maddy and reluctantly pulled her boots on, finding it difficult to keep her eyes open. She'd followed Maddy's advice and fell asleep in her clothes.

"Here, Jessie, here's your jacket," Maddy said, helping her put it on. "Now go!"

Jessie pulled her jacket closed, quietly going to the front door. She stepped out into the cold night air, and onto the front porch.

"Hi, pretty girl." Mike grinned up at her, standing down at the bottom of the stairs. "You were sleepin', haw?

Jessie walked down to him, yawning. "It's cold Mikey. Where are you taking me to?"

"My cars warmed up, I got the heater on." Mike wrapped his arm around her. "Come own, baby. We're going to a party at my friend, Gary's house." He bent down and pecked her cheek. "Thanks for coming outside," he said, walking her to the car and opened the door.

"Party? I'm tired, Mikey."

"You'll wake up, I wanna show you off. Git in, baby."

Jimi's, *All Along the Watch Tower,* was playing on the radio, and Kevin and Jenny were sitting in the back seat.

"Hey, Jessie," Kevin said, grinning.

"Hi." Jessie barely answered. She leaned her head against the seat and closed her eyes. Mike stroked her cheek with his finger and drove away.

~

Mike could not have been prouder to be seen at a party with anyone, but Jessie. All the major girls and jocks from school were there, and everyone was surprised seeing Mike come in with a girl; a beautiful girl.

"Wonder where he found her?" He overheard Michelle Morgan say to Lisa Salas, walking past them.

Jessie was tired, but the music was loud, and she wouldn't be for long. Lynard Skynard's, "Gimme Three Steps" was blasting and a bunch of the guys were in the kitchen, shouting the words out-loud.

"Miller!" Gary yelled, going over to him.

"You remember Jessie, don't you, Gary?" Mike shouted, with his arm around her.

"Yeah, who could forget? Hi Jessie," Gary said, taking her hand. "Come get a beer, Mike."

"Hey, Mike," Victor said, patting Mike's shoulder as they walked past. Sissy was hanging on his arm.

Mike nodded at Victor. "Hey."

Taylor sneered at them, and Jessie gave Taylor the evil eye.

"Who's the little fox?!" Jeff yelled at Mike from across the table, as Gary handed Mike a beer. Jeff, who was a bit smaller than Mike, sported a long, straight mane of blond hair, and played defense on the team.

"This is my baby girl, Jessie!" Mike announced, loudly.

"Does Jessie want something? Gary asked.

Jessie looked up from under Mike's arm. "Pepsi, please."

"Baby girl?" Nicki Mercer whispered to her friend Kathy. Nicki was there with her new boyfriend, *Tommy.*

Kevin held up a bottle of J.D. "Want a shot, Mike?"

"Naw, not tonight." Mike sat down at the end of the table, with Jessie on his lap. Jessie laid her head back on Mike's shoulder. She was sure she didn't want to be there.

"Hey, fucker," Andy said to Mike, coming from behind and sat down next to him. "I hope you got your shit together, fuck-off. Tomorrow night's an important game, you sorry-ass linebacker." Andy Bass was the varsity team's captain and quarter back this year. He was built sort of like Luke, but he was a bit shorter, and had shorter brown hair. His face was cute, but not quite as handsome.

Mike took a swig of his beer. "Don't worry about it, Bass. I'll be there kickin' ass."

"Yeah, well you better be, or I'll kick *your* fuckin' ass. Who's the cute little chick, man?"

"This is my girl, Jessie," Mike said, squeezing her against him.

Andy raised his eyebrow at Jessie and whistled. "Hey, sweet stuff." Andy grinned. "What the hell are *you* doing with this ugly asshole?"

Jessie shrugged and pushed her face into Mike's chest, frowning at Andy.

"Don't you think you have this little one out past her bedtime, Miller?" Andy asked, taking a drink of beer. "No wonder your head's been up your ass lately. Steady jail bait and football don't mix, man."

Mike grinned. "Watch your dirty, fuckin' mouth around my little girl, fucker. I might have to kick it in."

Taylor was creating quite a scene with the girls in the background. She was more than anxious to make Jessie look bad, telling everyone that Jessie was seeing Luke, too, and that she's the tramp that Luke dumped Sissy for.

"We gotta see this," Michelle said to Lisa. The girls who were all hot for Mike, slowly made their way around the room to get a good look at Jessie.

"Sit up, baby," Mike whispered to her. "Let's take your jacket off." He slid her jacket down her shoulders while Jessie pulled her hair out in front of her. It draped down one side and down her leg. She was just about the most stunning girl those boys had ever seen. Mike pretended not to notice the girls, all staring at the two of them. In fact, everyone in the room was curious about it. Mike bent down and kissed Jessie's neck, proud as a peacock.

A big, deep voice came up behind them. "Who ya got there, Miller?" He held his hand out to Jessie. "I'm Bobby." He smiled a big grin. Jessie had never seen an African American, or anyone quite as big before. Bobby was huge! He played lineman on the team. Jessie found him somewhat intriguing, and his smile was pleasant.

"Hi." Jessie smiled back, taking his hand.

"You ready to lose, *Jackson*?" Mike asked him.

"Not hardly." Bobby grinned. "Does the winner get a kiss from the perdy girl?"

"All right you Farm boys!" Gary yelled from the head of the table, holding up a shot glass. Which one of you losers takes the first shot?"

"Come on, vagina boy," Jeff said to Kevin. He sat down at the head of the table and held his arm up.

"What are they going to do?" Jessie whispered to Mike.

"Arm wrestle, bunny." He bent down and kissed her eye.

Jessie watched curiously at this strange ritual, which didn't last but a few seconds.

"Damn!" Kevin sounded, quickly losing the match. Grieved by all the heckling directed his way, he shook his hand, rubbing his arm.

Jeff laughed, taking his shot. "Kicked your ass again, Sheridan." He wiped his mouth and slammed the shot glass down on the table.

"Fat Boy, you need to work out some more. Get out of the fuckin' winner's seat." Andy said, taking Kevin's place, practically shoving him out of the chair.

"Hey, watch your cheatin', fucking arm, *Basshole,*" Kevin whined.

Andy and Jeff grinned at each other, grasping each other's hands, and Gary yelled out. "Go!"

Andy and Jeff were both bearing down hard on each other, their faces turning red.

"You fuckin' pussy's!" Victor yelled, laughing. All the spectators were shouting.

"Come on, take him down!" Kevin said to Jeff, who was giving it his all.

Andy tried to keep a straight face and grunted at Jeff, "Get out of the seat, if you can't take the fuckin' heat." Their faces were red, and the veins were popping out of Jeff's neck. The tension was building when Andy grinned at Jeff and slammed his arm down.

"All right, vagina boys! Who's next?" Andy held up his arms, flexing his muscles. "Somebody get me a fuckin' shot!" The boys were howling, and Victor took Jeff's place.

Jessie found the wrestling frightening, and violent. She watched intensely, observing how *into* it the guys were. "Are you going to do that, too, Mikey?" she whispered. She took the cigarette out of his hand and took a puff. The girls were bewildered. Mike never let anyone touch him, let alone his cigarette. He wouldn't give a cigarette out to a dying bum.

"I'm the Champion, baby," Mike said. "The last guy has to beat me." He squeezed his arms around Jessie and rubbed his face against hers. Jessie put her head back against his shoulder and took another drag of the cigarette. Mike kissed her ear, and went to take the cigarette, but she pulled her hand away.

"Well, let me have a drag, then, tittie girl." Jessie put it up to his mouth.

Two girls walked past the table to go into the kitchen. Jessie saw them and grabbed Mike's shirt. She quickly buried her head in Mike's chest. "Take me out of here!" she said to Mike in a panic.

"Why, what's the matter? Aren't you having fun, baby?"

Jessie squeezed Mike's side. "No! Take me out of here, Mikey."

"I cain't leave yet, baby," Mike said, grinning at her. "I still gotta beat all these losers."

"No! I want to go home! I want to go, now!"

Mike pulled her face out of his shoulder. "Baby, what's wrong?"

Jessie looked over at the girls. "You thee that girl, over there?"

"Yeah."

"She's the girl. She's the bad girl who hurt me at school."

"Tammie?"

Jessie nodded. "Please take me home, Mikey, I'm scared."

Mike glanced at Tammie and then back at Jessie. "She's not gonna hurt you, baby. Don't worry about it." Mike looked at Tammie, who just then recognized Jessie. "I'll take care of it," he said, taking a drink of his beer.

Jessie put her head back in his shoulder. "Don't do nothing, Mikey."

"I won't. Not here." Mike turned back to watch the match.

Tammie had tried to make a few unsuccessful moves on Mike herself and wanted to get a look at the big deal Taylor was carrying on about. When she realized who Jessie was, she took her friend and quickly walked out of the kitchen. She must have left the party, because Jessie never saw her there again.

There was a lot of cussing and howling from the Peanut Gallery, at what normally would have been the main event of the evening. The gripping, final match was down to Mike and Bobby. Mike's face was rigid. He made no sound, no expression, as Bobby leaned into the table, gripping it tightly with his left hand.

Bobby was trying not to smile as he snorted like a bull, even slobbering a bit. His arm quivered, bearing hard against Mike's, which was as tight as an iron I-beam. The music had stopped. Sweat was pouring down their faces; the crowd was silent with anticipation. Mike's jaw bulged as he gritted his teeth and slammed Bobby's arm down hard on the table. Even though Bobby was bigger, Mike had more upper body strength, and his pride would not allow him to lose, especially, with Jessie watching.

In the meantime, *someone* had given Jessie a beer, and Mike wasn't happy about it. He sat with her and went to take it from her. "I don't want you drinking that, Jessie. It'll make you sleepy."

"No, it won't," she said, pulling it away from him, taking a drink.

"Yeah, it will."

"I can drink, Mikey. I'm at a party *you* took me to." She frowned, getting up off his lap.

"Come own, baby," Mike begged, trying to pull her back down, "I don't want you to drink."

She pushed his hand away. "Mikey, leave me alone."

"Let her drink the fuckin' beer, man," Andy said to Mike, listening to them. He'd been sitting next to Jessie, staring at her for the last twenty minutes.

"Fuck you," Mike said, realizing Andy's attentiveness toward her. Frustrated, he watched as Jessie walked over to Gary. She was tired of all these girls giving her the evil eye.

"What kind of music do you have?" she asked Gary.

"Oh, I got all kinds." He took her over to the console stereo in the living-room and showed her his albums.

"Can I play one?" she asked, looking through them.

"You bet, play whatever you want, babe. Do you know how to work this?"

She shook her head, holding on to Al Greene.

"Here, let me show you."

"I want to hear *Let's Stay Together*." Gary put the song on for her. She walked over to Mike and took his hand. "Come dance with me, Mikey."

"I don't dance, baby."

"I'll dance with you, sweet thing," Andy said, half lit. Mike was thinking of punching him in the mouth and was just about to when Jessie pulled on his arm.

"Come on, Mikey," she said smiling. "You just stand; I'll dance on you."

Mike reluctantly followed her out to the living room and Jessie began to move her hips to the music, reaching up to hold Mike's shoulders. Seductively, she rubbed herself on Mike, who stood, looking down at her.

"I thought you wanted to show me to everyone, Mikey?"

He swallowed the lump in his throat as she swayed to the music, closing her eyes. Jessie turned around and rubbed her butt on Mike's legs. Mike took her hips when she began to pull her sweater up, getting into the music. Then she swayed down Mike's body and back up, pulling on her sweater, moving it up higher. An audience was developing with eager eyes, anticipating her next move, suddenly turned on as they stood watching this new main event.

"Let her take it off, man!" Jeff shouted.

"Yeah, man, let her take it off!" Andy said, and staggered over closer.

"Come *on,* Jessie!" Kevin howled. Soon, they were all hollering, "Let her take it off!"

Taylor was disgusted, standing with her hands on her hips, glaring at Jessie. Sissy rolled her eyes and tugged on Victor, who was also staring. The girls were appalled at this little tramp who was trying to strip in front of their boyfriends. Lisa grabbed Jeff and yelled at him for starting this whole show.

Some of the girls began to squabble and Mike realized things were about to get ugly. Just as Jessie was about to pull her sweater up high enough, Mike grabbed her hands and whispered in her ear, "You can show me later, baby." He pulled her sweater down. She turned around, and he picked her up, kissing her. "Let's go baby," he whispered.

Mike realized trying to show Jessie off didn't quite turn out the way he thought it would and decided he needed to take her out of there, before he lost his temper. Andy was pissing him off enough to beat the fuck out of him. Mike took Jessie over to their jackets and helped her put hers on.

"Let's go, Kevin," Mike said.

"Now?" Kevin answered, irritated. He was not ready to leave yet.

"Yeah, now."

"Come on you, fucker," Andy said to Mike. "It was just gettin' good. We're just havin' fun, man. Don't go off all pissed." Andy could hardly stand up; he was so drunk.

"Are you taking me home now, Mikey?" Jessie asked.

"No, baby, we're going to Jenny's."

"Are you going to have thex with me, Mikey?

Mike put his forehead down to Jessie's and rubbed her nose with his. "Yeah, baby."

"What if I'm still sick, Mikey?"

"Are you, baby?"

"I don't know."

"Well, we'll just fool around, bunny."

The guys were all heckling and booing at Mike as he turned and flipped them all off. "In your dreams… losers," he said smiling, as they walked out.

On the way back to Jenny's, she and Kevin were fooling around in the backseat. Kevin was whispering, and she kept giggling.

"Whatever you two are doing back there, why don't you save it?" Mike said. "You're fuckin' grossin' me out."

Jenny giggled, and Jessie wanted to go home. When they got inside Jenny's place, Kevin sat at the table while Jenny set up the coffee pot for in the morning.

Mike sat on the couch with Jessie and took their jackets and boots off. Jessie got up and went to sit at the table.

Kevin looked up at them. "Andy sure wanted you, Jessie. I thought for sure you were gonna hit that Basshole."

"That's why we left, dumb fuck. I still gotta play ball with the fuckin' pervert."

"All those girls were staring at me," Jessie pouted. "I was getting tired of it, so I wanted to make them mad."

"You did," Jenny chuckled. "I bet they're all fighting now."

"That's cuz you were with Mike, Jessie," Kevin said. "They all wanna make it with him, you know?"

"That's what everyone keeps telling me," Jessie answered.

Mike rubbed her neck. "Stop listening to all that bullshit, Jessie. Kevin's drunk."

"They're just jealous of you, Jessie," Jenny said, rubbing herself all over Kevin.

"Yeah, those chicks all wanna rub your hot, little body." Kevin was letting the alcohol do the thinking. "Jenny does. Hey," Kevin said, with a lustful gleam in his eye, "why don't you two girls make out, and let me and Mike watch?"

Mike couldn't believe Kevin said that, and Jessie didn't quite know what he meant.

"Oh, I'd love to make out with you, Jessie." Jenny grinned. She was drunk herself and Kevin had been filling her head with nasty sex all night. Mike was a little turned on by the idea.

Jenny took Jessie's hand. "Let me make out with you, Jessie, and let them watch. You know how much guys like that, don't you?"

Jessie pulled her hand away from Jenny. "Do they, Mikey?"

"Yeah," Mike said, "Only if you dig it, though."

"Come on, Jessie," Kevin said. "Don't you wanna turn your big boyfriend on?"

"Do you want me to, Mikey?" Jessie asked, not sure if they were serious.

"You do whatever you want, baby." Mike smiled at her.

"Do *you* want me to?" she asked again.

"Yeah, baby, I want you to," he whispered, more turned on then tuned in.

Jenny took Jessie's hand. "Come on, Jess." She anxiously pulled Jessie along, and ran up the stairs. Kevin grinned at Mike and raised his eyebrow at him. Kevin and Mike followed them up the stairs. Mike wasn't sure how he really felt about this, it might end up awkward, but, as usual, he was thinking with the wrong head and ignored his conscience. The three of them were swiftly aroused and their adrenaline was racing with the anticipation of this new naughtiness.

Jenny took them into her room and turned the lamp on next to the bed. Mike pulled the bedroom chair out from under the window and sat down. Kevin lay down up across the pillows.

Jenny sat Jessie down at the foot of the bed and kicked her shoes off, while Jessie watched, quite unsure of this whole thing. She felt embarrassed to look at Mike and didn't feel this was right, but she wanted to please him. Jenny reached down and unzipped Jessie's jeans. Then sitting next to her, she started to kiss Jessie. Jessie pulled away, but Jenny pulled her back over to her.

"You just let me do everything," Jenny whispered, and kissed her again.

Jessie's heart was racing. She didn't like this now, but maybe that's what kind of girls Mike liked.

Jenny put her hand up Jessie's sweater, pulling it off over her head. Jessie couldn't move. She felt paralyzed. Jenny stood up and quickly undressed, lying down with Jessie on the bed. Jessie was terrified. At this point, Mike was feeling anticipation, but a bit apprehensive, too. Jenny laid down half way on top of Jessie and started to kiss her again, caressing her body.

Kevin was all into it and leaned his head up on the bed. Mike was kind of half watching. The look on Jessie's face made him feel uneasy. His heart was beating fast. He had his foot up on the bed and was biting his thumbnail. He'd watched chicks make out before, but this was Jessie. *Fuck*, he thought, just then remembering the fight with Luke. *This isn't love, this is bullshit. I'm a fuckin' piece of shit.* He stood up to stop it.

Jessie started to cry, remembering the three big girls in the bathroom. "Mikey," she whined, looking at him with big tears. "I don't like this, Mikey."

Mike picked Jessie up and took her out of the room. "I'm sorry, baby. I'm sorry for that," he said, kissing her face. He took Jessie into the guest room, laying her on the bed, and shut the door. "I'm sorry, peanut," he said, laying over her.

"I don't like that," Jessie pouted. Her eyes were all watery with tears.

"I know, baby. We won't ever do that again, baby, I'm sorry." He pulled her close, kissing her head and face.

Jessie couldn't stop crying. "Jenny's a bad girl, now. I don't like her no more. She's like Tammie. I thought she was nice, but I don't no more. Take me home now, Mikey. I don't like to be here."

"God, Jessie. I'm so sorry baby, please don't cry. Please, stay here with me. I never should have put you in that situation. I was thinkin' with my dick, not my head, not my heart. Do you still want me now, Jessie?"

Jessie didn't answer. She pulled the blankets over her head. "I'm bad now, Mikey."

"No, bunny. I'm bad. I'm bad for not thinking for you. I'm sorry, Jessie. Please, I won't do that to you, again." Mike was trembling, worried he'd ruined whatever he had with her, and with Luke as competition, he knew he had to be more careful. "I know I have to think better for you. I haven't been very smart. I'm so used to being a fuckin' dick."

He lay his head down on her chest. "You're so willing to please me and I take advantage of you, you're so sweet. I'm such an asshole."

His eyes were watering. He moved up to Jessie's face and kissed her. He smoothed her hair back on her head and held her face, looking in her eyes. "I'm sorry about what happened to you in the bathroom. I love you, Jessie. I love you so much. Please forgive me for being an asshole to you all night. I get so stupid when I'm around you. You've been through so much already, abused, hurt, taken advantage of. I don't know what's the matter with me." Tears were running down his nose and he was sniffing.

Jessie reached up and wiped his nose off. "Don't cry, Mikey. It's okay."

"It's not okay, peanut," he said, kissing her face. "I laid in bed all night last night, worried about you, and then I do this fuckin' shit. My little Jessie, my sweet little Jessica, I don't deserve you. You show me what a fuckin' prick I am." His kept sniffing his runny nose.

"Go in the bathroom and wash your face and blow your nose, Mikey," she said, running her hands through his hair. "Don't cry no more."

Mike went to the bathroom and when he got back in the bed, Jessie put her hand down his pants and squeezed him.

"Dicks are for chicks," she said, smiling up at him. "Remember, you told me that?"

Mike sat up and took his shirt off, getting his rubber out of his wallet. He set it on the night stand and lay back down and kissed her. "You feel so good in my arms, Jessica."

"Put your muthles around me, Mikey."

Mike was afraid to do anything. He just wanted to hold her. The guilt he felt was unbearable. She was so vulnerable, and he had a hard time not taking advantage of that. He adored her innocence and how eager she was to please him, but tonight she was scared, and he made her cry.

"I don't blame you, if you don't want to see me again, bunny. You shouldn't even be here. Maybe I better take you home, now." He hated that. Saying good-bye to Jessie was heartbreaking and it got worse every time, and now he was worried. Worried she'd start to have second thoughts about him and not trust him. Luke would never hurt her like that.

"Luke is mad at me, Mikey," Jessie said, getting up on her arms, looking down at him. "I don't want Luke," she gasped, "to be mad at me."

"Shit, Jessie. Why is he mad at you?"

"Because of you."

Fuck. Mike felt like she was stabbing him with daggers. "What does that mean, Jessie?"

"He, he told me, stay away from you."

"He can't tell you that. What did you tell him?"

"I told him, I told him I don't try to see you, but, when you love me, I can't…Mikey, I don't want Luke to be mad at me, I love him. I don't want him to be sad."

"Jessie, you say you love Luke, what about Ricky?"

"Mikey, I miss Ricky," Jessie panted, her voice was shaky. "Ricky would be tho sad, wouldn't he, Mikey?"

"Most likely."

"Will you tell on me to him?"

Mike lay over Jessie, holding her face up. "No. Why can't you stay away from me, Jessie? Why are you telling me this, now?"

"Because, you want me, and I want you, too."

"You don't make any sense to me," Mike said, thinking about what she was trying to tell him. Apparently, that's where her mind was going at the moment, and she needed to talk about it, and he needed to hear it. "What is Luke like to you? Why do you love him?"

"Luke loves me. He takes care of me…and he will buy me a house. He takes me to the doctor and buys me clothes. He gives me good food for lunch and takes me to good places. He goes to my school and talks to my teachers about my work. He tells me wear a bra. He takes me to the mall, and to get my pictures. He loves me. He buys me chocolate and tells me pretty things to me. He keeps me alive, Mikey."

Mike didn't really want to hear all of that, but he needed to. He needed to understand Jessie. "What's Ricky like to you?"

"Ricky loves me. He's my best friend, and he loves me, and I love him. He tells me to don't wear a bra." Jessie smiled.

Mike kind of grinned. "He does, huh?"

"Yeah, I told him Auntie says I have to wear one or I'll look like a Africa lady. Luke says I have to wear one, so I don't look like his Mom. Auntie says proper young ladies don't show off their nipples to everyone. They might think ideas about me. Ricky came to see me at my school, but I don't want him to. I don't want him to come on that motorcycle."

"Does Ricky make you cum?"

"Jessie coyly nodded and smiled. "He's like you, Mikey."

"Do you think if a guy makes you cum, that he's nice to you? That he loves you?"

"Yes."

"Is that why you like Ricky?"

"No, Ricky loves me. He's my best friend in the world and he cares about me. He told me, he says he wants to kill my dad. Will he?"

"I wanna murder that fucker myself. Why do you like me, Jessie?"

She didn't answer right away. In the back of her mind, as dreadful as it was, that was a subconscious expectation. Maybe Mike could protect her and free her from her dad. It wasn't something she really contemplated. It was more of a feeling. "Because, you want me...Because, you're my Mikey...Because all the girls want you, but, only I get you...only I get you, Mikey...Because, you're strong, and your arms are tho big around me. You're quiet and you ask me about me and you still like me. And people are afraid of you like I was before. Like, when you kissed me the first time," Jessie smiled, whispering. "My tummy was tickling, and I was so scared of you. You were tho handsome. I wanted to kiss you, but I was scared of you. I was going to faint, and I had to run away." Jessie stared into Mike's eyes, her face was so intent. "I would be so sad if you didn't want me no more, Mikey."

Mike realized it was his own fault. He should have left her alone. Then she wouldn't be having feelings for him, too.

"I'll always want you, Jessie. But I don't think I want to share you, either."

"I won't choose, Mike. I told Luke I won't choose. I'll run away. *I'm not going to choose!* I can't!"

"Well, don't choose then!" Mike snapped. He didn't want to share her, but he didn't want to lose her either. "I don't want to talk about this anymore, Jessie. Let's just fuck, before you have to go home."

Jessie scowled. "I don't like that word."

"Sorry. I just don't want to hear any of this crap right now."

Jessie got up to leave. "Well, you asked me."

"Where are you going?"

"Leaving."

"You're *not* leaving," Mike gulped.

"I don't want you no more, Mikey," she said, heading toward the door, but he was angry, now. He shot out of bed and grabbed her, struggling to get her back to the bed.

"Don't you *ever* say that to me!" he snapped, trying to keep her from hitting him.

Jessie hit at him. *"I don't want you no more!"*

"God dammit, Jessie, don't do this. This fuckin' baby shit!"

Jessie struggled to get away. "Let-me-go!"

"Stop it, Jessie!" He straddled her body on the bed, holding her arms above her head. "I'm sorry," he said, letting go. "I'm sorry, shit, damn-it, I'm sorry, Jessie."

Jessie looked up at him. Her tearful eyes became still. "Are you going to hurt me, Mikey?"

"I'm not gonna hurt you." He took a breath. "I'll never hurt you, again." Desperately, he kissed her. He smoothed his hand across her forehead, gazing into her eyes. "I get frustrated, cuz I want you. I want you, Jessie, all to myself, but…Luke's my brother, and I can't do this anymore. I'm not right for you."

Jessie's eyes were sad as she stared into his eyes. "You can't love me no more, Mikey?"

"I'll always love you, Jessie, but this ain't gonna work. I have to choose for you, baby."

Jessie's sad little face was tearing him up, as her tears rolled down the sides of her face. Mike began to kiss Jessie and caress her body. She moaned with sorrow and sniffed. He felt so tender for her, feeling her pain. Overwhelmed with passion, he began to undress her. He was getting worked up and put the rubber on. He started to enter her and then stopped. "Are you still sore?"

She nodded, looking up at him.

"Maybe we better wait, baby." He kissed her neck, breathing heavy in her ear. "I don't know if I can wait, I want you." He took a deep breath. "I don't want to hurt you anymore. I'll just hold you."

Thursday, January 3, 1974

Mike woke up heated and sticky with sweat, holding Jessie against him. It was four o'clock in the morning and he had to get her home. Some dogs were barking on the next street over and Jessie's body was trembling.

"Wake up, peanut," he said, kissing her ear.

Jessie was weeping in her sleep. Luke was barking. The shadow in the trees and the spiders in the wood bin were tormenting her sleeping thoughts. "The spiders, the spiders, they're coming. Spiders are coming," she said, breathing heavy.

"Come own, baby, wake up. You have to get back, before everyone wakes up."

"No!" She clenched her head between her hands. "I don't want to. Mikey, make those dogs be quiet!"

Mike started to get up. "Come on babe, get up."

"NO!" Jessie grabbed on to him. "No! I won't go! I want you. I want you, Mikey, keep me." She pushed herself into him as close as she could get.

"Jessie," he said, hugging her. "I want you, too, baby, but don't do this right now."

"I don't want to go," she cried, hitting him in the chest. "No. No." She grabbed his arms and squeezed, hard. "I want you! Put me in your muthles, Mikey."

Jenny knocked on the door, opening it. She brought in Jessie's sweater. "I'm sorry, Jessie," she said, feeling ill at ease, and seeing them both naked. She went back out the door.

Mike took a deep breath and kissed Jessie's forehead. "You can have a fit if you want, but I have to take you home, Jessie." He started to get up again, when she put her arms around him.

"No Mikey," she cried. "I'm not going to leave you. I have to stay with you. Don't make me go, Mikey. I'll *die* if I have to go home. *I'm gonna die there, Mikey,*" she sobbed, "And you won't keep me. You have to take me away. Please, put me in your car and take me away."

"I wanna take you away, Jessie. I'm gonna take you away, I promise, but not now, bunny. I think about it all the time, but I can't right now, baby." Mike held her face, kissing her tears. "Don't you know that?"

"There's no place for me, Mikey."

"There will be Jessie. I promise you."

"Keep me, Mikey."

"I will, baby, but, fuck! We gotta go, right now." Mike got up and struggled to put her pants and boots on her, while she laid there, glaring at him. He had to pick her up and carry her out to the car. She leaned against the seat, glaring at him, pouting.

"Don't make that face, Jessie. It's tearing me up."

She ignored him and continued the entire way home.

When they pulled up in front of his house, he carried her over to her front steps and went to kiss her. She was sniffling and closed her eyes. She wouldn't kiss him. She pulled herself out of his arms and sat down on the grass. He backed away from her.

"Go upstairs, Jessie," he said, walking away. He got out to the street and she lay down in the grass, looking at him, pouting. "Jessie, *go upstairs.*"

She ignored him.

"Dammit!" he said under his breath and walked over to her. "You can't lay here in the grass." He squatted down in front of her and she pushed on him, making him fall back. She started to run off when he grabbed her.

Maddy was inside waiting for them at the window. She went out on the front step.

"Let me go!" Jessie squirmed, trying to pull away. "*Let- me- go!*" she whined, pushing on his chest, when she fainted. Mike picked her up and Maddy waived at him to bring her upstairs.

He carried her to Aimee's bottom bunk and laid her down. He kissed her lips, stroking her face.

"What's the matter with her?" Maddy asked.

Mike stood up and shook his head, looking at Jessie. "She just don't want to go home." Mike put his hand on Maddy's shoulder. "Take care of her, Maddy," he said, and left.

Mike went into his room and closed the door. It was apparent to him that he had messed with the wrong girl, and now it was too late, he had deep feelings for her. Jessie was cursed. She was bewitching. Not just to him, but obviously, anyone who got swept up in her path. Unfortunately, it was not intentional. If she'd been some manipulative little seductress, it would be easier. He could have
just played the game and left. He kept doing the wrong things with her, because he never cared about it before. He'd never known anyone like her. She needed him to take her away. How in the hell could he do that? Maybe he needed to grow up, get his shit together, and stay away from Jessie, for her sake. He wasn't really the right guy for her. Maybe it would have been better if she'd never come down off Genoa's Peak.

There were a few adult magazines on his bed. He threw them against the wall and sat down, lighting a cigarette. He looked up at his wall, plastered with naked women. He chuckled, knowing his mother couldn't stand to go in his room. He got up and started ripping them all down. "Sorry, Ladies," he said, taking it all out and burned it in the fireplace. He spent the morning cleaning his room.

Chapter Seven –
Waking Up

Friday, January 4, 1974

Jessie woke up depressed. She stared up at the bottom of Aimee's bed, thinking about Mike. She was sorry she told him she didn't want him anymore, and that she had a fit that morning. Her Aunt could have seen her, and everything could have been bad. Mike was crying, and she understood maybe she hurt his feelings, and he would think she really didn't want him anymore. Maybe she shouldn't want him, anymore. He didn't have very good ideas.

Maddy came in the room wanting to talk to her. "How was your night, Jessie?" Maddy asked, sitting next to her on the bed.

Jessie shrugged. "I wish I would not have gone."

"Why, what happened?"

Jessie's eyes began to tear. "Maddy, I'm bad for having thex. I wish I never met any of them. I wish I could go back in time, and never have met them. I would never have been pregnant or lost the baby, and now bad things are happening."

"Was Mike being mean to you?" Maddy asked. What was going on this morning?"

"No, I was mean to him. I told him I don't want him no more, and he was mad at me. I don't want to leave when I'm with him. I want to stay with them forever, but I always have to go, and I never know if I'll see any of them again. I can't think anymore. I love all of them, and I don't know how to think anymore. I think I'm crazy, I feel so torn up."

"Well, I guess that's what you get," Maddy replied sternly. "You need to learn, Jessie. Girls aren't like boys who can go around having sex, and not even care about who they're having sex with. Girls aren't like that. We do it because we actually like the idiot, and hope they like us back, but it doesn't work that way. Why did you tell him you didn't want him anymore, Jessie?"

"He asked me why I love Luke, and Ricky, and I was trying to tell him how I-I love them. He didn't know what I was trying to tell him, and he got mad. He said, 'I don't want to hear this crap', and it hurt me. I told him I don't want him no more. He cried last night, Maddy. H-he cried, and it made me s-ad." Jessie's voice faltered.

Maddy looked mournfully at Jessie. "Well, then he shouldn't ask questions, if he can't handle the answer. Why did he cry, Jessie, because you said that to him?"

"No. Because-because, Kevin and Jenny, and Mike, and me, we did something bad last night, and I got scared. Mikey was sad after that and we were bad. He was afraid I wouldn't want him no more."

"What did you do, Jessie?" Maddy asked sternly.

"I'm afraid to tell you, Maddy."

"Just tell me."

"Well," Jessie said, fidgeting with the blanket. "Jenny told me, have thex with her so they could watch us."

"What?! And did you?"

"Dis for a minute." Jessie sadly nodded. "But I didn't like it, and I cried, and Mikey picked me up and took me away. He said sorry for doing that to me and he cried."

"Whose brilliant idea was that?"

"Kevin's."

"Creep." Maddy scowled. "Why did you agree?"

"I wanted to make Mikey happy."

"Well, you didn't, did you?"

"No. I feel awful," Jessie sniffed.

"I bet. You're really a mess, aren't you, Jessie?"

Jessie nodded, pouting. "Maddy, I don't think I should come here no more. I'm so sad when I'm at home, because all I can think about is getting back here, and I can't. But, if I never leave my house anymore, maybe this will all go away. Maybe, after a while, I will forget everything and go back to what I was used to, and I won't do bad things no more."

"That won't work, Jessie. You'd go insane, because you'll never forget. You have to move on and look forward to the future. You have to do things differently from now on. I know it's hard for you, but, Jessie, you're going to have to pick one of those boys. You can't keep tormenting yourself or them. It's not fair to any of you, and Mike should be more careful with you, anyway. I think you should stay away from him. He's not someone you can count on."

Jessie didn't want to hear that, but she looked up at Maddy. Maybe she was right.

Jessie's face told Maddy how painful that was for her. "Today, just try to have fun and don't think about it. Us girls are going out shopping, and we should just think about that."

"Do you miss Jake when you're not with him, Maddy?"

"Yeah, a little; I'm not in love with him, though. I don't know if I'll ever love anyone like I love Mike, but, I have to give that up, too."

"I'm sorry, Maddy. I know how you feel…he's--unforgettable." Jessie smiled at Maddy. "I hope someday you meet someone, Maddy. Someone you love more than Mikey."

"Oh, I hope so too, Jessie, seein' as how you ruined that for me." Maddy smiled at her. "I suppose he had sex with you last night, even though you just had the miscarriage?"

"No. He said he would wait till I'm better."

"Really? Well, at least he had some sense. Come on, let's get dressed, Mom's waiting."

"Are you going to tell Jenny I told you?"

"I don't know. Jenny's gotten kind of weird lately. I think Kevin is a bad influence on her. I think Mike is a bad influence on you, Jessie. You should think about that. If he really cared about you, he would leave you alone and stop putting you in these situations. You know, I used to think Mike was special, someone I could look up to, but I'm not sure anymore…Well, it's kind of my fault, Jessie. I made you go." Maddy stood up, realizing she was just as guilty, "I think you should pick Luke. He really loves you the most and he would take really good care of you."

Maddy left the room while Jessie sat up thinking about what Maddy had said. Jessie didn't think she could tell which one loved her the most, or which one she loved the most. There was no way possible of ever knowing that.

Debbie took the girls to Mr. Burke's office first thing in the morning. As soon as he met Jessie and the girls, he realized he had to do everything he could to help Debbie get custody.

Debbie explained to him about Jessie playing with the band at the Festival, and that she needed to be able to practice. John told her that the possibility might be slim, but he would get together with Hank's lawyer, and Mark, and try to work out an offer that might be suitable to Hank.

The rest of the day was spent getting manicures, shopping, and looking at different bedroom styles. Debbie wanted Jessie to pick out a theme for her bedroom. At *Weinstocks*, they saw a bedroom set that had a Hawaiian theme. Jessie fell instantly in love with it and decided right then that's how she wanted her room to look. She was excited now, about having her own room at her Aunt Debbie's house, her Momma's house; her house.

Saturday, January 5, 1973

Harry and Debbie took the family to Lake Tahoe. They wanted to show Jessie the cabin. Debbie showed Jessie all around the place, and Jessie tried to be surprised, but all she could think about was Luke, and how much she suddenly missed him, and how sweet and protective he was of her. Maddy was probably right.

After looking at the cabin, they went to have lunch on the riverboat, *M.S. Dixie*. Jessie was fascinated at actually being on a boat. She pretended she was on a big ship in the ocean, going off to a tropic island. The family was chattering, but Jessie wasn't paying attention. She looked out across the lake as they sat waiting to be served, imagining sandy beaches with palm trees and hula girls. She remembered reading an article about Hawaii in *Sunset Magazine* and dreaming for weeks about living in a grass hut with her mother, lying on the beach in the warm sun, eating coconuts. As she looked out, she began to see a soft glow that was far out above the water. She watched as it grew brighter and seemed to be moving toward the boat. As it grew near, it seemed to evolve into a figure, the figure of a woman. Jessie's eyes grew big as she stared at the image. Slowly, a soft face appeared and a beautiful woman, all aglow, was floating before her. She had luminous blue eyes, and shining, golden hair. Her smile was as bright as the sun. She wore an elegant crystal gown, shimmering with golden glitter. Jessie felt a comforting warmth inside her and knew she was in the presence of a familiar being. She smiled. "Mother," she whispered. The woman nodded, smiling ever so gently and then faded.

"Are we having the Super Bowl Party at our house this year, Dad?" Eli seemed to blurt out suddenly and Jessie's attention turned toward the question.

"That's what we've planned, Son. Tom's invited a few people, and Pete will be there," Harry answered.

"What's the Thuper Bowl Party?" Jessie asked.

Debbie wished that Eli had not brought that up, knowing Jessie would be back home then.

"It's that last football game of the season," Eli answered. "This year is Super Bowl VIII. The Dolphins are playing against the Vikings."

"The Dolphins are your favorite team, aren't they, Eli?" Jessie asked.

"Yep, Larry Csonka is my all-time favorite fullback, and they're gonna kick butt!"

"Is it like Thanksgiving, when everyone is there, eating together?" Jessie turned to her Aunt.

Debbie looked at Jessie, with a sad smile and nodded.

"I wish I could come," Jessie said sadly, looking out at the lake. "Will Ricky be there?"

"You'll get to see plenty more Super Bowls, Jessie," Uncle Harry assured her. Debbie watched as Jessie's face became heartbreakingly poignant.

"That's right, Jessie," Aunt Debbie answered. "We have many years to watch Super Bowl Sunday, and enjoy Thanksgiving, and Christmas, and all the rest of our wonderful days ahead."

Jessie was not so convinced, and Debbie could see her pain at not trusting that, knowing she would be alone at home.

After lunch, intent on keeping Jessie's mind distracted from depression, they drove back through Carson City and went to the Nevada Museum, the State Senate building, the Capitol building, and that night, they went to the movies.

Sunday, January 6, 1974

Meg and Tom drove to Reno early in the morning, to pick Ricky up from his grandmother's house. It was going to be a sunny day outside. The air was still a bit nippy, but the sky was clear. Ricky was glad to be home. He dropped his backpack on the coffee table in the living-room and took his travel bag to his room to empty it. Mike was sitting in the recliner, half asleep, watching TV. Neither one said anything to the other. Ricky knew Mike would just make some smart-ass comment about something, and Mike was suddenly looking at his little brother differently.

Ricky had a few souvenirs from the Grand Canyon in his backpack that he'd gotten for his Mom and Jessie. When he went back out to get it from the coffee table, he looked out the window and noticed Jessie and Eli coming down the front stairs of their house. They were bundled up in jackets and Eli was holding a football.

Ricky dropped his backpack and ran out the door, slamming it. His face looked panicked, and Mike looked out the window to see what was going on. So did Luke, who'd seen Ricky run out the door as he was coming down the hallway to greet him home. Ricky ran over to Jessie as fast as he could. He grabbed her and picked her up, twirling around with her in the yard, then sat down on the front step with her, desperately hugging her.

"RICKY!" Jessie laughed, kicking her legs, holding him tight.

"Jessie, no one told me you were here!" Ricky said out of breath.

"I know, Ricky. They didn't want you to know. I *miss* you, Ricky." Jessie laughed, wrapping her arms tightly around him.

"I thought about you the whole time I was gone. I couldn't wait to get home! I hated being so far away from you. How long have you been home, Jess?"

"All week."

"You've been here a whole week? God damn-it that pisses me off!" Ricky snapped, looking over at his house. "And I suppose you're leaving tomorrow?" he asked, looking back at Jessie.

Jessie nodded, pouting up at him.

"They knew I wouldn't go if I knew you were gonna be here."

"I guess it was 'portant for you to go with your grama, Ricky," Jessie said, looking up at him, and stroking his chin with her fingers. "I miss my grama."

"Not that damn important. I was miserable the whole time. I couldn't stand how far away I was from you. I kept looking up at the stars at night, knowing you were somewhere under the same moon, but I'm so glad to see you now." Ricky hugged Jessie tightly and kissed her face. "I couldn't wait to get home, so I could come see you at school. That's what I was planning, soon as I got home."

Jessie sighed, laying her head on his chest. Clenching his arm, she sat up, "Ricky, I saw my Momma."

"You saw your Mom?"

"Yeah, she was like a angel. She came to me yesterday, on the boat, and she smiled at me when I called her Mother."

"Wow, Jess. Are you sure you weren't just daydreaming?"

"No. I saw her. I knew who she was. Ricky, don't say God no more like that."

"I'm sorry, Jess." Ricky noticed Elijah, tossing the ball up in the air. "Hey, Eli," Ricky said to him.

"Hi, Rick. Did you like the Grand Canyon?" Eli asked, already understanding he didn't. "Jessie and me were just gonna play catch, wanna play?"

Luke stood at the front room window looking out at them, not saying anything. He had his hand on his hips and was thinking. Mike sat back down in the recliner, tired from being awake all night, thinking of Jessie and what an idiot he was.

"Call Gary, see if he wants to play a game of football, Mike," Luke said, still looking out the window. "Call Kevin, too."

"What for? She's with Ricky right now."

"For Jessie." Luke went over to the phone and called Ryan. Then he got his jacket and walked outside to Debbie's yard. "Toss me the ball, Eli!" he yelled. "Go get your jacket, Rickus, we're gonna play."

Ricky looked at Luke, surprised.

"Go on, Ricky," Jessie said. "Go get your coat so we can play football in the yard!" She stood up and pulled on his hands to get up.

"All right, I'll be right back!" Ricky said, and ran home.

Mike called Kevin and Gary to come over. Yeah, he wanted to hang out with Jessie too, before she had to go home tomorrow. It would be their last day to see her, for God only knew how long.

Luke smiled and winked at Jessie. "I love you," he whispered to her, throwing the ball back at Elijah.

Jessie smiled back. "Thank you, Luke."

Maddy was looking out the living-room window, when Mike and Kevin walked over. Just then, Gary and Ryan showed up in their cars.

"Mom!" Maddy hollered. "Can we have the Miller's over for dinner?"

Debbie came out of the kitchen, wiping her hands on a towel. She noticed Maddy looking intently out the window. She walked over to her and saw all the boys in the yard. "What are you thinking, sweetie?" she asked, looking very curiously at her.

"For Jessie; she has to go home tomorrow. I think we should all be together today."

Debbie looked down at Jessie, who was playing football in the yard, laughing and smiling. "Sure, we can." Debbie grinned at Maddy, stroking the hair along her face. "I'll call Meg."

Maddy put her jacket on and went outside to join Jessie. The boys welcomed Maddy into the game, and she was realizing she didn't have to miss out anymore.

Jessie spent one of the best days of her life, with all the people she loved. It was good for everyone to see Jessie smiling and laughing, something she seldom did. A sense of peace and harmony had come over everyone that day. They all understood they had to make that day special for Jessie. Mike and Luke tackled her as often as they could, and Ricky got pissed.

They all sat around the dinner table, talking and laughing. For some reason, it felt like a holiday, and Jessie adored every minute of it. She sat next to Ricky, holding his hand and smiling at him. He smiled back at her. She looked around the table at all the faces she loved so much, and they all looked at Jessie in their own way and felt as though they were in the presence of an angel...

Chapter Eight – Things That Go Bump in the Night

Mike felt something bump his bed. He felt the bed bump again and heard a little voice.

"Mikey," Jessie whispered. She was standing at the edge of his bed, in her pajamas, holding Teddy.

"Hey, baby." He smiled, happily surprised. He held up the blankets for her. "How'd you get in here?"

"Magic," Jessie said, and snuggled up close to him. "Mikey, I'm sorry. I'm tho sorry, Mikey."

"Why are you sorry, peanut?" he asked, snuggling her close.

"I'm sorry, Mikey." Jessie started to sob. "I'm sorry I don't want you no more, and I had a fit in the morning."

"Well, do you, or don't you?"

"What?"

"Want me."

"I do want you. I have to go home tomorrow."

"It's okay, baby. I know how you get sad when you gotta go home. It makes me sad, too. It makes everyone sad. I'm sorry too, baby. I'm a fuckin' idiot." Mike said, kissing her head.

"Are you going to Uncle Harry's Thuper Bowl Party on next Sunday?"

"I don't know, peanut, I'll probably have to work all day."

"I can't be there, Mikey. I have to be at home. I might not ever see you again."

"I don't know if you should see me again, Jessie. I'm a stupid fuck."

"Maddy said I should not see you no more."

"She did, huh?"

"Yeah, Mikey, I'm afraid."

"What are you afraid of, peanut?"

"What if I don't ever thee you again?"

"You're with me right now, bunny. Did you lock the door?"

She nodded, with her sad eyes looking up at him.

Mike wrapped his arms around Jessie, kissing her. "My little bunny lovins'," Mike whispered, immediately caressing her breasts. "My beautiful little, tittie girl," he whispered, kissing and caressing her madly.

Jessie started to pant and whine and make her usual love noises.

"You gotta be real quiet, bunny," Mike said to her softly.

Jessie was so enraptured and emotional, she couldn't stop breathing heavy, and moaning. "Mikey," she was saying over and over. He could tell she was upset. He began to rub her back and whispered to her.

"Let me help you turn off your little cry baby engine, peanut," he said, caressing her. "It's okay, Jessie. Just breathe, just relax, baby. I'm right here."

"I'll be a good girl, Mikey, I promise. I won't make a fuss." She sniffed with tears going down her face.

"I know you're a good girl," Mike said, kissing her face. "Too damn good. You're so beautiful, baby. God damn, you're beautiful. You make it so hard, Jessie, not to want you; are you sure, baby? I don't want to hurt you."

"Mikey, I love you plugged in me. It feels like electric. Don't say God, though," she whispered.

Mike grinned, trying not to laugh. She held her hair up over her head, squirming and cooing. He tried, but had zero will power, she was too wanting, too beautiful, too bewitching. He protected himself and moved slowly. Jessie loved how powerful he felt, pushing his arms down against the bed, he squeezed her hand, and lay down over her.

~

"I have to go home, tomorrow, Mikey, and I don't know if I'll ever see you again. I don't know if I'll ever get to come here again." Jessie's eyes were as sad as could be.

"Sure, you will, baby." Mike stroked her face. "Momma's workin' on that…Jessie," he whispered, kissing her. "Will you go steady with me? We could end all this bullshit…and I'll be good to you, Jessie…I'll try real hard. I know I been real stupid, but you mean so much to me. I could ask your Momma, and then we wouldn't have to sneak around, anymore."

Jessie looked deeply in his eyes. They were desperately begging for an answer. "Yes, Mikey, I will," she whispered. "I'll go steady with you, Mikey…when I'm big. But, what if after a while, you don't want me no more?"

"I'll always want you, peanut, but what do you mean? When will you be big enough?"

"I don't know. When I can stay here, and not leave. Momma says I don't have to choose right now, because I'm too young, and well, my friend, Paula, told me that boys only go steady for a while, till they pick someone else."

"Yeah, I guess little boys do that. But I'm not a little boy, and you're not just anybody. What are we all supposed to do, Jessie? Wait around?" Mike rolled over on his back, looking up at the ceiling. "I wanna make babies with you, someday."

"Babies?" Jessie giggled. "I want a baby, Mikey. I want a little boy."

"Yeah, then I won't have to wear these fuckin' things anymore," Mike said, taking his rubber off and putting it in the trash. "What are we gonna name him, bunny?"

"Mikey. We're going to name him Mikey...Mikey," Jessie grinned. "I'm in your room with you."

Mike thought about that for a second, glad that he'd cleaned his room. He felt like it was a sign.

"I'm in your bed, where you sleep, Mikey, me and Teddy." Jessie was smiling, so happy.

"I know you are, bunny girl. I love having you in my bed."

Just then, Mike's dad knocked on the door and they both jumped, startled. "What's going on in there, Michael?"

"Shit," Mike whispered, irritated. "Nothin', Dad, I got a girl in here."

"Oh," Tom sighed, and went back to his room.

"Sorry, my dad's a pervert," Mike said, tracing Jessie's lips with his finger.

Jessie rolled over on her back, holding Teddy against her chest. Mike lay on his side, leaning over her, admiring her. "You have the prettiest blue eyes I've ever seen. They're not even like human eyes, they're like—like…"

She sat up and looked around Mike's room. "Where's the beaver shots?"

"Beaver shots?" he laughed. "I don't have 'em anymore."

"What are all those things?" Jessie asked, pointing toward the end of the bed.

"My weights."

"What do they do?"

"I lift weights, so I can have big muscles for you."

"Oh? Does it hurt?"

"Sometimes."

"You have a lot. Can you show me 'em?"

Mike climbed down the bed, picked up a barbell, and showed Jessie how he lifts it. Jessie could see the big muscle in his arm.

"Boy, that does make your muthles big."

Mike put it back and lay down on the bed, pulling Jessie close to him. "I lay awake at night, wondering what life is like for you. What you were like. How you're so little and…unprotected. I'm gonna be a cop, Jessie," he said, stroking his finger up and down her stomach and in between her breasts.

"A cop? Like Therpico?"

"Mm hm."

"Why?"

"That's what I wanna do, catch the bad guys. Catch all the bad guys for you, Jessie. I always thought about it, and I really think I wanna be a cop."

"It's dangerous."

"Not here. It's a good job, and I can take care of you, and all our babies."

"I don't think I would like that."

"Well, I guess you're not the boss, are you?" He smiled. "Would you want me to be a criminal, instead?"

"No. No, Mikey."

"My Uncle's a cop, down in Texas. He loves it. Everyone says I'm like him."

"And you will take care of me?"

"Of course. I have to have a good job, and *I* will buy you a house."

"Okay, Mikey. You be a cop. But you're tho handsome. You won't look like my Mikey no more."

Mike laughed, "You won't still love me, baby?"

"What if you meet a lot of ladies?"

"There's no woman that could take me away from you. There's no one out there like you, bunny. The only way I'd want another woman, is if I couldn't have you anymore, and even then, it would never be the same. I don't wannna think about that."

"What if you get shot?"

"I don't know. I'm gonna do it, Jessie, be a cop. I gotta go take a piss, I'll be right back, baby." Mike got up and put his boxers on. "You want a Pepsi or something?

"Yes, please," she said, holding teddy up with both hands.

He leaned over the bed and whispered to her, "You be quiet, and don't leave, I'll be right back."

Monday, January 7, 1974

Jessie woke up and saw it was four-forty-five on the radio/alarm clock. She quietly moved, watching Mike. It was a bit difficult, wiggling out from under his heavy arm. She wanted to cry but was trying to keep her promise of not making a fuss. She bent over Mike and kissed his sleeping mouth, looking at how handsome he was. "Good bye, Mikey," she whispered, quietly leaving the room.

At seven am, Mike stood looking out the front-room window, watching Jessie in her school uniform, get in Debbie's car and drive away. A horrible sense of fear and loneliness moved across his brain, actually feeling a tingling sensation in the back of his head. He swallowed the lump in his throat and leaned his head against the window. He closed his eyes when he could no longer see the car. "Good-bye, bunny," he whispered, wondering if he'd ever see her again. He thought to ask Ricky to drive to school with him in the mornings, like he used to ride with Luke.

Luke was in the bathroom, taking a shower. Ricky had already been to Debbie's and kissed Jessie good-bye. He rode his bicycle to school.

Chapter Nine –
God Only Knows

For some reason, that Monday didn't seem as bad as they normally did when Aunt Debbie took Jessie to school. In fact, Jessie seemed to have a sense of peace, and felt happy, because she was starting to understand that maybe, she *was* going to keep going back. Nothing could stop that now. Aunt Debbie loved her now and assured her she *would* be coming back. Luke was going to be there at lunchtime, so she had that to look forward to. Her own new bedroom would be finished soon, and maybe she would even be practicing with UnSed. She was starting to understand that her dad couldn't keep her away forever, and she didn't dread going home so badly. Mother Magdalena was glad to see Jessie happy for a change that morning.

Her first three classes went by quickly, but toward the end of third period, Jessie couldn't stop watching the clock, waiting for the eleven-thirty bell to ring. Anxiously, she watched the second hand go around the last minute, and as the bell rang, she hurried out to the main doors, but didn't see Luke's car. It was cloudy outside, and the air was cold. She felt a surge of fear and became panicked, standing on the steps. She didn't believe that Luke would forget her, and worried that something was wrong.

She walked over to the gate and looked down the road. She stood watching for about five minutes, worried about Luke. She remembered her dream and started to go back to the office. Maybe she could call his work to see if he left there. Just then, she heard his car coming up the road. She turned to see it was him and had never felt so relieved in her life. She ran over to his car door as he opened it. He pulled her in and sat her on his lap.

"Sorry, babe," he said kissing her, wiping her tearful eyes. "Don't cry, baby, I couldn't get out of the store on time. These customers keep talking, and you can't get away from them."

"I was scared, Luke. I was alone," Jessie sobbed. "I was worried about you."

"Don't worry, darlin', I'm here. I could never forget you." Luke pulled her close to him. "I was listening to a song on the way here, and it made me smile. It's gonna be my song to you."

"What song is it, Lukiss?"

"My Love, by Paul McCartney."

Jessie buried her head in his chest. "I want you to make love to me, Luke."

"We really have to be careful, Jessie. I don't want you to get pregnant again."

"But I miss you touching me," Jessie whined.

"Don't you want to eat, darlin'?"

"No. I want you to hold me."

Luke smoothed her hair back. Her beautiful, blue eyes were begging him. "Okay, Beautiful, get in your seat. I'll just love on you for a while."

Luke drove up the road some ways and pulled onto a dirt road. He stopped behind some trees and locked his doors. He took Jessie into the back seat and held her on his lap, kissing her. Jessie put her arms around his neck.

"Luke, I'm still bleeding from the miscarriage. I only have a few more pads to wear. Do you think I will bleed for a long time?"

"I don't know, darlin', you can ask the doctor tomorrow. Do you wanna go buy some?"

"No. I want you to hold me, Luke."

"Baby." He smiled. Luke slid his hand inside her blouse, caressing her, kissing her mouth, whispering, "Bubbles…Hello, little, soft bubbles."

Jessie put her hands up Luke's shirt, stroking his chest, and then ran her fingers through his hair, cooing to Luke's gentle touches. "I love you, Luke," Jessie whispered looking up at him. "I love how you love me, Luke."

Luke stopped kissing her and stared into her eyes. Jessie held on to his arm muscles, squeezing them. Luke let Jessie down on the back seat, lying over her. "Pretty baby," Luke whispered. Jessie put her arms over her head, cooing at Luke.

"Mm," Luke exhaled. "We better not do this, darlin'." His eyes were rolling back in his head. "I'm gonna get too hot. I can't wait till you're on the pill, Jessie. I'm gonna go insane."

"Am I gross now, because I'm bleeding? Is that why you don't want me?"

"Jessie, I would never think that. You could never be gross to me. That's normal anyway, Love. I just wanna be careful with you, cuz I love you so much."

"Okay, Luke," she whispered, closing her eyes. "Dis love on me though."

"I love you, baby."

Jessie opened her eyes and smiled up at him, stroking his face with her fingers. "You're so beautiful, Luke. Thank you for not forgetting me…we made love in the car before."

"If that's what you call it, Bubbles." He smiled. "I'm sorry it was in the back of the car the first time. I wanted it to be more special. What I really wish is that we were married first, and I would take you on a romantic honeymoon, to Hawaii or somewhere beautiful."

"In Hawaii?" Jessie asked, pondering. *How wonderful would that be?* "Anytime you touch me, you love me, Lukiss. Luke, I didn't feel so sad this morning going to school. I knew you were coming to see me."

"I won't be late tomorrow, Beautiful."

"Except I'm feeling sad now, Luke. We can't have no honeymoon in Hawaii, now."

"We could still have a honeymoon, Jessie. You could marry me."

Jessie longed to give Luke the answer he wanted, but everything was all messed up now. "Luke," she pouted, not really wanting to ignore his question. "I have to wait all the way till tomorrow to see you again, now. You're tho far away from me. I can't talk to you whenever I want. I was okay this morning, but now I'm not. I don't want to go home."

"I know, baby. I don't want you to go home, either. I'm never far away from you, though. You can call me at the hardware store during the day, in between classes. I could come stay with you tonight. I could watch to see if your dad comes home and stay with you."

"What if he came home, Luke?"

"I would just go out the back door."

"I wish you could do that. But I would be too scared."

"Jessie, if you would just marry me, you'd never have to go there again. You could live with me in our own house."

Luke eyes were desperate. Jessie wished it could be that easy. She wished she could just say yes to Luke, and never have to go back to that place again. But the thought of hurting Ricky or Mike now, was unbearable. *She would never be able to be close with them again.* That was too painful and complicated for Jessie to think about. Luke parked in front of the gate and gave Jessie a long kiss good-bye before he let her go. "You got my hair all messy." He smiled, looking in his rear-view mirror.

Jessie grinned. "You look beautiful." She smoothed her hand across his chest and kissed him. He pulled her down and held her tight.

"I love you," Jessie whispered.

"I love you, Jessie," Luke replied with a lovesick gleam in his eyes.

Jessie sadly got out of the car and ran to the bathroom. Luke wished he could drive away with her.

Tired and gloomy, Jessie sat down next to her dog, on the front porch steps of the cabin. It was the twilight of the evening, and quails were cooing somewhere in the brush next to the driveway. She'd already started the washing machine on the back porch, and the chickens were heartily pecking at their grain. They looked gangly, and she figured they hadn't eaten in a while.

"Poor old dog," she said, smoothing Luke's face. "I'm sorry I was gone away from you."

She handed Luke the last bit of her egg sandwich and he swallowed it whole. It was too much trouble to cook any big dinner tonight, and her mood was of hopeless despair. The all-too familiar sense of doom and loneliness swept over her like a long-lost friend. The breezy air was cool, and the sky was a bit cloudy, adding to Jessie's lonely depression. She looked down the road, listening to some little, black wrens up in the Aspen trees, wondering how long she was going to have to live there, and wishing she could just walk down it and never come back.

How wonderful it would be to be a little bird and fly away, she thought, looking across the cloudy sky.

There were no leaves on the Aspen's, and the large pines facing the cabin were like dark, old Ent's, groaning in the wind. They frowned down at her, with their big arms stretched out wide. She frowned back at them, sticking her tongue out to the big, nasty one. They always blocked the evening sunbeams, now hiding what would have been a pretty, yellow sunset. At once, she noticed an eerie silence as the birds had stopped singing. A chipmunk quickly scurried by on the grass, and Luke put his head up and puffed. They watched it run across the road and up one of the old codgers, as if it were running from something, when a big ugly crow, flying overhead, cawed loudly. It frightened Jessie and she could feel the hair on her neck stiffen as its lonesome wail vanished into the thicket.

"I hate crows," she said to Luke. Luke looked up at her with his eyebrows twitching. She petted him and sat still in the silence, only to be broken again, by the sound of a high branch crackling above, over in the north pines. She turned to hear it crashing through the trees as it fell, and thud, as it dropped to the ground. She shuddered with sudden fear, scanning the dark trees, when a shadow caught the corner of her eye. She fixed her eyes, and there, holding on to a tree from behind, was *the monster,* glaring at her with his red, beady eyes. His long, thick claws were drumming the tree trunk.

Her heart was pounding, she was frozen, unable to move. Her eyes opened wide as he began to creep out from behind the tree, growling.

Luke put his head up and barked at Jessie, and the monster shrinked back. Jessie got up and ran into the cabin, locking the door. Cautiously, she peeked out the front window, hiding behind the curtain, but only saw Luke, licking his leg on the porch.

Her heart was still pounding furiously in her throat as she tried to catch her breath. She decided she better leave Luke outside, to patrol the yard. She ran and made sure the back door and all the windows were locked, and then took out her dad's .22 rifle, leaning it up next to the front door. She peeked out the window again, but only saw Luke, now resting his head on his paw. She took a deep breath and got her books off the end table and sat at the kitchen table, frightened.

She tried but was having a hard time concentrating on her homework, listening for any strange sounds. She was wishing like crazy that she had let Luke come stay with her, almost hoping to hear her dad's truck. She wasn't about to go get the laundry out of the washing machine. She would just have to wear the same uniform tomorrow. She put her head down, closing her eyes and prayed for Jesus to come take the monster away, and get her away from there, forever.

She couldn't think about her homework. The wind outside was disturbing, and the creaking from all the old wood in the cabin made her jump at every little sound. All she could think about was how weary she was of being frightened and worrying about her safety. She realized she couldn't stay here anymore. No one could help her, so she would have to do it herself. She would have to run away, but how?

She put her books away; there wasn't any use in trying to complete her homework. She was contemplating her escape, now.

I won't get on the bus tomorrow, after school. I'll hide in the bathroom. I'll leave before it gets light and walk to Reno. She went to her room and got her overnight bag out of the closet and began packing a few clothes. Then she went to the kitchen and took some bread, crackers, and the jar of peanut butter, and began to organize her bag. She'd have to leave some of her clothes; there wasn't enough room for all of them. She thought as she packed, *I can't leave Luke here, so I can't do it after school. I have to come home and get him first. No, I'll go in the morning, soon as it's light. How will I walk down through the canyon? I'll take the rifle. Maybe I won't go down through the canyon, maybe go down the south road, past the meadow. There's not as many trees. It's longer, but it goes to the same highway. Oh, I have to leave my family. I have to leave, Luke and Mikey...and Ricky...and Momma.*

She took her Mother's picture, looking at it and began to cry, whispering to herself. "I can't stay here. *I'll die here*, I have to do it. When I get through this, and I'm older, I can call them. I don't know what to do, Jesus, you have to help me. You have to take care of me, now."

She put her Mother's picture in her bag, realizing she'd left the new picture frame from Luke at her Auntie's. "Oh..." she remembered, "I *have* to go to school tomorrow, because Luke is taking me to the doctor. Oh," she sighed, "that means one more night here, then I'll go." She hid the overnight bag under the bed and laid down, afraid to change into her pajamas.

Tuesday, January 8, 1974

Hank never did come home, and Jessie had a long night of restlessness and anxiety. She woke up with a horrible, uneasy feeling. It was so pressing on her that she started to go into a mild depression.

She forced herself to get ready for school, washing her face and putting her hair up in a ponytail, trying to remind herself she would get to spend the whole afternoon with Luke. *I'll never see him again*, she thought, looking in the mirror. She couldn't stop thinking and hurting about that.

She was getting a terrible headache as she pulled the frozen clothes in from the machine, telling herself not to cry. Then she went out front to quickly feed the chickens, watching the trees. It was cold, and her hands were frozen. She looked around with an unnerving sense that something was wrong. She put the bucket of chicken feed down and looked under the porch. Luke hadn't come out to greet her.

"Luke," she called, not seeing him. She went around to the back of the house, calling him, "Luke! Come here, boy!"

He wasn't lying on his blanket. She noticed some blood in the dirt. Jessie got a chill and looked over to the north pines.

Walking down toward the meadow, she began noticing a trail of blood, and tufts of black hair blowing across the road. "No," she whispered, and started running, terrified. She followed the blood trail south, along the road. It went across the creek into the meadow.

After about fifteen feet, she saw what was left of Luke's body, lying in the tall grass. She stopped. She could hardly breathe and didn't want to see what she was seeing. "Luke!" she shouted, running to him, scaring off a magpie that was pecking at him. Jessie fell on her knees, bent over what was left of the dog. The coyotes had ripped him to shreds, or was it coyotes? His old age and arthritis had been catching up to him, and Jessie didn't think he was going to live much longer, but she didn't want him to die like this! She bent down with tears pouring down her nose and smoothed her hand across his head.

"Oh, Luke," she sobbed, and put her head down on his. "Luke," she cried, breathless. She lifted her head toward the hills, and then to the cabin. She had to get to school, with no time to bury him, but she didn't want the coyotes, or those magpies to get the rest of him. She ran to the cabin and grabbed his blanket; her tears were pouring like the rain.

Gently, she put his remains on the blanket and wrapped it around him. She carried him to the burning barrel, and as she went to kiss his nose, she broke out in uncontrollable crying.

"G-o-ood-b-y-ye, L-u-uke," she sobbed all the while, as she took the blanket holding Luke's body and placed it in the barrel. She ran under the awning, getting the gasoline can and matches, unable to wipe away enough tears to see clearly. Quickly, she poured some gas in the barrel, lit a match and dropped it in. The barrel went up in hot, white flames, exploding and crackling. She cried in aguish, shaking her head. Her body was trembling as the smell of death carried on the smoke, surrounded her. She heard the bus coming up the canyon. "Good-bye, Luke," she whispered. She hurried into the house to get her books and ran down to the bus stop.

Jessie gazed out the window of the bus, watching the trees down through the canyon go by, as tears ran down her face. She kept wiping her hand across her runny nose and couldn't stop sniffing. Her heart was broken, wishing she would have brought Luke in last night. Now, more than ever, she had to leave. She was no longer safe at home. Luke could no longer protect her. The pain of leaving her loved ones, and the uncertainty of her fate was at hand.

The bus stopped along Highway 28 to pick up a few students, one of whom was Candy. Candy sat in the seat behind Jessie and leaned up against Jessie's seat.

"Why are you crying, Jessie?"

Jessie looked at her for a moment and turned away, "Coyotes killed my dog," Jessie sniffled, wiping her little, red nose, looking out the window.

Candy handed Jessie a tissue from her purse. "I'm sorry, Jessie."

Jessie turned to look at her. Candy's face was mournful. Candy was really apologizing to Jessie for her youthful mistake.

"Thanks," Jessie said, wiping and sniffing her nose.

"Forgive me?" Candy asked, truly sorry.

Jessie bit her lip and nodded at Candy, turning back to the window.

Jessie went directly to Mother's office and knocked on the door.

"Come in," Mother answered, intently reading something on her desk. She looked up to see Jessie in deep distress. She got up from her desk, going to her. "What is it, child?"

"Coyotes killed my dog last night, Mother," Jessie said, sobbing, starting to cry again. "I...I couldn't do my homework."

"You poor dear." Mother put her arm around Jessie's shoulder and squeezed her close. "Sit down, Jessica. Let me go get you a drink, and some tissue."

Mother left the room, but quickly came back with a glass of apple juice, and a box of tissue. She handed the glass to Jessie and set the tissue on the desk in front of her. She took out a tissue and handed it to Jessie. "It's okay to cry, dear, you just go ahead," she said, going to sit back down at her desk.

"I don't want to go back home, Mother," Jessie sobbed. She suddenly and very desperately wanted to tell Mother about all her troubles; the sex she'd been having, the miscarriage, about the monster, and how torn apart she was over the Miller boys. God was punishing her. She closed her eyes, trying to think of how to word it, when Sister Kathryn came in.

"Oh, there she is," Sister Kathryn said. "I was just coming to tell you that Jessie wasn't in class."

"Yes, Jessie's had a tragedy this morning. Her dog was killed by coyotes last night and we were just drying up the tears," Mother explained.

Sister Kathryn put her hand on Jessie's shoulder. "I'm so sorry, Jessie. My dog died when I was a little girl, too. I know how you feel."

Jessie looked up at Sister Kathryn. She had never thought of it before, she always thought the sisters were sisters, not little children. "Thank you, Sister," Jessie said. "Did you cry, too?"

"Yes, but I know I'll see him again." Sister Kathryn smiled, and Jessie thought of never seeing Mother or the sisters again.

"We've all lost a pet at some time in our life, dear," Mother said. "You'll see him again, child. We'll say a silent prayer for him, and for you, today at mass. Do you think you'll be all right going to class now?"

Jessie nodded, finishing her juice. "Thank you, Mother." She half smiled, still distressed and followed Sister Kathryn to class.

~

Jessie stood mournfully, leaning her face on the gate post when Luke pulled up at eleven-thirty. She was completely exhausted, and her eyes were red and puffy. Luke got out of the car and went to her.

"Baby, what's wrong?" he asked, wrapping his arms around her, wishing to see her smile.

Her body was trembling, and she couldn't stop shaking. "Those coyotes finally killed my doggy, Luke. I had to burn him in the burning barrel this morning."

"Dammit," Luke said. "My poor baby." He bent down to kiss her puffy eyes. She laid her head against his chest while he pulled her tightly against him, rubbing her head, rocking her in his arms.

Jessie was terrified. She'd been thinking all morning, *it wasn't the coyotes. It was the monster, and he will come kill me too, now. Now Luke is dead, there's nothing to stop him.* She wanted to tell Luke about the monster, but was too frightened, and it didn't matter now. What she had to do, was the hardest thing in the world.

"I wished I'd been there with you, darlin'." Luke gazed into her sad eyes and stroked her cheek. "I know you haven't been eating, Jessie. I want you to try and eat something today," he said, walking her to the car.

"I don't think I can eat anything, Luke. I'm so tired, and I feel sick." He reached over and buckled her seat belt. "I was scared last night, Luke, and Daddy never came. I wish you would have came."

"Me too, darlin'," Luke replied, squatting down in front of her. "I had a creepy feeling last night, worrying about you. Jessie, do the coyotes ever come around while you're outside?"

"No." Jessie shook her head.

"Do you have a gun, Jessie?"

"My daddy's rifle."

"Do you know how to use it?"

"Yes, Luke."

Luke got in the car and buckled his seat belt. He turned to look at her. "Jessie, I been trying to figure out how to get you away from there." Luke looked out, down the road. "It's not safe for you, baby." He turned looking at her and took her hand, kissing it. "Not all alone like that...if you'd just marry me, I could keep you with me. You'd be safe, darlin'. You wouldn't have to go back there; ever, don't you know that, baby?"

Jessie desperately wanted to say yes, and she almost did, but bit her lip. Her mind was racing. She had contemplated all morning, deciding she was not going to get on the bus after school. She was going to hide in the girl's bathroom and sleep there. In the early morning, she would walk to Reno. She'd left her overnight bag with the food and clothes, but it didn't matter anymore. She would *not* go back home. It wasn't safe there anymore. She couldn't tell Luke her plan, because he would stop her. She had to go away now, because she couldn't marry Luke. Mike and Ricky wouldn't understand. She had to start her own new life, and not see any of her loved ones anymore. They couldn't keep her anyway. Not until she was older and then, maybe it would be okay, when they didn't love her anymore.

"I'm gonna start sleeping outside your door, Jessie," Luke said, backing the car out onto the road. "I'm bringin' my sleeping bag, and I'm gonna sleep on your porch."

"No, Luke, you can't," Jessie said, with her sad eyes gazing up at him. "My dad..."

"Yes, I am," Luke insisted, looking down the road. "You won't let me take care of you, but I'm going to, whether you like it or not."

"Luke..."

"Don't argue about it, Jessie. I wouldn't be no kind of man, if I left you another second, unprotected. I want you to eat something."

Jessie leaned her head on the window, silently looking out.

Luke was suffering, worried about Jessie's health and safety, and she seemed to be so sad all the time, now. The recent events in her life were wearing her down and she *wasn't* safe at home. Anything could happen to her there, and no one would ever know. He wanted her to smile. He wanted her to be forever happy, if she would just marry him. He knew he had to be patient. They all had to be patient and hope that Debbie could get custody of her. They went to the Frosty Stand, but neither of them could eat anything.

~

Burying his face behind a *Time* magazine, Luke sat in the waiting room of

Doctor Russell's office, trying to keep the receptionist from staring at him. Jessie finally came out of the door and Luke got up, putting his arm around her. "Everything okay?"

Jessie nodded, glumly.

"That's good," Luke sighed. "Are you healing okay?"

Jessie nodded.

"Well, did-did you ask the doctor how long we have to wait to make love?"

"No," she answered, quietly.

"Baby, we gotta ask." He took Jessie over to the window where the receptionist smiled up at him. "Can I talk to the nurse?"

"Sure," she said, and went to get the nurse. The two of them came back to the window. Luke tried to ignore the receptionist, who sat back down, smiling at him.

"Is she healing? How long will she be bleeding?" Luke asked the nurse, wishing the receptionist would go away and mind her own business.

The nurse nodded. "She's healing fine and should stop by the end of the week. If she doesn't, call us, or if she gets a fever, call us right away."

"Well...how long do we have to wait...to...you know?" he stammered, glaring at the receptionist.

"At least a month for the pill to become effective," the nurse answered. "Jessie still needs time to heal from the miscarriage."

Luke nodded, and the nurse started to walk back down the hall. Suddenly she turned and came back out. "Oh, Mr. Miller," she hollered, and came out the door to the lobby. She walked over to Luke and spoke softly, "The doctor's a bit concerned with Jessie's mental state. It's probably just from the miscarriage, but she seems depressed. If she doesn't perk up, he'd like to see her again."

"Well, besides the baby, her dog died last night," Luke told her.

"Oh, I'm sorry, Jessie." She put her hand on Jessie's shoulder. "I guess that would certainly explain why."

Luke looked at Jessie. He knew things weren't right with her. Not just because of the dog, or the miscarriage, but having to go home. Not being able to stay with her Aunt was so hard on her. Luke answered for Jessie. "Thank you." Deep down, he knew it was because of the three of them, pulling at her heart.

"It's forty dollars," the receptionist said.

Luke took his wallet out and gave her two twenties'. She handed him a receipt, not letting go of it, smiling.

Luke gave her a dirty look and let go of the receipt. She set it on the windowsill. He took it and put it in his wallet.

"Come own, baby," he said to Jessie, kissing her forehead. The receptionist watched them walk out the door.

Man, she's annoying," Luke said, as they walked to the car.

"Who is?"

"That girl at the window; she keeps staring at me. Can't she see I'm with you and that you're so beautiful?" Luke held the car door open for Jessie.

"I think she only thees how handsome you are, Luke."

"You have to take your pill every day, darlin'." Luke said, backing the car out of the parking lot. He pulled out onto the highway.

"I know, the doctor told me." Jessie's face was so gloomy, and she had little tears streaming down her cheeks, knowing she would never see Luke, or anyone she ever cared about, again.

"What did he say about you, Jessie? I mean are you healing and everything?"

"Yeah, he...he said when I get older, I might have to think about a histertomy."

"What? Oh, you mean, remove your female parts?"

"I think so. He said mine are no good," Jessie answered, trying desperately not to cry.

"I'm sorry, darlin', but I love you so much, anyway. You don't have to go back to school today. I think we should go buy you some pads, B*ubbles*." Luke smiled at her, trying to cheer her up. "And some chocolate."

Highway 28 was also the main street through the town of Smith Valley. Most of the local businesses were located on both sides of the Highway. If you turned west, you would be heading toward St. Thomas and Genoa's Peak. To the east would be going toward Mining. They drove east through town over to the Smith Valley Drugstore. Luke didn't care about buying Jessie pads. He felt proud to be part of her life that way. He also bought her a *Hershey's* chocolate bar with almonds.

"I didn't mean to snap at you, baby," Luke said to Jessie outside the store. He held her close, gazing into her eyes. "I know you're scared, and I know you don't want me to sleep on your porch, but damn-it, Jessie, I don't know what else to do. I want you with me, where I can protect you."

Jessie looked up at Luke, unable to answer. Her sadness was tearing him up.

"I wish you'd say somethin'." Luke stroked her face. "What do you wanna do, baby? We could go get our room at the motel and watch TV and take a nap. Maybe even stay the night again. We could go see if your dads at the bar?"

"I'm scared, Luke. I wish I could, but..."

"Let's just go see if he's there, all right? I'll take care of you, darlin'."

Jessie's thoughts were racing. Her plan was not turning out right. Staying at the motel with Luke sure sounded better than what she was planning, but it would only prolong things, and she couldn't go back home now. She would be killed for sure, now.

"Luke, I have to go back to school and wait for the bus," she said, unable to control the tears falling down her cheeks.

Luke sighed, and stroked her face. "Baby, what is it? I know you're sad, honey, but I'm scared right now, Jessie. There's something else, something you're not telling me. What is it?"

Jessie closed her eyes and Luke wiped her tears. "We're gonna go drive by the bar, Jessie. I'm worried. I wanna stay with you tonight."

She shook her head, "No, Luke."

"Shhh, hush, Jessie, don't argue." Luke took her arm and walked her to the car. Jessie struggled with her thoughts, trying to think of what to tell him. "Get in, baby."

"Luke," Jessie started to speak, as she reluctantly got in. He shut her door.

"I love you, Jessie," he said as he sat down and buckled his seat belt. "Buckle up, baby."

"But, Luke…" Jessie fettered anxiously, buckling her seat belt.

Luke started the car and quickly pulled out. He made a turn east onto Highway 28. He was driving faster than usual, when Jessie noticed a motorcycle racing toward them on the highway.

"Luke!" she shouted. "That's Ricky! There's a truck!"

"Shit!" Luke gasped, swerving the Cuda, as they saw a semi-truck barreling down the hill. It wasn't stopping! It made the intersection just as Ricky was crossing. In a panic, Luke veered over to the side of the highway, going down into the ditch. The truck began to brake; its tires were smoking, squealing an ear-piercing sound, but not soon enough. The front of the truck smacked right into Ricky. Luke jumped out of the car, racing toward him.

"RICKY!" Jessie screamed a blood curdling scream, as they both saw Ricky and the bike fly up and crash down in the field on the other side. Ricky wasn't wearing a helmet! The truck swerved trying to brake, and jack knifed in the field next to the highway. RICKY!"

The world stopped turning. Luke felt himself, running in slow motion. His breath echoed in his ears, like a horse running; pounding the ground in desperate measures. The light faded like dark wind blowing through a dense hollow.

"R-i-c-k-y," he heard himself say, muffled and slow.

Jessie's screams pierced his ears like a deep siren. Luke's mind was spinning with images from the past, a whirlwind of memories sped through his mind.

Luke fell on his knees beside Ricky. Blood was pouring from the side of his head; his legs were twisted up under his body. Luke put his hands out to him but couldn't touch him. His body trembled, and he felt Ricky's throat. There was no pulse, no breath. "NOOOO!" Luke yelled, as the sound carried across the sky. "NO, God, NO!"

Jessie came running over, screaming, "RICKY! RICKY!"

Luke stood up and grabbed her, pulling her away from Ricky. Luke was half conscious as Jessie struggled to get away, screaming and crying. The images were surreal. The truck driver radioed for help and had gone over to Ricky.

"Baby, no," Luke said, holding her tight. "Baby, no."

Jessie was hitting Luke, pushing on his arms. "Let me go!" she yelled. "Let me go to Ricky!" She kicked her legs at him, screaming, "RICKY!"

Luke let go of her and she ran to Ricky. She knelt and put her head on his face. "Ricky, my Ricky," she cried. She put her hand on his forehead and kissed his mouth, lying her face down on his.

Two Sheriff's vehicles came tearing up the road, sirens blaring, then a fire truck, and then an ambulance. There were sirens, and lights, and people were suddenly all over the place.

Luke picked Jessie up and carried her over to the side of the road, holding her tightly against him.

"NO!" Jessie screamed. "Let me be with Ricky!"

"Baby," he cried, burying his head in her body. "I'm sorry, baby."

~

Jessie lay motionless in the hospital. Her vital signs were unstable, and the doctor told Debbie they were going to keep her. Hank was nowhere to be found. Luke stayed by her side all night, in despair.

In the morning, Harry and Debbie went to see John Burke to ask for an emergency custody order. They took a letter from the hospital. The judge granted Debbie a month's temporary custody of Jessie.

Meg's doctor prescribed some tranquilizers for her and Tom stayed by her side. She was inconsolable.

The rain had filled the ditch with mud and it took some negotiating, tolerance with Kevin, and bravery to keep his head, as Mike and Kevin pulled Luke's car out of the ditch. But on the way home, Mike could barely see the road through his tears, and the rain hitting violently against the windshield. The storm outside didn't compare to the storm in his heart. He didn't want to believe it, but nothing he could tell himself would make it less true. As hard as he tried to search for any good memories, all he remembered was being a pain in the ass to his little brother. After bringing Luke's car home, Kevin and he quickly got *out of their mind* drunk at Gary house, until they both passed out. Mike stayed gone. His boss let him hang out late at the Chevron station with Kevin, putting the headers on his car, and then getting drunk again. He didn't want to think about it. He couldn't deal with losing his brother, and there was no way he could handle seeing Jessie or his Mom grieving. He just kept drinking and passing out.

Jessie stayed incoherent at the hospital for three days, sedated most of the time. When she did wake up, she was hysterical. Luke, Debbie, and Eli, stayed by her side, only taking turns leaving to help Tom with Meg, who couldn't get out of bed.

♥

Friday, January 11, 1974

Ricky was buried. Many of his friends, classmates, and teachers came to the funeral, including Luke and Mike's friends. Sissy and Taylor, Pete and Lisa, Burt the Sheriff, and a few deputies they knew. Jessie never got to go, and Debbie thought that was for the best.

Mike came with Kevin and Gary long enough to comfort Meg, and went back out again, to get drunk.

On the third day, they didn't give Jessie any sedatives. The doctor wanted her to wake up. He requested a counselor to come speak with her and Luke, as well as Debbie, and her children. Luke was exhausted, but he wasn't leaving Jessie's side. When Jessie woke up, she was quiet. She didn't talk or move. Luke kissed her face. "Jessie," he whispered. She looked at him and lay there quietly.

Debbie held Jessie's hand. She gazed lovingly in Jessie's eyes, stroking her forehead. After a few minutes, Jessie looked at Eli, seeing his tears and his face looking down, so forlorn. She looked at her Aunt. "Ricky's dead, isn't he, Momma?"

"Yes sweetheart, he's gone." Tears were rolling down Debbie's face as she held Jessie's hand. Eli stood by her bed, trying to be brave.

"Ricky died for me. He was coming to see me, wasn't he?" Jessie closed her eyes. "You saw him, didn't you Luke?" Jessie turned to Luke.

"We both saw him, darlin'."

"I kissed him good-bye, didn't I?"

"Yes baby. You kissed him good-bye," Luke answered, rubbing Jessie's arm.

"He was coming to thee me," Jessie said, somberly. "Ricky's in heaven with my Grandma's and my Mommy, isn't he Momma?"

"Yes, he is, Jessie." Debbie smiled, rubbing her hand. "They're all up there together, honey."

"I'm going to be up there too, aren't I?" she asked her Aunt. Luke looked at Jessie panicked.

"Well, not for a while, sweetheart, but yes, we'll all be up there, too, someday. Mother Magdalena was here to see you."

"My baby and my doggy are there, too, aren't they Luke?" Luke kissed Jessie's hand, that wiped the tears rolling down his cheeks.

"What does she mean, Luke?" Debbie asked him.

Luke looked at Debbie, unsure how to answer. "Jessie's dog was killed by coyotes the same day as R-Ricky, Debbie," Luke said, hoping she missed the *baby* part.

"My Lord," Debbie sighed. "You mean there's coyotes…" Debbie started to ask, when the counselor walked in the room and introduced himself.

"Gary Smith," he said, taking Debbie's hand. Luke couldn't have been more relieved at not having to explain what Jessie meant. "I'm here to talk with all of you about Ricky," Gary said.

"Ricky?" Jessie asked, mournfully. "Did you see him?"

Gary shook his head and softly said, "No." He took Jessie's hand. "It's okay to be sad. Our sadness is an expression of the love we have for Ricky."

Gary spoke with them about the grieving process and how it's different for each person. He asked Jessie if she'd been eating anything. Jessie told him she wasn't hungry. He explained to her that she needed to eat a little something every day. Even if it was just ice cream or something yummy. "You have to eat before they let you go home," he told her.

"Home?" Jessie looked up.

Luke saw the panic in Jessie's eyes and immediately told her she was going to stay at her Auntie's for a long time.

"Yes, Jessie," Debbie said. "I've been granted temporary custody of you. You're going to be with me for a whole month, maybe longer."

"Really?" Jessie's eyes looked up. "What about my school?"

"I've already spoken to Mother Magdalena. She knows you'll be gone awhile."

"Custody?" Gary asked, and Debbie quickly summarized Jessie's situation.

He asked Eli if he and Ricky were good friends. Eli nodded, and squinted tear drops down his cheeks. Jessie felt sad for Eli and held her hand out to him, taking his hand. She could see now, she wasn't the only one sad, seeing Elijah, Maddy, and Aimee, all with tears in their eyes.

Gary asked Jessie some questions about staying at her Aunt's house and what did she like about it. Jessie told him how good she felt at her Aunt's, until she remembered she had to go back home, and then she remembered Ricky on Thanksgiving.

"Ricky won't be there no more, will he?" she asked, with tears welling up and rolling down her face. "I want Ricky." Jessie started to cry.

"I know you do," Gary said to her. "We all want Ricky back, but it's not ever going to be possible for Ricky to come back to us."

"I can't stop thinking about that and crying," Jessie said.

"It's okay to cry, Jessie, Eli, Maddy, and Aimee, he said to all of them. As much as you want, it's important to cry and grieve."

"I can't ever stop," Jessie said. "I can't ever stop wanting Ricky back."

"You don't have to stop wanting him, Jessie, but in your own time, you'll be able to find a sense of acceptance. Ricky wouldn't want you to be sad the rest of your life, would he?"

"No," she sniffled.

"Do you believe you'll see him again?" Gary asked.

"Yes, I do. Ricky died for me, he died for me, so I could stay with you, didn't he, Momma?"

Debbie smiled at Jessie, stroking her hand, unsure of how to answer that.

Gary turned to speak quietly with Debbie. "Has Jessie's hair always been this white?"

"No, when we first met her it was more golden, and I wondered about that myself when I noticed it turning a while ago."

Luke wondered about that, himself.

"Hmm." Gary pondered. "So, it's been a while. I was thinking maybe it was from the trauma she's just had. Sometimes when people have had extreme shock, their hair turns white."

"I know she's unhappy at home," Debbie said, "but she won't talk about it, and it worries me that bad things are happening to her, but she's afraid to speak of it."

"Well, I'd like to see her again. Maybe, we can help you with your custody."

"Yes, of course," Debbie answered.

"How are you doing, Luke, is it?" Gary asked, putting his hand on Luke's shoulder.

Luke nodded. "I'm all right."

"You should probably go home and get some sleep."

Gary left, and Luke went over to Debbie. "Jessie can't go back there, Debbie. If coyotes killed her dog, they could kill her, too. She's too little to protect herself, and her dad doesn't come home to protect her. She's not safe there."

"Yes, Luke, I know." Debbie began to weep. "Jessie needs to be able to speak up for herself, and I don't know how to get her to."

"I don't either." Luke turned to Jessie and went back to sit with her.

Saturday, January 12, 1974

The hospital released Jessie on the fourth day, and Debbie and Luke drove her home. Home to her family.

Jessie seemed to be okay the first day home. The family stayed together all day, talking about Ricky, and remembering him. They even laughed a little. During the night though, the memories had become painful, and Jessie was having severe anxiety. She got up and ran over to the Miller's house. She ran into Ricky's bedroom and laid down on his bed, crying into his pillow. Luke heard her and went to her. He lay on the bed, holding her and caressing her back, speaking gently to her.

Jessie went into a deep sleep and lay frozen on Ricky's bed. No one could wake her, and no one moved her. Debbie called Gary and he advised her that if she didn't wake up on her own within the next few days to get her to the hospital. Debbie stayed at the Millers, watching Jessie, and caring for Meg.

Sunday, January 13, 1974

Super Bowl Sunday came and went this year, without the Millers and the Ashworths.

Tuesday, January 15, 1974

Meg called for Luke, who wouldn't leave Jessie's side. He went to his mother's room and sat down on the bed next to her, holding her hand.

"Who's in Ricky's room, Luke? I don't want anyone going in there."

"It's Jessie, Ma. She's been sleeping on his bed for a few days, now. She won't wake up."

"I don't want her in there." Meg started to cry. "If he hadn't been trying to go see her, he would…he would still be alive!"

"Momma." Luke trembled, surprised. "Ricky *loved* her, that's why he wanted to see her. It wasn't anyone's fault."

"I don't care!" Meg snapped. "I want her out of there. I want her out of this house!"

"You can't blame her for this!" Luke shouted. "She didn't know he was coming to see her." Luke pointed his arm toward Ricky's room. "She's in there, in his room, sick from grieving! She loved him, as much as we do. Don't blame Jessie for this." Luke paused, shaking his head, looking into his mother's eyes. "I'm sorry, Momma." Luke stroked her cheek and took her hand. "I'm sorry, I didn't mean to yell. I know you're grieving too, Momma."

"You're right, Son," Meg sobbed, squeezing Luke's hand. "I'm just hurting."

"I know, Momma." He kissed her hand. "I love you, Mom, I'm sorry. We all are. Mike hasn't been home all week."

"Please make him come home, Son. Tell him I need to see him."

"I'll try, Ma." Luke bent down and kissed his mother. He went back to see Jessie. She was still in the same position, frozen. Luke covered her up and decided to go look for Mike.

Mike walked in the front door just as Luke went out into the living-room.

"You look like shit, man," Luke said. Mike's face was scruffy, and his eyes were red and weary. Luke and Mike hugged each other. "Mom wants you, she's in bed."

Mike walked down the hall, into his parent's room. He bent down over his Mom and hugged her tightly. "I'm sorry, Momma." He couldn't help from crying.

"Where have you been, Michael?"

"Just out, Ma. I gotta take a shower." Mike kissed her cheek and went to his room to get clean clothes, and then into the bathroom to shower. When he came out of the bathroom, he saw Jessie, lying on Ricky's bed. Luke was sitting at Ricky's desk chair, watching her.

"What's she doing in here?" Mike asked, holding his dirty clothes.

"She ran over here and laid down on the bed. She won't wake up. The doctor said if she doesn't wake up by tomorrow, to get her back to the hospital."

"Shit," Mike said rubbing his forehead. "Doesn't she have to go home?"

"No. Debbie has temporary custody right now. She's not going to school for a while, either."

Mike walked to his room to put his dirty clothes away. He grabbed Teddy, who was still on his bed, and went back into Ricky's room, lying down next to

Jessie. He stroked her face with his finger. Luke got up and walked out.

"Bunny," Mike whispered. "Wake up, bunny girl," he said in her ear, kissing it. Jessie didn't move and neither did Mike. He was exhausted. He put his arm over her and fell asleep.

~

Mike woke up to Jessie, holding him tight. "Mikey," she whispered. "I need you, where were you, Mikey?"

"I'm right here, bunny," he said, handing her Teddy.

"Mikey, my Mikey," she said into his chest, squeezing Teddy.

"I missed you, baby. I was listening to a song on the radio by the Beach Boys yesterday. They sang about how God only knows where I'd be without you, and I knew I needed to come home and see you."

Jessie pulled herself as close to Mike as she could get. He wrapped his arms around her, kissing her head and rubbing her back. "How did you know where I am?" she asked.

"I didn't. Just relax, baby. I'm right here now." Mike held her, softly stroking her head as she drifted off back to sleep.

After about an hour Jessie started to tremble and was moaning in her sleep. It woke Mike up and he put his head up, looking at her little face. She was in deep distress.

"Baby," he said, stroking her face.

Jessie moved up on her knees, pulling herself tightly into a ball. She started shaking, almost violently. Sweat began to pour from her body.

Mike was going to get up and leave; it scared him, but he couldn't do it. He put his arm around her and pulled her close. "Jessie, tell me what you saw. Why were you and Luke there? What was Ricky doing there? Did you see what happened, Jessie?"

Jessie stopped crying and looked at Mike, wiping her face.

"I need to know, Jessie. What did you see, peanut?"

"Lu-uke took me to the doc-tor," she trembled, barely able to speak, "so I could get the pills, and he could check me. Luke was driving me when I saw Ricky on his motorcycle coming at us on the road. The truck didn't stop. It didn't stop, Mikey, it ran into Ricky, and his motorcycle went up in the air. I was screaming, 'Ricky!' and Luke ran to him. Luke wouldn't let me see him, but I had to see Ricky. I kissed him, I kissed him good-bye." Jessie turned her head toward Mike, crying into his chest.

"I'm sorry, baby," Mike said, rubbing her back. "Don't cry about it anymore."

"My doggy is dead. My poor little doggy got killed. I had to burn him in the barrel because I had to go to school. My doggy and the baby are up in heaven with Ricky. Where did you go, Mikey? I needed you."

"Little bunny. I had to go cry by myself," he whispered, stroking her face. "I can't stand to see you hurting, Jessie. It tears me up. I'm not strong. I was scared."

"Even if you have big muthles?" Jessie sniffed, wiping her nose.

"Muscles don't make a man," Mike said, and stared off in thought. "It's what's in his heart that makes him a man."

"What's in your heart, Mikey?"

"You. You're all that's good in me, bunny."

"I want to be in you, Mikey, where no one can see me."

He gently lay over her. "I love you so much, Jessie. You're the only girl I'll ever love, Jessica. You're my little girl. I'll never love anyone else, bunny. You're my only love. I can't live without you, Jessie, my beautiful baby."

Jessie felt safe underneath Mike, and his heart became so tender for her. "Don't go away from me. I'm safe with you."

"Marry me, Jessie," Mike asked, holding her hands together on her chest. "I want you to marry me."

"I want to marry you, Mikey. I want to be Jessie Miller. I want to live with you and I want you to be a cop and take care of me. But I can't, Mikey. I can't," Jessie cried.

"Jessie, yes you can."

"No, I can't. I want to marry Luke, and live with him, too. Mikey, can't I dis live with you here, in this house? Can't I dis be Jessie Miller and live here in the Miller house with you and Luke?"

"No, Jessie, you can't do that."

"Why, Mikey?"

"You just can't baby. It doesn't work that way."

"I have to let you both go then, Mikey. I have to let you both go," Jessie said, weeping. "I can't live with this pain; it hurts too much. My head hurts. Mikey, my head hurts."

Mike ran his fingers through her hair, massaging her head.

"I'm not gonna let you go, Jessie. Close your eyes now, just relax."

Mikey, my head hurts. There's something in my brain that hurts." Jessie took Mike's hands. "*My head hurts.*"

"I'll go get you some aspirin, bunny."

Luke didn't want to be without Jessie, either. He lay miserable in his bed, knowing Mike was in there with her. They'd both begun to accept that that's the way it was going to have to be for now. There was no happy ending, no solutions, nothing to make it right. Jessie didn't mean to love them both, but it was tearing Jessie apart and breaking her down. It was starting to affect her health. The entire trauma was becoming too much for her little body, and her childish logic.

"We can go get a puppy, Jessie," Mike said, after a long spell of silence.

"Can we?"

"Yeah, we can."

"Can his name be Luke?"

"Yeah."

"Where is the puppy going to live, Mikey?"

"Right here."

"How come the puppy gets to live here, but not me?"

Mike couldn't answer her. It didn't make sense to him, either. "Why don't you come to school with me this week, Jessie?"

"Go to school? With you? Yeah, Mikey, I want to go to school with you. You could drive me in your car. We could go to lunch together...Oh." She suddenly lost her enthusiasm.

"What's wrong, Jessie?"

Jessie looked sadly up at Mike.

"Luke," Mike said, confirming Jessie's thoughts. "Well, he can't take you to lunch, not till you go back to St. Thomas. You come to school with me. You can go with me to all my classes and help me. I would really like that, baby," Mike kissed Jessie's smiling face. "We'll ask Debbie about it tomorrow."

"Okay, Mikey, but can we still get a puppy?"

"Yeah, we'll still get a puppy, bunny." Mike tickled her nose with his.

Tom knocked on the bedroom door. "Everything okay in there, Michael?" he asked, holding a glass of water.

"We're all right, Dad."

"All right, Son," Tom answered, and went back to bed.

Jessie giggled, "I'm hungry."

Mike got up and made them both a ham sandwich.

Wednesday, January 16, 1974

Debbie got up early. She hadn't been able to sleep, and the stress was wearing on her. She was going to have to take Jessie back to the hospital. She sat at the table drinking her coffee and broke down crying. "Lord, I know I don't talk to you much, and I'm sorry. I'm sorry to come to you, now, in sadness, but please be with us, Lord. Please be with Jessie and help her to heal. Be with me and give me strength. Help us to get custody of Jessie, and keep her with us, where she is loved. Please be with Meg and her family. I know that little Ricky is in your loving care."

As she was praying, Jessie and Mike came in the door and Debbie looked up at them. "Jessie, oh thank God," Debbie said, and went over to kiss her. She walked Jessie to the sofa and sat with her. "When did you wake up, sweetheart?"

"Last night. Mikey came home and woke me up. Mikey wants to take me to Mining school with him this week, Momma," Jessie said to her right away. "Can I go to his school with him, now?" Jessie's eyes begged her Aunt.

Mike stood nervously at the doorway. Debbie thought it was odd that Jessie was asking to go to school with Mike, and that Mike was with her. She looked at Mike who was smiling at Jessie. *Shit. Mike's in love with Jessie.* "I don't know, Jessie."

"Please, Momma," Jessie said, looking at Mike. "He thinks it would be good for me to go to his school."

Mike spoke up, "I just think doing something different for a few days would take her mind off things." He wanted to ask Debbie if he could see Jessie, as in dating, but he felt maybe it was too soon, and he didn't know how. He felt maybe he needed to prove himself first.

Debbie was unsure and sat looking at Jessie and Mike for a moment. "I don't know if you're ready for that."

"Please, Momma."

"Why don't you just go with the girls, sweetheart?"

"I want to go with Mikey. He wants me to go with him," Jessie answered.

"I'll bring her right home," Mike said. "She can go with me to all my classes, as my guest, and do all my homework for me," he joked, smiling at Jessie.

Debbie was not at all prepared to make a decision. She didn't have the heart to upset Jessie, after the trauma she had just been through, but she didn't know enough about Mike to trust him. Jessie looked so much better, though. Debbie thought somehow being with Mike must have done something. Jessie was awake and talking. Maybe it would be a positive thing if she really wanted to go. It might help Jessie heal, and help her with her socialization. Mike was probably sad too, after losing his brother. Debbie was willing to do anything to help Jessie get better. "Well, I guess we could try it tomorrow, and see how it goes."

"Oh! Thank you, Momma!" Jessie said, hugging her aunt. "I want to stay at the Miller house for a while. I want to help them. I want to help take care of them."

"Well you can't stay there, but you can go visit, Jessie," Debbie answered. "We have to find out how Meg feels first."

"Oh," Jessie said, disappointed.

"We need you here with us, Jessie."

"All right, Momma."

"I'll see you in the morning," Mike told Jessie, leaving her with Debbie. Jessie ran after him out the door and stopped on the porch.

"What should I wear, Mikey?"

Mike went back up the stairs to her.

"Can I wear *real* clothes?" she asked, anxious about the answer.

"Yeah, wear *real* clothes." He smiled.

"Do I have to put my hair in a pony?"

"No, little bunny."

They smiled at each other and Mike went back down the stairs. "Bye, Mikey," Jessie said, softly. Mike turned and winked at her.

"You're feeling better aren't you, Jessie?" Debbie asked as Jessie came back in. She took her hand. "What happened?"

"Mikey came home. He was gone for a while because he was so sad. I woke up and he was there with me. He asked me about the accident and I talked to him about it, and he talked to me about it. It made him feel better, I think."

"I'm glad, sweetheart." Debbie looked out the window at Mike, going into his house. "I think it made you feel better, too."

"Yes, Momma, I do feel better now."

"You must be starving. Are you hungry?"

"No, Mikey made me a thanwich. I need a shower now."

Debbie gave her a long hug and kissed her cheek. "All right, sweetheart. I'm going to call the doctor to tell him you're awake."

"I love you, Momma."

"I love you, Jessie. My little, Jessie."

Jessie took a long, hot shower. She wanted to get back over to the Miller's and help Meg. Debbie was curious that Jessie wanted to spend so much time over there, but she didn't question Jessie. She wanted her to do what made her happiest and heal the quickest. And Jessie suddenly felt as though she had a purpose; she was needed.

When Jessie entered the Miller's front door, Meg was sitting back in the recliner, in her white, terry robe. She'd finally gotten out of bed.

"Hi, Meg," Jessie said nervously, closing the door. She walked over to Meg, who was watching her. "Can I sit with you, Meg?"

Meg put her hand up and Jessie laid down next to Meg on the recliner. She put her arm across Meg's shoulders and her eyes began to weep.

"I'm sorry, Meg."

Mike had been trying to sleep in his room, but he was so dehydrated, he'd come out to get a drink of water. When he got down the hallway, he saw Jessie sitting with Meg, and stopped, leaning on the wall to listen.

"I know you are, Jessie," Meg said. "I know that my boys have all been kind of rough on you. I guess they're all in love with you, Jessie. I don't blame them. I love you, too."

"Meg," Jessie started to cry. "I had thex with your sons."

"Jessie," Meg said. "I slept with Tom's brother before we were married."

"You did? You did, Meg?" Jessie sat up looking up at her, her eyes were wide open.

"Yes, I did," Meg said, stroking Jessie's arm. "You don't have to share that with anyone."

Mike was biting at his thumbnail and stopped to put his head up when he heard that.

"I won't, Meg. How did you – how did you pick, Meg?"

"Well, I don't think I was ever in love with Mike."

"That was his name? Mike?"

"We named Michael after him."

"What happened to him?"

"He's a police officer in Texas."

"Oh, Mikey told me about him." Jessie thought for a minute. "You mean you didn't choose him, and he became a cop, anyway? He still went and did what he wanted?"

Mike wanted to hear this conversation, hoping it might help Jessie decide what she needed to do.

"Well, we really weren't in love, Jessie."

"But I love Mikey. Mikey wants to be a cop, like his Uncle."

"He does? Did he tell you that?"

Jessie nodded. "I love Luke, and I love Mikey, and I love Ricky. I don't know how to pick, Meg." Jessie lay her head back down on Meg. "I'm afraid to pick. I think God is punishing me for having thex and making everyone unhappy."

"Jessie, I don't think you've made anyone unhappy, and I don't think God punishes us that way. I don't think God is punishing me, and still, he took Ricky from me. I think he has his own reasons; things happen the way they're meant to."

"I don't understand that, Meg."

"I don't either, Jessie."

"I want to help you today, Meg. What can I do to help you?"

"I think you've already helped me, Jessie. I think you should go home now and spend some time with your family. We only have so much time with our loved ones, we can't waste it." Meg began to cry.

"Don't cry, Meg. We'll all be together again, just like I'll be with my Mommy one day."

"You go home, now Jessie." Meg smiled at her. Jessie nodded, realizing Meg was right. She should spend time with her family.

"Okay, Meg, but I want to help you, if you need me."

Jessie left, and Mike came out from the hallway. He went to his mom and kissed her cheek. "Is that why dad doesn't like me, Ma?"

"Tom is your father, Michael. He's your father. He loves you, Son. It's just that you two are so much alike," Meg said, holding Mike's arm. "You're like two negatives pushing against each other. That will go away in time, Son."

"Momma, I love Jessie so much." Mike got down on bended knees. "There's no god damn solution to this shit that's happening, and I can't even think about Ricky. He comes in my head and I just stop thinking. Should I just let her go? I don't want to let her go."

Meg could see Mike was in complete agony and distress. "I don't know, Son, are you strong enough to let her go?"

"I don't know. I'm not like Luke. I don't get back up again, so easy."

"Nothing is certain is this life, Son, but, we'll help each other get through this. Is it true you want to be a cop, Mike?"

"Yeah, I do, Mom."

Meg stroked Mike's face and smiled at him. "Then do it, Michael, get back up. You'll be a good cop. Don't do it for anyone but yourself. Good things will follow."

Mike lay his head down on Meg's stomach, putting his arm around her and she rubbed his face.

"You don't have to be like Luke, Son," Meg said, closing her eyes. "You're a good son."

Meg fell asleep, and Mike went into Ricky's room. He wanted to find the photos he was sure Ricky had taken of Jessie. He looked on the top shelf of Ricky's closet. He found an old baseball mitt that he had given Ricky when he was eight or nine. He looked through all of Ricky's drawers, trying not to cry, and focus on his mission. He looked under the bed, and around his desk. He sat on Ricky's bed, thinking. Then he lifted the mattress and found a blue folder. He opened it and there were the pictures. He quickly closed it, went back to his room, and shut the door.

He was glad he found them before anyone else could. He leaned back on his pillow and opened the folder. The pictures of Jessie were so beautiful. He'd seen that look on her face many times and took extreme delight in them. He stroked his hand across the two close-ups of Jessie smiling. They were good photographs, and Mike was totally turned on and in love. They were the most exciting and captivating *girly* pictures he'd ever seen. Ricky had taped them on a black piece of construction paper and put them in a sheet protector. In another sheet protector behind the photos, was a story of some kind that Ricky had written about Jessie. Mike read the story:

I met this girl one day. That was the day the world stopped. Her name was Jessica. She was the most beautiful girl I'd ever seen, and I felt like I'd been struck by lightning. Her eyes were like blue diamonds, sparkling, and her face was like an angel. I knew that Jessie was different right from the minute I met her. She was so beautiful; she didn't look like a real person. The next day, we were at the beach and I couldn't keep my hands off her. All of a sudden, she smiled at me and said, 'You're cute,' and ran away from me. I chased her and she was screaming and laughing. I picked her up and threw her in the water. I wanted to make love with her right there. It felt like my heart was coming out of my nose. There's something so magical about her, and I'm under her spell. I would do anything to be with Jessie, forever. Later, I discovered that Jessica Nelson wasn't really her name. Her real name is Angel and she comes from the planet Erotica in a galaxy beyond our own universe. The inhabitants of planet Erotica are only the most desirable, most beautiful women in any universe, anywhere. Every million years their queen sends one of their most desirable young girls to earth to mate with a male earthling, and I happened to be that guy. The queen has to put a spell on the young girl to make her look ugly so that humans are able to look at her without going insane. Still, even with the spell, she's more beautiful than any earthly woman. Angel keeps me tormented. Every time I get close to her, she takes off and goes to a black hole somewhere that I can't get to. I never know if she's coming back out or if she's gone for good, back to Erotica where I'll never see her again. I need to tell their queen that she needs to wipe out the memory of the human male who lives in hell for the rest of his life because of this wonderful, horrible, tragedy. I can't grasp Jessie. Every time I get a hold of her, she slips away, leaving me on fire. I love you so much, Jessie.

Mike couldn't stop the tears from running down his face. He often had similar thoughts about Jessie. Not that she was from Ricky's Erotica, but she certainly seemed like she was from another world; an unreachable world. Mike felt sorry for Ricky, knowing he never got his chance, understanding the pain of being so deeply in love with Jessie. He lay down on his pillow, staring at Jessie's beautiful pictures, feeling Ricky's same frustration. He wished he'd stayed at the beach that day. If he could have gotten to Jessie first that day, maybe he could have stopped her from having sex with Ricky and Luke all together, and she would be his. *Only his,* and Ricky might still be alive. He was such a prick to her that day. He hated himself for that. She was so sweet and innocent, and he was a big asshole to her. She just wanted to show him her nail polish and he made fun of her. He wanted to hold her and tell her how sorry he was for that. He put the pictures down on his chest and fell asleep, fantasizing about making love to Jessie.

~

When Jessie went inside the house, Eli was sulking on the couch, not doing anything. That wasn't like Eli. He was always happy, enthusiastic, and full of energy. She saw he was sad, and realized her purpose, now more than ever. "Do you want to go catch some football, Eli?" Jessie asked him.

"Naw, not really."

"Come on, Eli, I do," Jessie said, feeling sorry for Eli, and wanting to cheer him up, somehow.

"Okay," Eli sighed, and went to his room to get his ball and jacket. Jessie went to get her jacket.

"You didn't stay very long, sweetheart," Debbie said, coming from the hall. "Is everything okay?"

"Yes, Momma. Meg said she loves me, now."

Debbie smiled, stroking Jessie's hair. "Is she up, now?"

"Yeah, she said I need to spend time with my family, because we only get a little time together, and she's right. I need to help my family."

"She is right; we all need each other."

"Yep, I'm going to go play ball with Eli, because he needs me, now."

"All right, sweetheart." Debbie smiled.

The two of them were out in the yard playing catch, uneventfully. "Who won the Thuper Bowl Sunday, Eli?" Jessie asked, tossing him the ball.

"The Dolphins," Eli answered, unenthused.

"They did? Really? Did they kick the Vikings butts?" Jessie asked, excitedly.

"Yeah, twenty-four to seven."

"Isn't that so great, Eli?" Jesse grinned.

"Yeah," Eli chuckled.

"Eli, you're like my brother." Jessie smiled at him. "You're a good brother."

"Thanks, Jessie. You're a good sister."

Luke came up the street in his Cuda and parked in front of his house. He'd gone to work, but came back home, worried about her, and tormented by the fact that Mike was in the room with her all night. He was surprised to see Jessie outside, playing catch with Eli. He got out of his car and went to them.

"Jessie," Luke said, grinning. "You're awake…and playing catch."

Jessie smiled at him holding the ball. "Hi, Luke." She cocked her head with her blue eyes sparkling in the sun.

Luke didn't care about anything at that moment. Who was watching, or what they'd see. He wrapped his arms around her, kissing her. She dropped the ball, putting her arms around him. Eli was surprised and embarrassed.

"I'm so glad you're awake, darlin'," Luke sighed. "I've been so worried about you, baby."

"Don't worry, Luke. I'm okay … Play with us?" Jessie's blue eyes smiled up at him.

"You bet I'll play with you." Luke grinned and bent down, picking up the ball. "Catch!" he yelled at Eli. "You two against me, and you're both gonna loose!"

"How are we gonna play with only three guys?" Eli asked, catching the ball.

"I wanna play," Maddy said, coming down the stairs.

"Aright," Luke said, "Maddy and me against you two and you're *still* gonna loose."

"*I* want to be on *your* team, Luke!" Jessie snapped, pouting at him.

"Nope," Luke said. "I can't tackle you if you're on my team."

"Oh." Jessie smiled back at him. "Come on, Eli," she yelled, running over to Eli. "Let's kick their butts!"

Jessie and Eli had the greatest time, tackling Luke and dog piling him. Even Maddy did some dog piling, too. Eli's spirits lifted, because Luke was letting them win, and Jessie was laughing, which was contagious. Maddy felt happy, too. She was learning not to live her life through Jessie's fun and to have fun herself, plus, Luke was nice to her.

Luke tackled Jessie every chance he got, whispering, "Bubbles" in her ear, every time he took her down.

"Stop it Luke," she said, when he took her down for the fifth time. "You're going to make me want you."

"That's the whole idea, baby," he said, growling in her ear and getting up.

"Luke," Jessie whispered, pulling down on his jacket. "I miss you. I want you."

Jessie and Luke felt like they were flirting with each other for the first time. Luke was trying to figure out how to be alone with Jessie. It seemed so long since they were together, and it was getting more difficult now, with her being at her Aunt's house. He got the brilliant idea to take them all to the movies.

~

The four of them piled in Luke's car that afternoon to go see American Graffiti. It was quite a treat for the Ashworth kids, to be going somewhere with Luke Miller in his Barracuda. The movie had been running almost four months straight, and there weren't many people in the theater. Luke spent a fortune on candy, popcorn, and soda, trying to spoil them. Luke picked seats at the top row, in the corner.

"You little kids sit down there," he told them, pointing to the row in front of him. "I wanna make out with Jessie." He grinned, with his arm around her.

"Eww, gross," Eli complained.

Maddy was a bit insulted at being called a little kid, but she knew he didn't really mean it that way. All three of them looked at each other and giggled, moving down to the next row. Aimee shrugged and looked back at Jessie, who was now sitting on Luke's lap, with her head resting on his chest. Maddy turned around and said, "Why don't you just ask Momma if you can take her on a date? She knows you like Jessie. Momma *likes* you, Luke."

Luke smiled. "Thanks, Maddy, I think I will." Deciding right then, that's exactly what he was going to do. "I'm gonna ask Momma to take you on a date, baby." Luke grinned.

"We are on a date, Luke." Jessie smiled.

Luke whispered in Jessie's ear, "This is fun, isn't baby? Are you remembering to take your pill?"

"Yeth, Luke, I took one this morning, after my shower."

"Good girl. Please don't forget, darlin'."

Aimee and Eli kept trying to spy on Jessie and Luke, but they weren't doing anything.

"You two knock it off, will ya?" Luke kicked the back of Aimee's seat. "Eat your popcorn." He turned to Jessie and smiled. "Nasty little kids."

Jessie giggled, and put her hand on his neck, tickling it with her fingers. "I'm going to school with Mikey, tomorrow, Luke," Jessie announced, suddenly remembering about it.

"What?"

"Momma said I can go to school with Mikey, tomorrow. I want to go to your school and see what it's like."

"Fuck," Luke said, under his breath. Jessie seemed so damn happy about it.

"Don't you want me to go, Luke?"

"I don't know, Jessie. I don't want you to be with Mike."

"I'm not picking, Luke. Momma says I don't have to."

Luke sat stewing, with jealous aggravation. "Why did you wake up for Mike, and not me, Jessie?" He didn't mean to ask her like that, but it was heavy on his mind.

"Because, I knew you were safe with me, Luke. You were home, safe. But, I didn't know where Mikey was."

Luke understood that Jessie lived in the moment and thinking about people's feelings for her was limited. He knew that when she was with him she loved him, but when she was with Mike, she loved Mike. "Jessie," he said, "please stop telling me when you have plans with him. I don't want to know about it."

"Luke, love on me, please," Jessie whispered, quickly changing the subject. She kissed his neck. "I love you, Luke. I love making out with you at the movies. I like to be in your lap, Luke." She put her feet up on his legs and curled up tight against his chest. He couldn't resist her.

Chapter Ten-
Demons

Jessie woke up in the middle of the night, frightened by a bad dream. The house was dark and all too quiet. She took Teddy up and spoke to it.

"I'm scared, Teddy. Mikey will save us." She quickly got up and ran over to the Miller's house.

Mike was waiting for her and held open the blankets. "Hi, Baby." He lay over her, rubbing his nose on hers. He'd been imagining Ricky's photos, and his fantasies were still in his head. "I was just thinkin' 'bout you."

"Mikey," Jessie whispered, looking up at him. "I want you. Put your muscle around me, so me and Teddy won't be scared." Her magical eyes were squinting, sparkling up at him. They were like wolf eyes or something and were drawing his thoughts out of his head. Mike got a chill looking at her. Her eyes deepened. "*Oh, Mikey. I saw you…I saw you, Mikey. I saw what you were doing to me…you're nasty.*"

Mike puffed, bewildered. "You didn't see anything." He grinned, intimidated that Jessie might really have seen what nasty thoughts he was just having, wondering if maybe Ricky was right. "You're scary, Baby," Mike said and caressed her face with his lips and kissed her. For an instant, he thought to show her Ricky's photo's, but realized that would only make her cry.

He wanted to tell her how much he wished he'd stayed with her that day on the beach, so he could've made her his. Unfortunately, the conversation took off in a different direction, when he called her his little Playboy Bunny.

"Playboy Bunny?" she asked.

"You don't know what a Playboy Bunny is, bunny?"

"No, what is it?"

"They're the girls in Playboy magazine."

"The ones with beaver shots and no clothes on?"

Mike laughed. "Who told you about beaver shots, anyway?"

"Ricky. He said you have beaver shots all over your wall. Where are they, Mikey?"

"Baby," Mike said, grinning. "You're so adorable. I took 'em all down, remember?"

"Oh. Mikey, is that why you call me bunny? Because I want to be a Playboy Bunny, now?"

"What?" Mike stopped smiling. "I thought you didn't know what that was."

"I want to have pictures of me in the magazine," Jessie answered, naively.

"Why do you wanna do that?" Mike asked, invidious.

"So you can put me on your wall. Isn't that what you like? Because I'm tho beautiful and you like to show me naked? When Luke got my pictures, I looked beautiful." Jessie was laying there so soft, looking up at Mike. "'Member when we were at the party and you wanted to show everyone, me?"

"No. I don't want to show you to anyone. When did Luke take you to do that?"

"Before."

"What else did you want to show everyone?" Mike felt jealous anger, remembering Andy, and how he was all over her, and not quite on the same page as Jessie.

"I don't want to show me to no one," Jessie answered, nervously tapping her finger on her mouth. "I dis thought you like the girls in the magazine and…and," she gulped, "you would like me, too. Don't you want me a Playboy Bunny?"

"No." He smoothed her hair off her face. "Sorry, bunny. Don't do things to please me, anymore. I don't want you to show other people your body. I love you more than that. You please me just the way you are… I get distracted so easy with you, and I forget to think."

"Mikey, I don't want to be a Playboy Bunny."

"I know, baby, I'm sorry. I'm a jealous idiot, and I forget how you talk sometimes, the way you word things. I love you. Jessie…" Mike gazed into her eyes with a troubled heart. "Promise me you won't have sex with any other guys. Promise me, Jessie."

"What do you mean, Mikey, not even Luke?"

"*Don't let anyone else have sex with you.* If Andy or anyone ever tries to touch you, you promise me you'll run away from them. You scream and run away, Jessie. Just because a guy wants to have sex with you, doesn't mean he likes you. You have to be careful not to let that happen anymore."

"I promise Mikey. I don't want nobody else. I want you." Jessie rubbed his arms. "Kiss me, Mikey, love me."

"Damn-it, baby," Mike sighed. "You're so fucking beautiful, you're so beautiful. You're so damn good, Jessie." She put her feet up and he held them in his hand, rubbing her little toes.

"I want to be your baby, Mikey."

"You are my baby."

"I was never a baby. My dad hates me," Jessie said, looking up at him.

"I don't think he hates you, he's just a dick."

"He never picked me up and put me on his lap. He never smiled at me or rubbed my head or my toes. He dis points his finger at me and yells. He hates me."

"He must have been nice to you, sometimes."

"No." Jessie shook her head. "He never bought me no toys, or played with me, or laughed with me. All he ever says
is 'do your chores and shut up.' He never lets me talk to him. I tried to talk to him about my school, but he always says, 'Don't pester me. Can't you thee I'm reading?' All he ever does is read when he's home, and says 'get me a beer', and throws my libary book in the fire. He never says thank you for cooking or cleaning."

Mike looked down at Jessie. "No toys, ever?"

"No, only you ever bought me a toy."

"Teddy?"

Jessie nodded. "Where is Teddy?"

"Right here," Mike said, picking him up off the bed and handing him to her. "I think we've been neglecting him."

Jessie squeezed Teddy against her face, while Mike gazed down at her little face. "I think my dad's in love with me, compared to your old man. I'm sorry, baby, but *I* love you. It doesn't matter what he thinks. He's a selfish prick. You're gonna grow up and live your life without him, anyway. Why'd he throw your library book in the fire?" Mike rested his chin on his hands, on top of her chest, while she twirled his hair in her fingers.

"I don't know. Whenever he's mad about something he…he yells at me. He said it was thmut."

"Smut?" Mike grinned. "Why, you readin' dirty books, peanut?"

"No, a love story."

"My dad's kinda like that, sometimes. What do you do at home, Jessie?"

"Well, I have to do my chores. Clean out the chicken coop, and feed the chickens in the morning, and put the eggs away, cut the firewood and stack it up."

"Cut firewood? You?"

"Yeah. One day I pretended you were helping me."

Mike smiled, caressing Jessie's face. "Then what, baby?"

"Then I do my homework, cook dinner, and wash my clothes when I get home from school, and put them on the
clothes-line. Then I have to clean my daddy's room and the bathroom."

"What do you cook for dinner?"

"I cook a lots of eggs and fried potatoes, and Daddy likes steak, tho he buys a lot. Sometimes, I make cookies, if he buys sugar." Jessie smiled, raising her eyebrow.

"I like steak, and eggs, and potatoes, too." Mike smiled. "I bet you're a good cook. You'll have to cook some up for me." Mike looked softly into Jessie's eyes, and stroked her face. "So, if you have any spare time left after all those chores, then what? Watch TV?"

"I asked Daddy for a TV once, but he got mad. It was going to be summer time. I told him since his work was good maybe we could buy a TV, so I wouldn't be tho bored. He said, 'No, you're going to paint the house. That will keep you busy.' But when I was painting the house, guess what?" Jessie smiled.

"What?" Mike smiled at her.

"Well, I found a guitar in my daddy's closet, with a speaker. I took it down and it worked when I plugged it in, and I started to play it. It was electric, dis like when you plug into me," Jessie snorted, giggling. "I play it every day now, when he's not home. I have to put it back up, though. I'm sure he would be mad about it."

"When are you gonna play the guitar for me, bunny?"

"Whenever you want me to. What do you do for spare time, Mikey?"

"I'm a bum compared to you, Love. I don't know, hang out at the bowling alley, play pinball. Sometimes we bowl. I guess we're kinda spoiled...Your world is so shitty, Baby, and yet, you're so sweet. I'm a spoiled, asshole."

"I don't know what pinball is. We have to play bally ball at school, but I don't like it. I always get pushed down."

"Is that what you do all summer, baby?"

"Well, I take my doggy for a walk in the meadow. But he's dead now, tho I can't take him no more. I climb in the big tree in the meadow and look out, wondering about other places. The fairies lives in the oak tree. I made them a house, but some *thing* keeps breaking it. The monster in the trees, I think. He does *not* like the fairies."

"Fairies, Monster? Is that why you don't like trees?"

No! I hate the pine trees, Mikey." She cringed, whispering, "They're dark and mean…The monster lives in the pine trees. He watches me when I'm outside. He killed my dog!" Jessie frowned.

"What do you mean, a monster in the trees?"

Jessie's face turned frightened as she got closer and whispered, "He lives in the dark trees." Jessie's eyes were getting bigger.

"He watches me," she took a deep breath, "when I get off the bus, he follows me up the road…in the trees to my house…and stays there, watching…I hear him in the wind, when the sticks crackle and he growls at me."

Mike felt a chill as he watched the fear welling up in Jessie's eyes. He moved up closer to Jessie's face.

"There's no such thing as monsters, Jessie. Are you sure there's something there? I thought coyotes killed your dog."

Jessie shook her head. "No. He was there, and next morning, Luke was dead. He's always there, since I was little. He growls and hides behind the trees, I can thee his shadow move…and hear him in the wind." Jessie's eyes were watering and filled with terror. She started to cry. "I couldn't fix the chicken wire," she gasped. "It keeps coming apart every time I fix it. I can't stay outside long enough…because he might come out and take me. The chickens gets out because I can't fix the wire. Now Luke is dead…and the monster will come out now and kill *me*."

Mike sat up and put Jessie in his lap. "What does the monster look like, Jessie?"

"He looks, he-he looks," Jessie said, sniffling. She closed her eyes. "I don't know what he looks like…He looks like a
pig." Jessie swallowed. "He's black, I don't know. He growls like a *werewolf*. He has long fangs and *pinchers* and his eyes are…his eyes are…red. I don't know what he looks like," Jessie said, holding her hand over her eyes.

"Does he have black glasses, Jessie?"

Jessie opened her eyes and looked up at Mike. She gazed off across the room.

"I don't think it's a monster you see, Jessie. I think whatever happened to you when you were little is messing with your head. Did it happen in the trees?

Jessie looked up at Mike, worried and puzzled. "No! It's a monster! And he will never go away, and you don't believe me! He killed my dog, and he will come get me and take me, because no one can help me! And I'm not ever going there again! I'll run away, and no one will find me!"

"I believe you Jessie, yes there is a monster and I'm going to make him go away, and then, I'm gonna take you to a doctor, Jessie. One that can help you figure it out."

Jessie sniffed, wiping her eyes. "A doctor?"

"One that helps you figure out what's going on inside your head, bunny. I'm gonna make Luke go, too."

"You mean, me and you, and Luke, all together?"

Yeah, all of us together, we all need help."

"What's the doctor going to do to my head, Mikey?"

"He's not gonna do anything to your head, bunny. He's just gonna talk to you and find out what's hiding in it."

"I'm afraid about that," Jessie gasped. "I don't want no more doctors, Mikey."

"I know you don't, baby. But we're gonna go anyway."

"Mikey," Jessie said, looking in his eyes. "Did you take the monster away?"

"Not yet, but I will. I'll find him, and I *will* hurt him. Do you want me to go with you in the trees, Jessie? I'll show you he's not there."

"No! I'm not going there ever again. Momma's going to
keep me, now."

"I'll go with you, baby, you'll see, he won't be there."

"That's because he's afraid of you, Mikey. You're tho big; he won't ever come out when you're there."

"Well, when I find him, he's gonna be more than afraid, and he won't be alive to come out, again."

"You're going to kill the monster, Mikey?"

Mike glared out across the room. "Yes baby, I'm gonna kill the monster in your head."

"Lay on me, Mikey, tho no one can see me."

Mike lay down over Jessie, not sure what to think.

"Mikey, I don't want to go back there…I don't want to go there no more. Keep me, Mikey. Please, keep me."

"Jessie, I wanna take you away so bad, baby. I know you don't want to be there, but I can't right now. We don't have anywhere to go right now. You won't marry me, so what can I do?"

"Mikey, you have money…don't thend me back there."

"Shhh, you have to be quiet, baby. I'm not sending you anywhere, Jessie. I been saving all my money, so I can take you away. But right now, your Aunt is doing everything she can to help you, maybe for good. We're gonna figure this all out, baby. You're not going back there right now, so please, just relax and don't cry, no more. You're right here with me, you're not going anywhere, right now. Tomorrow, we're gonna go to school together, remember?"

Jessie sniffed, "Okay, Mikey, I'll be a good girl. I won't cry no more."

Mike exhaled. "Baby," he whispered, lying his head down on her. "You're not bad because you cry."

Jessie lay there for a moment, thinking about going back home, and the wood bin, and the monster, and if Ricky could die, then she could too, and going to the doctor who was going to look in her head to find the monster. Her head was tingling. She couldn't breathe and started to hyperventilate, worrying herself into a full-blown panic attack. She began to cry, again. "You're going to thend me back home, aren't you, Mikey?"

"Baby, please stop. I don't have no say over that, baby. You know that."

"Mikey." Jessie panted and wiggled out from under him, getting up off the bed.

"Where you going?" Mike sat up. "You said you were gonna be good."

"I'm not going back there, I'm not going there no more, Mikey…You won't take me away, Mikey. And Momma can't keep me. People just say that, no one can keep me. I have to run away." Jessie was trembling and ran out the door.

"Fuck!" Mike quickly pulled his Levi's on. He ran out of his room, and opened the front door, where he saw Jessie's silhouette go around the bend of the street in the cold, dark, night. Chasing after her, he swooped her up in his arms.

Jessie struggled as he swiftly started back. "No Mikey! Let me go!"

"Damn you, Jessie. *Damn you!* What the *hell's* the matter with you?

Jessie kicked her legs. "I don't want to go home! You won't keep me! You don't want me! You won't let me stay with you!"

"Stop it, Jessie!" Mike said, holding Jessie as tight as he could. He got to his car and sat with her until she could be quiet and calm down. "Jessie, do you want your Aunt to see you? Stop it, now! You're going to wake up the whole neighborhood. I can't believe you did that, Jessie. Don't you ever do that, again!"

"Because, you won't let me stay here!"

"Well you can't stay with me if you're running off down the fuckin' street! I don't have any fuckin' say about that, why can't you understand that? Be still, dammit!"

Jessie stopped struggling and started to cry. "You could take me away, Mikey…you could keep me in your room. Why can't you?" Jessie buried her head in Mike's chest.

"Where would we go, baby? Where would we live right now?"

"I don't care. In the Miller house, Mikey. I don't want to go home. I don't want to be alone."

"I know you don't want to be alone." Mike sighed, rubbing her head. "I don't want you to be alone, but where'd you think you were gonna go, bunny? You gotta marry me baby, then you can stay with me."

"I'm cold, Mikey," Jessie pouted, shivering.

"No shit, baby. Are you gonna be quiet now, so I can take you back to bed?"

"I want my teddy."

"Come own, baby, you dumb, little girl," Mike said, kissing her face. He took her back upstairs to his room and pulled the blankets up over her shivering body.

Jessie put Teddy up to her face, squeezing him. "Don't get up, Mikey."

"I'm not getting up, Jessie."

"Mikey my head hurts tho bad."

Mike ran his fingers through her hair and massaged the top of her head. Jessie's eyes were watering.

"My head hurts tho bad…It hurts."

"Why do you keep havin' headaches, peanut?" Mike got her some aspirin and laid back down, rubbing her head until she fell asleep, agonizing over how he was going to take Jessie away.

Thursday, January 17, 1974

It was about three in the morning when Luke came in Mike's room. He leaned over Jessie, who was asleep. He bent over and slid his hands under her.

"Luke," Jessie said, opening her eyes.

"Shhh, come own, baby," Luke whispered. He picked Jessie up to take her in his room, when Mike woke up.

"What the fuck are you doing?"

"I'm taking Jessie," Luke said, picking her pajamas up off the foot of the bed.

"The fuck you are," Mike snapped, throwing the blankets off him and sat up.

"It's okay, Mikey," Jessie said. "I have to see Luke, now."

Mike was stunned, not sure how to react, as Luke left the room with Jessie. He let out a heavy breath, knowing this was bound to happen sooner or later. He'd been thinking a lot about having to share Jessie with Luke and wondered if he would be able to endure the torment of watching them together, if she should ever actually choose one of them. Luke had been thinking the same thing, wondering if they could really have a normal life, again. Mike's mind was spinning, and he felt helpless. Jessie was so adamant that she wasn't going to choose.

Luke laid down on his bed with Jessie, pulling the blankets up over them. Softly, he kissed her face.

He wasn't going to ask her anything about all the noise he'd been listening to and didn't really give a shit about Mike's feelings. Luke gently stroked her face.

"My Luke," Jessie said.

"Jessie," Luke whispered, "I think about you all day, all night. I just want to hold you in my arms, forever. I see your beautiful little face, and your precious little ways, and my heart aches for you. I can't stand the minutes we're apart."

"Luke, I runned away."

"Why? Is that what you were doin'?"

"Because, you and Mikey always thend me away, you won't keep me."

"I don't want to send you away, Jessie, I want to marry you."

"Why do I have to be married? Why can't I dis stay here, Luke?" Jessie closed her eyes. "You say you can't be away from
me, but you always send me back there, and I'm not going there, ever again. You say you don't like it when we're apart, but I don't like it when we're apart, and you send me away, anyway. You say how you feel, but you don't know how I feel, Luke. I'm scared, and I don't want to be there, and no one cares, and Auntie can't keep me, either."

"Baby, I'm sorry. I know you're scared. I know you don't understand, but Jessie, there are laws. Laws that say I can't keep you...not unless we're married. Laws that say Debbie can't keep you, not unless she has custody. We do care, baby. We care so much. I understand it's a hard choice for you to make, I know that, baby. I wish I could help you, but I can't. All I can do is love you and wait for you." Luke kissed Jessie's cheek, as she blinked the tears from her eyes and closed them. Apparently, no one was going to help her. She cuddled her back up against Luke's chest, and he wrapped his arms around her.

Jessie woke up with Luke, kissing her face. "Mornin', beautiful. You gotta get up, now," he said.

"I know, but I don't want to. I'm tho happy right here, with my Luke, in the Miller house."

"Remember, you're going to school with Mike, darlin'."

"Oh, I am, haw? I'm going to go to school with Mikey." Jessie smiled.

"Yeah, so you better get up."

"I want to go to school with my Mikey. Luke, don't forget to ask Momma about the date."

"I won't forget. I'm gonna talk to her today. Come on, darlin', get dressed." Luke said, helping Jessie put her pajamas on.

"I have to tell Mikey something, for a minute."

Jessie went down the hall to Mike's room. He was leaned up on the headboard, smoking. She leaned over and kissed him. Mike pulled her down on him.

"Jessie, I want you to wear your uniform today."

"Why Mikey? You said to wear my *real* clothes."

"Just today, baby. I want people to know where you're from, and how cute you are in your uniform."

"K, Mikey," Jessie said, disappointed. "If you want me to."

"We're leaving at seven, so be ready."

Jessie went back to Luke's room and sat on the bed as he pulled his jeans on, standing over her. "When are you gonna come to my room, Jessie?"

"I'll come to your room, Luke," Jessie said smiling. She looked around the room. It was clean and organized. Luke picked Jessie up and carried her to her house. He set her down on the front porch and kissed her good-bye.

"I'll see you, tonight, and baby, I'm gonna think about you all day."

"Bye, Luke." She pouted, standing at the door, as he ran down the stairs in his jeans and bare feet. When he got back inside his house, Mike was looking out the window.

"I think Jessie's getting worse," Luke said, wiping the dirt off his feet. "And we're not helping her any."

Mike looked out the window, nodding.

"I think Ricky's death is triggering something in her head, and she's dealing with it by regressing," Luke said. "She's becoming more of a baby, if that's possible."

"Yeah, I wonder why?" Mike answered, smartly. "I wanna take her to a psychiatrist." Mike looked at Luke. "I want you to go, too. I think we all need to go, we're all fucked up."

Luke was surprised that Mike would consider that, and he nodded. "Maybe that's a good idea."

"It's a fuckin' brilliant idea. She's talking about monsters; a monster that follows her." Mike looked back out the window. "She's been having bad headaches. She ran off down the street last night, trying to run away."

"It's us, Mike…I'm glad you know nothin' good's gonna come out of this," Luke said, heading toward the bathroom.

Chapter Eleven -
At Mining with Mikey

Jessie went right away and quietly got ready for school. She sighed, putting her icky, old uniform on, and then put her hair up in a pony.

Still too early to go, she lay down on the couch with George and Gracie cuddled up beside her and fell asleep.

Mike started his car at ten to seven. The new headers on his car were loud enough to wake up the whole neighborhood. Jessie awoke, startled by Mike's noisy car. She sat up and looked out the window. George and Gracie were barking their heads off.

"Well, someone's been up early, excited to go to school," Debbie said, sitting on the couch next to her. Aimee came walking out from her room, yawning.

"Gracie! George! Hush up!" Aimee shouted.

"Why are you wearing your uniform, Sweetie?" Debbie asked.

"Mikey says it's a good idea, so everyone can see where I'm from. Just for one day."

"Well, go get your jacket. I think he's coming up the stairs."

"How come you're leaving so early?" Aimee asked, sitting at the table in front of a bowl of cereal.

Jessie shrugged. "I don't know." She raced to the bedroom to get her fuzzy white jacket and ran back to the front door. "Bye, Momma!"

"Jessie," Debbie said, "I'm going to call Mother to let her know you're going to Mining, for a few days, just to let her know how you're doing."

"Okay, Momma," Jessie said, just as Mike knocked on the door. The dogs went off again and Jessie yelled, "HUSH!" as she stepped out onto the porch. Mike was wearing his Levi's, old white Nike's, and a black Grateful Dead T-shirt. Jessie felt shy, because he looked so handsome. "Noisy dogs," she said, smiling at Mike. "I'm sorry 'bout what I did last night, Mikey."

"Which part?" Mike asked, looking down at her.

"When I runned away."

Mike smiled, taking her hand. "I know, baby. Don't do it again. Let's go get in your car, bunny."

He didn't want to talk about it. He didn't have it clear in his head. Mike opened his door for her, and she climbed in, over his seat. Mike pulled away from the curb, driving up the road like a maniac.

"Mikey, you'll scare my Auntie," Jessie said, leaning her head against the seat, looking at him. Debbie went to the window, regretting her decision.

"Do I scare you?" he asked, backing off the throttle.

"No," she said, quietly. Her beautiful blue eyes twinkled up at him. "I like you in black."

Mike grinned. When he got up the road some ways, he pulled over and stopped. He leaned over her and said, "Good morning, sweet thing." He smiled, taking her chin in his hand, and kissed her. "I like you in anything, or nothing…I hope I never scare you, Jessie."

"Why did you want me to wear my uniform, Mikey?"

"Because, I don't want anyone gettin' any ideas, gettin' all hot and horny."

"They don't do that at school, do they?"

"Well, you don't go to school with a bunch of dicks. Come 'ere, baby, scoot over here next to me."

Jessie slid over next to him and he took off, back down the road, rubbing her leg. Impulsively, he put his hand up her skirt and into her panties.

"You make me so crazy, baby. Hold your panties out of the way," he said, looking out at the road, and quickly shifting with his driving hand.

"I'll just take them off."

"No, just hold 'em over to the side. Your panties are pretty."

"Mikey, you can't do me and drive."

"Yeah I can. Put your legs up, baby."

"No," Jessie said, digging her fingernails into his arm.
"I think not. I'm a good girl, now."

"Aright, baby, I'm sorry. I don't mean to be a pig." Mike rubbed his arm. "Damn, bunny, you scratched the shit outta my arm."

"That's because I'm a *tiger*, and I will *scratch* you," Jessie growled.

"A tiger?" Mike chuckled; her little voice was so cute and serious.

"Why did you do me like that?"

"I don't know. I can't keep my hands off you, baby." Mike answered, trying to swallow the lump in his throat. "My brain fuckin' shuts down when I git around you, and my dick goes into overdrive."

"Mikey?" Jessie asked sitting up in her seat. "I don't want you to call me tittie girl."

"Why, baby? You're my little, big tittie girl."

"Because I don't want to be tittie girl. Can I have a cigarette?"

"We're almost there, baby. We'll smoke outside. You don't have to sit over there, stay here by me…Jessie, you remember what I told you, don't you?"

"Yeah, no, what did you tell me?" She asked, sliding next to him.

"About guys trying to touch you. You run away, remember?"

"Even you?"

"No, baby. You're *my* bunny."

"Mikey, you're not going to leave me alone, are you?"

"No, just in case something happens, though."

"What will happen, Mikey?"

"Nothin'. You stay with me."

Mike pulled up into the parking lot of Mining High School. He revved the engine and turned the car off. Taylor was waiting for him, standing on the curb with Amanda and Julie Butcher. It was Mike's first day back at school since the accident, and Taylor wanted to tell Mike she was sorry about his brother. Instead, they all stood glaring at Jessie, when Mike got out and took Jessie's hand. She pushed her skirt down.

"Mikey, I forgot my backpack."

Mike bent down and kissed her, "You don't need it, peanut," he said, shutting the door. He walked her toward the smoker's section of the parking lot, barely noticing Taylor and her friends. Jessie did. They were giving her dirty looks.

Amanda sneered. "What's she doing here?"

Jessie looked back at them as Mike pulled her along.

"What's the matter, Jessie?" he asked, seeing she was looking back.

"Those are means girls." Jessie frowned.

He looked back toward them. "They're stupid little bitches, don't pay attention to them, little peanut."

Mike's friends all patted him on the back and told him they were sorry about

Ricky. Jessie became sad, being reminded about him.

"Hey, Jessie," Kevin said, leaning back on the front of his blazer.

Jessie frowned at Kevin, hiding behind Mike's arm. She did not like Kevin anymore.

"You guys all remember Jessie, don't you?" Mike said, taking out a cigarette and lighting it. He handed it to Jessie. She shook her head, not wanting it, now.

"How could we forget?" Jeff asked. "Hi, Jessie."

Bobby took Jessie's hand. "Nice to see you again, Jessie."

"Hi, babe." Gary smiled.

"How come you don't park over here?" Kevin asked Mike.

"Cuz, I don't want you shit heads sittin' all over my car."

"Hey, Miller," Andy said, coming up and patted Mike on the shoulder. "Sorry about your bro, man." He looked at Jessie, staring right down at her blouse. "I see you brought your yummy girlfriend." Andy raised his eyebrow, smiling at Jessie.

Jessie squeezed Mike's hand and stepped behind him, looking out at Andy from under Mike's arm.

"Look all you want, Bass, but don't touch," Mike said, taking a drag of his cigarette.

Andy winked at Jessie. "I'd pay a lot of money for a piece of that."

"Well, I appreciate your honesty, fucker, but I'll kill you, if you ever touch my little girl."

"Yeah, well, I'm not sure you're man enough, Miller." Andy said, standing up straight, trying to impress Jessie.

"Let's find out!" Mike snapped, instantly hot headed, ready to swing.

"Hang on!" Kevin yelled, grabbing Mikes arm. "Andy's just fuckin' around, Mike."

Andy held his hands up. "Yeah, man. I'm just fuckin' around."

"Well, keep your mouth shut, Bass," Bobby told him.

"Hey." Andy held up his hands again. "I'm just a playboy, you guys all know that. I'm a lover, not a fighter, unlike some people." He looked at Jessie. She felt something was menacing about him.

"Some people aren't as fuckin' ignorant," Mike replied. "At least I never did that ignorant bitch, Taylor."

"Well, maybe you missed out on a good piece of ass," Andy smirked.

Mike chuckled. "I truly doubt that, man. You must've been fuckin' high off your ass, to want a piece of *that*." Mike sneered. "How could you even compare that ugly skank to my little girl? Just get the fuck away from me. I'm through talkin' to you, Fuck!"

Mike took Jessie's hand, practically dragging her up toward the school, with Kevin following behind.

"Damn, he's got a lot of nerve," Kevin said.

"I'm gonna kill that stupid fucker one day." Mike threw down his cigarette. "You stay away from him, you hear me, Jessie?" Mike turned to her, yanking on her hand.

"Mikey," Jessie gasped out of breath, trying to keep up with his long legs.

Mike stopped and bent over Jessie, hugging her. He could see she had a frightened look in her eyes, and now he felt stupid for already ruining her first day at school. "I'm sorry, bunny," he said, kissing her. "I didn't mean to scare you. I got a bad temper."

Bobby got up off the hood of the car he was sitting on and looked down at Andy, who was watching Mike and Jessie walk away.

"You better watch yourself," Bobby said.

"Well, he's still gotta play ball, he better watch *himself.*"

~

Mike's first class was Principles of Mathematics, which was a ridiculously easy class. The teacher, assistant coach Reed, rarely gave out homework, made the assignments easy, and talked about football for most of the forty-five minutes of class.

Mike walked Jessie over to a desk where Brad Schaeffer was sitting.

"Move," Mike ordered him.

Brad reluctantly got up and moved over to another row. The whole class was staring at Jessie.

"Sit down, baby," Mike said.

"Why did you do that?" Jessie whispered, sitting down.

"Do what, baby?" He sat in the seat behind her.

"Make people move."

"Cuz, I wanna sit by you."

"Are you a mean boy, Mikey?"

Mike looked back at Brad for a second and then stroked Jessie's face.

Coach Reed walked in and began writing some words on the board. He was a husky man, with short curly black hair, and a round face. He turned to look at the students, who were still coming in, making noise. "Who's your friend, Mike?" Coach asked, going over to them.

"This is my Jessie. She's gonna come to school with me for a few days."

"Nice to meet you, Jessie, and Mike, we'd all like to tell you how sorry we are about Ricky," Coach said. "We'll all miss him."

Some of the students said out loud, "Yeah, Mike, and sorry,"

"Thanks," Mike said, looking at Jessie, who had turned around, pouting at him. Mike winked at her and blew her a kiss.

Coach went back to the board and told the class to turn to page two-hundred-fifteen. Mike handed Jessie his book. When she turned to the page, she couldn't believe that students in high school were learning such simple math.

"Why do you take this class, Mikey?" she turned, whispering to him.

"So I can play football, baby."

"Oh." She turned back around, ignorant as to what that meant.

"Quiet down," Mr. Reed told the class as he finished putting the words up on the chalkboard. The class was to have memorized their meaning.

The Different Branches of Mathematics

Arithmetic	Trigonometry
Algebra	Probability
Geometry	Statistics
Theory of Games	Symbolic Logic
The Calculus	Topology

Coach pointed to Arithmetic. "Can anyone tell me the definition of Arithmetic?" No one raised their hand.

"Mr. Logan?" He pointed to a student.

"Um, No, Sir," came the reply.

"Miss Avery?"

She stared at him, shaking her head.

"Well, I'm sure Mr. Miller has no idea what we're talking about. How 'bout you, Jessie?" Coach Reed smiled with the class, who were chuckling.

Jessie timidly, looked down. She did not want to be talked to. "Um, yes Sir,"

Coach looked surprised. "Please tell us, Jessie."

Jessie looked down at her desk and spoke softly. "Arithmetic deals with the properties of numbers and groups of numbers, and with the operations used to combine them."

"Wow, that's terrific, Jessie." Mr. Reed smiled and pointed at the word Trigonometry.

Mike gently pulled at Jessie's hair, surprising her, but she ignored him.

"Can anyone tell me about trigonometry?" Mr. Reed asked the class, knowing full well that no one had learned the words.

"Miss Crawford?"

"No."

"Mr. Chavez?"

"No."

"Well, does anyone know where in the book to find the definitions?" he asked, and everyone started turning pages in their books.

"How about you, Jessie?" Coach asked Jessie, again.

"Yes, Sir," Jessie timidly answered.

"Go ahead, Jessie." Coach Reed smiled.

Jessie answered, shyly looking down. "Trigonometry deals with the property of angles and the relationships between the thides and angles of triangles."

"Smart ass," Mike whispered to Jessie, who did not turn around. Jessie had proper school conduct and did not feel comfortable visiting with her neighbor during class.

"Remarkable," Mr. Reed said. "Jessie, can you tell us the meaning of calculus?"

"Yes Thir." Jessie was fidgeting, and wanted to be left alone, but she took in a deep breath. "The Calculus may be divided into two basic studies. Differential calculus deals with changing rates of change, such as non-uniform velocities and actthelerations. Integral calculuth is used to find areas, volumes, the center of gravity of a mass, and the equations of curves."

Mike leaned over. "I know the equation of your curves, bunny."

The boys in class were captivated; she could feel their eyes roaming her body, while practically every girl was giving her the evil eye.

"My guess is you could tell us the meaning of all of these words, Jessie?" Coach Reed asked her.

"Yeth, Sir." Jessie nodded. She was not about to look at anyone.

"And can you perform any of these branches of mathematics?"

"Yeth Sir."

"Which ones, Jessie?"

"All of them, Sir."

"It must be an honor having you as a student, Jessie. You go to St. Thomas?" Jessie nodded.

"It's an honor having you, period, Jessie," Mike whispered.

"Apparently, none of *my* students were concerned about their future in the world of knowledge this week," Mr. Reed grinned. "So, can anyone tell me what two times two is?" Mr. Reed wrote the equation on the board and then another one. 367 1/2 X 432.

"Mr. Davis," he asked, "come to the board and show the class how to perform this equation."

The young man came to the board and began processing the problem. Coach put some other problems on the board and asked various students to come and solve them; even Jessie. She didn't solve her problem, she just went up and immediately wrote the answer down and returned to her seat.

Mr. Reed took out his calculator and found her answer correct. "Jessie," he said, typing on his calculator. "What is 785 X 563?"

Jessie answered without hesitation, "Four-four one, one thousand, nine five-five."

Mr. Reed typed again, and asked her, "12,564 divided by 456."

"Twenty-seven point five, five," Jessie answered without pausing.

Mr. Reed was fascinated and asked, "Are all of St. Thomas' students as remarkable as you, Jessie?"

"Yes, Sir," Jessie answered, realizing everyone was staring at her.

Mike was not surprised at all anymore about Jessie. He sat resting his head on his hand, smiling. Jessie felt shy and nervous about being the center of attention. She could feel her palms start to sweat and rubbed her hands on her skirt. Mr. Reed sensed her uneasiness and told the class to have page two-hundred-fifteen done for homework, tomorrow.

Being totally unprepared for class, as usual, Mike grabbed the pencil from the student behind him. "Gimme a piece of paper," he said to her, which obviously, was something he did quite frequently. She handed him a page from her notebook, and he wrote down: 'You're the cutest little Einstein. Will you go out with me?' with XOXO, and 'write me back,' on it, and dropped it down on Jessie's lap. He decided he was going to write her love notes all day. It was going to be fun, having never done it before. He handed the pencil back to the girl. "Thanks," he said.

Jessie didn't know what to do with the piece of paper. She read it under the desk and folded it, terrified of getting in trouble. She didn't write notes at school, but a lot of girls did. When they got caught, the teacher would read it out loud, and they would have to do detention.

"Aren't you gonna write me back, hot stuff?" Mike whispered.

Jessie shook her head, not turning around. Mike tickled the back of her neck. Jessie smiled to herself, shrugging.

Coach began discussing a football game that had taken place during his junior year at USN in Las Vegas. Most of the students were passing notes and whispering to each other, in particular about Jessie, and wondering what Mike Miller was doing with her, and why was he acting like that?

A few of the boys were interested in Mr. Reed's football game. Normally, Mike would have been interested in it, too, but he had a big fat boner and couldn't think about anything except his amazing, beautiful Jessie this morning in the car, and her cute little butt that was hiding under that skirt, and her beautiful breasts that he knew were wiggling around under her blouse.

After class, Mike took Jessie to his locker, switched his math book for his history book, and handed it to her.

"Aren't you 'spose to carry my book?" Jessie asked, looking around at everyone staring at her.

"Yeah." Mike took the book back. "You're supposed to write me back on the love note, baby," he said, closing the locker.

"Love note? I don't want to get in trouble, Mikey." Jessie's face was innocent, and her eyes were so serious.

"You're not gonna get in trouble, bunny." He smiled at her, pulling her blouse out to look down the front of it. "Write me back, baby. I never got to write love notes to a girl at school."

"Never?" she asked, pulling her blouse closed.

"Never," he answered, pressing her between himself and the lockers. He put his hand up her skirt and squeezed her.

"Mikey, stop it! Stop touching me." She pushed his hand away. "I thought you don't want me thexy?" Jessie whispered, looking around. "You're getting me in trouble and everyone is staring at me."

Mike picked her up so he could reach her face with his. "I'm sorry, baby. I know, I'm a pig. You're always thexy." He rubbed his nose on hers. It dawned on Mike that Andy was in his next class.

Mike was greeted by Mr. Leland with the same sympathies regarding Ricky and he pleasantly shook hands with Jessie. They were studying the *Battle of Bull Run*, and once the class was settled, Mr. Leland started a discussion on it. He asked Jessie if she was familiar with the subject.

Jessie blushed, fretfully disappointed that apparently, she was going to be the center of attention all day. Trying to be brave, she answered, "Yes, Sir," and somehow, from there, it got around to Jessie, giving a detailed account of Colonel Jackson's major tactical stand on the hill that won the battle, captivating the entire class. Mr. Leland was awestruck, yet he sensed something peculiar. Jessie's account, though correct, was mechanical and lifeless, as though well-rehearsed. He asked Jessie what Colonel Jackson might have been thinking. Jessie couldn't answer. Her logic only went as far as remembering facts.

He found Jessie fascinating, and so did Andy. Andy couldn't keep his eyes off her, fantasizing her breasts, her legs, her long silky hair and beautiful face. The sound of her voice was more than he could stand. She was the most beautiful girl he'd ever seen, and he could barely breathe looking at her, but he couldn't stop. In fact, every guy in class was staring at Jessie, adjusting themselves.

Mr. Leland was curious about Jessie's abilities. He sensed Jessie might not speculate on personal thought or emotion and tried to think of a simpler scenario. He asked her, "Does your dad hunt, Jessie?"

Jessie was worried. The sisters never made a spectacle of her, but it seemed Mr. Leland didn't understand her timidity. Maybe he didn't feel it was important to be as guarded with her. She looked down at her desk, quietly answering, "Yes, a lot."

"Does he hunt for sport or food, Jessie?"

"I don't know. I don't think he likes them. I don't like coyotes, so I have to shoot them."

"Oh. And when you shot at them, did you shoot to kill or shoot to scare them off?"

"I don't know." Jessie tried not to fidget.

"Say you shot one, but only injured it? Then what would you do?"

"Um, probly kill it," Jessie answered. "'Less it ran away."

"Why would you shoot to kill an injured coyote?"

"To kill him."

The class laughed, and Jessie felt very intimidated. Mike was getting upset with this.

"Settle down," Mr. Leland said, giving the class a stern look. "I apologize, Jessie, for my rude students. Why do you need to kill him if he's injured?"

"To make him dead?" Jessie asked, embarrassed. She had no idea what he was getting at.

"God, she's stupid," Taylor whispered to Nicki, who was sitting in front of her. Mike turned around and glared at her. Taylor stopped laughing, chewing on her gum, and twisting a strand of hair around her finger. She gave Mike a silent, blank look.

"Mr. Leland…" Mike started to say.

"Hang on, Mike," Mr. Leland said, putting his finger out to Mike.

Jessie was thinking, not sure what Mr. Leland was asking. She was terribly nervous. She sat up in her seat and said, "Because, I probly shot him outside of sixty-five yards."

"What caliber?" Andy spoke up.

"Well," Jessie looked around and took a deep breath, "For a .22 caliber to kill, he has to be inside sixty-five yards, if you shoot him in the head."

Mike was truly impressed with Jessie, regardless of what Mr. Leland was trying to do.

"What caliber rifle do I need to shoot a deer, Jessie?" Erick Greene spoke out, being a smart ass. Andy, and his dad were avid hunters, and he couldn't wait to hear this conversation.

"Where are you hunting?" Jessie asked, looking at Erick. Mr. Leland leaned against his desk, crossing his legs.

"What difference does that make?" Erick asked her.

"Because, if you're hunting in Nevada, we have only white tail or mule deer," Jessie answered.

"In Nevada," Andy interrupted.

Jessie turned toward her desk and looked down. "There is no perfect rifle. A lever action thirty-thirty is one of the most popular choices."

"Will you go hunting with me, Jessie?" Andy asked smiling, leaning on his arm. He was completely mesmerized by her.

Jessie glanced over at Andy. Mike was totally in awe of Jessie, and totally wanted to go beat the shit out of Andy.

"I think we're getting away from the point I was making with Jessie," Mr. Leland spoke up. "Don't answer right away, Jessie. I want you to think about it. Why wouldn't you just let the coyote go off injured?"

Jessie didn't answer, she sat thinking. Some kids started to snicker, and Mike was about to say, 'shut up' when Mr. Leland said, "Quiet, give Jessie a chance to think."

Finally, Jessie answered, "Because I don't want him to thuffer?"

"Yes, that's it. You got it, Jessie." Mr. Leland smiled.

Jessie assumed Mr. Leland was looking for a more complex answer. She had not been asked to use her brain before or think for herself. She was used to memorizing facts, and the nuns hadn't taken notice that Jessie really wasn't thinking for herself.

Mr. Leland had discovered that within a few minutes of talking to her. Mike was realizing that Jessie had difficulty feeling for things outside of herself, which was probably why she could lay in his bed and then go off with Luke, without any remorse. And him allowing her to do it only reinforced that.

She seemed to love him, was she able to love him? He didn't want to care, he loved her.

Mike understood what Mr. Leland was doing and wasn't irritated with him anymore. He was really pissed at Andy, though, arrogant fuck. Mike never liked Andy to begin with, taking Luke's place as Captain and all, and now he really had it in for him.

~

Mike and Jessie went with Kevin and Gary to lunch at *Denny's*, their usual hang-out. The place was buzzing with kids from school, including Andy and Jeff, Andy's girlfriend, Katie Hart, and her friend, Lisa. Katie was a pretty girl with golden-brown hair. Her friend, Lisa Salas, had long black hair with big black eyes. Andy kept staring and winking at Jessie.

"What do you want to eat, bunny?" Mike asked, looking down at the menu.

"I'm not hungry," Jessie answered. She was sitting under his arm, trying to hide. She felt uncomfortable and sweaty.

"You're gonna eat something, you don't eat enough, Jessie. That's probably why you have headaches."

"Don't order me nothin', Mikey, I won't eat it." Jessie fidgeted, holding on to Mike's arm. She never felt like this at lunch with Luke.

Kevin and Gary were trying not to stare at Jessie. Neither one of them wanted their face bashed in.

"What's the matter with you, baby?" Mike whispered. "Why do you keep fidgeting, how come you're so sweaty?"

She put her mouth up to his ear. "My panties are all wet."

"What, baby?"

"My panties are wet."

"Well go in the bathroom, baby, and wash off."

"It's not going to help, Mikey. They'll just be wet again."

"Bunny, go in the bathroom and wash off."

Jessie went to the sink in the bathroom and wiped her face over and over with cold water. Her hands were sweaty, and she felt weak. She sat on the toilet, trying to soak up the wet in her panties with toilet paper. She didn't think she wanted to go to school with Mikey, anymore. Not if it was going to be like this. She was embarrassed in Mr. Leland's class. He was trying to make her answer questions she didn't know the answer to, and it made her extremely uncomfortable. Reluctantly, she went back out and sat next to Mike.

"What do you keep staring at?" Katie snapped at Andy, noticing that he put his head up when Jessie sat back down.

"Nothin'," Andy answered, playing with his fork. Katie and Lisa both turned and glared at Jessie.

"Well, stop looking over there." Katie turned back around, with a defiant sneer. "You're staring at that girl with Mike."

"No, I'm not."

"Yes, you are, Andy, quit it!"

"I'm not fuck*in'* staring at her, and don't *fuckin'* tell me what to do!"

"Shhh," Jeff hissed, looking around. "Come on you two, everyone's looking over here."

"You stare at her again, and I'm leaving," Katie said to Andy.

"Don't fuckin' threaten me!" Andy threw his fork down at the table. "Go then, I don't give a fuck."

"Come on, let's go," Katie said to Lisa, getting up. The two of them left the restaurant. Kevin turned behind him and watched Katie and Lisa leave.

"Looks like Andy just lost his girlfriend," Kevin said to Mike, taking in a big mouthful of his cheeseburger. "I think he needs his face kicked in."

"He is getting pretty ballsy," Gary said, stuffing a handful of French fries in his mouth.

"He better back off my girlfriend, or he's gonna lose his fuckin' balls," Mike answered, glaring at Andy, shaking the salt and pepper everywhere. Mike cut a piece of pancake and put it up to Jessie's mouth.

"No, please, I'm not hungry," Jessie said, pouting up at Mike.

"Eat dammit."

Jessie put it in her mouth but wanted to gag. Her eyes were watering.

"What's the matter with you, baby?" Mike whispered, squeezing her close to him.

"I don't know, Mikey, I dis want you." Jessie's heart was pounding. "I don't know what's wrong."

Mike handed her his water. "Here, drink some water. I want you too, baby."

"I don't think I better go to school with you, tomorrow, Mikey. Everyone is looking mean at me. It's because of my uniform."

"Fuck that, let them stare. Eat just a few more bites, please, baby. You'll feel better tomorrow, with your real clothes on. I'm sorry about that, bunny. It's my fault for messin' with you this morning. I wasn't thinking. They're staring at you because you're beautiful, that's why, bunny."

~

During fifth period, Jessie sat on the bleachers, watching the boys practice football. She was shivering cold, tucked inside Mike's big jacket, and couldn't get comfortable. Mike felt bad for her and kept running over to ask if she was okay. Jessie nodded, but she felt like her panties had stuck frozen to herself. She was miserable.

By the end of the day Jessie was exhausted. She had to go to the bathroom and Mike waited for her outside the girl's restroom. While she sat on the toilet, she began reading some of the writings on the wall and became upset by what she saw. The whole stall was covered in nasty stuff about her Mikey. When she finished using the toilet, she looked in the other stalls and found more ugly things on the walls about Mike. She went out to where Mike was smiling at her. He put his arms around her, grinning from ear to ear.

"You ready to go make some bunny-lovin's, tittie girl?" he asked, rubbing his nose on hers, being all lovey-dovey.

Jessie pointed to the bathroom door. "Michael, do you even know what's on the walls in there?"

"I don't know, baby, what is it?"

"Do you want to go thee?"

"Is anyone in there?"

"No, come on." Jessie took Mike by the hand and pulled him into the bathroom.

Mike was surprised. He always figured his name was in there somewhere, but not like this. "Damn," he grinned, rubbing his chin. "I didn't know I was that good-lookin'." He bent over reading something in small print. 'Mike Miller is a lousy fuck.' He was pretty sure he knew who wrote that.

"Mikey." Jessie frowned. "This is very *rude!* How could they say these ugly things about my Mikey?"

Mike looked down at Jessie's cute, little pouty face. "Well, Luke's name is up here a few times, and a few other guys. Don't worry 'bout it baby, it don't bother me. It's all just bullshit."

"Because I'm mad!" Jessie snapped, frowning. "I don't *want* your phone number on the wall. It's not their business about my Mikey."

A girl came in the bathroom and saw Mike standing there. Mike waved at her and her eyes got big as saucers.

"Come on, little bunny. We got some bunny-lovins' to make." Mike smiled, taking her hand. "We gotta hurry though, cuz I promised your Aunt I'd bring you right home."

"Where are we going to go, Mikey?"

"We're gonna go down the road in our car, and you're gonna sit on my lap, Jessie Miller," Mike said, with his arm around her as they walked down the hall.

"Mikey," Jessie giggled. "Did you call me Jessie Miller?"

"Yeah."

"Mikey, I don't want you to be a cop."

"Why not, baby?"

"Because I dis want you to be my boyfriend."

"You want me to be your boyfriend?"

"Yeah, you could dis stay home and be my boyfriend."

"I'd love to just stay home and be your boyfriend, bunny, but how are we gonna get money then? Where we gonna live?"

"We can live in the Miller house. Your momma can give you money and you can be my boyfriend."

"I don't want my momma to give me money. I want my own money. I wanna be a cop."

"Then how will you be my boyfriend if you're a cop?"

"Baby…"

Chapter Twelve –
All is Not Fair in Love and War

Debbie was going over Jessie's hospital bill when she heard the little dogs in the backyard start barking, and then a knock at the door. She answered it to find Luke standing there, looking distraught.

"Well, hi, Luke," she smiled. "Come in."

"Hey, Debbie." Luke cleared his throat. He seemed quite anxious.

"Is everything okay? How is Meg, today?"

"I think she's doin' better…Debbie," Luke stammered, twisting the watch on his wrist. "I, I wanna ask you if I can take Jessie out tonight?"

Debbie paused for a moment, not expecting that just then, but then, maybe she was. "Take Jessie out," she said, somewhat hesitant.

"Yes, ma'am, I'd like to date her, Debbie."

"Come sit down, Luke. Let's talk." They both went to the table and sat down.

"You know, Luke, Jessie's just a young girl."

"Well, yes ma'am, I know she's young," Luke answered, trying not to seem nervous and keep his voice calm.

"You're in love with Jessie, aren't you?" Debbie couldn't help but ask. She could see it written all over him, especially since seeing his behavior toward her after the accident.

"Yes, ma'am, I am."

"And so is Mike," Debbie replied.

"Mm, yeah, I guess so."

Debbie had mixed emotions about the whole thing. She wasn't quite sure how to answer. She didn't want to seem anxious for Luke to date Jessie, and she wanted to gauge his seriousness. "Well, as long as we're talking, I really think you both need to back away from her. I already have enough to worry about, trying to get custody of her, and I don't have a lot of say when it comes down to it. I'm in charge of her when she's here, but I don't know what happens when she's not, and you know, Jessie has a lot of trouble in her life as it is."

"I know that and I've thought about it," Luke replied. "I've thought about it a lot. But, Debbie, I don't know how to back away. I can say that I will, but I don't think it'd be honest. I've tried, and I can't do it."

"Are you and Jessie, mm, intimate, Luke?" Debbie asked mournfully, hoping not, but realizing now, they probably were, and knowing that Jessie, like her mother, was damn near impossible to resist.

"Yes ma'am." Luke swallowed, almost choking. "Well, Debbie, I guess you should know…Jessie's on the pill. I took her to the doctor a while ago." Luke thought that would make him seem responsible, but then regretted saying it.

"My, Lord," Debbie sighed, "When was that?"

"Well, it was the same day of the accident. That's what Jessie and I were doing out that day."

Debbie took a deep breath. "Well, I appreciate you telling me, Luke, but I think Jessie's too young, and I expect you to refrain from having any more intimate relations with her."

"Yes ma'am." Luke wished he hadn't had to answer that. "I'm sorry, Deb."

Debbie watched Luke's fretful face. "I was a teenager once, Luke. I know what it's like. I just wish it wasn't happening now, so soon. Where were you planning on taking her?"

"Just out to eat, somewhere special."

Debbie hesitated, again. "I can see that you'd like to be Jessie's steady boyfriend. What does Jessie think about that? She seems to like Mike, as well."

"Well, I'd like to be her steady boyfriend, Debbie...but all I can do right now is date her and let her make up her own mind."

"I guess you really care for Jessie to be willing to wait. It must be difficult for you, with Mike as competition. I don't know, Luke. It just seems like so much to worry about."

"Yes ma'am, it is, but like I said, all I can do is give her time. I'm not trying to force her into a decision, Debbie. I just want her to know how much she means to me."

"Well, I'd rather it be you, than anyone else. I've always respected you, Luke. I just hope you understand that."

"I do. I'll wait a long time, Debbie. I love her."

"I can see that, Luke. I guess if you really wanted to hide things from me you wouldn't have told me what you did, and I don't believe you're that kind of person."

"I love her, Debbie. I love Jessie, so much."

"All right, Luke, I'll allow you to *date* her, but don't keep her out late. She's got school in the morning."

Luke's eyes lit up and he almost tripped over himself, standing up. "Yes, ma'am, I'll take good care of her. Thank you, Debbie. Tell her I'll pick her up at five-thirty."

"Why don't you call her and tell her yourself?"

"Aright, ma'am, and thanks, Debbie," Luke answered, in a hurry to leave.

"Good-bye, Luke," Debbie said, smiling.

"Bye and thank you!" Luke's smile widened as he walked out the door.

Debbie knew Jessie was young, but if she were going to get with someone, she was happy it was Luke, and maybe too young was better than giving her too much time for every jerk in the world to mess up Jessie's life, like Hank did to her sister. Debbie was pleased that it was Luke. Surely, that would keep Mike away. Now she just had to deal with Madison, who was going to be upset. She was going to have to talk to her as soon as she got home from school.

~

Jessie ran up the stairs, anxious to get in the shower, and Debbie was relieved. Maddy and Aimee had stopped to gossip with their friends in the hall about Mike and Jessie. They didn't get home quite as fast.

Getting out of the shower, Jessie wrapped a towel around her and went to her room. Aimee was in there changing her clothes.

"Jessie, practically every girl at school was talking about you today," Aimee said, pulling a clean blue t-shirt over her head.

"What were they saying, Aimee?" Jessie asked, trying to pull her panties up under her towel.

"About how beautiful you are, and how lucky you are to be going to school with Mike, which I think is questionable."

"Aimee, what do you think about all the writings on the walls about Mikey in the bathroom?"

"I don't know, I guess I'm used to it."

"Well, I don't like it, it's mean."

"I guess Mike's been pretty mean to girls, Jessie, which is why I wonder about you and him. It's his own fault, you know. He's not really very nice."

"Well, he can't help it if he's so handsome. He's really not like that at all, Aimee. He's really a sweet person." Jessie fastened her bra and pulled the straps up over her shoulders.

"Well, maybe to you, Jess, but not anyone else," Aimee replied just as the phone rang. Aimee ran out to get it.

"Jessie!" she yelled, "It's for you!"

Jessie quickly put her jeans on, pulled her pink sweater over her head, and ran out to get the phone. "Hello," answered Jessie's small, voice.

"Hi, bubbles."

"Luke!" Jessie grinned. "You're calling me on the phone! I love being at my Auntie's, where people can call me!"

"I am calling you, baby. I'm calling to tell you that I love you so much."

"Oh, Luke," she whispered. "I love you, too, and I miss you, too."

"I'm picking you up at five-thirty, Jessie girl, so you be ready."

"Luke, did you talk to my Momma about the date?"

"Yes baby, you be ready. I love you, darlin'."

"Okay, Luke, I'll be ready. Good-bye, Luke."

Maddy was in her bedroom with the door closed, yelling at her mother, when Jessie went back down the hall to brush her hair in the bathroom.

"It's not fair that Jessie's fifteen and you're allowing her to go out on a date, when I'm almost eighteen and still haven't gone on a date!" Maddy yelled. "And, you let her go to school with Mike!"

"Maddy, "Debbie said, "It's because I love you, and I wanted to protect you as long as I could, but I realize now, you're growing up, and I have to let you make some decisions. Things are different now, and well, Jessie's situation is different than yours."

"Why?" Maddy snapped. "Because she's beautiful and I'm not? Because guys like her and not me?" Maddy began to cry.

"Oh, Maddy." Debbie hugged her. "Not at all, sweetheart. You *are* beautiful. I love you so much. I just want to make sure you're ready and that you're not going to get hurt. I do understand, you know. I was jealous of my sister. I know I never talked about it, because I loved her more than I was jealous. But I was, horribly jealous. She got all the boys and I was pretty much ignored."

Maddy looked up at her mom, surprised.

"That didn't last long though, Maddy. Look at what a lovely man I found in your father. My sister never found anything but pain. That's why I wanted you to wait, because you *are* beautiful."

"What are you saying? You don't love Jessie, or care about her then, Mom?"

"Madison," Debbie said with a stern look. "You know I love Jessie, I care very deeply for her. Jessie's been through a lot. She's gone without most of her life, with no one to care for her, and I- well, I have a hard time telling her no. I can't be too tough on her right now. Not until I get custody and I feel safe that she knows we love her. I guess that doesn't always seem fair, but don't you understand why?"

"I guess. So, you're going to let me date now, Mom?" Maddy sniffed. Thinking about it, she was relieved that at least it *was* Luke that asked and not Mike.

"Yes, of course. But I still need to know who you're dating."

"I know. I'm not dating anyone right now."

"But you will be, and I want to know he's a good person, and well, Luke seems to love Jessie, and I like Luke. I think he's well suited for her. I think he would take good care of her, and well, if I can't get her away from her dad, maybe he can...does that make sense?"

"I suppose." Maddy frowned, sitting on the bed, looking down at the floor. She looked up at her mom. "Does that mean you're going to let Aimee date?"

"Mm, good question. No, I don't think so."

"Why not?"

"Well, Maddy, you tell me, do you think Aimee's old enough to date?"

Maddy paused for a minute, looking at her mom. "Well, I guess I see what you're saying, it must be a difficult situation for you. But still, they're both only fifteen."

"You're right; it is a difficult situation and not really my decision to make with Jessie. If she had been with me all these years, I would have more say, but you understand how different her circumstances are?"

"Yeah, I guess."

"I'll allow you to date, but remember, we've known Luke for a long time. I have to know who you're dating, and I want you to start taking birth control if you do. Not that I'm encouraging you to have sex, because I certainly think you're too young, and I hope you'll wait until you're married, but I think it's a responsible way to look at it. Do you understand, Maddy?"

"Well, if I ever have anyone to date, then of course I would be on the pill, and yeah, I know what you mean." Maddy got over her temper, realizing she didn't have anyone to date right now, and maybe that's why she was upset in the first place. Jake was really kind of boring and immature. She didn't get to see him that much anyway, since he lived in Reno.

"For the hundredth time, you'll find your true love, someday soon. College is a good place to meet a husband, you know?"

Maddy nodded. "I hope I don't have to wait that long."

"It's *not that long*," Debbie sighed. "You never know what can happen between now and then."

"Mom, there's something else I want to ask," Maddy said, intently. "Why does Jessie get your room? I'm the oldest. Shouldn't I get the room with the bathroom?"

"Hmm, I think you're right, Maddy. Certainly, you should have the bathroom." Debbie smiled.

"And, Mom, can I dye my hair blond?"

"Blond? Why? Your hair is beautiful."

"Because, I just want to. I think I'll feel more attractive as a blonde."

"Maddy, you're beautiful." Debbie smiled. "But, if you want to *bleach* your hair blond then you can go get it done this weekend."

"Thank you, Momma!" Maddy hugged her Mother. "I'm gonna call Jenny and tell her the good news!"

Debbie took a deep breath and exhaled walking down the hall. She stopped in the bathroom doorway and asked Jessie, "How was school today, sweetheart?"

"Good," Jessie answered, brushing her hair.

"Was everyone nice to you?"

"I think tho, I guess. The teachers all asked me questions."

"And did you know all the answers?"

"Yes, of course."

"Did you get your phone call, Jessie?"

"Yes, Momma, thank you."

"Jessie, I talked to Luke for a while today. He told me you two have been intimate.

"Intimate?"

"Having sex, Jessie. I think you're too young to have sex, you know that, don't you?"

Jessie nodded, feeling embarrassed. "I wanted to tell you, Momma, but I was scared."

Debbie put her arms around her. "Jessie, please don't be afraid to tell me things I need to know. How can I be your Mom and help you, if you don't tell me what's going on in your life?"

"I won't, Momma, I'll try. Thank you for telling Luke yes about the date."

"Jessie, I think you're too young, but…well, at least you're on the pill. You take it every day, don't you?"

Jessie nodded. "Yes, Momma."

"*Please don't forget.* I want you home by eleven, Cinderella," Debbie said, kissing Jessie's cheek.

"The Virgin Mary was a teenager, Momma," Jessie advised her Aunt.

Debbie looked at Jessie somewhat surprised. "I understand, Jessie. But you're not the Virgin Mary. You're my little girl and I think you're too young. Come into the kitchen, Jessie, we're all going to have a girl talk."

Debbie pulled the three girls into the kitchen and they all had a long, overdue discussion.

~

Luke took Jessie to the cabin, which is exactly where she wanted to go. She wanted to pretend she lived there with Luke, and that she was a grown up, in her own house. The drive was quiet. Luke thought all day about taking Jessie from Mike the night before. It was weighing heavy on his mind. He asked Jessie how school went, but she didn't seem real excited, she just said, "Okay." He still felt timid around her sometimes. He couldn't quite get over her beauty.

Luke carried her in the door. The cabin was warm and there was a fire already going. A dozen pink roses were sitting on the coffee table, with a little envelope that read: "Bubbles".

"Luke, you already came here," Jessie said smiling, as he set her down on the sofa.

He grinned, sitting next to her. "Yes ma'am."

"*Are you romantic?*" she asked, coyly. Her eyes were twinkling up at him.

Luke chuckled. He leaned over Jessie and softly, he kissed her. "I'm very romantic...I love you so much, Jessie," he whispered to her mouth, gazing into her eyes.

"I love *you* so much, Luke."

Luke took off his jacket and went to put more wood on the fire. Jessie sat up getting the envelope from the flowers and opened it. Luke had written:

I would die for you, Jessica Michelle Miller.
I'll always be in love with you, baby. Lucas Craig Miller.

Jessie looked at Luke. He was gazing at her with an ache for her in his eyes. Jessie took off her jacket. Luke sat by her, pulling her close.

"I wanna eat you up, baby," Luke whispered, kissing and caressing Jessie, bubbling over with desire.

Jessie felt like a stick of butter and melted in his hands. "Oh, darling," she said, putting her arms around his neck. She was trying to sound grown up, and romantic. Luke smiled at her with complete adoration.

"Momma says I get to have Maddy's room now, because Maddy's the biggest, so she gets to pick."

"Well, I guess that's only fair, love bug."

"Luke, I want to be Jessie Miller and live here with you, Luke. I want to be grown up and live here with you."

"Maybe someday we'll have our own house, baby."

"Luke, this is where you first wanted me. I want to live here with you *now*."

"Okay, baby, we live here now, just me and you." Luke pulled her sweater up over her bra-less bubbles. "Mm. You know how much I love your bubbles, baby?" Luke kissed them ever so softly, caressing them gently in his hands.

"I didn't wear my bra."

"It's okay, baby," he whispered, picking her up. "When you're with me, I don't care."

"Do you have ideas?"

"Oh yeah," Luke grinned. "I got ideas, *bubbles*." He carried her into the bedroom downstairs and made such sweet love to Jessie. Every moment he had with her was precious...

They lay in each other arms, gazing into each other's eyes. Jessie shyly smiled, turning her head. "Luke, I'm shy when you look at me like that."

Luke grinned. "Me too, baby, you make me shy, too."

"Can we go sit by the fire? It's tho beautiful out there."

"Okay, lover girl." Luke took the white, cotton throw off the end of the bed, wrapping Jessie in it, and carried her out to the sofa. Jessie watched as he put more wood on the fire. His body was beautiful. His skin was dark and smooth. His thick black hair shined in the glow of the fire. His face was handsomely steady, yet gentle.

"I brought one of my albums," Luke said, going over to the record player on the shelf. "I want to play you a song that I've been listening to." He lay down over Jessie and began to sing the song as it played, gazing into her eyes, and stroking her face.

Jessie smiled as he sang, running her fingers through his hair. When he had finished, Jessie snorted her little giggle. "Luke, you sang to me so pretty. Am I your lady?"

"Yes, Jessie, someday, I hope for good." Luke stroked her hair, admiring her gentle beauty. "It's a song about a man in love with a Polynesian girl, but it makes me think of you. It's how I feel when I'm with you." Luke sighed, softly kissing her face. His eyes were intent, stroking her cheeks. *"I'm so in love with you, Jessica,"* he whispered, deep in a love trance.

Jessie was enraptured and torn as she gazed into his loving eyes. "It's beautiful, Luke. Thank you, for my romance."

Luke smiled. "Are you hungry or anything, Jessie Miller?"

"I'm thirsty."

Luke got up and went to the refrigerator. He took out the Pepsi and a chef salad that he put in there earlier and brought it out to Jessie. He knew she would eat salad if nothing else. They both huddled under the cotton throw, watching the fire and listening to the album. Jessie felt so far away from her own meager dwelling. Every second in this beautiful cabin, sitting next to Luke, was like a dream that wasn't real. She hated time and how she had no control over it. How quickly it slipped away when she was in heaven. Luke was so good to her, and so thoughtful; she didn't believe he could be real. He catered to her so desperately. Her heart broke for him, seeing how much he loved her. She realized she would always love this beautiful, handsome, young man. "Look at my bubbles," Jessie said, looking down at herself. "They're glowing in the firelight."

"They're beautiful, baby."

Jessie giggled and put the plate down on the coffee table.

He took a rose out of the vase and softly stroked it against Jessie's breast. "They're more beautiful than this pretty pink rose...Mike says you've been having headaches, have you?"

"A little bit."

"He said you told him about a monster, too."

"I can't talk about that right now. I'm happy right now." Jessie rested her head on Luke's chest, while he caressed her face.

"Jessie, I want you to be happy and never sad again. I know you don't want to talk about things, but we have to. Last night when I took you to my room, I was trying to see if I could share you with him, and that's what he was doing, too. I know that's what you want, baby, isn't it?"

Jessie felt confused about answering that but nodded.

"It's not something I would ever really do, if I didn't love you so much," Luke said. "I never imagined I would have to share someone like you with my brother. Sometimes it really freaks me out and scares me." Luke pulled Jessie down on his lap, so he could look at her face. "Is that really what you want, Jessie, because I'm not ever gonna let you go."

Jessie nervously tapped her finger on her lip. "I don't know, Luke. I want you and Mikey, is that ugly, Luke? Sometimes I think about that. Even a lot of times now. No, Luke, it's not what I want, but I can't go back and make it better. I can't go back and fix it, now. You both kept loving me, and I didn't know how to stop you, or even think about it. I wanted you both, and now I love you both, and everything is messed up, now. How did that happen, Luke? That doesn't happen to people, and now I'm ugly."

"It was just the time and the situation, baby. None of us had any control over it. And you're not ugly, that's the problem. We never should have touched you. You're an angel, and we never should have touched you."

"And Ricky too, Luke, and Ricky too. I think I went after Ricky, he didn't come after me."

"He would have eventually, but I think he did, Jessie. The problem is that you're so damn beautiful. Guys are gonna want you wherever you go. It's just the way it is. You're not just beautiful to look at, you're beautiful all over. Your movements are so graceful and elegant. The minute you open your mouth to talk, or look at someone with your pretty eyes, they're in love with you. Your heart is so pure, and kind, and loving. You're so innocent, and it makes men crazy for you…Jessie, that day on the beach, when we first met, I thought you were so precious, like a diamond or a big hunk of gold that I found in the sand. If I had been thinking ahead, thinking clearly…I shouldn't have gone back to Sissy that night. I should have stayed with you on the beach and kept you distracted from Ricky or Mike. I should have known anyone as beautiful and precious as you are, was too valuable to walk away from. I should have put you in my pocket that very second and kept you there. My heart is yours, Jessie Miller."

"I liked you too, Luke. That first day you came to get me at school. I looked in your eyes and I saw you loving me. I thought how magic you were to come to me in time, in my world, and take me to a better world, and I knew I had someone to care about, and I didn't hate myself anymore. I didn't know I was like how you say I am. I didn't know how boys would think about me like that. How can I not be like that, Luke? I'm afraid of it happening again. I can't help it, Luke. Why am I like that? I don't want no other boys."

"I don't know baby, but it scares me, too. Maybe now that you know about it, you've learned to stop it before it happens. You can't let every guy out there get close to you. You have to learn to be kind of mean, maybe. Heh, that would only make it worse," Luke laughed. "Guys are stupid. They like to be treated like shit. Maybe you shouldn't go back to school with Mike."

"I have to go. How will I go to college if I can't go to school with boys?"

Luke smiled. "Baby, the only thing you can do is to find one person. One person that you love, and one person that loves you, and live happily ever after. That's what happy people do, Jessie, like your Aunt and Uncle, like my mom and dad."

"That's what Momma says. She told us about sex and love today. That's what I want to do, Luke. I want that. I just don't know how to stop loving someone that loves me. I don't know how to choose, Luke, because someone will be hurt, and I will be hurt, too, and sad…Luke." Jessie's eyes began to tear. "I love you, Luke, and I want to live with you, and be with you forever, and not ever go back there. And- I love you, Luke…and when I love you, I feel happy and not scared, but…I feel sad, too…because, um, I love Mikey, too, and I'm afraid. I'm afraid about what will happen, that Mikey will be sad, and I will be sad, and you will be sad, forever. And if I choose you, I can stay with you in our house, and not go back there. And what will happen, Luke?"

"I don't know, baby," Luke sighed, sitting up. "I don't have an answer, Jessie. I wish I did. All I can tell you is that I love you, and will always love you, and I will always want to take care of you and keep you happy. But that's up to you, now. You're just gonna have to hurt one of us, and let one of us go, and then it will be up to us to deal with it."

"I'm sorry, Luke. I don't want to hurt one of you. If I go away, and don't come back, then…"

"Jessie, it's not really your fault, and I'm sorry, too. It's not fair, is it? Mike told you about the psychiatrist, didn't he?"

"Psychiatrist?"

"The doctor."

"Yeah." Jessie pouted, worried about that.

"We have an appointment next week."

"Why do I have to keep going to the doctor, Luke? Because I'm retarded?"

"Jessie, why would you say that? Why would you even think that? Baby, because your dad didn't take care of you right, and now the people that love you have to…have to fix everything he messed up."

"I don't think I want to go, Luke. Mikey says he's going to look in my head."

"No, darlin'. He's not going to look in your head. He just talks to you to find out how you think about things. Maybe he can help you understands things better. Help all of us out."

Jessie held Luke's arm tightly and her voice trembled. "Luke, when I have sex, then I feel loved, and not scared. Will I not want sex no more? Will I still want you, Luke?"

"I hope so, baby. I know I'll always want you. I love you whether we make love or not, and I wish you weren't afraid. I don't want you to be afraid. Besides, everyone wants sex, baby, that's normal." Luke stroked Jessie's face. "I don't think you want sex so much, but love and attention, because your dad treats you so cold. Because he never showed you love the way a father should love his daughter, and now you try to get that love from other people, and when someone pays attention to you, you're like a dry sponge, soaking up water, you don't have any control over it. Do you know what I mean?"

"I think so, Luke...I love you, Luke, because I feel good when you love me. And I love you, too, Luke, because you're so good. Someday, maybe we can dis talk about happy things, because there won't be any more bad things. Maybe someday my daddy will be dead, and I'll be free to fly. I'll be free to fly away."

Luke wiped the tears from her cheeks. "Where will you fly to baby?"

"To heaven...to heaven, and I'll have wings like the angels...Like my mommy. Do you think my soul is black and I will go to hell, Luke, for having tho much thex?"

"Baby, you haven't had that much sex. Shit, I've had more sex than you. Nothing, compared to any other person in the world. We're all doomed to hell if that's the case. Anyway, Jessie, people as perfect as you don't go to hell, and how 'bout if you fly away somewhere a little closer to me than heaven. Like, to our new house."

"But, I want you, but I don't want to be bad."

"It's not bad when you and me make love. We're in love and we make love. But, having sex and making love are two different things. Making love should be something special between only two people; a man and a woman, a husband and his wife. I been thinking a lot, Jessie. It's gonna be hard for me, baby, but I think we should probably not make love for a while. I promised your Aunt, and I just think maybe we should wait till you're able to decide. There's other reasons, and I'm not gonna go into that right now, but..."

"Luke, you mean you won't love me no more?"

"Jessie, I'll always be in love with you, but I, I can't share you that way. It makes me feel sick inside."

Jessie looked out across the room. "You mean you won't see me no more?"

"Of course, I'll still see you, baby. That's why I asked Momma to date you. I promised her I'd do the right thing, and that way you can have time to make up your mind, and I can show you how much you mean to me."

"We have to go soon, don't we?"

"We should leave pretty soon, since you have to be home by eleven. I'm glad your Momma said I could date you, Jessie. We can see each other all the time, now."

"Luke, that's so wonderful, isn't it? It's a good thing to talk about."

"Jessie, I think things are gonna get better and better."

"Me too, Luke. Will you still kiss me?"

"I'll kiss you as much as you want. I'll kiss you, forever."

"Kiss my toes."

~

Mike called Maddy on his first break.

"Hey Maddy, it's Mike."

"Jessie's not here."

"I know, she's out with Luke, isn't she?"

"Yes…Mom said he could date her now." Maddy's tone was not only vindictive, but she felt quite pleased at telling Mike that.

Mike paused for a moment. "Yeah, well I need you to do me a favor…Hey, Phil!" he yelled at his co-worker.

Why don't you do me a fuckin' favor for once? Maddy thought. "What is it now, Mike?"

Mike chuckled. "Have I been that bad?"

Maddy had to clear her throat and thought, *did he really just ask me that?* She decided to be brave. "Well…you haven't exactly been so nice that I have to keep doing favors for you."

"I'm sorry, Maddy. I'll try to be more careful…Hey!" Mike turned his head away from the phone and hollered at his co-worker, Phil. "Can you put that impact gun over there by the Buick? I still need to tighten the lugs on that back wheel." His voice echoed through the garage.

Maddy just about threw her heart up out of her throat. His damn voice was so deep and sexy. She felt herself turning flush, imagining him in his uniform, with his big hands all black and greasy. A tear rolled down her cheek. "What do you want me to do, Mike?" she asked, trying to keep her voice from faltering.

Mike could hear the sorrow in her question and he felt bad all of a sudden.

"Well, if you and Aimee would meet me and Jessie in front of the girl's restroom, in the upper hall, tomorrow, after fifth period. I have a surprise for Jessie."

"In front of the girl's restroom?"

"Yeah, I need your help with the surprise."

Maddy sighed. "Okay, Mike. We'll be there."

"Thanks, Sweetie, see ya tomorrow," Mike said, and hung up.

Maddy broke out in an uncontrollable, emotional outburst and couldn't stop crying. She ran to her room and called Jenny.

"Hello," Jenny answered.

"Jenny! Mike called me sweetie!" Maddy said, still crying.

"What do you mean, he called you sweetie? Why?"

"That son of a bitch, mother fucker called me sweetie! How *dare* he talk to me like that?"

"Maddy, calm down and tell me what happened."

Friday, January 18, 1974

Mike found Jessie and Teddy sleeping in his bed when he woke up to go to the bathroom. He bent over and kissed her ear. "Can't we ever just be alone, bunny? Why does there always have to be a threesome?" He smiled and got up to go pee. When Mike came back, he locked the door.

"Hi, big thexy boy." Jessie held her teddy up to Mike as he laid down over her.

"You and your funny little lisp."

"Mikey, I don't lisp!" Jessie snapped, frowning.

"Shhh." He smiled. "Be quiet, bunny. Yes, you do."

"Mikey, no I don't. You are the one who talks funny."

"I don't talk funny."

"Yeth you do. You thay '*come own baiby.*'" Jessie cocked her head. "It's not *own*, it's on, and it's not *baiby*, it's baby."

"Well, I guess we're even then." Mike smiled. "You were so beautiful at school today, *baby*. I'm sorry if I wasn't as sweet to you as I could be or anything. You know how I get real stupid around you, but, I'm so proud of you."

"You want me to help you do your homework, Mikey, so you won't be stupid?"

"I would love to have you help me not be stupid," Mike chuckled. "Besides, I already did it."

"Mikey, I want to go to the libary when you have football."

"Wi baby? Don't you wanna watch me?"

"No. Those boys hurt you at football. I don't want to watch that. And, it's too cold."

"Well, I don't want you going anywhere by yourself. We'll take a blanket. They don't hurt me, baby. That's just part of the game."

"But it's scary. Scary when they hurt you."

"Jessie, they don't hurt me. Don't worry about it, peanut."

"Okay…um, Mikey, I'm sorry about Luke last night, Mikey."

Don't be sorry about Luke to me, and don't be sorry to Luke about me, baby. Just don't talk about it."

"Mikey, Luke says he can't make love to me for a while. He says I have to pick now, first. He says I have to hurt one of you…Mikey, are you going to stop, too?"

Mike hesitated, looking at her. He stroked her face. "Eventually, I guess you're gonna hafta hurt one of us. I don't know, Jessie."

Jessie's sad eyes gazed up at him, her mouth quivered. "I dis want you to know, how much I love you, Mikey. I dis want you to know how special you are to me. You're such a good boy, Mikey. You always make me feel better. You always take away my headaches and the monster, and I love you tho much, Mikey." Jessie began to cry, and her voice was winded. "And I love you tho much, Mikey. Luke is tho sweet and good to me, and he loves me more than anything in the world, and I love him so much, too, and he keeps me alive, and I have to see him, because if I don't, then I'll be sad, and he'll be sad, Mikey, and I can't never hurt Luke. I'll never hurt Luke; I'll never, ever hurt Luke, but Mikey, you…you…I love you; I want to be inside you. I want to be inside you and never come out." Jessie closed her eyes holding teddy against her face, squeezing a tear out from under her eyelid. "But I love Luke, too, Mikey." Jessie couldn't stop crying and sniffing her nose. "And I will never hurt him, not ever, and I don't know what to do. Because if I don't see you, then you won't see me, and I won't see you, and Luke won't see me."

Mike had been waiting and was hoping to hear what he thought Jessie was telling him. His heart jumped for joy when she said it, but then he understood how difficult this was becoming, not just for her, but for all of them.

"I do love Luke, Mikey, so much and I tell him I love him, because I do, but…everyone loves you, Mikey. Everybody loves you, but only I get you, only I get you, Mikey. I loved you the very first thecond I saw you, right from the first thecond, when you… when you were mean to me on the beach and…and you had that chain…and…"

Mike lay over Jessie and smoothed the hair from her face. "Don't cry now, baby. I'm sorry I was mean to you on the beach. I'm a stupid fucker. I don't know why you love me. I'm glad you do, but I don't know what you see in me. I wanted to go back to you that night. I really wanted to go back to you, but Kevin was being a dickhead and wanted to go to that stupid party. All I could think about that night was you, Jessie. I wanted you so bad. I wanted to be the one in your tent. I know if I would have gone back to you, you would have let me in your tent. You never would have had sex with Luke or Ricky and you'd be mine, only mine."

"Mikey, Luke says that, too, and I think about that, too. Why couldn't it have been like that, Mikey? Why couldn't it have been like that? If I would never have come to my aunt's, then I would never have met you. Because now, I love you both, and I don't know what to do."

"I don't know, baby. I don't want you to love Luke, but I can't make you stop, can I? All we can do is just be happy with what we have right now, and right now you have me and I have you. We have to just live it one day at a time."

"Mikey, you're tho handsome," Jessie said, stroking Mike's face. "You're tho pretty. That's why everyone wants you. But they don't know how beautiful you are, and I do. I do Mikey, I know how beautiful you are, and you love me. You love me, Mikey. And I love how you thay 'come own baiby'. Mikey, if you have thex with thomeone else, please remember that. Remember we're going...steady."

"Are we going steady?"

"Yes."

"Baby, you're the only girl I've ever loved. I'll never love anyone else, ever. I'll never, ever love anyone but you. I know that in my heart. If I lost you, I'll never love anyone else. Even when I've had sex with someone else, I just think about you. There's no one as good as you, baby."

"Mikey, are you going to have some more thex with thomeone else?"

"I don't know, baby, I hope not. I'm not good like Luke. I don't think like Luke. I have a bad temper and I do a lot of things I know I shouldn't do. Like this morning, in the car. Then I get mad at myself. Like the things I do to you all the time. I know I'm an asshole. I don't mean to be, baby. You're so sweet to me, bunny, I don't deserve you at all, and sometimes I think I should just let go of you, because I know how good Luke would take care of you. I know he would always love you and treat you right, and then you wouldn't have to choose anymore."

"Mikey, don't talk like that, oh Mikey, please don't talk like that. I can't be without you. I don't care what you do to me, even if you have more thex with someone. I'm not going away from you. I'm your bunny girl, Mikey. *I'm your bunny girl."*

"Yes, baby, you are my bunny, my only little bunny girl."

"Mikey, don't call me tittie girl." Jessie pouted.

"I love your titties, baby. When I think of you, you're so little and your titties are so beautiful, I just wanna hold you."

"And you only love my titties, Mikey?"

"No, baby, I love all of you. I love every bit of you, especially you inside. That's just why I call you tittie girl. It's not just how you look, baby, it's how you are. How you're my sweet little Jessie girl. Baby, it's not just that. It's everything about you, everything. The way you talk, and think, and treat me.

And …you know what makes you really special to me?"

"What?"

"Well," Mike looked deep into her eyes. "Because you're my little virgin girl. Because I was the first one with you, and that makes you a part of me. We're bonded, Jessie, and no one can ever take that away from us. Our bodies were married the first time we made love, and that will never change."

"You mean; we're married already?"

"Yes, baby, forever."

"How do you know that?"

"It's just the way it is."

"Because you believe in God, now?"

"I'm not sure about that, Jessie. I'm sure about you."

Jessie looked sternly at Mike. "Mikey, you have to be. If you don't, then how will you get to heaven with me when I go?"

Mike didn't say anything. He didn't want her to stop believing in heaven, for her sake. But he had doubts.

"Mikey when I have a baby, I'm going to let him drink my boobs. Don't you think?"

Mike laughed, "Are you, baby? Why do you always catch me off guard with these questions? I forget how your brain thinks."

"Yeah, because that's how you're s'pose to."

"You mean breast feed him."

"Is that how it's called?"

"Mm hm. Sometimes there's a different meaning behind what you say, and if you put it wrong, people might get a different idea about what you meant."

"Oh, did I say it wrong?"

"No, not for me cuz I know you. But it doesn't matter, bunny. I don't talk very good either, and it don't matter what people think. You talk how you want, cuz that's something I love about you."

"Okay, Mikey. But, Mikey, I want you to not cuss no more."

"Not cuss? I don't cuss."

"Yeah, because you always cuss, and say the F word, and God's name, and I don't want you to no more now, because I don't want the baby to say the F word, and God's name."

"Mm, yeah, but it's gonna be awful hard. I don't even know I'm doing it."

"Well, you have to. Someday, if we have a little boy, his name will be Michael. Michael Ricky. Can we name the baby that?"

"Why don't we just name him little fucker?" Mike grinned. "Then I don't have to worry about it.

"Mikey, no."

"Aright baby, Michael Richard. What if it's a girl?"

"Then her name will be Juliana."

"You don't want to name the baby Jessie?"

"No, no more Jessie's. Jessie's are sad, like me and my mom, and I don't want my baby to be sad. I want her to be happy. I want her daddy to love her, and kiss her, and pick her up, and tickle her, and talk to her, and not cuss to her, like a good daddy is s'pose to. Are you going to be a good daddy to my Juliana, Mikey?"

"I'll be the best daddy in the world to her, baby," he whispered, kissing Jessie's neck.

Chapter Thirteen - Luke, Mike and the Baby Doll

Jessie woke up to use the bathroom at four-thirty, after which she went into Luke's room, remembering her promise. Climbing under the covers with him, Luke smiled, and she cuddled up next to him as he wrapped his arms around her.

"Mm, I wanna wake up with you every day, my baby doll," Luke sighed, squeezing her tight. "Speaking of baby doll, let's put on that nightie. I was gonna bring it last night, but I forgot it. I really wanna see you in it, again, baby."

"Go get it," Jessie said, yawning.

Luke went to the closet and took the Fredericks bag off the top shelf, and carefully took out the sheer white baby doll with the white feather trim and silk straps. Jessie sat on her knees on the bed as Luke slipped it over her head. He wrapped the long white boa around her shoulders and swirled each end around her wrists. "Now go look how pretty you are, Bubbles," Luke said, sending Jessie over to the mirror on the closet door.

"Oh, Luke, look at me. I'm tho beautiful." Jessie looked amazed at herself in the mirror.

"I'm lookin' babe, trust me. I don't think I'll be able to stop." Luke lay on his side on the bed, resting his head on his arm, feeling very proud of his beautiful little angel baby. "Come lay on the bed and show me how pretty you are."

"I'm beautiful," Jessie whispered, as she crawled up on the bed and lay down next to Luke.

"Mm, yes you are."

She put her arms above her head, with her hair spread out on the pillow; the little boas around her wrist looked so cute against her pink nail polish. Jessie smiled, squirming her body, feeling beautiful. Luke pulled Jessie in his arms and leaned up against the headboard. Jessie quietly looked up at him twirling a strand of her hair in her fingers. Luke was completely enamored. She put her feet up, and Luke held them, rubbing her little toes. "I wanna show you something, Beautiful girl," he said getting up. He took out a black leather album off the top shelf of his closet. He lay on the bed next to Jessie and handed her the album.

"Oh, Luke," Jessie giggled quietly. "Look at me...that's me...that's me in there."

Mike was more than pissed when he woke up finding Jessie gone, and hearing her giggling in Luke's room. *What kind of game is she playing, anyway?* Mike thought. *She tells me I'm the one, and that we're finally going stead, and the minute I fall asleep, she runs to Luke.* "Dammit!" Mike stammered, getting up.

They both looked up at the door, when Mike came in, wearing his white boxers.

He shut the door, leaning on it. He swallowed the lump in his throat. All Mike could do was stand there, and stare at her. He was definitely a lingerie man, and Jessie was absolutely the sexiest thing he'd ever seen.

"Hi Mikey." Jessie smiled up at him. "Luke bought me this pretty."

Mike wanted to be pissed that instead of coming back to his room, she ended up in Luke's bed, looking like a bunny that just stepped out of a magazine. He cleared his throat, speechless, accepting the fact that Jessie was hot, and it would be best for him to stay cool.

"Come look at me in my book, Mikey," Jessie said, totally oblivious of the impending situation.

Mike took a deep breath, adjusted the glasses on his nose, and sat next to her. He was blown away by the most gorgeous pictures of the most gorgeous girl he'd ever seen in his life. Jessie touched the pictures with her fingers. "I'm a Playboy Bunny, now, Mikey."

"Yeah," Mike answered, his mouth hanging open. "What d'you spend on all that?" Mike asked Luke.

"A lot."

"How much is a lot?"

"Twelve-hundred."

"Damn," Mike said, rubbing his chin. "My car wasn't that much. They sure are worth it though." He shook his head, biting his bottom lip.

"Fuckin' A," Luke answered.

"Who the hell did you get to take pictures of a minor like that, Luke?"

"Why?"

"Cuz I'm gonna go beat the fuck out of him. Fuckin' pervert."

Luke chuckled as they watched Jessie turned to the last pages. There were the four pictures of her and Luke, together. Jessie got tears in her eyes; they were so loving and beautiful. They looked so perfect, happy, and in love, together. Even Mike hated to admit, they were a good-looking couple. Jessie was so in awe of how wonderful they were, she couldn't stop smiling.

Luke took the album and set in on the nightstand. Jessie lay down and looked up at Luke, and then at Mike, playing with her finger in her mouth. She began rocking her breasts back and forth under the sheer, silky fabric. Jessie closed her eyes. Wearing that nightie and being in the same room with Luke and Mike brought on an overwhelming arousal. She put her hands down between her legs and began caressing herself.

"Oh, oh..." she began to pant and coo. "Ooh...oowee…" she whispered. Neither one could take their eyes off her as she began to breathe and moan. Her face was beaming with sensual ecstasy. Mike and Luke were both paralyzed, and dumb. She quietly giggled to herself and smiled up at both of them, her eyes twinkling, like some bewitched creature.

Mr. Miller knocked on Luke's door and they all jumped, half senseless. "What's going on in there, Luke?"

"Wouldn't you like to know?" Luke laughed quietly, and Jessie giggled. "Go away, Dad. I have a girl in here," Luke yelled out, grinning at Jessie.

Mike, who was trying not to cum in his boxers, or laugh, smiled down at Jessie. He leaned over and kissed her, rubbing her butt. "Go get ready for school, bunny." He left the room, to go jack off in the bathroom.

"Oh, man, you gotta go, baby," Luke said, trying to breathe. He put the album back up on his closet shelf. He went over to help Jessie take off the nightie. "You wait till I get you alone, you little vixen." Luke stroked her neck with his nose and kissed it. "Rrrr," he growled.

"Luke, how come you don't keep my nightie in your drawer?"

"I will if you want me to," he answered, gently pulling the nightie up over Jessie's head.

"Yes, Luke, keep it in your drawer. We can have a drawer together."

"Aright, baby." Luke bent in front of her, pulling her pajama pants up her legs.

"Can I put it in there?"

"Sure." Luke cleared his throat looking at Jessie, re-playing the 'Jessie baby-doll show' over again in his head.

Jessie took her nightie and put it in Luke's top drawer with his boxer shorts and socks.

"Does it belong in there, now, Luke?" Jessie asked, as he came up behind her, kissing her neck.

"That's where it belongs, darlin'."

"Carry me home, Luke. I don't want to go home alone."

Luke carried Jessie across the street, and up the stairs to her porch, kissing her good-bye. The little dogs were barking, and Debbie was sitting at the dining room table, drinking coffee, when Jessie came in.

"Hi Momma," Jessie said closing the door, looking like she was in big trouble.

"Jessica Ashworth! Did you go over to Luke's house last night?" Debbie asked, trying to look stern. She had watched Luke carry Jessie home from the window.

"Yes, Momma," Jessie answered, walking slowly toward her.

Debbie held her hand out to Jessie. "Come here, Sweetie."

Jessie went over to her Aunt who took her hand. "I should just give you a spanking." Debbie half smiled. "Just...don't...I understand how your young raging hormones get, but, it makes me nervous, you're just a baby."

"Why are you up, Momma?"

"Well, I couldn't sleep. You have to start rehearsing with your band right away. The concert is less than a month away, and I have to go over the paper work with John today. We have to get your dad's permission as soon as possible."

"Momma," Jessie said, smiling. "I think things are getting better, now."

"So do I, sweetheart, but no more running over to Luke's in the middle of the night!"

Jessie didn't answer. *She was formulating a plan, and she would never have to choose.* She ran to the bathroom to take a shower before anyone else got up. She put a light pad on, and took another one for her backpack, in case she had the same trouble as yesterday. She put on her Levi's, thinking as she was buttoning them. She took off the chain from her waist and put it around her neck, so everyone at school could see it. Then she put on her bra, her white tank-top, her white, number thirty-six, football jersey, and her white sneakers. She was much more comfortable than the day before. She made sure to bring her backpack, because Mr. Leland had given her an assignment to do. She already had a notebook and some pencils inside, she knew Mikey wouldn't be prepared.

She was ready by six a.m., just when Maddy was getting out of bed. She sat on the couch with the dogs, watching cartoons. Eli came out from down the hall, in his blue plaid pajamas, yawning, with his hair sticking up. The sight of Eli suddenly made Jessie remember Ricky, sitting with her on the couch, peeling potatoes on Thanksgiving Day, and playing catch in the front yard. She panicked and started to hyperventilate.

"Momma, Momma! I can't breathe!"

"Jessie, what's wrong?" Debbie asked, running over to her.

"I can't breathe. I saw Ricky in my head and I started to breathe funny."

"You're hyperventilating, Jessie," Debbie said, sitting beside her. "Sit up and relax, take in some deep breaths. Breathe in and count to ten."

"I'm scared Momma. My brain is tingling; I think I have to run."

"You're okay, Jessie." Debbie stroked her forehead. "You're just breathing too fast, and not getting enough oxygen. Just relax and take deep, slow breaths."

Jessie put her head on Debbie's shoulder and began to breathe slowly, closing her eyes. Debbie held her, softly stroking Jessie's face. "You're alright, Jessie. Just relax…you feeling better now, sweetheart?"

"Yes Momma." She took in a deep breath. "I just got scared. Momma, if Ricky died so easy, we could all die so easy. One day he was sitting over there at the table, and we were peeling potatoes, and then next day, he's gone forever. I miss
Ricky, Momma, why did he go?"

"I know, sweetheart, we all miss Ricky. Just cry if you want, honey."

"I can't cry now," Jessie said, sniffing her nose and wiping her cheeks. "Mikey will be here, and he hates me to cry."

"What do you mean, Mike hates you to cry?"

"He says it makes him sad when I cry."

"Well, you can still cry if you want, it doesn't matter what Mike thinks. Do you still want to go to school? You can stay here with me if you like."

"No, I want to go to school, Momma. I feel better now. I have homework to turn in."

"All right, but why don't you eat some cereal or something, before you go."

Jessie made herself a bowl of Cheerios, and sat next to Eli on the couch, watching *Merrie Melodies* cartoons.

Chapter Fourteen - Mikey Loves Jessie

At six-fifty, Jessie heard Mike's car roar. She ran in the bathroom, quickly brushed her teeth, and grabbed her white jacket out of the bedroom.

"Bye!" she yelled, running out the front door. She practically knocked Mike down off the step, in front of her.

"Whoa, bunny, you're gonna hurt someone," Mike said, taking her backpack.

"I brought you a pencil and paper, Mikey," Jessie said, as they walked to the car.

"Thank you, peanut."

Mike drove off slowly this time. Jessie pulled her legs up on the seat, leaning her head on the back of it, staring at Mike.

"Don't you want to scoot over here by me, baby?"

"No, not today."

"What's the matter? Come over here and sit by me. I just wanna be close to you, you're so beautiful. I think that more and more every day, Jessie."

Mike drove up the road a little way and pulled over. He shook his head, gazing into her beautiful eyes. "You take my breath away, you're so beautiful. I don't believe you're real sometimes...Jessie," he said, leaning over to her. "What you did this morning was about the sexiest thing I've ever seen. Come 'ere, baby."

Jesse moved over next to Mike and he smoothed his hand across her face, and up her neck. "Baby, you are the most beautiful girl in the world. Sometimes

I wanna die, you're so beautiful." He took her chin in his hand and gently kissed her mouth. "You're wearing my chain around your neck, bunny?"

"Yeth, but it's mine, not yours. Mikey, are we going to smoke by the parking lot?"

"Yeah," Mike chuckled.

"Can we get coffee first?" Jessie asked, rubbing his chest.

"You bet, peanut."

"At 7-11?"

"Yeah." Mike smiled.

"Mikey, I have a pimple." She pointed to a tiny spot on her cheek.

"Where?" Mike asked looking, wrapping his arms around her.

"Right here. I have to go to school with a pimple. Is it gross?"

"Yeah."

"Am I gross, now?"

"Mm hm."

"And you don't like me no more, now?"

"Nope."

"Mikey?"

"Hm?"

"You don't like me no more?" Jessie's face was so serious, it took every ounce of strength Mike could muster not to smile at her and remain serious.

"Baby, I'm teasing you. Didn't I just tell you how much I love you? I don't give a shit if you have a pimple. It's not a pimple anyway; it's just a little red spot. Where do you get these silly questions?"

"Maddy says boys don't like no girls with pimples at school."

"Well, I guess they better stay home then, Jessie." Mike laughed so hard his eyes were watering. "Maddy's just a dumb girl, bunny, I wish you'd listen to me."

"You like girls with pimples?"

"Jessie."

"Am I a dumb girl?"

"Yeah."

"But you do like me?"

"I love you. You don't 'member nothin, do you?" Mike gave Jessie a thousand little kisses on her face, kissing all of her invisible pimples, and turned smiling, shifting into gear.

Jessie was ecstatic to go to 7-11. She decided not to have coffee, but one of those fascinating blue, *Slurpee* drinks instead, and Mike happily showed her how to pour it.

A smooth, psychedelic sound came on the radio in the car and Mike turned it up. "I dig this song," he said and started singing it.

"What's it called?" she asked.

"Time of the Season," he sang.

The morning was going well, and Jessie was happy. When they pulled into the parking lot, it seemed that every guy in school was standing out there, whether they smoked or not, waiting to see Jessie. Mike looked around at all of them and put his arm around her. Andy and Jeff stood in their own group, although Andy couldn't take his eyes off Jessie, either.

"I wonder what's with that little bear she carries around," Andy said to Jeff.

"Yeah, it's kind of weird," Jeff answered.

"She's cute, like a little girl. I bet she sucks her thumb."

"I wouldn't fool with her, Andy."

"She would've shown us all her big tits at the party that night, if Mike hadn't stopped her," Andy said, watching Jessie.

"I wonder what else she would have shown us." Jeff grinned.

"Yeah, me too. I wonder what else she sucks. Damn, she's a fox. Look at her hair, she's so tiny. My fuckin' dicks gonna be hard all damn day."

"Well, stop staring at her, dumb ass," Jeff said, throwing his cigarette on the ground. "Katie's really pissed at you, and Mike would kick your ass."

"Fuck her. I don't give a shit about her. I'm not gonna rest till I can fuck that sweet little girl with the big tits."

"Man, you're gonna get yourself killed."

"I'm not so sure about that. Mike's not so tough. I think she's kind of dumb. I bet she's easy. I bet if you got her alone, she'd be so easy. She must be really hot, to keep Mike hangin' on her." Andy threw his cigarette down. "Doesn't she live with Maddy Ashworth?"

"Yeah."

"Let's go," Andy said. He purposely walked past Jessie and smiled at her. Mike caught it but didn't say anything. He didn't want to upset Jessie like he did the day before. He pulled her close to him, kissing her neck.

~

Mr. Leland had given Jessie a special assignment. Nothing he was going to share with the class, just a couple of factual questions, and a few common-sense questions. Mr. Leland was learned in psychiatry and thought maybe he could talk to Mother Magdalena about his observations. He didn't ask Jessie to answer any questions out loud today, and Jessie was glad about that. Mike kept writing Jessie love notes, handing them to her under his desk.

"Hey foxy little girl, would you go out with me?" he whispered, softly pulling on her hair. "I sure would like to go out with you."

Jessie shook her head. She didn't turn around, but she smiled. Mike was thoroughly enjoying flirting with her.

"No? Oh, you're gonna break my heart, little girl. Are you sure you won't go out with me? I'll buy you something pretty...I'll buy you chocolate."

Jessie giggled, but then she blushed, hoping no one heard her. Nicki and Taylor were passing notes back and forth, disgusted at how sickening Mike was being.

Mike leaned over and whispered, "Hey, baby. Do you fool around on the first date?"

Jessie tried not to laugh but squeaked for a second and shook her head and then nodded.

Andy leaned his head on his arm, staring at Jessie. Her eyes kept going over to him.

Not because she liked him, but because she was afraid of him and wanted to see if he was still looking at her, like she did with the monster. Every time she looked, he would smile or wink, or lick his lips. She could feel her hands getting sweaty and couldn't wait to get out of there.

When the class let out, Mike wrapped his arms around Jessie from behind, trying to tickle her as they walked down the hall.

"Mikey, *stop!* You're trying to make me thexy again!" Jessie snapped.

"Is that what I'm doin', little tittie girl?" he said, kissing her ear.

"Yeth, I'm trying to be a good girl, today, Mikey."

"I'm sorry, baby. You are good, I just can't help it. Especially after seeing you this morning in that little white thing, doing what you did. Mm," he said, rubbing his face on hers. "I had to go jack off in the bathroom, baby."

"Really?" Jessie asked, turning to look up at him. "Mikey?" She held up her finger and curled it for him to come close. He bent down and put his head on top of hers. "Can I see you do that?"

Mike stood up and looked at her. That wasn't a usual question for a cute little girl like her to ask. In fact, he'd never heard of that at all. He got a lump in his throat. *Shit,* he thought, *now what's she gonna want?* "We'll talk about that later," he swallowed. "We gotta get to class right now."

~

Jessie ordered a salad at lunch and ate all of it, not looking at Andy at all this time.

"You are a little bunny, aren't you, baby?" Mike asked, smiling. "I think we found something you'll eat."

"I feel better today, Mikey. I put a pad on, so my panties won't get all wet."

Mike chuckled, hugging her.

They got back to school early from lunch and sat under a huge maple tree in the big grassy area next to the football field. Jessie laid her head in Mike's lap. He caressed her face, gently pulling out strands of her long hair, smelling it.

"Mikey?" Jessie asked, stroking his chin.

"What, Love?"

"Who was the girl in math that was looking so sad at you?"

"What girl?"

"The one who was looking sad at you. She had a red shirt."

"Mm," Mike said, looking off. "She's just a girl I been with, sometimes." He turned and kissed a strand of her hair.

"You been with her?"

"Yeah."

"A lot?"

"Yeah, baby."

"Is she your girlfriend?"

"No, Jessie."

"Because she's not pretty?"

"She's all right, in bed anyway."

"Did you take her on a date?"

"Once. Not really a date. I took her to a party once. She just fucks me Jess, that's all. She don't harass me."

"And that's why she is sad now?"

"I don't know, maybe. I told her not to get involved or start havin' feelings for me, cuz I wouldn't do her anymore."

"What is her name?"

"Why?"

"I dis wonder is all."

"Deborah."

"Are you going to have some more thex with her?"

"I don't think so, baby. I might...I might if I can't have you anymore, I might if you keep having sex with Luke."

Jessie tapped her lip. "Um, Mikey, is…is your car blue?"

"You know my car is blue, baby."

"Um, Mikey, but you don't have no thex with her, now?"

"No, I got you, now."

A little tear ran down her face. "And you don't like her no more, and she will cry?"

"Why are you crying, peanut?"

"Because, you won't like me no more."

Mike looked lovingly at Jessie, stroking her face. "Baby, I never liked her that way, I like you."

"Then why did you make thex to her?"

"Cuz, she let me. Baby, I love you, forevermore."

Jessie pouted, tapping her mouth with her finger. "Um, don't you want my name, Patti?"

"Patti?" Mike chuckled, "No. Why would I want that?"

"I don't know."

"Where did you hear that name?"

"I don't know."

"I like your name, peanut."

"And you want my name peanut?"

"Sometimes."

"Because you don't like my name Jessie?"

Mike looked in Jessie's eyes loving her so much. He grinned and kissed a strand of her hair.

"Do you want my name Deborah?"

"No," Mike scowled. "Jessie quit it. I love your name. Don't be so upset about it, baby. I love you, and you're only Jessie to me."

"And peanut?"

"Mm hm"

"And bunny?"

"Mm hm"

Jessie frowned. "Not tittie."

"Sometimes."

"You want my name, Thomas?"

Mike broke out laughing. Her face was so seriously cute. Jessie smiled because she knew she was just joking now, and she liked Mike to laugh.

"Sometimes I think you just say these things baby, to crack me up."

"I do." Jessie grinned, tapping her finger on her mouth.

"I'll have to try 'n remember that, you funny bunny. Yes, Jessie, I want your name to be Thomas. Mrs. Michael Thomas Miller."

"You mean I get to have your name, too, and we both will be Michael Thomas Miller?"

"Yes, my love, you and me, are one in the same."

"Because I live in you?"

Mike kissed Jessie all over her little face. "Yes."

Jessie looked out in space, pondering that, while Mike smiled at her cute little expressions. "And you will call me Thomas?"

"Baby, I love you more than anything in the world. You have no idea."

"I have ideas, Mikey, like you have ideas."

"What do you want for your birthday, peanut?"

"To come live in the Miller House."

"I'd like that, Jessie. Maybe someday you will. What else do you want?"

"Mm, I want makeup, like Maddy."

"Make-up? You don't need no makeup. You're already too beautiful. I love you too much already.

"Oh? I want to play a game, Mikey."

"What game, bunny?" Mike asked, playing with her hair.

"I want to play, 'Mikey can't catch the bunny girl in the grass," she said, getting up. Then she pushed Mike down, and started to run, giggling. "Come get me, Mikey!"

Mike chased after her as she ran around the tree, trying to escape him. "You can't get me." She laughed, just as Mike tackled her down.

"I got you, Patti." He smiled down at her, and they laughed. "I like this game, bunny."

"You're not 'pose to catch me, Mikey. Bunnies are faster than you," she said, getting up.

"Well, that's no fun if I can't catch you."

Jessie pushed Mike again and ran off laughing. Mike chased after her, but she put her hand up, giggling and out of breath. "Stop, Mikey, stop. Don't catch me, I'm scared."

Mike stopped, resting his hands on his knees, breathing heavy. "I wanna catch you, bunny."

"No, you're a *hound dog*, you can't catch a little bunny," she said, and ran off again.

The students watching couldn't believe that Mike Miller was chasing a girl around. Taylor was beside herself, sitting in the bleachers, watching with the rest of the cheerleaders.

Mike caught Jessie and picked her up, whirling her around in the grass. "This ole hound dog caught me a bunny."

~

Aimee noticed Mike and Jessie in the hall, on her way to fourth period. She ran to ask Jessie if she would go to band with her. Jessie was excited about that, but Mike said, "No".

"What do you mean, no?" Aimee asked. "You can't tell her no, she's my cousin."

"Please, Mikey?" Jessie pouted.

"I don't want you going anywhere without me, Jessie."

"She'll be with me, Mike," Aimee said. "You can come get her right after class."

He couldn't resist Jessie's pouty face. "Aright, peanut, but don't go anywhere else, you be right here after class."

"I will, Mikey," Jessie said, grabbing Mike's arm. She jumped up to kiss his face.

Aimee took Jessie and introduced her to Mrs. Willis, the band teacher.

"Yes, I remember you Jessie, from last year's spring concert," Mrs. Willis said. "Would you like to practice with us today?"

"Yes, please," Jessie answered.

Mrs. Willis gave Jessie a violin to use. Some of the kids asked Jessie if she would play a solo for them and she agreed, playing "Vivaldi, Concerto in A minor". While listening to it, Mrs. Willis was thinking.

"Jessie?" she asked, when Jessie had finished playing. "Sunday night we have a football game, and the student who was scheduled to sing the "Star Spangled Banner" is out ill. Would you like to play it on your violin, for the game?"

"Yes, Mrs. Willis!" Jessie answered, with a sparkle of excitement in her eyes.

"Will you play it for us, now?" the teacher asked.

"Yes, I will!"

As Mike walked toward his next class, he noticed Tammie, standing at her locker. She was with some weird looking guy. Mike wondered why he hadn't seen her around. Maybe she was avoiding him. He stopped and glared at her.

"What the fuck are you looking at?" Tammie sneered at him.

"That's what I was wonderin'," Mike said, hovering over her with his hands on his hips. "I think you and me might have some settlin' up to do." He rubbed his hand across his chest.

She turned, slamming her locker shut. "I don't know what you're talking about."

"I think you do," Mike said. "I think some other people might be interested, too. Or maybe I'll just take care of it myself."

She glared at him. "Are you threatening me?"

"I hope so."

"What makes you so fuckin' righteous, asshole?" Her eyes were full of guilty hatred. She walked off with her long-haired, skinny, wasted, looking friend. "Fuckin' prick," Mike heard her say to him. Mike didn't need to say anything more. She knew what he meant.

~

After fourth period Mike ran to his car to get the blanket for Jessie and ran back to meet her in the music room. He stopped to watch Jessie, who was playing a tune on the piano. He didn't know the piece, but it was beautiful. She was beautiful. As class let out, Jessie walked shyly toward him.

"Hi, Beautiful," he said, with a lovesick gleam in his eye. "That was beautiful, Jessie. You're beautiful." Mike stroked her head, and taking her hand, he kissed it.

"Mikey, you didn't tell me you have a football game, on next Sunday."

"I meant to tell you this morning, but all I could think about was you in that little white thing. I wanna buy you something pretty like that white thing, Jessie," he said in her ear, hoping Aimee wasn't listening. "I want you to come to my game, bunny."

"Well, she's going to be there, anyway." Aimee smiled. "See you after school, Jess."

"Bye, Aimee." Jessie waved. "Mikey! You'll never guess what! Mrs. Willis asked me if I would play the "Star Spangled Banner" on my violin at the game on Sunday!"

"That's far-out, bunny. I can't wait to hear you." Mike hugged her against him as they walked down the hall to go to the gym. "My little bunny's gonna play at my game."

~

Jessie wrapped up in the blanket on the bleachers, watching Mike's practice. Andy kept messing with Mike, aggressively tackling him, and trying to hit him with the ball. Mike was trying to keep his cool, but Andy was becoming more aggressive.

"Is that how you're gonna play, Sunday, Miller?" Andy asked, throwing his shoulder into Mike.

Mike had had enough. He threw Andy down on the ground, holding his arm up against his back. "What the fuck's the matter with you, asshole?"

Coach Reed ran over to them. "You boys need to run a few laps?"

They both got up, and Andy put his hands up. "I'm cool," he said, looking at the coach.

Mike didn't say anything. He glared at Andy and then looked over at Jessie, who was now lying on the bleachers, shivering under the blanket.

"Jessie looks miserable, Mike," Coach said. "Why don't you take her to the office?"

~

After practice, Mike walked up to the counter in the office. He stood quietly watching Jessie, who was sitting at one of the desks, quite busy. Mike cleared his throat and Jessie looked up at him.

"Mikey, I have work," she told him quickly, getting back to it.

He grinned. "Oh? What kind of work, bunny?"

"She's quite the little helper, Mike," Mrs. 'C' spoke up. "She's almost completely organized my whole office."

"I'm making folders, Mikey," Jessie said, quite seriously.

"Well, come on, babe. We got something important to do, now."

"Mikey, I'm not finished."

"That's all right, Jessie," Mrs. 'C' said. "I'll finish it. Thank you for your help."

Mike walked Jessie out to the car and put the blanket in the backseat. "Let me see your backpack, Love."

Jessie handed him her backpack. "Mikey, do we have homework?"

He grinned and walked to the back of the car, opening the trunk. Inside was a box containing five cans of forest green spray paint, and one can of white. He stuffed them in Jessie's backpack.

"Where did you get those, Mikey?"

"At the hardware store, come *own*, babe," he said, taking her hand.

"What are they for, Mikey?"

"You'll see."

Mike took Jessie upstairs to the girl's restroom. Kevin, Maddy, and Aimee were there waiting, wondering what Mike was up to. As soon as the bell rang for sixth period, Mike told Aimee to go see if anyone was in the bathroom.

"There's no one in there," Aimee said, coming back out.

"Come on," Mike said, and they followed him into the bathroom. He handed everyone a can of green paint. "We're gonna paint over all this bullshit on the stalls. But don't fuck around, we gotta get outta here." Mike walked over to the window, opening it.

All three girls smiled and giggled, and Jessie gave Mike a kiss.

"*Come own, baby,*" he said, on purpose. "Hurry up."

They all snickered and giggled at the excitement of the deed. The intrigue of getting caught was pure bliss as they hurried to get it all done. When they finished, Mike took the can of white paint, and clear across the front of the stalls, he wrote in big letters: MIKEY LOVES JESSIE.

Kevin kept a look out by the door. Mike finished just in time when Kevin said, "Let's go, someone's coming."

The boys ducked out of the bathroom in front of the girls, and they all ran down the hall, down the stairwell, and outside to the front grass, laughing and screaming. They were all out of breath. Mike dropped down next to Jessie, lying in the grass. "I love you, baby," he said, kissing her.

Maddy was enjoying the adventure, but the sight of that kiss, reminded her how sad she was over Mike, and turned away.

The last bell rang and they were all sitting in the grass, watching as the students made their way out of the school. Mike said to Jessie, "Mikey Loves Jessie." Then Aimee started to giggle and then Jessie. Even Maddy joined in, not wanting to feel left out. Kevin was being a dork, talking in a funny low voice and they all began laughing hysterically at themselves. All the kids walking by stopped to look at what a bunch of idiots they were.

~

After feverishly making out in the car, Mike dropped Jessie off at home and drove out to the Sheriff's Department on Highway 50.

The desk sergeant, Joe Harrison, stood up to meet Mike at the counter.

"Hey, Mike. We're sure sorry about your brother."

"Thanks," Mike answered, mostly being a man of few words. "Is Burt in? I'd like to talk to him a minute."

Hello, Mike," The secretary, Barbara Buhler said, smiling up at him. "How's your mom?"

"She's better." Mike nodded at her as she went into Burt's office to announce him.

"Come on around," Joe said, holding the counter gate open for him. Mike stood up straight as he walked into the Sheriff's office.

Burt smiled up from his desk, chewing on a toothpick.

"Hey, Mike, how ya doin'?" He reached across his desk and shook Mike's hand. "Come in, Son. Take a load off."

Mike sat down in the chair in front of Burt's desk.

"We're all real sorry about your brother, Mike. Everything okay at home? Your Mom doin' okay?"

"She was takin' it pretty hard. She's been on some pills...tranquilizers or sleeping pills."

"Well, send her our love. I'm looking forward to the game, Sunday." Burt said, not letting Mike get a word in. "That Andy's a piece of ass wipe, compared to Luke."

"Yeah." Mike cleared his throat and smirked, agreeing with Burt.

Burt leaned his fat belly back in the seat, folding his hands behind his head. "What brings you here, Mike?"

Mike was a bit nervous, anxiously bouncing his long legs, and rested his arms on the arm rests of the wooden chair.

"Well, Burt, I'd like to get on here after I graduate this year. Do you think you'll have any openings?"

"As a matter of fact, Mike," Burt said, sitting up, "the commissioner's approved four new positions that should open up in July." Burt took a pen, tapping it on his desk calendar. "Come down and apply. It's better if you got some college or military first, but, you can still apply."

"Well, what do I gotta do, Burt?" Mike asked, needing more information.

"Let's see here." Burt put his glasses on and pulled out a handbook. "You gotta have your high school diploma or GED, a clean record, no felonies or Class A or B misdemeanors." Burt looked up over his glasses at Mike, and then looked back at the handbook. "A valid license, with a good record, score at least seventy percent on each section of the written exam, pass the Officer's Ability test, physical, and psychological exams." Burt looked up at Mike. "Guess you'll do good there. Submit to a polygraph and background." Burt handed Mike the book and leaned back in his chair. "Give a good Oral Interview, to make sure you know what you're doin', then if you get hired, you'll have to go to P.O.S.T. training down in Carson. The county pays for it. You have to work in the jail a few years before they put you out on the street."

Mike nodded, already knowing most of all that. "How long does the background take?" he asked.

"Couple weeks. You're a good kid aren't ya?" Burt leaned over his desk.

"You'll have to cut yer hair…quit smokin' dope, and no more speedin' tickets."
He smiled at Mike. "You boys and yer damn hot rods," Burt said, shaking his
head.

"Yeah," Mike chuckled, forgetting about that ticket last week. Mike nodded,
thinking about Jessie. He was thrilled to hear about the new positions. "Thanks,
Burt. I'll be here in July," he said, getting up.

Burt got up and walked with Mike toward the door.

"How's things down at the station?"

"Aright. This Oil Embargo is kind of messin' things up,
though. We had to shut down a couple days, last month."

"Yeah, I talked to Bill about that. Damn Arabs." Burt smiled and put his
hand on Mike's shoulder. "Don't wanna be a grease monkey forever, eh, Mike?"

"No, Sir, I don't."

"Tell your dad I said 'hi'. What's that Luke been up to, anyway? Still at the
hardware store?"

"Yeah, I think he's gonna make a career of it."

"Too bad, he should play college ball."

Joe and Barbara looked up at Mike as he left the front desk.

"Good luck, Sunday, Mike." Joe said. "We'll be there."

Mike nodded. "Yeah, well, thanks, Burt," Mike said, shaking Burt's hand.

"Alright, Mike, you take care now. Come back and see us."

~

Mr. Burke had been over to see Jessie's dad. Immediately after, he called
Debbie to explain what had transpired between them. He told Debbie that he
thought it odd that Hank never asked him about the temporary custody order
she had gotten for Jessie. He also found it disturbing that when he explained
Jessie was ill and had been hospitalized, Hank said nothing, nor showed any
concern. Debbie didn't think it was odd and thought it best not to mention that
to Jessie. Hank did advise Mr. Burke, however, that he had met someone, and
he was going to take her to Mexico in about a week or two, for a month, and
that Debbie could keep Jessie until he got back. He also signed to allow Jessie
to rehearse with the band and play in the concert. They had written in the
contract that he would keep any monies earned. Debbie was completely and
happily surprised with this news and was beside herself with relief. She couldn't
wait to share the good news with her family.

Harry and Debbie took the kids to pizza and a movie that night. At dinner,
Debbie told them all the good news. Jessie didn't care about the money. She

was completely delighted and shed happy tears with the news that she wouldn't be going back home for a long time. Everyone was overjoyed. Jessie couldn't have been any happier. She felt as if the whole world had been taken off her shoulders. She told her family about playing the "Star Spangled Banner" for Sunday's game. They were all thrilled to go support Jessie and have a family night at the game. It was one of the best days of her life!

Jessie stayed home with her family that night. After pondering a bit, she was curious, and felt a little jealous about this new woman her dad was seeing, *and*, he was taking her to Mexico. Jessie thought that was strange and a little suspicious. She was so exhausted from the late-night movie and the events of the week that she fell asleep as soon as they got home and didn't wake up until the morning sun was shining on her face through the bedroom window.

Chapter Fifteen -
Trouble in Paradise

Saturday, January 19, 1974

Maddy was elated! She was going to the beauty parlor at the Country Mall to get her hair bleached blond! In her excitement, she invited Jessie to go with her and Jessie was delighted. Jessie had wanted to buy teddy an outfit that she'd seen at the clothing store that day with Mike. She was finally beginning to feel like a member of a normal family, experiencing the freedom that she longed for when she first found out that Maddy had her own car. Maddy took Jessie under her wing that morning and decided that she and Jessie should match.

Maddy had two, silky, mini-dresses that she bought a while ago, but hadn't worn yet. One was light green flowered, and the other was light pink flowered. Maddy picked out long sweaters to wear over them. She gave Jessie the pink dress with a white sweater and she wore the green dress with the black sweater. They both wore their slip-on sandals. The neck-line was elastic, meant to be worn off the shoulders, like a peasant blouse. Jessie had put her bra on and the straps were showing.

"You don't wear a bra with that dress, Jessie," Maddy said, showing her how to wear it. "It's sexier without it."

"Well, that's not what Momma says," Jessie answered.

"Come on, Jess, we have to be *daring* today. I'm starting a whole new me, today!"

Maddy couldn't wait to be blond, start attracting guys, and go out on dates. She desperately wanted to live some of the life that Jessie had been living.

While they were getting ready, the phone rang. It was Luke calling for Jessie, to ask her to come meet him for lunch, and Maddy agreed she would bring her. They went back in the bathroom, and while Maddy was helping Jessie put mascara on, the phone rang again. Aimee answered it.

"Is Jessie there?"

"Jessie!" Aimee shouted, "Phone call! It's Mike!"

Maddy clicked her tongue and scowled at Jessie. "How are we supposed to get ready if you keep getting phone calls?" Maddy followed Jessie out to the phone as soon as she heard Aimee say it was Mike. Aimee smiled and shrugged as Jessie walked past to get the phone.

"Mikey," Jessie's small voice answered.

"Hi Jessie, what are you doing today?"

"I'm going to the mall with Maddy, today, Mikey!"

"What mall are you going to?" he asked.

Suddenly, Jessie realized it wasn't Mike. Mike's voice was deeper than the one on the phone. "Who are you?" she asked, looking puzzled.

Maddy gave Jessie a curious look. "Who is it, Jessie?"

"It's Andy," he answered, "Don't you remember me?"

"Yes," Jessie answered, now frowning. "I'm not allowed to talk to you, Andy."

Andy chuckled, "Why not, sweet stuff?"

"Because, Mikey said tho," Jessie scowled.

"Mike's not your boss, is he? You can talk to me, I like you."

"No. Mikey's going steady with me and he *is* my boss. I have to go now." Jessie hung up the phone.

"Was that Andy Bass?" Maddy asked. "How did he get our number?"

Jessie shrugged. "I don't know." She started walking back to the bathroom when Maddy stopped her.

"Well, what did he want, Jessie?"

"He said what I was doing today. I thought it was Mikey, but it wasn't. I told him Mikey said I'm not allowed to talk to him...Mikey told me never talk to Andy, Maddy."

"Jesus, Jessie, now we're going to have every guy at school calling here for you. Mike should have never taken you to school."

Jessie gave Maddy a worried look.

"Come on, Jess, let's go finish getting ready. My appointment's in a half hour. Did you say you and Mike were going steady?" Maddy asked when the phone rang again.

"I'll get it!" Maddy snarled at Aimee and pushed past her, thinking it was Andy calling Jessie back. "Hello!" Maddy snapped.

"Damn," Mike said. "What's wrong with you?"

"Oh, hang on, Mike, here's Jessie." Maddy handed Jessie the phone.

"Hi Mikey," Jessie answered.

"Hi, baby. How's my beautiful bunny today?"

"Mikey, do you have work today?"

"I am at work, peanut."

"I don't want you to go to work."

"Well, I have to work, baby, to pay for that car of yours, and buy you a house."

"Mikey, I have money you can have."

"How much money do you have, bunny?"

"Momma gave me twenty dollars, you can have it."

Mike chuckled. "Bunny, that's not enough."

"How much is it then?"

"It's more than twenty dollars, punkin'."

"Mikey, what do you do at your work?"

"Fix cars."

"Mikey, how long do you have to go to work?"

"Till five, bunny."

"Five o'clock? That's the whole day."

"I tried to call you last night, but you weren't home. I had so much fun at school with you yesterday, baby. I have some good news to tell you."

"What is it, Mikey?"

"Well, you'll have to come see me tonight, and I'll tell you."

"Mikey, you'll never guess what!?" Jessie exclaimed, suddenly excited.

"What, baby girl?"

"My daddy is going away to Mexico for a long time!" Jessie squeaked. "He said I can stay here and play in the band!"

"Mexico? No shit, baby?"

"My Momma told me."

"That's far out, peanut. That *is* good news."

"I'm going to start playing on Monday night!"

"Right on. That's really cool, babe. You get to stay with us for a long time?"

"Mm hm."

"Baby, that's the best news, ever. I'm happy for you, little peanut. You have to come see me tonight, so we can celebrate. Well, I have to get back to work now, Beautiful. I just wanted to tell you I love you, and I can't wait to see you again."

"Mikey, are you still going to buy me a pretty?"

"I can't wait to buy you pretties, baby, on Friday."

"I love you, Mikey," Jessie said, while Maddy impatiently stood there, rolling her eyes.

"I love you, too, baby. Will you come see me tonight, bunny? I missed you so much last night."

"Yes, Mikey. She's waiting now, Bye." Jessie hung up the phone.

Mike tried not to feel insecure at Jessie's lack of phone etiquette; it w*as* so damn cute. He was happy about Jessie's news, though, and that made everything okay.

~

The two girls pulled into the parking lot of the Mining Country Mall in Maddy's little blue Volkswagen bug, and parked right in front of the Mountain Clothing Store.

"You come right over there to New Age, as soon as you're finished buying the outfit," Maddy told Jessie, pointing to the beauty parlor. "Momma went on and, on this morning, making sure I kept an eye on you, so hurry up."

"Okay, Maddy," Jessie answered, closing the car door. She walked into the clothing store as Maddy walked over to New Age Hair Salon, two doors down. Jessie felt grown up now, carrying her pink purse with real money in it, and she was shopping all by herself!

Jessie leaned over, looking at the little bear clothes on the shelf. She didn't see the outfit she wanted to buy, so she looked for something else. Her dress was a little too short, and her panties were showing as she was bent over. She heard someone whistle behind her. She stood up to look and was startled. She thought it was Luke at first; he was wearing a black and red Mining Jacket.

"Hi Jessie," Andy said grinning, pulling at the bottom of her sweater.

"Hi," Jessie answered automatically, but at once, was frightened. She remembered what Mike told her, 'Not to ever go near Andy, and if he tried to touch her, to scream and run.'

Andy smiled and ran his hand down along her dress.

"You sure look cute in that dress, Jessie." He took Jessie's hand, but she pulled it away. "Don't be shy, Jessie," Andy said, taking her hand again. "How 'bout a soda?"

Jessie pulled her hand away. "No!" She wanted to scream, but she felt unsure. She looked around and then back at Andy. He was just smiling at her, and she felt embarrassed to scream. She decided not to buy anything and go see Maddy. She turned to leave when Andy grabbed her arm.

"Come on, little fox, let's go have a soda." Andy took Jessie and walked toward the back of the store.

"Wait!" Jessie snapped, trying to pull away. "I'm not s'pose to go with you."

Andy chuckled. "I just wanna buy you a soda or something. We could sit and talk for a few minutes," Andy said, pulling her along. "Come on, just for a minute? You're so cute, Jessie." He smiled, walking backwards, trying to distract her.

Jessie *was* distracted and dropped her purse, trying to free her hand from Andy. It fell under a rack of clothing.

"My purse!" Jessie said, trying to get it. Andy didn't stop and kept talking, hastening now, to take her.

"I was really impressed with you the other day, and I hear you like chocolate," Andy said, walking Jessie out through the back door of the store. It went into a large, empty hallway that led to the business office of the mall, and some public restrooms.

"Let me go!" Jessie yelled, trying to pull free from Andy. "Why are you going back here? I have to go thee Maddy."

He squeezed her hand tight, pulling Jessie over to him and she let out a loud scream. Andy put his hand over her mouth and picked her up. Jessie kicked at him, struggling to get free, and one of her sandals fell off in the hallway.

Maddy was getting worried. It had been almost a half an hour, and Jessie still hadn't come to meet her. She couldn't leave, because she had toner in her hair, and she was waiting for it to process. She knew it couldn't take Jessie that long to buy the bear outfit. *What is she doing?* Maddy asked herself, feeling anxious.

The hairstylist could see that something was bothering Maddy and asked her if she was okay.

"Yeah," Maddy answered. "I'm just worried about my little cousin. She was supposed to meet me here almost forty-five minutes ago, and I'm getting worried."

"Well, I just have to put the conditioner in and you're ready."

Maddy didn't wait for the stylist to dry or style her hair. She left New Age and ran over to the Mountain Clothing Store. Jessie was nowhere in sight.

Maddy could see the whole store, because it was an open area with small racks of clothing, but she went around through it anyway. She walked right past Jessie's purse, but didn't notice it. Then she ran up to the cashier at the counter and asked her if a girl fitting Jessie's description had been in and bought one of the little bear outfits. The lady said, "No," she hadn't seen anyone who looked like Jessie, and no one had bought a bear outfit. Maddy started to panic, remembering about Andy calling this morning, and Jessie telling him where she was going. She ran to the phone booth outside the store and called the Chevron station. The phone rang about five times. Maddy was terrified, waiting. The station manager finally answered and Maddy asked to talk to Mike.

"Hang on," the man said.

Maddy felt like she'd been waiting for ten minutes, even though it was only a few seconds when finally, Mike answered.

"Yeah, this is Mike."

"Mike, it's Maddy! Jessie's missing!"

"What?" he snapped. "Missing from where?"

"I took her to the mall and she was supposed to meet me at New Age, almost an hour ago now, but she never showed up. The lady at the Mountain Clothing Store, where I dropped her off, said she hadn't seen her. I can't find her anywhere!"

"She probably just went to another store."

"No, Mike! I made her promise to meet me right after she bought the outfit for her stupid teddy bear! She already knew which one she wanted. The lady at the counter said she never saw Jessie, and no one had bought a teddy bear outfit. *I saw her go in the store*!"

"Fuck," Mike exhaled.

"Mike," Maddy stuttered, "I'm...well, Andy called our house this morning and asked to talk to Jessie."

"What!?"

"She thought it was you on the phone at first. He asked her what she was doing today, and she told him, thinking it was you."

"But I called her this morning, how could she think..."

"Mike!" Maddy interrupted, "It was before you called."

"I'm on my way! Keep looking for her!"

Mike got there in about ten minutes, barely skidding into a parking space. He immediately spotted Andy's white Ford pickup. It was jacked up for four wheeling and had a spot of gray primer on the right front fender.

Maddy was waiting outside the clothing store and ran over to Mike. Mike jumped out of his car with grease still on his hands and face, and ran over to

Andy's truck, pulling open the door. The truck was empty. Maddy followed him as he entered the back door of the mall where the restrooms were.

"There's her shoe!" Maddy exclaimed, picking it up. Mike ran to the men's room. The door was locked. He could hear noises through the door. Jessie's cry was muffled by Andy's hand squeezing her mouth.

"JESSIE!" Mike yelled, hitting the door.

Jessie screamed under Andy's hand.

Mike pulled on the door, "JESSIE!" he yelled, again. "OPEN THE DOOR, MOTHER FUCKER!" Mike hit the door again. "I'M GONNA KICK YOUR FUCKIN' ASS!"

"I'll let you *try* to kick my ass, Miller, as soon as I'm done with your girlfriend!" Andy yelled back.

"Mikey!" Jessie screamed, kicking and struggling with Andy. Mike stepped back and kicked at the door. His body was trembling with rage. He kicked at the door again, this time flinging the door open against the wall. It went to slam shut when Mike pushed it back. Andy was standing, just zipping up his jeans. Jessie was curled up on the bench, panting and terrified. Her top was pulled down below her breasts.

"She wanted it, man," Andy said, defiantly. "She told me to meet her here."

"That's a lie!" Maddy snapped.

Mike immediately slammed his fist into Andy's face. *"I'm gonna kill you, Mother fucker!"* Mike grunted, pulling his fist back, again.

Andy tried to block it but, Mike flew into Andy, pinning him against the wall, punching him in his sides. Andy rammed his head into Mike's chin and forced his arms out and was able to push him off, kicking him. Mike flew back against the sink.

"Mikey!" Jessie screamed. She had gotten off the bench and was huddled in a corner on the floor, holding teddy with her hands over her head, terrified that Mike was getting hurt.

Andy ran at Mike to head- butt him, but Mike brought his knee up into Andy's face and hit him in the back of the head with both fists clenched together.

Maddy was outside the door in shock, not knowing what to do. She tried, but couldn't get to Jessie, because the boys were all over the bathroom.

Andy fell over and Mike kicked at him. Andy grabbed Mike's leg, pulling him down, and punched him in the face twice, hitting Mike's head against the tile wall. Mike kicked at Andy, and got up, pulling Andy up by his jacket so he could punch him in the face some more. He punched Andy, four or five times in the face until it was bloody, and Andy fell back against the wall, not able to get up.

"You're a stupid Mother Fucker, you know that?" Mike said, going over to Jessie. She was crying, holding her hands over her head. Mike pulled her top up, and picked her up, grabbing her sweater off the bench. He was about to leave through the door when Jessie yelled.

"My panties! I want my panties!" she cried, pointing to them under the bench. Maddy ran in and grabbed them and handed them to Jessie.

"It was worth it, man," Andy said, wiping his mouth. He was out of breath, sitting against the wall, all bloody.

Mike ignored that and carried Jessie to his car and sat down in the driver's seat, holding her in his lap. Jessie buried her face in Mike's greasy blue uniform, crying, "I want my Mikey, I want my Mikey."

Maddy got in the passenger door, leaning over the seat.

"Andy's lying, Mike. Jessie never said that to him. I was right there."

Mike gave Maddy a strange look, seeing her with blond hair. He looked down at Jessie and stroked her face. "Mikey's right here, baby." His hands were shaking.

"I want my panties on," Jessie whimpered, barely able to breathe. "I want my panties." She had a small, bleeding cut on her mouth.

"My Jessie," Mike said to her face, trying to put her panties on her, but his hands were shaking and were so greasy he didn't want to touch them. "Oh," she whined, "I lost my purse."

Maddy helped him, sobbing, "I'm supposed to take her to meet Luke for lunch at the hardware store."

"I'll take her," Mike said. He pulled some wadded-up money out of his pants pocket and handed it to Maddy. "Do you know which one she was gonna buy?"

She looked at Mike's fat, bloody lip, and cut black eye. "I think so," she answered, taking the money.

"Go buy it real quick, please, and look for her purse," Mike said. He wrapped his arms around Jessie. "Don't cry, baby. I'm here now. I'm sorry, baby, I'm sorry." He put his face down to hers. "He didn't hurt you did he, Jessie? Did he hurt you? He didn't hit you, did he, baby?" Mike asked, wiping her lip.

"Yes...I want my Momma; *I want my Momma.*" Jessie dropped her head back and fainted.

Mike heard Andy's truck peel out of the parking lot. He looked back at it as Andy took off down the road. Maddy came back with an outfit, and Jessie's purse.

Mike wiped his hand under his nose. "I'm gonna take her to the hardware store now, Maddy. What time is she supposed to be home?"

"I told Momma we'd be home about two. I'm gonna follow you over there."

"Aright." He laid Jessie in the passenger seat. He took the blanket from the back seat and put it over her.

Mike pulled up in front of the store, and Maddy's car pulled in next to his. Mike went around and picked Jessie up in the blanket, while Maddy held open the door. He carried her to the back of the store, upstairs to John's office. John had a cot set up in there. He laid Jessie down on the cot, when Luke came storming in, behind them.

"What the hell is going on?" Luke snapped.

Mike sat down at John's desk. His face was bloody and swollen. He put his head down on his arm, while Maddy explained to Luke and John, who was now standing in the doorway, what happened.

Luke bent down over Jessie, rubbing her forehead. "God dammit," he said, under his breath. He was furious, and beside himself with grief, worried now, that she had gone back into shock, and was going to sleep for days, again.

"You should probably call the police, Mike," John said, folding his arms against his chest.

"No," Mike said. "I don't want Jessie standing up at some rape trial or going through some rape exam at the hospital. She can't take that." Mike leaned back on the chair, lighting a cigarette.

"He's right," Luke answered, stroking Jessie's face. "She's got enough bullshit going on right now. I wanna go *kill that fucker!*" Luke looked up at Mike with anger in his eyes.

"I don't think Andy will mess with Jessie, again," Maddy said, leaning on her hands against the file cabinet. She was looking over in awe at Mike, the hero.

"Here, Maddy, sit down," Mike said, getting up. "I gotta get back to fuckin' work." He went over to Jessie and squatted down in front of her, stroking her face with his black injured hand. "I love you, baby," he whispered, and kissed her cheek. "I hate to leave you, bunny, but I gotta go." He got up and left the room.

"This poor little girl," Luke said, kneeling in front of her, smoothing back her hair. "She's so frail and helpless. She just can't seem to get any happiness out of this life." Tears began to roll down his face as he put his face next to hers. "I wish you would've called me, Maddy." Luke looked up. "I would have brought my gun."

"Mike beat the shit out of Andy, Luke. I'm surprised he's not dead," Maddy said, hoping somehow that would make Luke feel better. She couldn't imagine how bad she felt for Jessie, thinking it was probably her fault, and realizing, maybe Jessie wasn't really having so much fun.

Luke glanced at Maddy not able to reply and turned to Jessie. "Wake up, darlin'," he whispered. "Please don't go back to sleep."

John brought Luke a cold, wet washcloth, and a glass of water. Luke wiped Jessie's mouth, her neck, and forehead with the cloth.

"Luke," Jessie said, trying to open her eyes. She could see the tears on his face. "I'm okay, Luke. I'm okay. He didn't hurt me. I'm all right, Luke."

"My sweet baby," Luke whispered, holding her hand. "Do you want a drink of water?" he asked, holding up the glass.

She nodded, sitting up to take the glass, and took a drink. "Maddy," Jessie said and smiled. "You're here…and you're a blonde."

~

Maddy took Jessie home and had her take a shower. Jessie had a bruise on her cheek and her lip was swollen.

"What in the world happen to you, Jessie?" Debbie asked, examining Jessie's face.

"Jessie tripped in the parking lot, Mom," Maddy said, and Jessie nodded. Luke had asked Maddy not to say anything to Debbie just yet. He wasn't sure how to handle it, yet.

Jessie slept all afternoon until dinner, and then she barely ate anything. Deep depression had settled inside her head. Debbie was worried and suspicious. She didn't quite believe Maddy. After dinner, Jessie sat on the couch for a while with Eli and Aimee watching *All in the Family*, while Debbie was in the family room with Harry, discussing Jessie. The phone rang, and Aimee ran to get it.

"It's for you, Jessie."

Jessie was slow getting to the phone. "Hello," Jessie said softly, barely able to speak.

"Baby?" Mike asked, "I can hardly hear you, are you okay, baby?"

"I'm tired, Mikey."

"Please come see me, Jessie, I need you."

"I'm tired, Mikey."

"I'm sorry, baby. I need to talk to you."

"Mikey, I can't. I'm tired. I want to go to sleep, now…I'm okay, Mikey."

"I don't know if I can go another night without you, bunny."

"Mikey, I have to go to sleep now…my head hurts."

"Take some aspirin, baby, and go to sleep."
"Bye, Mikey."

A whirlwind of unwanted thoughts were racing through Mike's head. Maybe Jessie *did* somehow provoke Andy, and maybe she didn't do enough to try to get away. She hadn't done what he told her, or she would've gotten away. He didn't want to think those horrible things, but he was so jealous. He understood her weakness, when anyone paid attention to her, and how easy she was to seduce. He tried not to believe what Andy said, but was finding himself obsessed with the idea that maybe Jessie did like Andy, and that's why she told him where she was going. But he was horrified at what happened to her, and thankful she wasn't seriously injured. He kept telling himself, it couldn't have been Jessie's fault. It's stupid to even think it. Andy was all over her, and he knew what a creep Andy could be. Jessie was too tiny to get away from him. He really wanted to call the Sheriff, but didn't want to put Jessie through all that, especially, with her dad finding out. He was seriously contemplating murder. He needed to talk to her, to ask her what happened. He couldn't sleep all night, suffering anxiety.

Luke tormented all night as well. He couldn't decide if he wanted to turn Andy in, or go kill him; or at least beat him up some more. His heart was aching and hurting for Jessie.

Sunday, January 20, 1974

In the morning, Jessie woke up on the couch, with Eli sitting at her feet. He was eating a bowl of cereal, watching Lassie on television. George and Gracie were watching him, begging for food. There was a knock at the door, and the dogs went off like a couple of wild banshees screaming. Eli yelled at them to be quiet and went to open the door. It was a flower delivery for Jessie.

Eli brought in the beautiful bouquet of six, dark, red roses, in a lovely, clear, red vase. He set them on the coffee table. Right away, Jessie knew they were from Luke, and sat up, taking the card off the holder. She opened it and it read:

I'm sorry I didn't get there soon enough, baby.
I wish I was better at protecting you.
I love you, bunny. Mikey

Jessie put the card back in the envelope, and took it to her room, hiding it in her backpack. Then she put the flowers on the dining room table, touching one. Debbie came into the kitchen and smiled. "Who sent you flowers, sweetheart? Luke?"

Jessie nodded. "He felt bad about me hurting myself yesterday."

"Well, you don't seem very happy about them, sweetheart. Are you feeling any better today?" Debbie asked, hugging her and re-examining her lip.

"Yes, Momma," Jessie answered glumly. She was quite depressed.

"Well, smile, Jessie, they're beautiful, and don't be sad. You get to stay with us for a long time! Your Uncle has a contractor coming this week to start working on our bedroom downstairs, and it won't be any time at all until you have your own room!"

Jessie wanted to be happy about staying there a long time, and having her own room, but it seemed at times she was not anymore happy there than she was at home. The incident the day before was so traumatic that her body felt like it was shutting down. She didn't want to feel unhappy at her Auntie's house, because that's where she wanted to be. She didn't quite understand her own feelings. She wasn't free and there was guilt and too many secrets to keep. She was tormented by the feelings she had for the boys and couldn't see an answer. All she could feel was pain and sadness. Everything reminded her of Ricky, and it was so hard not to think about him and cry. There was a sense of emptiness. It was a lot of work having so many people around her. She was used to being alone and only having to think about her chores or homework.

She felt tired all the time now, and her headaches were more painful and more frequent. Her relationships with Mike and Luke were causing her to feel so torn apart. She loved to be with each of them, but when she was, she felt sad, like it was hopeless and didn't see if there was a point or a direction.

When she was with Mike, all she could think about was that she was going to have to leave him again, and the future with him was black with no sense of a peaceful ending.

When she was with Luke, she felt like she couldn't give him what he needed and deserved, like she had gotten in the way, keeping him from his destiny, holding him back from being whatever he was meant to be. Her experience with regular school made her shiver. It seemed so erratic, not the controlled environment she was used to. She was finding that the outside world was scary, that boys are not always so nice, and although she was going to be at her Aunt's for a while, even that was uncertain. Maddy was desperate to have a boyfriend and be like Jessie, but Jessie wanted to tell her that having a boyfriend was painful, and that being Jessie was sad and uncertain. She felt like she'd been neglecting Jessie, too, not practicing her violin or guitar, or listening to music. Not drawing or reading. Not going to school with Mother or seeing Luke at lunch anymore. The only constant thing was her Aunt, who she hadn't been paying enough attention to and she wanted her to know how much she loved her.

Luke came to see Jessie in the morning. He had taken the day off and wanted to spend it with her. He wanted to know she was okay.

"Thank you for the flowers," she told Luke when he came in the door, giving him a look.

He smiled. "You're welcome, Jessie."

"Come sit by me, Lukiss," Jessie said, and he sat next to her on the couch. She put her head on his shoulder. "They're from Mikey," she whispered.

"I know." He put his hand around her head, kissing her eye. "I was gonna buy you some, too, till I heard Mike this mornin' on the phone."

"Luke, I don't remember if I told you about my Daddy going to Mexico and letting me stay here and play in the band."

"Mexico? Really, baby? You get to stay here?"

"Yep, I have to start rehearsing tomorrow night."

"I wonder why you're Dad has suddenly let you go so long."

"I don't know, and I don't care. I'm glad he did... Well, he said he was seeing some woman, and I'm suspicious about that."

"Suspicious? How come?" Luke smiled.

"Why is he doing that?"

Why do you care, baby? Luke thought. "I don't know, baby. I think his ideas of what's important are kinda jaded."

Luke could see that Jessie's face was changing. Not that she'd ever been a really happy girl, but somehow, she seemed different, distant. He didn't know how to take that away. He couldn't be with her enough to keep her safe.

"Jessie, I want to talk to you, today."

Jessie looked up at Luke, knowing he was going to want to talk about *them* again, and maybe this time he was going to tell her she had to make a choice.

"It's not about that," he said to her right away, seeing the worried look in her eyes. He stoked her cheek. "I wanna talk
about *you*, darlin'. I think you just need to talk, and maybe you'll feel better. Get dressed, baby, and we'll go somewhere."

Jessie nodded glumly and went to get dressed.

"I'd like to take Jessie to Reno today, if that's all right?" Luke asked Debbie, who always seemed to be in the kitchen.

"Reno, is it," Debbie said, pouring herself a cup of coffee. "Those roses are beautiful. Going anywhere in particular?"

"No, just to go," Luke said, deciding to take her to the cabin. He wanted to be alone with her, and she liked it there. She had things going on in her head, and maybe she just needed to talk about them, freely. After what she had gone through yesterday, he wanted her to know she was still a good girl, and that it wasn't her fault.

Jessie fastened her seat belt and looked up at Luke as he started the car.

"Luke, this is just like before, when you would come get me at school, isn't it?"

"Yep, only better, darlin'."

"This time, we don't have to hide, Luke. This time we're not hiding."

"Nope. We can see each other almost whenever we want now, baby." He smiled at her. He looked back and pulled away from the curb.

"Isn't that so wonderful, Luke? Are we going to the cabin?"

"Is that okay, baby?"

"Yes, I want to go there, to our house, just me and you."

"You wanna eat first, darlin'?"

"My tummy hurts, I don't think so."

"You really need to eat more. I think you're losing weight, and you don't weigh anything as it is."

"Are you hungry, Luke, because you can go eat if you want?"

"Yeah, I'm hungry."

They stopped at the Golden Nugget before leaving town. Jessie was quiet and only ate part of Luke's breakfast, and drank some apple juice. The ride to the cabin was a quiet one. Jessie lay back in her seat, closing her eyes. She was so tired. Luke held her hand all the way there, except to shift gears.

The cabin was chilly inside. Luke turned up the thermostat and started a fire right away. Jessie plopped down on the sofa, one leg on the sofa, and one leg hanging over the side. She didn't understand why she was so tired. Luke sat down above her and took his boots off, putting his feet up on the coffee table. Jessie laid her head in his lap. She put her hand up to his mouth and caressed his face.

"You're tho handsome." She smiled up at him. "I feel safe here, Luke. Nobody knows where I am, 'cept you."

Luke smiled and gently traced Jessie's lips with his finger.

"Your mouth is all hurt. I love you, Jessie. I wish I could take yesterday away from you. I don't want you going anywhere alone anymore, baby."

"Luke, I miss you picking me up at school. That feels like such a long time ago. I liked it when you would come get me. You helped take away my sadness from leaving my Auntie's house. I don't want to go back home, but I miss being with you."

"That's one of the reasons why I came, Jessie. I knew how lonely you were. Sometimes I felt like it only made things worse for you, though."

"Is that why you stopped coming for a while?"

"Yeah, that, and because I knew you were with Ricky," Luke answered, caressing Jessie's face.

"I was tho sad when you didn't come. I would wait by the steps, but you didn't come."

"I didn't know if you really wanted me to, darlin'."

"I didn't know either; I dis knew I was sad when you didn't come."

"I wish I would've known that, Jessie, I would have come.
I hate you to be sad. But you're at your Aunt house now, baby. You don't have to feel that sadness anymore.

"Lay down by me, Luke."

Luke lay down next to Jessie, leaning his head up on his arm, looking down at her pretty little face.

"Luke, sometimes I feel like I wasn't really meant to go to my Auntie's. I feel like it was not the right thing. Like a mistake in time."

"Why, baby?"

"Because, all I did by coming is made people unhappy, and I think it wasn't really 'spose to be for me to come." Jessie's eyes were filling up with tears. "And now, you and Mikey are fighting, and you don't like each other, now, and it's my fault. When I'm with you, I want to be Jessie Miller and live
in our own house and go to college together. And when I'm with Mikey, I want to be Jessie Miller and live with Mikey in our own house and I know how awful that must be for you and Mikey, because I love you both so much...I can never really be with either one of you." Jessie put her hand over her mouth, tapping her finger nervously on her lip, trying not to cry, but her voice was trembling. "That's why I think I wasn't really meant to come...I think something happened that was a mistake. Because if I never came...then Ricky would still be here, and I wouldn't have ruined your life." Jessie could barely contain her tears.

"It wasn't your fault about Ricky, or Mike and me fighting," Luke said, stroking her hair away from her face. "Don't ever think that, my sweet, little love, and you haven't ruined my life, darlin'."

"Yeth, I did. You used to have a normal life, with your own girlfriend, and now, you don't… Now, you don't have…everything looks black to me when I think about the future, like it's black and there's no light, and I don't want to be at my home, either, because I know I don't belong there, either. I don't really belong at my Auntie's either, because I'm not like them. I feel like someone looking in the window. I don't think I really belong anywhere, because there's no real place for me to be. I know I'm stupid and I'm not normal, and if my Daddy would have died and not my Mommy, I don't think I would be this way. I think I was 'spose to die with my Momma, but I didn't and now here I am, in the wrong place…I feel like I'm falling, and I miss Ricky."

Luke's heart was breaking for Jessie and he wanted to comfort her just then, but he wanted to let her talk and try to work it out in her head.

"Luke, do you think it's my fault that Andy did that to me? Because I didn't do what Mikey told me to do? I didn't run away and scream. I didn't do that right away. I let Andy take me away, and I didn't scream, because I didn't know what he was doing, until he picked me up and put his hand on my mouth. He said I was flirting with him, because I kept looking at him," Jessie sobbed, shaking her head. "But I only looked at him…because I was afraid of him and…I wanted to see if he was still looking at me."

"What happened, baby?" Luke asked, holding her hand and stroking her face.

"Then he took me to the bathroom and locked the door and put his hand on my mouth because I was screaming. He kept saying he wasn't going to hurt me, he dis wanted to make love to me, but I kept screaming, and he said, 'I don't want to hurt you, but I will if you don't stop screaming', and he hit my face and pinched my lips together. Then I dis laid there, because I was afraid he would hurt me, and he was so heavy, and I kept saying no, you're not 'pose to touch me, and he was hurting my arms and being ugly to me."

Luke could see Jessie's arms bruised and it took every ounce of strength he could muster not to freak out. "Well, Jessie, you don't love Andy, do you?"

"No!"

"See, you don't love everyone that has sex with you."
Luke smiled. "You didn't do anything wrong, baby, and no, it wasn't your fault at all."

"You're right, Luke, I don't. Luke, you're right."

"Come sit up here in my lap, darlin'," Luke said, pulling Jessie up close. "What Andy did to you was wrong. Mike and I did the wrong thing, too, Jessie. We both did the same thing Andy did, just not *like* he did. We both had sex with you by seducing you, and not letting you decide if that's what you wanted. Mike and I ruined *your* life, Jessie. You didn't ruin ours or anyone else's. Mike and I should have known better, because we knew more about it than you did.

Everyone around you has done the wrong thing with you, baby. You haven't done anything wrong. You're the good girl that all the people are bad to, because you love everyone so much." Luke's eyes began to water, and he sniffed. "So, if our lives are unhappy, it's our fault, not yours, and you can go anywhere, live anywhere, and love whoever you want, and if one of us gets hurt, then it's our own fault, not yours. You have a God given right to make your own choices in life, Jessie, and do what you want, not what we want you to do. Do you understand that, baby?"

Jessie nodded, and with tears in their eyes and sadness in their hearts, they stayed silent for a while, looking into each other's eyes, and after a bit, Luke said, "I think Andy should go to jail for what he did to you. What he did was against the law and he hurt you, he violated you. The only thing is…he won't go if you don't tell the police. If you tell the police, then your Aunt, your Dad, and everyone else will have to get involved. Then you'll have to go to the hospital to get checked out and go to court and tell them what happened. I don't know if you're strong enough to go through all of that, and I don't want you to if you don't want to. I'm only telling you this because Andy committed a crime against you, and if he gets away with it, he could do it again, to you or someone else, and maybe really hurt someone next time. Do you want him to go to jail, Jessie?"

"I have to think about that, Luke. I'm too tired to right now."

"It's okay, Jessie. I don't really want you to go through all that. I really want to go beat the shit out of him some more, though. Would that make you feel better? I know it would make me feel better."

"No, Luke. I don't want you to do that. Would you dis lay here and hold me, Luke?"

"I'll do whatever you want me to," Luke said, laying his head down on hers, holding her tight against him.

"When I'm with you, Luke, I don't feel tho dumb, like I do with Mikey."

"That's because Mike doesn't want you to grow up. He wants you to stay a little baby, because he knows he can't always do the right thing with you. I want you to grow up and be a successful young woman, because that's how it's supposed to be."

"Do you want to go to college with me, Luke?"

"I would like that a lot."

"I think I would be okay going to college with you, Luke. Not like when I go to school with Mikey. I need to learn things, not just memorize things. That's what Mr. Leland said."

"What do you wanna do when you grow up, Jessie?"

"I dis want to be like my Auntie, who takes care of her family, and makes them laugh and do what they're 'spose to do…Luke, I need you. I need you to take care of me. You're tho good to me. I want to be your little baby girl. I don't want to grow up right now."

"Well, it's too late, darlin', you're already growing up, every second."

"Luke, my Aunt and Uncle are making me my own room now, next week."

"Well then, I guess you do belong there, Jessie."

"I think I feel better now, Luke. I don't feel so sad now."

"That's good, baby. What happened yesterday would make anyone feel sad. I feel sad about it. You just need to talk
about things sometimes, and you can talk to me about anything. When you're feeling sad, remember it doesn't last forever. Some days we just feel sad, but usually we feel okay."

"I love you, Luke," Jessie said, putting her arms tightly around him. "Thank you, Luke, for loving me so much. Kiss me. Just kiss me and hold me, hold me tight, Luke."

At five p.m., the bleachers were starting to fill up and the boy's locker room was a little quieter than usual. Every so often, one of the boys would look over at Mike or Andy, but nobody dared to say anything, at least, not out loud. Coach Reed came in and noticed Andy's swollen, black and blue face. He was about to speak when Mike stood up off the bench after wrapping his knee and looked over at the coach. His face didn't look much better.

"I wanna see you two after the game," Is all the coach said, and turned around. "All right, listen up," he began as the boys all took their places around the room for their pep talk.

Twilight had also taken its place in the western sky, as Jessie stood with her family, Luke, and Mrs. Willis, down by the field. She was shivering cold and nervous, waiting to be announced. Luke stood behind her for a moment, rubbing her shoulders and whispered to her, "You'll be terrific, darlin'."

Jessie nodded and wiped her cold, runny, nose, sniffling. Sissy noticed Luke holding Jessie, and was perplexed, and still somewhat jolted.

There was a cool breeze on the field, and while the western sky was a still yellow, the eastern sky was darkening blue, and the stars in between began to twinkle. The bright lights were shining down on field with the school band, and the cheerleaders gearing up.

The teams walked out onto the field and began their warm-ups. The announcer came on over the loud speakers. After a discussion of both teams' stats, the teams lined up on the field, and the announcer finally introduced Jessie. His voice echoed loudly over the field.

"Ladies and Gentlemen, please stand with Miss Jessica Nelson of St. Thomas School, in the National Anthem."

Jessie stood up to the microphone and nervously looked around, astounded at how quiet the crowd suddenly became, as everyone stood up. She closed her eyes and began to play. She didn't want to look at anyone, especially Mike. Never the less, Mike's eyes were fixed on her. Midway through the song, her fears subsided, and she opened her eyes to glance over at Mike. Jessie's performance, as usual, was perfect, and the crowd cheered most profoundly. Jessie went to sit with her family, Luke, and Mr. and Mrs. Miller, in the bleachers. She was delighted to finally be watching her first football game; Mike's football game.

The announcer introduced all the players and the game got underway. After a listless first half, the score was tied at seven to seven. Luke was irritated and didn't feel Andy was giving it his all. He'd been explaining the plays to Jessie and she could tell he was not very happy.

"They're gonna hafta play a lot better than this, Jessie," Luke said, putting his arm around her. In the locker room, the coach ripped everyone a new one.

The second half began with the Miner's kicking off. The Mucker's received, running the ball to their own forty-yard line. Luke was beside himself, cursing, and Jessie had never seen him quite like this. The third quarter finished with the score, Mining seven and Tonopah ten.

Luke stood up as the Mucker's scored the last touchdown, hollering, "Come on you idiots, wake up and play!"

Mr. Miller and Uncle Harry both seemed unhappy as well and were also yelling down at the team.

In her excitement, Jessie stood up, too. "Yeah," Jessie imitated Luke, "Wake up, idiots!" However, after she realized she'd just called Mike an idiot, she put her hand over her mouth and sat back down.

The tension was building and halfway through the fourth quarter, Gary, the Miner's running back, and Mike's best friend, got tackled by the safety, running down the sidelines, near the forty-five-yard line, in Miner's territory. He fell back, twisting his ankle. The coach called a time out and the trainers ran out to check on Gary, who is noticeably distressed. They walk Gary off the field. The coach is out of options at the running back position. He scratches his head looking toward the field and yells to Mike.

"Miller! Take Gary's place!"

Andy looks over at the coach and snaps, "What?!"

The offensive coordinator sends in a running play. The ball is snapped, but Andy purposely hands it off to Mike low, and throws his shoulder into Mike, causing him to fumble. The Mucker's recover the ball on the Miner's forty-eight-yard line.

"What the hell was that?" Luke jumped up yelling.

"Did you see that?" Mr. Miller shouted. "What's wrong with that damn quarterback!"

On the sideline, with only three and a half minutes left in the game, the coach pulls Andy and Mike aside.

"You two wanna lose this game because you got some beef going on between you, you better think again, and get your shit together."

The Mucker's go three and out and punt the ball to their twenty-five-yard line. Kevin makes a spectacular run back to the Miner's eighteen-yard line. The offensive unit comes out with a minute left in the game. On the first play, Andy throws the pass out of bounds. With time running out, the coach sends in a running play, but this time Mike is on to Andy's attempt to discredit him. The ball is snapped. Andy turns to Mike, but Mike's ready. He leans forward anticipating that Andy will try to hand it to him low. Mike picks the ball off his shoelace. He knocks Andy over, running towards the Mucker's defense to score a touchdown just as time expires. The Miner's win the game at thirteen to ten! The sidelines run over and jump all over Mike. Andy picks himself off the ground, dejected and takes off his helmet as he walks over to Mike.

"Nice play, Miller," Andy says.

Luke jumped up hollering, and Jessie jumped up wrapping her arms around him. "We won the game, Luke!"

"Yes, we did, baby!" Luke smiled, holding Jessie and kissed her face. "Mike won the game."

~

Mike called Jessie at nine p.m. He was tired, but he was worried about her.

"Hi, Mikey." Jessie answered, glumly.

"Hi, Beautiful. What are you doin', baby?"

"Watching TV."

"I miss you."

"Mikey, I cut my hair."

"What? Baby, please, tell me you didn't?"

"Yeah, because I want it short like Aimee's.

"Baby, no. I love your hair. Damn-it, Jessie."

"I want it short, so boys won't like me, now, and I'll be ugly..."

Chapter Sixteen - Understandings

Jessie had to see Mike. She needed to feel his big, strong arms around her. She left her bed as soon as she felt it was safe. When she got to Mike's door, she pulled her jacket up over her head, so that her eyes were barely peeking out, and quietly, she went in. He was leaning up on his arm, waiting for her.

"Lock it," he said, putting out his cigarette.

Jessie locked the door and stood looking at him, as though she were in big trouble.

His face was stern. "Come 'ere. Let me see you... Whad'you do to yourself."

She ran over to Mike, falling into his arms. "Mikey," she pouted, looking up at him.

Gently, he pulled her jacket down off her head. He smiled. "I thought you cut your hair?"

"I did, right here, see?" She pointed to a finger-pinch of spiked hair, sticking up from her forehead. "I was going to cut some more, but Maddy yelled at me when she saw me with Momma's scissors in the bathroom."

"I would've spanked yer ass." Mike gazed lovingly into her eyes. "We gotta stop meeting like this, little girl." He smiled, smoothing his hands all over her body. "You sweet, young thing," he said, kissing her lips. "You could never be ugly, baby. Even if you were bald."

"Oh, Mikey," Jessie whispered, panting right away. "I love you, I love you, Mikey," she said, squirming in his arms, desperately wanting to be close to him. "Mikey, my big strong boy, my lover boy." She caressed Mike's chest and face, longing to feel his touch.

"Damn, Jessie," Mike said, breathing heavy. "Damn, baby," he whispered, kissing her neck. Mike stroked Jessie's face, gazing deeply in her eyes. "Baby I love you, I love you so much, baby girl."

"Hold me, Mikey, hold me tight." Jessie's face was distressed, and a tear fell down her cheek. "Don't be mad at me, Mikey, please, don't be mad at me."

"I'm not mad at you, peanut," he said, pulling her close.

"I think you are, Mikey. I think you are mad at me."

"Baby, tell me you didn't want Andy."

"Mikey, I didn't do it; I didn't, Mikey."

"Why did you have that dress on?"

"Because, Maddy gave it to me, so we would be matching. I-I screamed like you said, Mikey. Not at first, but then I did. He said he didn't want to hurt me, but he would if I didn't stop screaming." Jessie kissed Mike's face, wildly, rubbing his chest, crying with big tears running down her face. "He...he slapped me in my face...he...he hurt my mouth...Mikey, I don't know what you want me to do. You want me to be thexy, but you don't want me to be thexy. I don't know what you want me to do, Mikey. Please don't be mad at me. I would be tho afraid if you stopped loving me. Please love me, Mikey."

"I do love you, baby. Oh, baby." Mike wiped her tears and kissed her face. "I'm not mad at you, Jessie. I love you so much. I'm so sorry, baby. I know you're a good girl."

"I don't love Andy, Mikey," Jessie sniffed.

"I know you don't. I don't know why I asked you that. I know you love me. I'm just so jealous, I'm so damn jealous. I never thought I'd ever be jealous of anyone, but...you're so beautiful. I'm afraid someone's gonna take you away from me."

"Where are they gonna take me to, Mikey?"

"Jessie," Mike sighed, holding her tight. "I used to think I was too good for anyone, that no one would ever be good enough for me. I realize, now, I'm not good enough for anyone, especially not you, Jessie. I'm so sorry. I can't ever do anything right with you. I'm mad at me, Jessie, not you. You're such a good girl. Don't feel like it was your fault. I love you. I'm sorry he did that to you, baby, my bunny girl," Mike said, caressing her arms. A teardrop fell from his nose. "I want you to be sexy for *me,* bunny, just me. When I get stupid, just tell me, bunny. Tell me I'm being stupid...*sniff*... I used to dream about having a little blonde-haired, blue-eyed girl like you. I just didn't know she would be so beautiful. You're so beautiful."

"Mikey?"

"What, peanut?"

"Can I tell you something 'portent?"

"What, baby?" Mike asked, stroking the hair from her forehead.

"You're good enough. You're good, Mikey."

"I'm gonna buy you something pretty, Jessie. Friday, I'm gonna take you shopping and we won't go to school that day."

"And candy too, Mikey, because I like chocolate. Would you take me to *7-11*, and buy me a chocolate?"

"You like chocolate, don't you?" Mike smiled, kissing her nose.

"Mm hm." Jessie nodded, tracing his lips, with her finger. "Um, Mikey?"

"Mm?"

"You bought me flowers."

"Yeah."

"I love them."

Mike lay down with Jessie and sighed, "Jessie, I wanted to be mad at you the other morning for leaving my bed, and going to Luke's, but after I saw you in that nightie, and in those pictures, and doing what you did, well, I wasn't mad anymore. I was scared. I realized how lost I'd be without you. I'm sorry I don't think to do things for you like Luke does. He's had a lot of practice at being a boyfriend. Jessie, I haven't had any. It's not that I don't want to do things for you; I just don't think fast enough to do them. Baby, you're the only girlfriend I've ever had."

"I know, Mikey, I know, I'm you're only one."

"You are, baby. The only girl I'll ever want. I don't know what I'd do if I ever lost you. I'd be lost. Forgive me if I'm a little slow, I'm learnin'. Your Aunt talked about you all the time when we were kids, we just never paid attention. I wish I would have. I wish I would have asked her about you. You were there all along, Jessie, in another world. If we would have known you, maybe you could've been with us, and we would have all loved you then, like we do now. I'm sorry you weren't here with us. You needed us, and we needed you, baby. I'm so glad I met you, Jessie."

"Mikey, I'm so glad I met you too, but…sometimes I'm sad about it. I think sometimes I should not have met you."

"I know, Jessie. I know how you feel. When you're older, you'll be free, and you won't feel far away from us like you do now. You won't be taken away from us like you are now."

"My Auntie loves me, Mikey. She wants me to be her little girl, now," Jessie whispered.

"I know. She's always wanted you.

"You saved me, Mikey. You saved me from Andy."

"I didn't save you fast enough." Mike gently kissed her hurt lip, looking at the slight bruise on her cheek. He broke down and started to cry. "Oh baby," he said, and put his head down on hers. "I'm so sorry he did that to you, Jessie. I'm so glad you're okay. I was scared you wouldn't want me, anymore. I was scared you wouldn't want me to touch you, anymore."

Jessie stroked Mike's face, touching his black eye. "I'm sorry too, Mikey, that he did that, and you had to fight him. I was scared too, Mikey. I was scared he was hurting you, and was killing you, and you would be mad at me. Please love me, Mikey." Jessie turned and pushed her hair up over her head, so she could tangle her hands up in it. Mike caressed her back, kissing her neck, while she closed her eyes.

"Mikey, tell me about something nice. Tell me about Christmas, when you were a little boy. Did Santa Claus bring you a present?"

"Mm hm," Mike said, rubbing her arm.

"Because you were good and not naughty?" Jessie said, beginning to cry, again.

"I thought you wanted to talk about something nice. Why are you crying, peanut?"

"Santa brought you a present… because you were a good boy," Jessie sniffled.

"You and your little cry baby motor," Mike said, stroking her face. "You were a good girl, sweetheart."

"No. Santa Cl-aus, he ne-ever came."

"Jessie, how were you ever bad?"

"I don't know," she sniffed. "Because I'm stupid."

Mike took Jessie's face in his hand. "Jessie, can I tell you something 'portent? There's no such thing as Santa. Santa's not real, just like fairies or monsters aren't real. It's just a made-up person that parents tell their kids about for fun."

Jessie looked up at Mike. "I saw him in the book, Mikey. I saw him in my book and he brought all the good children presents, and I saw the fairies. Fairies *are* real! I saw all the fairies coming to me and…and…"

"Baby, your dad just never bought you anything, that's all."

"I know that, I know, Mikey." Jessie nodded, wiping her face. "But I saw the fairies."

"Is that what you think, Love? Your dad thinks you're stupid, and that's why he doesn't do anything for you?"

"Yeah."

"Well, it's not true. He's just not a good person. You just got stuck with an idiot for an old man. If he were good, he would know what a wonderful little daughter you are, and he would've done good by you. You have to stop caring about what he thinks now, and know how beautiful and sweet you are, and what a good person you are, and how much everyone else loves you. You know that?"

Jessie nodded, looking into Mike's eyes.

"I'll buy you a ton of presents, next year." Mike smiled.

"My Auntie bought me presents, and my Uncle, and Pete and Lisa, and your mom and dad."

"See, you're gonna have a lot of presents, Jessie, now that you have a lot of people that love you. I don't want you to call yourself stupid ever again, you hear me, Jessie?"

"Mikey, Maddy says you wouldn't love me if I wasn't pretty."

"Jessie, stop listening to Maddy, she's just jealous."

"Mikey, if I was ugly, but I was still Jessie, would you love me?"

Mike didn't want to answer that, because the answer would be sad and impossible.

"Yes, but probably not like I do now. You have to be attracted to someone first, before you find out if you like them or not. I don't know, baby. I'm in love with your inside beauty, Jessie, not just how beautiful you are.

"So, then you would think I'm just a stupid, ugly, retarded girl and you would be mean to me."

Mike's face became distraught, looking at her.

"Are you crying, Mikey?"

"Jessie, this question really upsets me. I can't imagine being without you, no matter what you look like. But I already love you, now. I was willing to get to know you because of how
attracted I was to you. It makes me terrified to think of what a
beautiful, sweet person I could have missed out on, if I wasn't attracted to you. In fact, it scares the hell out of me."

"Mikey, you are crying."

"It makes me sad when you think about yourself as stupid or retarded, you're brilliant, you have no idea how talented and wonderful I think you are...And don't cut your hair and try to be ugly. I understand why you thought that way, but don't. You be proud of the beautiful, little lady you are. I guess I just have to get to know a person before I think about how they look from now
on. I don't want to miss out anymore, baby. I think eventually, you would have made me care about you, because you're so sweet and beautiful on the inside. That's what makes me love you more. Is how beautiful you are inside, but I'm

glad you're not ugly." Mike smiled. "And you should be, too. Would you wanna make love to me if I were ugly?"

"You mean like Kevin?"

Mike laughed, "You think Kevin's ugly?"

"Yes," she pouted.

"Why, baby? He's not ugly."

"He's not?"

"Not really."

"But I don't want to make love to him." Jessie frowned.

"I'm glad, peanut." Mike grinned. "Cuz I'd beat his face in, and then he would be ugly."

"Kevin is stupid, Mikey, and he makes you stupid. You should not listen to him. He doesn't care about people."

"He is kinda careless. I guess I've been careless, too."

"Mikey, when you're a cop, are you going to get all the bad guys?"

"Oh…I forgot to tell you my good news, peanut. I talked to the Sheriff, Jessie. They're gonna be hiring more officers this summer."

"Mikey, what if the bad guys shoot you?" Jessie asked, just as some dogs over on the next street started barking. "They sound like the coyotes, why do they keep howling?" Jessie hid under the blanket. "I hate dogs barking."

"It's just dogs, Jessie, barking at each other. I'm right here." Mike rubbed her back. "It's just part of the job, babe, a risk you take when you dedicate yourself to being a good cop."

"Are you going there?"

"Yep, in July. I'm gonna apply and see what happens."

"Mikey, I'm afraid about that. I was tho afraid when you were fighting, yesterday. I was afraid you were getting hurt."

"I'll kill anyone that touches you. Don't be afraid."

"And you will kill Andy, now?" Jessie said, touching his swollen lip.

"No. He won't touch you anymore. I don't mean I'd really kill anyone, bunny, just mess 'em up real bad."

"Are you still taking me to school?"

"Course I am."

"Mikey, Luke said you won the game."

"Yeah, I guess so. I was proud of you playing the violin. It gave me goose bumps, listening to you play.

"I'm tired, Mikey. Lay on me, tho no one can thee me. Wake me up when it's time to go," Jessie yawned, closing her eyes.

Monday, January 21, 1974

"I feel soft, little kisses on my face," Jessie sang sleepily, still too tired to open her eyes. She felt Mike's warm breath on her face, as he smiled, admiring her.

He caressed her cheeks with his lips. "Good mornin', Beautiful, my sleeping beauty."

"Is tomorrow the doctor, Mikey?" she asked from underneath his warm body.

"At one o'clock, peanut." He said and petted the sides of her face.

"I don't want to go no more, baba. I don't need to go no more, now."

"Yes, we have to go, Jessie. You go get ready for school, now. Wear whatever you want, and we'll stop at *7-11*."

"I'm afraid to go home. What if Momma sees me? She said she was going to give me a spanking."

Mike laughed. "I don't know, baby. You'll just have to tell her. Come *own*, peanut, go get ready for school."

"All right, Mikey," she sighed, getting up. Quietly, she slipped out of the Miller's house and ran across the street.

Ready and waiting, Jessie ran down the stairs as soon as she heard Mike start the Chevelle. She was wearing her Levi's, tennies, and the pale-yellow, angora sweater that her Aunt bought her for Christmas. She ran over to her side of the car as Mike watched her get in. He was letting the car idle, with his long leg resting outside the open door, blowing smoke rings.

"These Chevy's are so damn cold-blooded in the mornings," he said, tossing his cigarette out and closed his door.

Jessie turned toward Mike, leaning her head on the seat with her legs folded up tight in front of her. Mike pulled away from the curb and leaned over, pulling Jessie to him. "You're so sweet, my tittie girl," he said. "Come sit by me."

Jessie moved over next to Mike and he put his arm in front of her, rubbing her leg. Jessie held onto his arm and leaned her head on his shoulder.

"You're so soft and cute in that yellow sweater, bunny."

"Mikey, your lip is still sore. Is Andy going to be at school?"

"Don't worry about it, baby. I'm not lettin' you outta my sight."

"Mikey, I don't want the doctor. I'm afraid he's going to make me pick, and I don't want to. I'm afraid he's going to make me not want you no more. That's why we're going, isn't it?"

Mike hesitated to answer. He held Jessie against him and

put his head down on hers. "It is one of the reasons, Jessie. It's scary for me, too, bunny, and I don't know what's gonna happen. But we can't go own like this forever, either."

"I don't want to talk about the monster, Mikey. I'm afraid."

"We have to, Jessie. I'll be with you, so you don't have to be afraid."

"Momma says I have to go back to my school next week. I'm going to miss you, Mikey."

"Me too, bunny," Mike said, squeezing her tight. "At least you get to come home to us, though."

Jessie nodded. "I start my practice with the band, tonight."

"Where are you practicing?"

"At Mark's house."

"Is he in the band? Who's taking you, Jessie?" Mike asked, suddenly worried about her practicing with strangers.

"Momma and Pete are driving me. I have to go almost every day."

"How many guys are in the band?"

"Four."

"What are they like? How old are they?"

"I don't know. Mikey, don't worry; I learned my lesson about you boys. Mark is the leader and he sings. He has long, gold hair and furry cheeks, like you," Jessie giggled. "Alex plays the bass. He's not too friendly. I don't think he likes me."

"Hmm, good, he's an idiot, but that's good."

"Chris is the drummer and Jeff plays the keyboard. They were nice to me. They mostly play Led Zeppelin songs, but they want to try out some Black Sabbath, because Mark said I play Sabbath tho good.

"That's far-out, Jessie. I'm proud of you but stay right with your Aunt. Don't go off by yourself with any of them."

"I'm not, Mikey, I know."

Mike was suddenly unhappy about Jessie playing in a band with four men. He wanted to go with her but knew that wouldn't be possible.

"I think Luke should go with you, baby. Just to make sure you're okay."

"Can't you go with me, Mikey?"

"I don't think your Aunt would understand that, bunny. I'll call Luke today, after school."

"Don't you work, tonight, baba?"

"Yeah, I do, bunny."

~

Andy came to school but avoided Mike. He skipped Mr. Leland's class. Neither one said anything much to Coach. Gary and Kevin asked Mike what happened, but he just told them 'nothing'. Jessie felt somewhat depressed all day and didn't talk much. She was anxious about going to the doctor, and about going back to St. Thomas. Mike could tell she was still upset about Saturday and did his best to be sweet to her all day. He would have killed Andy if it weren't for going to jail but decided to leave it alone for now. He'd been in a fight three times over Jessie and wondered if he was going to have to fight these stupid fuckers off her for the rest of his life.

~

When Jessie got home from school, there were two construction trucks parked in front of the house. She ran inside, excited to see how things were going. There were some workers making noise in the basement. She went right to the kitchen, where Debbie was starting dinner.

"Hi, Momma, are they making your room, now?" Jessie asked grinning and set her backpack on the bar stool.

"Yep, the sure are." Debbie said, smiling. "How was school?"

"Good. Can we go see downstairs?"

"Yes, after the men leave. I made some brownies; would you like one?" Debbie asked, setting the tray of brownies down on the bar.

"Yes, please," Jessie said, taking one. "Momma, do I have to go back to St. Thomas?"

"Don't you want to, Jessie?"

"No, I want to go to Mining, like the girls. I like Mining. People are nice to me."

Debbie stopped peeling her potato and wiped her hands off on her towel. She went to Jessie and wrapped her arms around her.

"I wish I could say yes, Jessie. With all my heart, I do. Hopefully, Sweetheart, you will soon. We'll just have to pray about it. I want you to go where you're happy."

"I know, Momma. I love you, Momma."

"I love you, so much, Jessie," Debbie said, just as Aimee and Maddy came in the door.

As soon as Eli got home, the kids all wanted to go see the excitement downstairs and were allowed to go look for a few minutes. Seeing the work get started on the bedroom downstairs, helped Jessie to feel hopeful, like maybe things would be better.

The phone rang as they were coming back upstairs, and Jessie ran to answer it this time.

"Hi pretty blue eyes."

"Luke!" Jessie said. "I answered the phone in my house!"

"It is your house, baby. I'll be there as soon as I get off work, darlin'. I already talked to Momma about going with you to your practice."

"You're going with me, Luke?" Jessie asked, excitedly.

"Of course, I am. You don't think I'd let you hang out with a bunch of guys without me, do ya?"

"I'm glad you're coming with me, Luke. I want you there, Luke. You belong there with me."

"I'll see you in just a little bit, love bug."

"Okay, Luke, my Lukiss."

♫

Pete came and drove Debbie, Jessie, and Luke to Mark's house. Mark had a big ranch style home out in Washoe Valley. He had turned the huge family room into a studio. Mark was professional and very serious about his music. He and his girlfriend, Ana, were more than hospitable, making sure everyone felt comfortable and at home. Ana, a health food junkie, kept offering everyone alfalfa and tomato sandwiches, with homemade vegetable juice. She was a new-age flower child, with long, ash blond hair and blue eyes. She was twenty, and not much bigger than Jessie. Luke was impressed and felt right away that Jessie would be okay with the band. Even Alex seemed to have changed since Jessie met him last time. They were all eager to start practicing for the Rock Fest.

Jessie was nervous at first and was worried about going to the doctor. Once they started playing, though, she felt more at ease, feeling good at finally putting her talents to use.

Luke noticed she seemed to lead without leading. He was anxious to see Jessie play for the first time. He and Eli were thrilled to come and watch. Luke had goose bumps all evening, totally impressed with Jessie. She knocked his socks off!

Debbie was pleased and happy for Jessie, but she was finding it difficult to get comfortable. The music was so loud.

Ana felt bad for her and gave her a tour of the huge house. Ana was creating a vegetable garden in the field out back. Debbie was quite impressed. Then Ana made coffee and they sat drinking it in the living area.

On their way home, Jessie leaned her head on Luke's shoulder. She was worn out, and began to worry, again. She whispered to Luke in the backseat of the station wagon, "I have to go to the doctor tomorrow, Luke."

"I'll be there with you, darlin'. Don't worry."

"Is he going to find out what's in my head, Luke, and then I won't have to go no more?"

"We'll see," Luke said, holding Jessie against him. "You're really good on that guitar, you know, baby? You're a hot little chick."

"Are we all going to drive to the doctor together, Luke?" Jessie asked, unable to focus on anything else.

"Yes, darlin', we're all gonna drive together. If you need to, come lay with me tonight, Jessie. I want to hold you, and help you relax."

"Okay, Luke." Jessie yawned.

Tuesday, January 22, 1974

Jessie did try to sleep in her own bed, but the fear of seeing the monster was overcoming her, and she eventually ran across the street and quietly climbed in bed with Luke. "Me and Teddy are afraid, Luke. I need you."

"I know, baby," Luke said, laying over her. "Do you wanna talk about it, or do you just want me to hold you, and rub your back?"

"I don't know. Hold me. Talk to me so I won't think about it."

"You were incredible, tonight, Jessie. I can't believe how damn good you are on that guitar, I was so proud of you. When you started playing that first song, man, I'm really impressed. You were like a whole new Jessie. I think you could be famous. Not just because you're so good, but you're a hot little chick, and the world would go *crazy* over you." Luke tickled Jessie's sides. "That makes me a little jealous, darlin'. I want you all to myself, but I could never keep you from flying,
Jessie."

"Luke, you're my good daddy. Thank you, Luke, for being my good daddy."

"Jessie, I don't wanna be your good daddy, I wanna be your husband."

"I want you to be my husband, too, Luke, and I can dis be Jessie Miller, and I could marry Mikey, too, and live here with you in the Miller house."

"Maybe tomorrow, the doctor can help us figure that out."

"Do you think so, Luke? That would be so good. I want to get all of this fixed out in my head, so I cannot see black no more when I think ahead. Thank you, Luke, for loving me so much. I love you, Luke. You're tho handsome. Lay on me, Luke, and don't get up."

Luke laid his head down on Jessie's chest and tried to think of things to talk to her about until she fell asleep.

Mike knew she was in there, but he was tired. He'd had a long night at work, and as much as he loved her, Jessie could be a bit exhausting at times. He fell asleep and let it be.

Chapter Seventeen - Mysteries Unfold

At one in the afternoon, Mike, Luke, and Jessie were sitting in the waiting room of Dr. Colby's office. They were anxious about what they would find out.

Luke sat leaned over on his legs, looking at a *Psychology Today* magazine, not really paying attention to it. Jessie was nervously fidgeting with her hands, tapping her mouth with her finger, and then looking down at her hands, rubbing them on her jeans when they would get too sweaty. She knew something horrible was going to happen in there and wanted to run out the door. She looked up at Mike, who was sitting back in the chair across the coffee table from her, with his foot up on his leg, nervously shaking it. He was deep in thought. She wanted him to take her out of there, but she knew he wouldn't. Jessie leaned over to Luke, who was sitting next to her, and whispered, "Luke, I want to go home now, daddy."

Mike looked over at her, sternly shaking his head. Jessie frowned at him.

"Jessie," Luke whispered, taking her hands and kissing them. "It's okay, baby. It'll be okay. I'm right here."

Jessie nervously tapped her finger on her mouth. She whispered back, "Um, Luke, why are you and Mikey dressed liked that? Is something going to happen?"

"No," he whispered. "We don't want to look like bums, darlin'."

"Oh…Luke, can we go home, now?"

"Baby, what did I just say?"

Jessie pouted. "You said we could go home, now."

A woman came out of the door and told them to come in. The look on her face was curious, as they all got up and went into the doctor's office.

It was a large room. There were five, brown leather, high back chairs, all facing one another. A large Cherry-wood desk sat behind the chairs, in front of a big picture window. There were bookshelves filled with books. In between two of the chairs was a round cherry-wood coffee table with a bronze statue of two mule deer running.

The doctor got up from behind his desk. He was a short, stout man with gray hair and a nicely groomed beard. "Dr. Colby," he said shaking hands with Luke and Mike, as they introduced themselves. "And you must be Jessie," he said, taking her hand. Jessie's face was distressed, she barely nodded.

"Have a seat wherever you want," he said, pulling up his pant legs and sat in what was obviously his chair. He held a pipe in his mouth, chewing on the tip of it. "So, tell me why we're all here," Dr. Colby said to Jessie, who sat in one of the chairs by the table next to Luke, the farthest away from the doctor.

Mike didn't like the way he put that question right off and was having second thoughts about being there. He didn't want Jessie to feel like she was being interrogated by a stranger, she was already frightened enough. Jessie looked up at the doctor for a second, not really knowing why she was there, and wondering why Mike sat in the chair far away from her. She fidgeted with her hands on her lap, looking up at the ceiling.

"We're here about Jessie," Luke spoke up. He was anxious and knew he had a lot to tell in a short period of time. He cleared his throat and began. "First of all, you should know that Mike and I are brothers, and we're not normally in the same room together, recently, anyway. We're both in love with Jessie, and she loves us, but she's not able, or capable of choosing either one of us. But, that just skim's the surface of why we're here. It is a big reason, but mostly because we think Jessie might have been molested when she was little, and we think it's messing her up right now. Which, I only just found out about this morning," Luke said, looking over at Mike.

The doctor took a pen and a small notebook from his shirt pocket and began scribbling notes.

Jessie pulled her tennis shoes up on the chair and wrapped her arms around her knees, burying her face in them. "Luke, don't tell him nothing," Jessie spoke into her knees.

"Baby, that's why we're here," Luke said, and turned back to the doctor. "She doesn't remember it really, she just knows it happened. And, well, the doctor we went to, to get on the pill, said she has scars, like she was badly injured, but she won't talk about it. Jessie lives with her dad up in the hills and hasn't had much human contact other than St. Thomas school. You know of it?" Luke asked the doctor. He felt nervous, like he was rambling on like an idiot. Mike noticed it, but he didn't care, better Luke than him.

"Yes, I know of it," The doctor answered, holding his pipe in his hand, with his leg pulled up on the other.

"Well, anyway," Luke continued, "last year Jessie discovered she had an Aunt, our neighbors. Her Aunt had been looking for Jessie since she was little, and just found her last year. Her dad is…well, he doesn't like Jessie to go anywhere, and has kept her isolated, in fact he's pissed that Jessie's been allowed to see her Aunt. She really has to fight to see Jessie. I think he's paranoid. I'm trying to make this short," Luke said anxiously, rubbing his forehead, still feeling like he was rambling.

"You're all right," Doctor Colby replied.

Anyway, it's really stupid I know, but…well, we both started seeing Jessie, including our little brother, Ricky, who was killed recently, on his motorcycle. And that hasn't helped the situation, but we didn't know about each other, or what we were doing, or how naïve Jessie is, till it was too late, and now we both love her, and she loves us, and can't choose, and she doesn't understand why she has to. She was traumatized when Ricky died and had to be hospitalized awhile. Jessie's mind is different. She's a genius at school. In fact, she's graduating two years ahead of her class. She has talents; I don't know what they all are. She has a photographic memory, she's a musical genius, she's a mathematical genius, but she's just a baby when it comes to any kind of social interaction." Luke looked over at Jessie, "Probably because she's lived all alone with an asshole for a dad. Anyway," Luke said, frustrated, nervously rubbing his head. "She has bad dreams and believes there's a monster that follows her at home. She's very…" Luke cleared his throat, "sexual, and we think it's because, well partly because she was molested, and partly because she's so damn irresistible. She just struggles with her thoughts, and doesn't always know how to express herself, only like a child. She doesn't eat; she gets headaches all the time. She doesn't look at people or talk to them unless she loves, knows you." Luke stopped to take a deep breath. He was so frustrated, and felt like he was sounding like a complete fool, knowing he had only a short time to fit it all in.

Mike was leaned over in the chair, resting his arms on his legs, holding his hands together. He cleared his throat.

"Jessie…Jessie," Mike started to say, trying to get the words out.

"Go ahead, Mike," the doctor said, "What about Jessie?"

Mike sat up nervously rubbing his legs. "One time she, well, she told me, she felt she needed to be punished for having sex, and thought I was going to hurt her when we…when we were in bed."

Luke's eyes got as big as saucers, looking at Mike. He looked at Jessie, who was still hiding behind her knees.

"She told me I could bite her, and pinch her, and she wouldn't be afraid," Mike continued. "She said, um…she's not supposed to do that, and says it's because she's stupid and a bad girl…And," he cleared his throat, "last Saturday, she was stalked, and raped by one of our classmates."

"I guess that explains your black eye?" The doctor asked Mike.

"We just think," Luke said loudly, sitting up, "If she could remember what happened, she could stop being so afraid all the time and…and," Luke couldn't finish, looking at Jessie, who was sitting paralyzed in her chair.

The doctor sat up and put his foot down off his leg. He looked at Jessie and took his pipe from his mouth. "Well, Jessie," he said. "You've had quite a lot going on. Do you want to remember what happened?"

"No." Jessie's muffled voice came out from her knees. She shook her head and took a deep breath, "I don't think tho," she said, rubbing her hands on her legs.

"Jessie, do you think you might put your head up, and speak with all of us like a big girl?" The doctor asked, noticing her immaturity right away.

Jessie slowly lifted her head, looking up at the ceiling. "Yeth," she said softly.

"All right, thank you, Jessie. That's makes it much easier for me to see you and understand. How old are you Jessie?"

"I'm going to be thixteen next month." Jessie's voice quivered, while she hugged her knees, bouncing her feet.

"Can you tell me what you think about all of this, Jessie?"

Jessie dropped her legs and put her hands up, pulling on her fingers. Her face was drawn up in distress, knowing she didn't want to talk about it. "I don't know," Jessie answered, unable to look at anyone. "They made me come here."

"You don't want to be here, Jessie?"

"No. I don't want to see the monster. I'm afraid. No, I don't want to. I don't want to pick. Mikey, can we go home, now?" Jessie asked, covering her eyes and pulled her knees back up.

"Jessie," the doctor said, and put his finger up to Mike, who was about to speak. "We would all like to know about the monster, and if you are willing to talk about it, then perhaps we can make him go away. Wouldn't you like that?"

Jessie put her hands down and pouted at the doctor. Slowly, she nodded.

"I think that's very good, Jessie. We'll all be here with you, and you'll be safe." He turned to Luke and then Mike. "Because this is possibly a criminal act, I'd like to tape-record Jessie. It will be kept confidential."

"Of course," Luke said, nodding. "Yes, of course."

"Jessie is that okay with you?" the doctor asked.

Jessie looked at Luke and he nodded at her. Jessie gulped and said, "Yes."

"Mike?" the doctor asked, looking at him. Mike nodded.

Doctor Colby went to a shelf by his desk and brought over a tape recorder, setting it on the table next to Jessie. He put in a new tape and started it, looking at his watch.

"Wednesday, January twenty-third, 1974. One-twenty p.m., Doctor Martin Colby," he said. "I'm speaking with Jessica Nelson, my patient. She's fifteen years old, and she's here with her friends, Mike and Luke. Jessie's been having nightmares and believes a monster has been following her. Jessie, do you understand we're tape recording?"

Jessie pulled her legs up again and nodded, tightly grasping her knees.

"You have to say yes or no, please, Jessie. The tape recorder can't hear you nod."

"Yes," Jessie answered timidly, looking at the recorder.

"Now Jessie," the doctor said, and sat down in the chair next to the table. "Tell us what you know about the monster. Remember, we're all here and he won't be able to see you."

Jessie closed her eyes, rubbing her forehead, and then looked over at Mike.

"Go own, baby," Mike said. "It's aright."

"He – he – he lives in the trees by my house," Jessie began quietly, with her eyes closed, her voice trembling, her body tightened, rocking herself back and forth. Luke sat up to listen, because he didn't know about the monster.

"He lives in the dark of the trees and howls in the wind. I can thee him watching me behind the trees. As soon as I get off the bus, he's waiting for me. I thee his shadow follow me up the dirt road to my house, and then he waits and watches." Jessie stopped, and looked at Dr. Colby.

"Does he ever come out of the trees, Jessie?" Dr. Colby asked.

"No. He was afraid of my dog, but now my dog is dead, tho I think maybe he might." Jessie's eyes were welling up with tears and she spoke so softly, nervously trembling and panting. "He killed my dog, and now, he will kill me."

"I need to hear you, Jessie. Can you speak a little louder, please? You say he will kill you. How long has he been there, Jessie?"

"He's always been there, since we lived there."

"How long is that, Jessie?"

"Thince I went to school, in kinergarten."

"Did you have the dog then, Jessie?"

"No."

"Did he come out before you had the dog, Jessie?"

"Yeth, no, I think he did once."

"Can you tell me, what does he look like?"

"I don't want to look at him," Jessie whispered, sitting back in the chair, holding her hands over her eyes.

"Jessie, I think if you look at him while we're all here together, it will be okay. He won't be able to see you, but we'll

be able to see him. Would that be okay?"

Jessie opened her eyes and looked at Luke, whose eyes were terrified. He nodded at Jessie and said, "We'll all be here, Jessie, you can look at him." Jessie looked at Mike.

"It's okay, baby, I told you I would be here."

"I want to sit in your lap, Mikey," Jessie said, pouting and tapping her finger on her lip. "The monster's afraid of Mikey."

"Jessie, I want you to relax in your chair," Doctor Colby said, getting up, and he squatted down in front of her. He took her hands. "I'm going to help you fall asleep for a few minutes. You'll feel safe and your body will be still. I'm going to ask you some questions and you'll be able to see yourself here, safe with Mike and Luke. Is that okay?"

Jessie reluctantly nodded. "Mikey, I want you." She pouted, looking at Mike.

"Be a good girl, Jessie. Listen to the doctor," Mike said. She looked over at Luke, who nodded.

"Okay." Jessie frowned, looking at the doctor.

"Now Jessie, close your eyes and relax. Put your arms down and feel your eyes getting tired. Breathe in slowly and let your breath out slowly."

Jessie closed her eyes and sat back in the chair, with her arms loose by her sides.

"Put your legs down and relax your body." The doctor said. "Breathe slowly. Your body is relaxed, and your very safe. You're falling asleep now, Jessie. I'm going to ask you some questions. You'll be safe, with Luke and Mike."

Jessie kept her eyes closed, breathing calmly.

"You're asleep now, Jessie. Jessie, I want you to remember when you were five, and you first went to school. Do you like school?"

Luke remembered Jessie's kindergarten photograph and was imagining her in kindergarten.

"Yes, I like school. But I don't want to talk to no one."

"Who takes you to school, Jessie?"

"Grama."

"Does Grandma live with you?"

"No, Daddy takes me to Grama's."

"Now, think about being home, when you're not in school. Who's there with you?"

"My Daddy and some other people."

"Do you know who they are?"

"One man is Jerry. He's nice to me. He plays the drums in our living room. One man is Robert. He plays the guitar in our living room. I like him. My daddy plays the guitar, too, and it's very loud. I don't like it." Jessie shook her head. "Daddy won't let me go outside where it's quiet. He says I have to sit and listen; tho I can learn."

"Is there anyone else there, Jessie?"

Jessie started to fidget with her hands and her face was in distress.

"Jessie, is there someone else?"

Jessie nodded.

"Who is it, Jessie?"

Jessie gasped, "It's the monster."

"What does he look like, Jessie?"

Jessie began panting and breathing heavy. "Breathe deep and slow, Jessie, just relax. Remember, Mike and Luke, are here with you."

Jessie took a deep breath, as did Luke and Mike, their bodies tightened with anxiety.

"He-he looks like a pig. He has a-a pig nose and big black glasses." Jessie started to squirm in her chair and her voice was shrill. "My daddy is yelling at everyone. He's very drunk. He yells tho much that everyone leaves, 'cept the man with the glasses. He's trying to talk to my daddy, but he keeps looking at me. I don't want him to look at me."

"What's happening now, Jessie?"

"Daddy yells at him and falls down in his chair, because he's tho drunk. Carl came to me on the couch and put his hand out to me. He said, 'Come here, little Jess, I want to show you something.'

"Then what happened?" Dr. Colby asked.

Jessie's body was sweaty, and she couldn't hold herself still.

"Relax, Jessie, remember you're here with Mike and Luke."

"I-I took his hand, and we went outside. Carl took me out

in the pine trees. We walked for a long time. No, I want to go back home."

"It's okay, Jessie. We're here and we're just talking. Then what happened?"

"Then-then we stopped, and he bent down. He told me, 'be quiet'. He said if I'm not quiet, I might get in trouble. He–he took off my dress and my-my…panties. He took a piece of rope in his pocket and told me, 'lay down'."

Mike and Luke could both feel their hearts racing. Luke was sitting back in his chair, squinting his eyes, no longer sure if he wanted to listen. Mike was leaned over with his head in his hands.

"Then what happened after you laid down, Jessie?" the doctor asked.

"He tied up my hands over my head. I was naked on the dirt, and the big pine trees were looking at me and the pines were sticking in me... I could hear the wind blow and sticks crackling. I don't want to be naked! I don't want you to see me! He has a stick! No, go away! Oh…oh, it hurts. Don't touch me, it hurts!" Jessie began to scream, "Come get me Mikey, I'm in the trees!"

Mike couldn't hold back the tears that slid down his face.

"Jessie," Dr. Colby said, rubbing Jessie's hands. "You're only talking now; you're only telling us what happened. Your body is still, and you feel no pain. What happened then?"

"He grabbed my face and squeezed it tho hard. He said, 'Don't scream or a monster will come get you.' He took the stick and… and, oh it hurts, hurts me." Jessie was panting, and was
having a hard time talking.

"It's okay, Jessie, we're only talking now." The doctor stroked her hands. "What did he do then, Jessie?"

Jessie rubbed her hand across her mouth and wiped the tears off her cheek. Luke's eyes were watering, and his face felt hot. All he could do was sit back in the chair, painfully watching Jessie's face. Mike couldn't look. He closed his eyes, leaning on his legs, feeling rage, and his heart pounding. Jessie's voice got higher.

"He was pushing it up higher…then he pushed me in my stomach." Jessie tears ran down her face. Mike and Luke both looked up at her, watching her face.

"He punched you in the stomach, Jessie? How many times did he do that?" Dr. Colby asked.

"He kept *pushing* my stomach, and my pee-pee was hurting tho bad. I couldn't put my hands down to get the stick out. Then he pinched me on-n-n my, on my, he pinched me on my… my gigi and on my pee-pee. I wanted to scream, but I didn't want the monster to come. Grama, Grama, where are you, Grama? I want my Grama… I want my Grama."

Mike remembered the dream of the little girl with the knife, and the man spanking her, and the terrified look on her face, and the old lady trying to help her.

"What did Carl do next, Jessie?"

Jessie sniffled and wiped her eyes. The doctor handed her a tissue, and she put it to her nose.

"Then he, he…he," Jessie whimpered, trying to speak. "Then he got up on his knees over me and made sex to himself, over my face, and then he went pee on my face. He went pee on my face, and my eyes were burning, and my nose was burning, and I couldn't see, and I couldn't breathe. Then he pulled out the stick, and picked me up by my hair, and dragged me across the dirt, and the sticks… It hurts tho bad…oh…oh… I want my Grama. I want my Grama."

"We're just talking now, Jessie. Then what did Carl do?"

"He picked me up. There was blood. Blood…is coming down my leg. The blood scares me. Blood…blood…he said…he said, *'You've been a very bad girl'*, Jessie said, deepening her voice. "The fairies came. They all came, and they were flying all around me, like lights. Like little Christmas lights. They told me, be still, to be very still and not cry, and the monster would go away. *'You been a very bad girl and now you're going to get a spankin'*. He grabbed my hair and spanked my butt. He…he said, I better not tell no one. Because if I tell anyone, he'll be watching me from the trees and he'll come out and get me and take me back in the trees."

"Then what do you remember, Jessie?"

"He took off the rope and put my dress back on me. He picked me up and ran and took me inside. He put me in the bath tub. He squeezed my face, and said I better remember the monster, and don't tell. He left. He didn't talk no more. I heard his car go."

"Do you remember anything else, Jessie?"

"I woke up in my bed, and Daddy was yelling at me to get up, to go to Grama's…No, Daddy, I don't want to go in there. Please, don't put in me there. It's dark and the spiders are coming. The spiders are coming. The spiders…the spiders. I don't want to go in there, Daddy. Please don't put me in there, it's tho dark, and I'm afraid of the spiders."

"Where does Daddy put you, Jessie?"

Luke and Mike both sat up, terrified and startled at this new information.

"In the wood bin," Jessie answered quickly, gasping. "I can't tell you … he'll put me in there, again. I don't want to go in there. It's dark and Luke is scratching at the wood bin. He's trying to get me out, but he can't. Luke is scratching and whining at the wood bin to get me out before the monster comes to get me."

"Why does Daddy put you in the wood bin, Jessie?"

"Because I'm a whore, because I'm a whore like my Momma. I won't be a whore, Daddy, don't put me in the wood bin. The spiders are crawling on me. Black widows are coming. Oh..."

"How did you get out, Jessie?"

"I pushed on the board. I kept pushing on the board with a log as thoon as the light came through the crack, and I got the tape off my wrist. I pushed on the board till my hands hurt. I heard the bus coming and I screamed, help me! But Luke was barking, and they didn't hear me. I kept pushing on the board till I could get out."

"Did Daddy put you in the wood bin more than once?"

"Yes."

"And does Daddy tape your wrists?"

"Yes, and my mouth."

"What does Daddy do when you get out?"

"He doesn't remember I was in there. He's gone. He doesn't remember. He forgets about me. Shhh, I can't tell nobody. I can't tell no one, he'll put me in there, again."

Jessie's body was trembling, and wet with sweat. Her face was red and drowned in tears. The doctor handed her another tissue.

"Jessie, I want you to relax. You feel completely peaceful. Breathe softly, now. We're here with you and you're safe. Jessie, I want you to imagine you're at home, looking at the trees. Luke is holding your hand, and Mike is holding your other hand. Are you there, Jessie?

"Yes."

"Jessie, look in the trees. I'm going to bring the monster out. Mike and Luke are with you. He's coming out now, Jessie. Do you see him?"

"Yes." Jessie cringed.

"What does he look like, Jessie?"

"He's black, he's all black hair. Oh, he's coming out. Oh....he's walking," Jessie gasped. "It's, it's Carl. He's turning into Carl. He's not black no more. He's Carl."

"Jessie, where is the monster, now?"

"He's not there no more. It's only Carl."

"Jessie, I'm going to wake you up, now, and you'll be safe, and peaceful. When I tell you to wake up, Jessie you'll feel much better. Wake up now, Jessie."

Jessie put her hands up over her head and stretched out on the chair, opening her eyes. "Don't look at me," she said to everyone in the room, putting her arms across her face.

"Why can't we look at you, Jessie?" the doctor asked her.

"Because, I'm disgusting. I'm bad."

"No, you're not disgusting at all, Jessie. You're a sweet, little baby. Carl is bad. Carl is disgusting, but not you. You're a baby, just a little girl."

"Little girls should not be treated like that." Jessie frowned, and began to weep. "He was bad to me, wasn't he?"

"Yes, he was, Jessie. He committed a terrible crime against you."

Jessie nodded, wiping her nose. "And there is no monster, is there?"

"No." He softly shook his head. "When children are afraid, or hurt, sometimes they remember things differently Jessie, sometimes in our thoughts we have vivid pictures that keep coming up, when we become frightened. Carl tricked you into believing it was a monster that hurt you, and it kept you afraid, so you wouldn't tell. You had a very bad thing happen to you, but you were a baby, just an innocent little girl. Now, you have to believe that you weren't the bad person, that you did nothing wrong, and move away from what happened to you. It's only a memory now, a memory that can no longer hurt you. Carl, the person that committed this crime against you, is a very sick person, and should be in jail. If your father locks you up, then he should go to jail, too, and not be allowed to have custody of you." Dr. Colby cleared his throat. Even he was horrified. "Telling people what happened is the best way to keep him from doing it, again, Jessie, because they won't let you go back there, if you tell. If he does things like that to his daughter, they won't allow him to take care of you, and you won't have to go back there. Do you understand that?" Dr. Colby took Jessie's hand.

"Yes," Jessie said, looking down. "But first, when I go there, he will put me in there, and there won't be no one there to help me. That's why I can't tell."

"Yes, Jessie, you can tell. You tell *now* before you have to go back, and then you won't have to go back, ever."

The doctor turned off the recorder and looked at Mike and Luke. He sat back in the chair, leaning on his arms. The doctor cleared his throat. "It occurs to me right away that Jessie suffers from PTSD, Post-Traumatic Stress Disorder and extreme anxiety, given her trauma, and never being treated. Does she have panic attacks?"

"Yes," Luke answered. "She hyperventilates and tries to run."

"Well, I can prescribe some medication for that. I can't say she does for sure, but I definitely think she should be evaluated for any mental disabilities. With all the trauma in her life, it's hard to say whether or not she has a disability, but she truly needs a lot of therapy. Either way, treatment will be difficult without finding out for sure. Jessie, you could just be a genius who hasn't been socialized, yet. With her living situation, she must have tremendous trust issues, as well as anxiety and depression, just from the isolation, alone. When a child's life is uncertain, and they don't trust their environment, or the future, and the only person she's had to depend on is unstable, that causes great fear and anxiety, among many other issues. I'd like to see her again, in any event. She would benefit greatly from therapy, and probably won't heal without it. Does any of this make sense to you, Jessie?"

"No. I don't know."

Neither Mike nor Luke could say anything at that moment. The shock of Jessie's molestation had made too big of an impression for either one to think clearly.

"I'm also concerned, Jessie, about this triangular relationship you seem to be in with Mike and Luke. What is happening between you three?

"I love them. I love them both," Jessie answered, looking over at Luke, then Mike.

"I see. Have you thought about how that's going to work out?"

"I dis want to live with them both. I want to live with them, together in the Miller house."

"Well," the doctor scratched his head, "there's actually more people than you think that do that, but usually, it doesn't work out. I imagine it makes life very difficult for all of you. You're not even old enough yet, Jessie, to have such a complicated problem, or to be having sex yet, none of you are. Unfortunately," the doctor said, looking at Mike and Luke, "early sexuality is a chronic result of child molestation. There's also a higher probability of rape occurring. Did you call the authorities?"

"Why is that?" Mike asked.

"Because they're more vulnerable to the attacker; they're not always able to tell the difference between wanted sex and unwanted sex. They'll even associate pain with love."

Mike looked lovingly at Jessie, feeling helpless. "No, we didn't call anyone. I don't want to put her through that. I just beat the fuck out of him."

"I think it's something you should reconsider, for Jessie's sake. It could help with her fears if she knows he's safe behind bars, both of the attackers. Do either of you know if this Carl is still around, in Jessie's life? Jessie, do you ever see him?"

"No, I never see him no more."

Luke almost said yes, but he knew Mike would want to go kill him immediately, so decided to tell him at a more opportune time. "We don't know," he answered.

"He can still be held accountable, and her Aunt needs to know about this." The doctor looked sternly at Luke. "Jessie will need to talk about it and let out all the feelings and emotions that she's been suppressing."

"Yes, Sir, I agree," Luke answered, looking at his beautiful little love. "We'll tell her."

"As far as the headaches, they could be a result of not eating. You're awfully thin, Jessie. Are you eating?" The doctor went to his desk to write out a prescription.

"I'm not hungry, food hurts my tummy."

"A low appetite is a symptom of anxiety, but a check up with a family doctor should be considered. This medication should help." The doctor handed Luke a prescription. "She may have an eating disorder." Dr. Colby turned to Jessie and took her hand, and then looked at Mike and Luke. "Again, I think Jessie needs further evaluation before any mental diagnosis can be concluded, and I highly recommend aggressive counseling with her." The doctor turned to Jessie. "I'd like you to come see me again, Jessie, so we can talk about how you're getting better, and growing up." Doctor Colby wanted to reach out and hug her, feeling quite compassionate. "You'll begin to feel much better, Jessie."

Jessie nodded shyly, quite unsure about all of this.

"Is there anything else you haven't mentioned, or any other questions?" The doctor asked, looking at his watch.

There were a million questions, but no one could think of anything to ask just then. Mike had something else he wanted to mention, but he was too distraught to remember what it was. They all got up to leave as the doctor walked them to the door, holding Jessie's shoulder.

"I think you two boys should think about what's best for Jessie. She does need friends, good friends, and I see you both care for her, but she shouldn't have to choose. I don't think she should be in any relationship right now. It's just going to add to her anxiety. I'd like to continue to see Jessie. She's not going to heal overnight or with one visit." The doctor shook hands with them.

"We'll make sure she gets back here. Thank you," Luke said.

"Jessie's not going anywhere by herself anymore," Mike said, breaking the silence in the car, driving home. "If she's not with her family or at school, she's gonna be with one of us."

Luke nodded, agreeing with Mike, as he looked out at the road, pondering.

Neither Luke nor Mike said another word on the way home, but their minds were racing with a hundred thoughts. Jessie fell asleep in Luke's lap.

He knew it was stupid, and somewhat selfish, but Mike was suddenly worried that Jessie would change. He didn't want her to change; he loved her the way she was. He wanted the monster out of her head; he just wanted her to remain his bunny girl, his little Jessie. Listening to the doctor helped him understand how easy it was for Andy to rape her. Maybe Dr. Colby was right. Maybe he wasn't the right guy for Jessie. His ego got the best of him too many times. He wasn't sure he could be as good to her as he knew Luke would be. Many times, he thought of letting her go, because he knew Luke would love her, and take care of her. Maybe if she did change, it would be easier for him to let her go. But that was only a fantasy. He could never let her go. One thing he did know, he was going to fuck up the mother fucker that hurt her; that monster that tormented her all her life. He didn't know how, but he was going to hurt him. Find him and hurt him. He was going to be punished, one way, or another.

Luke wanted to cry for Jessie. He had a difficult time hiding his tears on the way home. Every sentence, every word of Jessie's torment broke his heart. He pictured that sweet little face in her kindergarten picture, it did look sad. There was sadness in her eyes that Luke noticed when he first saw it. He was in so much pain, feeling the terror that Jessie must have suffered. He wished he could take it away. *How could anyone be so ugly to such a beautiful little angel?* Luke wanted Jessie to grow up and get better; to go to college with him, and become a successful young woman, with him by her side along the way. He knew she would never lose her sweetness or her beautiful sexuality. He never once imagined giving her up to Mike, or anyone. Mike would never be good enough for Jessie. No one would ever be good enough for Jessie. He would share Jessie with Mike until hell froze over, if that's what he had to do. He didn't care, as long as he could still hold her and love her, even if he did have to give up making love to her for a time. He agreed with Mike though. That fucker was not gonna get away with what he did, and he knew *who* the guy was, and *where* he was, and he was going to tell Mike as soon as he could.

"Jessie," Luke whispered. "We're almost home, baby. Wake up."

Jessie squirmed and started talking in her sleep, "Come on, Ricky." she said giggling, and got a smile on her face.

Mike and Luke both looked at her. "God, I hope this isn't gonna screw her up worse," Luke said, looking down at Jessie, rubbing her arms.

Mike looked back at the road, deep in thought. He was having a difficult time trying to focus. He did *not* want to picture what happened to Jessie in his head, ever again, *never*. He felt violent about it and didn't want to imagine it.

Instead, he was visualizing himself smashing the creep's face in, and choking the life out of him. He was also trying to quietly deal with Jessie, sitting in Luke's lap. Submitting himself to sharing Jessie with Luke was the strangest thing in the world, and he didn't know how long he could do it. He felt like he was being pulled in a thousand directions, and Jessie was becoming so obsessive about it. The doctor was right about her being in a relationship, but he wasn't sure about giving her up.

"Wake up, Jessie. We're almost home," Luke said, again.

"Mikey, don't drive us home," Jessie said, grabbing Luke's arm. "Drive us far away. We're all together, now. Take us far away…Luke; make Mikey drive us far away. Tell him, don't take us home."

"We gotta go home right now, darlin'," Luke said. "You need to go home to your family right now, that's the best way to get better, is being at home with your family. Your Aunt is expecting you back from school."

"No, you are my family. I'm Jessie Miller. I belong with you; you and Mikey."

"Jessie, we'll talk about that in a little while, but right now you have to go home. Sit up now, baby," Luke said.

Jessie reluctantly sat up between Luke's legs, leaning her head back on his chest, looking out the window.

"Maybe her Aunt should've gone with us," Luke said to Mike. "She might need to talk about this when she gets home."

"No!" Jessie snapped. "I'm not! Only you and Mikey can know. Only you and Mikey."

"We do have to talk to your Aunt about it, Jessie, but later, not now," Mike said.

"We can't talk about it no more, now, Mikey," Jessie answered, sullen, and looking out at the houses going by. "The doctor said to go away from it, now."

"Jessie," Mike said sternly. "He also said you have to talk about it. When do you want to tell her Aunt?" Mike asked Luke.

"Mikey, No!" Jessie snapped.

"Jessie, it's okay," Luke said. "We'll all be together, don't worry about it, right now. I want to ask Dr. Colby a few things, first."

Mike dropped Luke off at the hardware store. Luke was worried about taking her back home after such a traumatic session at the psychiatrist. Getting up out of the car together, he hugged Jessie and kissed her. "Call me at work today if you need to talk, darlin'. Do something to keep your mind off it for a while. Practice your violin, or guitar, or do something with Eli and Aimee." Luke took her face in his hand, "I want to take you out tonight, baby, right after work. I'll call you in a little while to ask Debbie."

Jessie looked up at Luke and nodded. "Okay, Luke," she said and smiled.

Her smile made him feel a little better. Luke kissed Jessie's face, and she got back in the car. He leaned his head in, looking at Mike. "I gotta talk to you. I'll call you when you get to work. What time do you get off?"

"Ten."

"Bye, baby," Luke said kissing Jessie's cheek. He closed the car door, and Mike left to take Jessie home.

"Mikey?" Jessie asked looking at him, leaning her head back on the seat.

"What, baby?"

"Remember when you first made love to me, at Jenny's house, and I was sitting on the couch when you came?"

"Course I do," Mike answered, stroking her cheek. "Sit over here by me, baby," he said, pulling Jessie close to him. Jessie moved over next to Mike, holding his arm.

"Mikey, you...you loved me, when you made sex to me."

Mike squeezed her next to his body. "Baby, I love you so much. Making love to you is beautiful. Even having sex, is aright, but what he did to you wasn't either one, baby. It was sick. I hope you can see that, baby, and he hasn't gotten away with it, Jessie. We know about it now, me and Luke. Jessie, you're a really brave girl. I love you. I'd never hurt you. I wanna protect you and keep you safe."

"Mikey, I want you." Jessie pouted, holding tightly onto his arm, rubbing her face on it. "I don't want you to go to work. I want you. I want you to lay with me and hold me forever. You and Luke are always telling me go home, now. Don't you know you are my home?"

"I don't want you to go home either, baby, but you have to for now, and I have to go to work. Even if we lived together, I'd still have to go to work, you know?

Jessie nodded her head against his arm.

"Don't you love your Auntie and your cousins?"

"I do. It's dis that when I'm with you, I don't want to leave you. You're my Mikey."

"That's because we can't be together whenever we want. We will someday, and then you won't always feel that way. Are you okay, bunny? Are you gonna be okay, today?"

"I want you, Mikey. I want to live inside you, and never come out."

"Me too, baby. Come see me tonight, so I can hold you," he said, rubbing her leg.

"I'm okay, Mikey." Jessie closed her eyes and rubbed her face on his arm. "Mike?" she asked, and it scared him, she called him Mike.

"What, baby?" he cringed.

"There's no more monster, is there?"

"No, my love, there never was." Mike stopped the car and pulled Jessie up on his lap. "Smile at me, Jessie," Mike said, smiling and smoothed the hair off her face. Jessie looked up at Mike and made half a smile.

"Is that all I get?" he asked tracing her lips with his finger. "I love you, baby. No matter what, I'll always love you. Do you feel better, now that you know there's really no monster?"

"Yes, baba. I'm sad though, what happened."

"I know, baby. I am too, but it's over and you're with me, and I love you. It's okay to be sad, but now that you remember, you can start to get better, and not be afraid, cuz he won't ever hurt you again, bet on it. You can talk to me about it anytime you want, K?"

Jessie nodded, but her face was sad.

"You're so beautiful," Mike said, stoking her face. "I'm always here for you, Jessie, even when I'm at work. You're always with me. Friday we're gonna go buy your pretties, bunny."

"And chocolate?"

"Mm hmm, and chocolate." Mike bent down and kissed Jessie, holding her close against him. Mike could see Jessie becoming unhappy. He felt so helpless about it. He wanted her to smile and be happy. He thought more and more about letting her go. He couldn't stand how painful it was for him to love her, and how he was only making things more difficult for her. She could never choose, so maybe he should just let her go. At least with Luke, she could marry him, and start to get a healthy life. He didn't want to, but he was hurting, seeing her so unhappy all the time and he felt like he was the main reason. He could never really share her with Luke. He was too jealous but having the balls to tell her was going to be tough.

Chapter Eighteen – War

Luke knew he was asking for trouble when he called Mike at work, but vindicating Jessie seemed more important. He knew exactly what Mike would want to do, and he wanted the same thing. He called the station as soon as Mike walked in the door.

"Phones for you, Mike!" Bill, the owner, yelled at him from inside the garage.

Mike picked up the phone. "Yeah, it's Mike."

"I know who it is, Mike," Luke said. "I know who the fucker is that hurt Jessie, and I think I know where to find him."

"*Where?! Who is he?*" Mike snapped, suddenly feeling himself trembling.

"After you get off, Mike. Have Kevin meet us at the house."

"We gotta get him right now!"

"No! After work, man, when it's late. Think about it, we can't be stupid."

Mike was pissed that Luke wouldn't tell him anything, but maybe Luke was right, they should wait till dark. "Aright, meet me at the house," Mike said, hanging up. He called Jessie.

"I want Jessie, please," Mike said to Maddy rather curtly.

"*Here* Jessie!" Maddy snapped, holding the phone up in her hand, sneering.

"Hello?" Jessie answered softly.

"Hey, baby."

"Mikey, I'm playing cards with Eli and Aimee."

"You're a good girl, bunny. Are you gonna come see me tonight, bunny girl? I miss you. I'm gonna need you, you need me, too...I wanna hold you."

"Yes baba, I miss you, too."

"Okay, baby. I gotta go. You okay?"

"Are you hanging up now, Mikey?"

"Yeah. Did you eat, baby?"

"I'm going out with Luke."

Mike was silent for a minute.

"Mikey?"

"I gotta go, bunny. I love you."

"Bye, Mikey." Jessie hung up before she heard him say,

"I'll see ya, baby."

The minutes felt like hours, as Mike tried to concentrate at work, waiting for ten o'clock. It dawned on him that what he wanted to tell Dr. Colby was the bathroom incident with Tammie, and he was irritated with himself that he couldn't think of it while they were there. He also kept remembering the name, Carl. He remembered Jessie telling him once that her dad calls Carl a pussy, so he must still have something to do with Hank. He kept trying to figure out how he could kill someone without killing them. He really wanted to hurt this creep, like he did to Jessie, but he couldn't think of anything cruel enough that would take a few minutes.

~

Luke picked Jessie up, straight from work. He pulled Jessie close to him as soon as he got in on his side of the car.

"I couldn't wait to get to you, baby. I need to know you're okay. Are you feeling all right, darlin'?"

"Luke, I'm okay," Jessie reassured him. She was talking into his chest; he was holding her so tight.

Luke took her shoulders, so he could look at her. "I'm just worried that going to the doctor today would upset you. I don't want you to hurt or be afraid of it anymore, darlin'."

"Luke," Jessie answered, calmly looking up at him. "I feel good, Luke. I feel better. I think I always remembered it, I dis forgot. I feel like I always 'membered it, somehow."

"Does it make you afraid, Jessie?"

"No, not no more, Luke. Not even the trees, now."

Luke pulled Jessie close to him, again. "I'm so glad, baby. I've loved you all your life, Jessie. I know I have. You've always been with me. I'm sorry I wasn't with you though, when you needed me."

"Luke." Jessie grinned, pushing on his chest, to look at him, "How could you be? You were a little boy."

"Are you smiling, pretty blue eyes?" Luke grinned at her. "What do you want to do tonight, Bubbles?"

"I want you to make love to me, Luke. I feel like I been away from you."

"Jessie, I don't think I can do that right now."

"Why? Please, Luke, don't stop loving me, now. Is that why you and Mikey took me? And now you don't want me no more, because what happened?"

"Baby, I'll never stop loving you. I love you even more, now. I just don't want to hurt you or do anything to you that makes you scared."

"I'm not scared of you, Luke. I want you. I need you to love me."

"Are you sure, baby? We can go do whatever you want. We don't have to do that."

"Luke, I want you to hold me and make love to me."

"Mm, Jessie, I wanna make love to you, too. I miss my little Bubbles." Luke said, kissing her face. "Where do you want to make love at, the cabin? We could go to the Pine Tree
Lodge, like before, or we could just do it right here in the car." Luke smiled.

Jessie giggled. "Let's go to the movie theater and have thex."

"Movie theater? Mm, that sounds fun."

Jessie giggled again. "Can I wear my pretty, Luke?"

"Mm, yeah. Wait right here, I'll go get it."

Luke drove Jessie to the Pine Tree Lodge and they had dinner in the dining room. Jessie actually ate and seemed at peace. Luke didn't ask her about anything. He was enjoying her smiling.

Luke carried her into the room and over to the bed. There was already a warm fire in the fireplace. He lay down on top of her, madly kissing her little face, caressing his hands all over her body. Luke was ever so gentle and tender with Jessie. He wanted her to understand that making love was a sweet, tender, intention between two people in love, that she would never have to be afraid of him, and he was happy that she still wanted his love. After, as he was laying over her, gazing into her eyes, he couldn't help himself, and tears started rolling down his cheeks.

"Luke, why are you crying?" Jessie asked, puzzled.

"I don't know," Luke sniffed, wiping his nose, "Lots of reasons."

"Why, Luke?"

"I hurt for you. I hurt for your life. I want you to be forever happy, Jessie, and I hate to keep bringing it up, but, baby, I know you're in love with Mike. You don't have to say anything, but I love you so much, Jessie. I won't ever stop loving you, even if you choose him."

Jessie's eyes were fixed on Luke's as she frowned up at him, stroking his cheek. "Luke, *I love you*...oh Luke, I love you so much. I could never go away from you, Luke. You're my Luke, and I-I need you."

"Jessie, do you know how impossible that is? Baby, that's so impossible." Luke said, gazing into her tearful eyes. "I don't think Mike is good enough for you, Jessie. You've been through so much, and you deserve the whole world. He won't take care of you right." Luke's eyes were watering, and his nose was running. He wiped his nose again, sniffing. "He won't do the right things to keep you happy...Jessie, I'm not gonna let you go. I won't ever give you up to Mike."

"I won't ever make you, Luke. I can't be without you. You're my Luke, and I'm your Bubbles, and you came to me, and I love you, Luke, I'm not ever going to choose. Remember, the doctor said I don't have to choose, and you said I can do whatever I want, and you'll just have to do whatever you want, because I can do whatever I want...and I don't want to choose, tho you dis have to do whatever you want."

"Jessie, there's a little house for sale in town, right by the hardware store." Luke stroked her face and hair. Hopeful thoughts were gleaming in his eyes. "It has lots of neighbors, and you can be close to me at work, and the stores, and grow pretty flowers. I want you to come look at it with me, tomorrow, after work."

"Okay, Luke. Are you going to buy it?"

"I am if you like it."

"And I can work with you in the hardware store?"

"Yeah, you could. You could be my cute little helper."

Jessie looked up at Luke, watching his eyes. "What about Mikey?"

"I don't care about him. He can do whatever he wants. You can come and stay with me, and we don't have to go anywhere else again, except to our own house."

"Okay, Daddy." Jessie smiled. "I'll go look with you...Luke?"

"What, baby?"

"My daddy told me, before I came to stay at my Auntie's, to stay away from boys, because all they want is sex, and I heard girls at school talk about boys like that. Do they?"

"Jessie, that's something I want you to understand. Sex and love are two different things, and not every guy thinks the same ways about it. We don't always understand that, till we're older, but yeah, we think about it a lot. I wanted to have sex with girls, not make love to them, but I wasn't old enough then, to really understand the difference. But, that's not why I love you, Jessie. In fact, when I first met you, I couldn't imagine having sex with you. I thought of you as someone so pure and innocent, it kind of scared me. It wasn't till later that I wanted to make love to you. Not have sex, but love you, and show you how beautiful making love is when you really love someone, like I love you. You've learned that some people can be creepy, and they don't always connect sex with love. If they're a bad person, with no love in their heart, that's when it's bad. It's hard to explain, baby, cuz not everyone thinks about it the same, especially sick people. Like the guy who hurt you. He's a sick person, ugly and cruel. But I want you to know, baby, that I love you and I would never hurt you, ever, and I never want anyone to hurt you. You're a beautiful, precious, little human being, and you only deserve to be loved. When I took you to the cabin the first time, I wanted to be romantic with you, and show you how much I loved you, and I was kinda glad you said no. I really wanted to ask you to marry me, cuz I loved you right away, but I couldn't because of Ricky. But yeah, guys think a lot about sex."

"Why?"

"Well, like I said, everyone is different, and situations are different, but I guess because we have more testosterone that kicks in when we reach puberty, and it makes us more sexually minded. It's a chemical that people have in their bodies, and guys have more than girls."

"And Mikey?"

"Yeah."

"And Ricky?"

"Mm hm."

"And even when you were little?"

Luke laid his head down on the pillow and put his arm around Jessie. "Well, I was about nine or ten when I started thinking about it. Not a lot, but it got worse in junior high."

"And Mikey, too?"

"No, he's always been a maniac, even in kindergarten."

"Luke, you lived by Aimee and Maddy when you were little. Did you talk to them?"

"Mm, not really. I kind of stayed inside more than Mike and Ricky. They were always gone outside, doing stuff. Mike was annoying to be around. I stayed in, mostly, watching TV, reading, playing with my toys. I liked to put model cars together, and I had this big erector set I liked to build stuff with. Well, I went outside to ride bikes and motorcycles, and do sports, as I got older. Ryan and me got to be good friends in seventh grade. I went to the hardware store a lot with my dad, and then I got into football and my car in high school, and then I met Sissy. I guess I talked to them a little, like when we went camping or whatever. Sometimes in the summer we'd all stay outside late and play hide and go seek. But I never thought about them that way."

"And if I lived with my Aunt, you would be like that to me?"

"No," Luke chuckled. "I don't think so, baby. I probably would've had a crush on you my whole life, and you would've tormented my dreams, and I would have been fighting Mike off you the whole time. It's funny, but I imagine you as a little girl, running to your Auntie, crying and pointing at Mike. Tattling on him about being mean. But then, I probably would've had you pinned up in a corner of the backyard, trying to kiss you, or in the fort, wanting to play house all the time."

"In the fort?"

"Yeah, me and Mike built a fort, and we had a secret club."

"A secret club? What kind of club?"

"A 'boys only' club."

"You didn't like no girls?"

"Oh yeah, we liked girls. We had all dad's *Playboys* in there. But, I would let you in our fort, so we could play house."

What's play house?"

"It's where we pretend we're married and play house together."

"Like at the cabin?"

"Yeah. You did have it so different than other kids, didn't you, baby?"

"I guess so. Maybe that's why God waited to bring me here."

"I don't know, baby. I don't understand why he didn't bring you here before he let anything bad happen to you. I don't know, Jessie. I feel like I've always been with you. What did you think about when you were little?"

"Oh, my Momma, heaven. I think about going to heaven, and being with God, and Jesus, and my Momma, and all the angels, and play music. I think about Fairies, reading books, being bored, and pretending I could fly over the mountains, and go to Hawaii and live there with my Momma on the beach. We would live in a grass hut with coconuts, and hula girls dancing, and go to the carnival. If I wasn't afraid of the monster, I always played in the meadow with the fairies when it was warm. I would make them a little fairy town by the stream, and oak tree, and I would climb the oak tree, and look out over the hills, and imagine places over them where something was happening, and people were doing things. Luke would come with me, and smell everything, and pee. It always snowed everywhere in winter. I made a snowman sometimes, but it was too cold, so I stayed in my room and read my books over and over, and drew pictures, when I didn't have school or work, or I played my guitar, too."

"I wish I could've been there with you, Jessie. Your little life was all made up, even the scary things, nothing real to believe in. If our families would have been closer, and your dad was different to your Aunt, maybe we could have come to visit you. Bring our dirt bikes and camp out."

"Luke, that sounds so strange, ugly even. I don't know if I like that. To imagine being happy there makes me feel sick."

"That's because you were so unhappy and frightened there, and all your life you just wanted to get away...even if it meant going to heaven or living in a make-believe world."

"That's why I was going to jump out of the tree. So my wings would come, and I would fly up to heaven."

Luke sat up and looked at Jessie, horrified. "My God, Jessie? What do you mean, jump out of the tree? When did you do that?"

"Yeah, because I was so sad last year, and I wanted to see my mom and not the cabin no more, or the monster or pine trees, and not be all alone."

"Last year? What stopped you, baby?"

"Luke kept barking up at me, and I was afraid the monster would come. Then I heard my dad's truck coming, and I didn't want him to see me, because he would be mad. So I hurried and got back down and ran inside before he could suspect me. Then I met my aunt, and I knew that's why God let me stay here. So I could meet you, and all of you."

Luke laid his head down on Jessie's chest, holding her. "Thank God you didn't. Baby," he said, getting up to look at her. "Please don't do that anymore, Jessie. Please don't ever think like that, again. You have me now, and I love you. I love you more than anything; more than life itself, more than I love me, or anyone, or anything." Luke stared deeply into her eyes, caressing her face. "You're my whole world, baby. I can't live without you."

Jessie held Luke's arms, stroking them. "Luke, you have to love God. You have to love God first, and then me, because he loves you, and then we can be happy."

"I want that more than anything, Jessie, for us to be happy, for you to be happy. If that's what it takes to keep you safe with me, then that's what I'll do."

"Good, Luke. So then when we do go to heaven, we can be together forever, and never be sad again."

Luke felt guilty just then, remembering what he was going to do. For a moment, he thought to tell her, but decided against it. Jessie wasn't vindictive, and it wouldn't mean anything to her now, except to stir up bad feelings. But it meant something to him and Mike. He couldn't stop thinking about it. He couldn't stop thinking about the monster that hurt his little girl. He wanted him to know he didn't get away with it. His conscience was bothering him, but the wheels were already set in motion, and there was no turning back. Even if he didn't go, Mike would, and he had to make sure Mike didn't get too carried away. "Baby, I have to meet Mike and Kevin tonight, so we have to leave in a while."

"See? "You're always telling me it's time to leave, I *hate* that!" Jessie pouted.

"I know, I'm sorry. Because you're just a baby, honey, and your Momma wants you home. If we lived in our *own* house, I wouldn't have to take you back home."

"You mean if I lived in our own house, I wouldn't be a baby no more?"

"You'll always be my baby."

"Why are you meeting Mikey and Kevin?"

"We gotta go help Kevin do something."

"Well, don't forget to put my pretty back in our drawer."

"I won't, darlin'."

"I better take it off, now… How am I going to wash it, Luke?" Jessie said, getting up.

"What does the tag say on it?"

Jessie sat up on the bed and pulled her nightie off, to look at the tag. "It thays to wash by hand in cold water. Maybe I should wash it first."

"I don't think it's that dirty yet, baby. I'll just put it back in our drawer."

"But you got the panties all wet." Jessie pouted, and her lips curled when she spoke.

"Well, go rinse out the panties in the bathroom sink, punkin'." Luke pulled her down under him, kissing her. "Let's go take a shower, so you can wash me by hand, too."

~

Kevin and Luke were waiting on the grass in front of the Miller's house, when Mike finally pulled up at ten-forty.

"It took forever to fuckin' shut down," Mike said, walking up on the grass. "Who is this fucker, and where is he, Luke?"

"He hangs out at the bar with Jessie's dad," Luke said, getting up. "I went in there one night, just to get a look at her old man. There was some skinny guy with him. He had a military buzz and thick black glasses."

"That's him. Let's go," Mike said, heading toward Kevin's blazer.

Luke grabbed Mike's arm. "Hang on a minute, Mike, don't be stupid."

"I'm gonna fuck this guy up! Come on, Kevin."

"WAIT, dumb fuck!" Luke snapped. "We gotta plan this thing out. You just can't go beat the shit out of someone. You wanna go to jail?"

"This guy's out there living and breathing the same air as Jessie. I can't deal with that, man. He's gonna pay."

"All right, he's gonna fuckin' pay. I want him to pay, too. But we're gonna do this right. We gotta find out if he's even there."

"Do you think Jessie should go?" Kevin asked, flicking his cigarette out in the street.

They both gave Kevin a stare that went right through him. "*Okay*, fuck, I just thought she might want to see this guy get the shit beat out of him, that's all." Kevin said, shrugging.

"You need to go change out of that uniform, Mike," Luke advised him.

Mike quickly went upstairs and changed, wondering how the night was going to play out. They couldn't get caught. That would mess up his chances with the Sheriff's department, and if he went to jail, he'd never see Jessie. Then Luke would have her all to himself.

Mike looked over at Debbie's house as they got in the blazer. Kevin drove them to Smith Valley. They took the blazer because it was black, and a little quieter.

"We're not going to kill the guy, Mike," Luke said, as they rode in the truck. "We just need him to know he hasn't gotten away with it."

"I know that."

"What if *we* get caught?" Kevin asked.

"We're not," Mike answered, glaring out the window.

"If it looks like things aren't gonna go down, we'll back off," Luke said. "Don't say our names, or their names, *and for God's sake, don't say Jessie's name! Keep your fuckin' head!* And, Kevin, I don't want you talking at all. We can't let anyone see anything. We gotta go out back, in the dark."

It was a little before midnight when they pulled into town. The streets were dark and empty, like a ghost town. As they got close to the bar, Luke pointed. "There's his truck."

They parked behind the Second Street bar, and all three got out of the blazer. Luke walked around to the front to see who was in the bar. Jessie's dad was sitting there with Carl, as usual. The sight of Carl instantly brought a rush of adrenaline. Luke had to shake his head, to stop himself from wanting to kill. There was no one else, except the bar tender. Luke went back to the blazer.

"They're in there," Luke told them. "It's just the two of them. We gotta get them out here, somehow."

"We could just wait till they come out," Kevin answered.

"We could be here all fuckin' night, too, shit for brains," Mike snapped.

"I'm gonna go around and open Hanks pick up door and then slam it," Luke said to Mike, stuffing an oil rag in his pants pocket that he found in Kevin's truck. "When they come out, Kevin and me will grab Jessie's dad and hold him, while you grab Carl. *And take them around to the back!* Don't fuck up and let anyone see you, Mike. That bartender knows who we are."

"Let's go," Mike said and started toward the Blazer.

"Mike," Luke said, grabbing Mike's arm, "Take your glasses off, and just a few hits, man. Don't try to kill him, and *not* Jessie's dad. He can't think this has anything to do with him, or he'll get suspicious. If anyone's gonna kill that mother fucker, it's gonna be me. And don't say anything about it being Jessie that got raped."

"All right, man," Mike said, yanking his arm away. He put his glasses in his back pocket. They walked up the side of the building, just to the sidewalk. Luke went over to Hank's truck and slammed the door. He opened it back up and left it, hurrying back to the side of the building.

"What the shit was that?" Hank yelled, in a drunken stupor. He got up and staggered over to the front door, with Carl following. "Who the *hell's* in my fuckin' truck?" Hank said, trying to stand still. They staggered outside toward the truck. Kevin and Luke quickly grabbed Hank and took him out back.

"What the shit is this?" Hank stammered. "Who are you fuckin' punks?"

"Keep your mouth shut," Luke said to Hank from behind, stuffing the rag in his mouth.

Mike towered over Carl, dragging him with his arm tight around Carl's neck. He got around back to where Kevin and Luke were holding Hank.

Carl was struggling, and his glasses fell off. Mike held Carl up by the throat against the brick wall. Carl grabbed onto Mike's hand, in an attempt to pull it off his throat. His legs were kicking, trying to get a grip on the ground. "Who the hell are you?" Carl choked.

"I'm the nightmare you been waitin' for," Mike whispered, deepening his voice, glaring at Carl. He squeezed his throat. *"I'm the monster you sent to*

torment my baby," Mike growled through his teeth, wanting to choke the life out of him.

Carl's eyes grew immense with terror, realizing he'd been discovered. He choked, panicking. Mike squinted, nodded his head, and whispered, *"You remember, you like to fuck little girls, don't you? Mother fucker*! Mike snapped, and backhanded Carl across the face with his fist. Carl slammed into the brick building, falling to the ground. Mike kicked him in the stomach. *"You fucking raped my girlfriend, you fucking freak*!" Mike picked him up, holding him by the throat.

"I'm sorry," Carl said, gasping for air. Mike began to strangle him, and Carl clenched Mike's hand.

"Sorry? How many other little girls have you fuckin' mutilated?" Mike grunted, looking down at him, clenching his fist. He wanted to choke him until his eyes popped out of his head.

"Come on! Let's go!" Luke yelled.

Mike hit Carl in the face again, and Carl dropped to the ground. Mike kicked him over on his back. "You need to die for what you did to my little girl," Mike said, stepping on Carl's arm. "Touch anymore little girls, *freak* and *I'll kill you.*"

Mike kicked Carl in the head, twice. He looked over at Hank, who was quite submissive, barely able to stand. Luke shoved Hank over by Carl, and the three boys walked to the blazer and sped off.

Hank took the rag out of his mouth, trying to balance himself over Carl. "You rape somebody's girlfriend, Carl?" Hank asked, leaning over him, barely able to stand. Hank kicked at him. "You could've got me killed, dumb son-of-a-bitch."

Carl knew exactly who it was, the boys came to vindicate. He pulled himself up; thankful they didn't kill him and followed Hank back inside.

"What's going on out there, God damn-it!" The bartender yelled.

"Nothin', Jack, not a damn thing," Hank said, slopping back down at the bar. "Seems Carl's puny-ass dick got his self in a little trouble, is all," Hank said, finishing his drink.

~

"That was barely worth it," Kevin said, driving home. "The guy was so drunk and puny; he probably won't even remember it."

"He'll remember it," Luke said, hanging on to the back of Kevin's seat. He was looking out at the headlights going down the dark road. "Tomorrow, when he wakes up with his ugly fuckin' face all kicked in. It's that son-of-a-bitch,

Hank, I want to kill!" Luke hit his fist on the roof of the truck. "*Man*, I wanted to choke the fuck out of him!"

"He's next," Mike said, feeling rather unsatisfied.

"The stupid SOB just sits there drinking, year after year with the same freak that molested his daughter," Luke said, in disbelief.

"Well, you two just keep an eye out for cops," Kevin said. "They're probably out looking for us right now."

"Quit freaking out, fuckin' pussy," Luke said. "They're not gonna call the cops. He's not gonna incriminate himself. Not in front of Hank." Luke glared out at the road. "Fuck, I just thought of something, Mike."

"What?" Mike answered, frustrated.

"Didn't Jessie say he locks her in the wood bin? That her dad locks her in the wood bin?"

"Yeah, she did," Mike answered, still focused on Carl.

"That's why she's so terrified. That's what she's been hiding from her Aunt! Jesus," Luke said, smiling inside. "Where's my fuckin' head? We know! We know what Jessie's been hiding! She won't have to go back to her dad!"

The two of them had been too traumatized in the doctor's office to put two and two together, and with only focusing on Carl, it took a bit before it sunk in. "And, we have the whole damn thing on tape!" Luke was overwhelmed with relief. They suddenly felt as if the world had been lifted off their shoulders. Jessie would be free!

"Turn around, Kevin." Luke ordered. "Let's go look at that wood bin!"

"What for?" Kevin asked. "What if he comes home?"

"Because we need the evidence, dumb fuck. Get back over to Hwy 28!" Mike snapped. At this point they didn't care if Hank came home, knowing most likely he wouldn't.

Luke could barely contain his anticipation as they drove down Highway 28. They couldn't get there soon enough for him. Mike was rattled and couldn't think. Once they got onto Genoa's Peak turn off, the drive up through the dark canyon, gave them all a chill. The moonless sky was dark, and they couldn't see a thing through the trees. The sound coming from Kevin's mufflers seemed noisier than usual, and it followed them with an unnerving loudness. The road seemed longer than Luke remembered.

"Christ," Kevin said. "She lives way out here? It's fuckin' dark."

A jack rabbit appeared in the headlights and ripped across the road as Kevin swerved to miss it. "Shit!" he said, on edge.

"There's the turn-off, right there." Luke pointed as they neared the dirt road up to Jessie's house. "Right past that tree stump."

Kevin pulled onto the road, and all three felt eerie. It was pitch black, except for the headlights of Kevin's truck. Mike was getting a better understanding of why Jessie always had such a fit about going home.

"I hate this fuckin' place," Luke said.

"*This* is where she lives?" Mike asked Luke as they pulled up into the driveway. He wasn't expecting to see such an old, run down shack. He'd never realized how far away she was from anything. This place was downright creepy, unnatural.

"There's the wood bin, Kevin," Luke said. "Put the headlights on it." Kevin parked right in front of it, and they all got out of the truck, going to the wood bin.

"Look," Luke said, pointing down. "There's all the scratches from the dog, trying to get her out."

Mike lifted the lid, seeing how dark and deep it was. The sound of spider webs crackling as they tore, gave Mike the creeps. "Shit, fuckin' spiders!" He snapped, pulling his hand away. The air was cold, and the darkness was un-real. The wind whistling through the trees above was haunting, and every little sound was amplified by the stillness of the deep black of the trees. Crickets were singing near the house.

"Do you have a flashlight, Kevin?" Mike asked.

"No."

"What the hell's the matter with you? You're supposed to keep a flashlight in your damn car." Mike snapped at him. Just then, a bat unattached itself from under the awning and flew over Mike's head. Mike put his head down, waving his hands over it. "Fuck! What the fuck was that?" he shouted. His heart was pounding.

"It was a god-damn bat!" Kevin flinched, watching it fly away.

"See all this firewood?" Luke asked them, standing over it. "He was making her split it. She did half of it herself, before she lost the baby. That's probably why she lost it, doin' all this work up here. She was so worried about getting it done. I brought her up here one day, instead of taking her back to
school, and finished it for her. Fixed that damn chicken coop, too," Luke said, looking over at it.

Mike looked over at the coop, still rattled by the bat. "Damn, it's creepy out here, "Mike said, looking around, rubbing his chest.

"No Shit!" Kevin exclaimed as Luke took out his lighter and walked over to the bench, looking for a flashlight. He found some pine branches and picked one up off the ground, lighting it. He held the branch over the wood bin as they all three looked inside. There were about ten logs at the bottom, wrapped in spider webs.

"Is that a piece of duct tape?" Luke choked, swallowing the lump in his throat.

Mike nodded and took the long ax that was leaning on the bin and moved some of the logs over, seeing something metal. It was the pry bar that Jessie had placed under the wood.

"There's the marks where Jessie knocked it loose," Luke said, looking at the front piece of plywood.

"Jesus fuckin' shit!" Mike snapped, walking away, rubbing his face.

Luke lit another branch, stepping on the spent one.

"Why don't we tear it down?" Kevin asked. "Then he can't lock her in there, again."

"Because we need the fuckin' evidence, Kevin," Mike said, wiping a tear off his face, walking back over to them. "What would he think if he came home and saw anything different? He'd get suspicious and get rid of it."

Mike was hard-pressed, trying not to imagine his beautiful little Jessie, lying in the bottom of that wood bin, desperately trying to get out, with the damn dog on the other side, scratching and whining, and bats, and fuckin' spiders. Goddamn spiders. Luke was thinking almost the same thing. Mike remembered Jessie screaming at that little spider. He felt his body trembling and wished now it would have been Hank that he messed up. He would have killed him, seeing what he was seeing here tonight. He walked over to the front porch and cautiously stepped up on it. The wood creaked under foot. He turned on the old door knob. It was wobbly, but locked. He peered in through the window, but it was too dark to see anything. He wandered around to the back of the cabin, trying to see out beyond the meadow, and get an idea of what Jessie lived with. Hurriedly though, he went back around to the front with Luke, it was too dark to see anything.

"How are we gonna keep this as evidence?" Kevin asked. "What if he does come back, and tears it down himself?"

"He doesn't have a reason to do that right now," Luke answered. "He doesn't know anything's different right now. But we have to tell Debbie and see how she wants to handle it. She'll need to get the sheriff up here to look at it as soon as possible. That's why we gotta leave it just the way it is."

"When are we gonna tell her, Luke?" Mike asked, wiping his nose.

"I don't know, Mike. I wanna call Dr. Colby first. I have some questions I need to ask him."

"Well, fuckin' get on it, Luke," Mike said and walked away from the wood bin. He glanced over at the trees to the north of the cabin. They were deep and dark, and the wind in the pines above sounded like spirits, moaning. He heard something like the crackling of pine needles being stepped on, and all at once, he thought he saw a flash of light; like eyes, staring at him and then move away.

"Fuck!" Mike snapped. "Let's just go, this fuckin' place is fuckin' creepy. Jessie's not ever comin' back here, if I have to kill every *mother fucker* in the world!" he yelled, walking toward the blazer. "There's no way I'm gonna ever let her come back here!"

Kevin followed him to the truck. Luke looked in the trees and saw a big, black, raccoon, gripping its claws halfway up one of the tree trunks. Its eyes glowed green. *There's Jessie's monster.* He thought.

Luke walked over to the chicken coop. There were five dead chickens, all, most likely starved. Then he looked in the burning barrel. He saw a piece of what was left of Luke's blanket and imagined Jessie's tears as she lit him on fire. Two coyotes started to howl behind the house in the meadow, and the wind was picking up.

"Let's go!" Mike hollered, getting in the blazer. They both understood it would kill Jessie to go back home now, and neither one was going to let that happen.

Wednesday, January 23, 1974

Mike couldn't sleep, he was too restless. It was already two o'clock in the morning, and Jessie still hadn't come. He wanted to hold her so bad and tell her he was sorry for making her go home, and tell her she would never go there again, even if he had to run away with her.

At two-forty-five a.m., Mike felt Jessie climb in under the covers.

"Hi, baby," Mike exhaled, pulling her under him. "I figured you'd sleep all night." He kissed her little face, putting his arms under her. "Oh, Jessie," he whispered. "My Jessie, girl." He kissed her mouth, satisfied at last to be holding her in his arms. He put his head up to look in her eyes. He felt like he could hardly breathe, she was so beautiful. He was contemplating on how he should let her go.

Jessie's eyes began to squint and sparkle, as if she could see right to his brain. "Mikey," she whispered, frowning. "What did you do? What did you do, Mikey?" She grabbed his arms. "You did something...No Mikey." She shook her head. "Don't leave me, Mikey." Her eyes quickly filled with tears and she squeezed Mike's arm, crying uncontrollably. "Mikey, don't leave, I love you, Mikey... Please don't leave me."

Mike trembled inside, his eyes watering, his nose running. He sniffed, wiping his nose. "Baby, you'd be so much better off without me. You'd be better with Luke, Jessie. I'm no good for you, Jessie. You're too good for me, baby."

"No, Mikey, I'm afraid without you. I'm afraid if you don't love me no more. *I'm your bunny girl.* I'm your bunny girl, Mikey." Jessie turned her head, unable to stop crying.

"Baby," Mike said, holding her face. "Don't cry, baby. I'm not gonna leave you. I can't leave you, you are my bunny girl. Baby, don't cry. I'm not leaving you. It's just, you deserve so much, and I don't ever want to hurt you."

"Hold me tight. Hold me tight, Mikey." Jessie panted.

"Jessie, I'm never gonna let you go back there, again. You'll never go to that cabin again, I swear to God, Jessie. You'll never go there again. I'll take you far away, far away, baby. You'll never call that place home, again. If your Momma doesn't get custody, we're gonna run away, far away."

"Mikey, my big strong Mikey...love me, Mikey, love me," Jessie cried, kissing Mike's shoulders.

"I love you, baby," Mike said, taking Jessie's lips in his mouth.

Jessie's eyes teared, and she moaned painfully. She couldn't bear the thought of being without him. She wasn't convinced that he wouldn't let her go. She could feel his thoughts, and her head was pounding.

"Don't get up, Mikey," Jessie begged. She wrapped her arms tightly around him. "Don't get up."

"Baby, I'm not going anywhere," he answered, kissing her face.

"Lay on me Mikey. My head hurts," she groaned. "Mikey, my head hurts tho bad. Will you get me a medithine?"

Mike got up and brought Jessie some aspirin and water, and laid back down over her, massaging his fingers around her head. "We gotta get you to the doctor and find out about these headaches, baby girl."

"No more doctors," Jessie moaned, and closed her eyes, squeezing out little tears.

The headache was so intense, that she couldn't relax, and her body was pouring out sweat. Mike kept massaging her head until the aspirin started working, and she was able to relax her body.

"Jessie..." Mike whispered, moving close to her face. "We have to tell your Aunt about your dad locking you up in the wood bin. Luke and I both know now, baby. You can't keep it a secret anymore."

"No, Mikey, don't tell her, he'll find..."

"Jessie," he interrupted. "He's not gonna do that to you anymore, I won't let him. You have to tell them. I'll be with you, baby. They won't make you live with him anymore."

"But, Mikey..."

"Jessie, we went to your house tonight and saw the wood bin. Me and Luke, we saw all the marks on it, just like you said; the scratches from the dog and the marks where you tried to get out. I'm not gonna let that happen to you again, baby. I think we're gonna turn Carl into the cops, too. If it wasn't for what your dad might do, Andy would be in jail right now, too."

"Is that where you went with Luke this night?"

"Yeah."

"I'm afraid…"

"Don't be, Jessie, he can't hurt you anymore. I'm gonna take care of you...Jessie, I want you to marry Luke."

"No Mikey, don't say that."

"Just listen; I want you to marry Luke, so you can live with him..."

"Mikey..."

"I'll still see you, baby, but they can't take you away if you marry Luke. Can't you see that? Momma knows about Luke and you. I don't want them to take you away."

"I want to marry *you*, Mikey…. I want to be Jessie Miller."

"I'll marry you, Jessie, today, right now, but I won't share you with Luke. I won't share my wife with Luke. You have to give him up…is that what you want?"

"You can't take care of me if I'm married to Luke." Jessie pouted, getting angry. "I don't know what you want. I won't marry no body, I'm gonna run away! I'll run away again, and this time I won't come back!" Jessie pushed on him to get up off her.

"Stop it, Jessie," Mike said, grabbing her arms. "You're not going anywhere, don't say that again."

"Don't tell me what to do! You don't know what I want!" Jessie struggled to get her hands out of his grip.

Mike got up and straddled Jessie, holding her arms down on the pillow. "Jessie, you don't even know what you want!"

"Yeth I do! I want you… and I want Luke and I don't care!"

"Shhh! I know you don't fuckin' care!" Mike yelled through his teeth. "That's the problem; you don't care what you're doing to me, or Luke. You just want what you want and fuck everyone else!"

Jessie lay still, looking up at Mike and started to cry. "That's why I have to go away, Mikey, because I do know. If I go away, then you can find thomeone else, thomeone who you don't have to share with Luke, and Luke can find thomeone else, that he doesn't have to share with you. That's why I have to go away."

"Jessie," Mike said, submitting, with painful tears falling. He lay down next to her, pulling her close. "Come here, baby. I don't wanna fight with you. I want to make your life better, not harder. God damn-it, I love you so much, bunny. You can't go anywhere." Mike held Jessie, caressing her. "I do understand, baby. I understand that you'd rather continue to live in hell, than hurt one of us. I know that's why you don't, you can't choose, but, baby, if you can't choose, then I have to do it for you. We can't keep goin' on this way, and I'm not lettin' you go back there. Can't you see that's more important than hurting one of us?"

"I don't want to hurt you, Mikey, I do love you. I don't know why I can't see you when I see you. Why do I have to choose all the time?"

"Because, baby, if you're married, you'll be free from your dad. Who knows how long it'll take, or if Debbie will even get custody? You have to be free, *now*."

"No. This hurts too much, Mikey. I have to think about it. Can I have a cigarette?"

Mike leaned up to get his pack off the nightstand. "I thought you didn't like cigarettes anymore?"

"But I want one, now. I want one, now."

"Does your head still hurt?" he asked, lighting the cigarette and handing it to her.

"Dis a little," Jessie answered, sitting up against the pillow.

"I think I'm what's giving you headaches." Mike lay down next to her. "How was your day, today, bunny? Were you okay, today? I worried about you all day."

"I was okay, Mikey. I have practice tonight. Are you working tonight?"

"No, it's my day off."

"I wish I could be with you on your day off. I wish you could tell Momma you want to take me out, like Luke."

"I don't think Momma would like that, baby."

"Luke is taking me tomorrow after work, to look at a house he wants to buy."

Mike looked over at Jessie. "I don't know what to tell ya, baby. I really don't. Give me that cigarette." Mike took it from her, holding it in his mouth. He lay his head back down, looking at the ceiling. He rubbed his hands across his chest. "I wish you'd quit readin' my thoughts. It scares the fuck out of me when you do that."

"Because I live in you, Mikey," Jessie answered, lying next to him.

Chapter Nineteen - Frustration

As soon as Jessie got in the car that morning, Mike kissed her and handed her a present. "I got you this the other day, babe."

Jessie took the present, looking up at Mike. "You bought me a present, Mikey? What for?"

"Cuz, I love you."

"What is it, Mikey?" Jessie smiled.

"Well open it, baby."

Jessie opened the present and looked at it. "What is it, Mikey?"

"It's a Barbie doll. Haven't you ever seen a Barbie?"

"Barbie doll," Jessie said unsure, examining the doll. "What is it for?"

"It's a toy, baby. Didn't you ever want a Barbie when you were little?"

"I don't know…Mikey," Jessie grinned. "You bought me a toy?" She smiled, holding the Barbie, looking at it. "You bought me a toy," Jessie giggled. "I'm going to keep this at my Auntie's house. Thank you, Mikey."

Mike stroked Jessie's face. "I love you so much, peanut." He pulled her over to him and kissed her, passionately.

"I want you to put your arms around me, Mikey."

"I am, baby."

"I want you to kiss me, Mikey."

"I am, baby," Mike said, with little kisses on her face and lips.

Everyone was getting used to seeing Mike and Jessie at school together. The teachers knew that Jessie was doing Mike's homework for him. Mr. Leland liked to show off Jessie's amazing facts to the rest of the class, and constantly asked her all the questions.

Some of the girls would even smile at her, and say 'hi', when they passed her and Mike in the hall. There were no new writings on the walls in the bathroom. Jessie would go to band practice with Aimee at fourth period, and then she helped Mrs. 'C.' in the office during football practice. Mike tried to make out with Jessie in the halls at every break, and wrote her love notes in every class.

Jessie kept them all in her backpack. Taylor and Amanda stopped waiting by the parking lot in the mornings. Andy avoided Mike and Jessie. He didn't really mean for things to go the way they did. He felt lucky that they didn't turn him in. It could have gone much worse for him. He did a real stupid thing though, and quietly handed her a note, walking past her that morning, while they were all smoking in the parking lot. It just read: "I'm sorry."

Jessie opened it, when Mike grabbed it away from her and lit it on fire with his lighter. He went after Andy and grabbed his arm.

"There's a reason why you're not in jail, Mother fucker, otherwise you'd be there right now, and you still might. You stay away from Jessie, and you stay away from me. Your sorry note is never gonna excuse what you did. You're a worthless piece of shit." Mike shoved Andy's arm and walked back to Jessie. Jessie didn't turn back to look at Andy. She pulled Mike's arm down, standing on her tip toes to whisper in his ear, "I love you."

~

Luke took Jessie to see the house on 3rd Street, when he got home from work. Mike watched them leave in Luke's car from the front-room window. He didn't know how much more of that he could take, and decided he and Kevin should go get drunk, since he couldn't spend his day off with Jessie.

The house was an old, Victorian one story, with white, clap-board siding, and gingerbread scrolls above the gabled front porch. There was an old-fashioned wire fence around the front yard with the remains of last season's sweet peas still clinging on it, and a little, red, plum tree in the corner of the yard. It faced west so the sun would always shine on it during the day, and it was just two blocks from the hardware store. The front door opened up to a very small living-room with a white fireplace, nicely kept hardwood floors, and a big picture window with French panes. An archway led to the dining-room to the left and past that, a kitchen. It had older kitchen appliances, white glass tiles on the counters, and the same vinyl tiles that Jessie's cabin had, only they were black and white checkered, and in much better condition. The bathroom had the same tile with Wainscoting, painted white, and a claw-foot bathtub. There were two bedrooms to the back of the house, both very small, and a laundry/mud room off the kitchen. The driveway led to a garage in the back yard, and a huge apple tree shaded the lawn.

Jessie fell in love with it and imagined herself living there with Luke. The small room could be a baby nursery, or maybe, a music room to practice in, or even best of all, Mikey's room. She tried to imagine how that would work. It wouldn't work at all. She didn't say anything to Luke. Not after her conversation with Mike. The whole idea made her feel kind of sick to her stomach. If she said anything about the house, she would have to get involved in making some kind of choice, and she was determined that was never going to happen.

Luke kept asking her, "What do you think about this, or isn't this neat?" Jessie just smiled and nodded. He was frustrated that Jessie wouldn't say anything. On the way home, he asked her about it. "Why won't you talk to me about the house, darlin'?"

Jessie just shrugged with her innocent little eyes looking up at him.

"You don't have to make any decision. I just want to know if you like the house. It'll be my house, and you can stay with me. We can come here from now on, instead of the cabin."

"Luke," Jessie's eyes saddened as she looked up at him. "If you live there, then you won't live across the street from me no more, and I can't come see you at night, and I'll feel like you're far away from me."

"Well, you haven't really come to see me that much, anyway," Luke said, a bit irritated.

Jessie gave Luke a hurtful look, pouting at him.

"I'm sorry, love bug. I didn't mean to hurt your feelings," Luke reached over to stroke her face. "I know, baby. I know you're not like me, I have to keep reminding myself."

"Momma has dinner ready, Luke. She said for you to come eat dinner with us, before we go to practice."

They were both silent on the way home, just until Luke parked in front of his house. Jessie's big blue eyes gazed up at him.

"Luke, I don't want you to move away from me right now. I'll come see you at night, I promise. I'll come thee you tonight."

Luke bent over, hugging Jessie, and gave her a kiss. "You're right, baby. I don't really want to move away from here, yet. Come on, let's go eat."

Jessie noticed that Mike's car was gone and wondered where he was. When they walked in the door, Maddy was walking past to go sit at the table. Luke noticed Maddy's blond hair right away.

"Wow, Maddy, your hair looks great."

Maddy smiled, surprised. "Thanks. It's been this way for a while, you saw me just the other day."

"Yeah, you and Jessie look a little more alike, with your hair that way."

That sent a thrilling wave over Maddy. That's exactly, what she wanted people to think. Luke sat down at the table next to Jessie.

Debbie set a bowl of rolls down on the dinner table. "Hi, Luke. I don't mind entrusting you to take Jessie by yourself tonight, that is, if you don't mind."

"No, of course not, Debbie," Luke answered.

"I love watching Jessie play, but the music is so loud. You don't mind if I stay home, do you, Jessie?"

"Well, I guess not, Momma." Jessie was watching Luke load up her plate with mashed potatoes, as if she were really going to eat all of that. She put her hand up to him to stop. "I like having you come, Momma, but you've done tho much for me, already."

"I'll come if you need me to, Jessie," Debbie answered, helping Eli get some roast.

"I think it will be okay if you want to stay home, Momma, I know it's loud."

"I can still come sometimes, Sweetie."

"I wanna go!" Eli jumped in. Maddy kept staring at Luke, while Uncle Harry was talking to him about the hardware store.

"*Can* Eli come, Momma?" Jessie asked, anxiously.

"I don't know; it is a school night."

"Just one time, Mom, please?" Eli begged.

"I guess; if Luke doesn't mind?"

"No, I don't mind. He can keep me company," Luke answered, taking a bite of potatoes. "Man, this is good, Debbie."

Luke didn't think he would at first, but he really enjoyed watching the band practice, and Eli decided he wanted to learn to play guitar. He was having a blast with the guys all showing him their equipment. Mark was very organized and kept everything running smooth. Jessie was adorable as a little rocker chick. She was so natural at playing the guitar, and she could move so smoothly without skipping a note. Chris had a very witty sense of humor and kept everyone laughing and light spirited. Even Alex was beginning to see how they really had a good band going, and how beneficial Jessie was. Mark thought of Jessie as an asset. Not only was she the most talented guitarist he'd ever known, she was great eye candy, and her talent and looks would draw in the crowds. She had a uniqueness that could bring them success. He wanted to bring out more of a 'rocker chick' image, though.

"I want to turn you into a little star, Jessie," Mark told her, after practice. "I've asked Ana if she would help you with your image a bit, is that okay?"

"Yes," Jessie said smiling, nodding at Ana, while Luke put her Gibson away in the case.

"When we get you on stage at the rock fest, you're gonna be the one drawing in all the fans, Jessie," Ana said. "We need to accentuate your appearance as a rock star; a super-hot rocker chick!" Ana smiled, enthusiastically. "I'd like to take you out shopping this weekend. We need to find some accessories for you. I like your jeans and cowboy boots; we just need to add a little style."

Luke had to hold his breath. He felt like he was plunging into the deep end of the pool or even greater, the ocean. He knew Jessie could really be something, but it scared the hell out of him.

~

Mike and Kevin started the night off at Gary's, just to hang out, and drink a little. Mike was frustrated, and a little more than jealous about Luke spending so much time with Jessie. He was also irritated at the fact that he had to sneak around with her. Ricky was allowed to freely be her boyfriend and now, Luke. He felt like some creepy toad or fiendish outcast. If she were a normal girl, he would have made her choose a long time ago, but she was Jessie, and he couldn't do that to her. He had only two choices, to share her with Luke in some distorted, polygamous relationship, or let her go, and he couldn't do either one. His friends all knew by now, the situation he found himself in. Gary sympathized with him and was talking to him in the living-room.

"Man, I know she's hot, but you gotta find yourself another girlfriend," Gary said to Mike.

"Girlfriend? You don't get it, man," Mike answered, sitting back in the armchair. "She's not just hot, she's Jessie. I don't want no fuckin' girlfriend, I just want Jessie." After three shots of tequila, he was almost in tears.

"Maybe you better not drink anymore, tonight," Gary said. "You're too down about this thing. It's gotta work itself out, eventually. Things always do, man."

"She's been through so much. She's such a little nymph," Mike said, closing his eyes.

"That's a good thing, isn't it?" Gary grinned.

"I used to think so. I can't keep up with her sometimes. She says she wants to watch me jack off. Man, I can't do that."

"Yeah, that might be a little awkward," Gary laughed. "I wish I had your fuckin' problem, *asshole*."

Mike chuckled at it, too. "She wants to do me and my brother at the same time," Mike hiccupped.

"Shit, are you serious, man? Did she say that?" Gary was curiously intrigued.

"No, she hasn't said it, but I know that's what she wants. Oh, fuck." Mike rubbed his forehead. He was anxious and wanted to tell someone. "We both laid down on the bed with her…the other day."

Gary listened intently, almost creaming in his jeans.

"She had this little nightie thing on; she looked so fricken sexy. The way she was smiling and squirming around on the bed. She wanted us both to touch her, but neither one of us could. I was so damn tempted; I was so tempted. I had to go in the bathroom and jack off."

"Doesn't sound like much of a problem to me, Bro; I would have done it." Gary grinned, taking a drink of his beer.

"Really?" Mike was shocked at Gary. "Man, that's fuckin' sick."

"Fuckin' A, man. I would have fucked her brains out."

"With your brother in the room?" Mike shuddered at the thought.

"Hell yeah, fuck that redneck, asshole. If I had a little chick like her, I'd do whatever she wanted. You got me all excited now, man. I gotta go find me some fuckin' *poon tang*." Gary laughed.

"Yeah? Let's go, man." Mike smiled. "I can show you some twenty-four hour a day pussy, over at Eddy's."

"I'm with you, man," Gary said, getting up.

"Hey Kevin, you monger!" Mike yelled, "Let's go, son!"

"Where we goin'?" Kevin answered, stumbling into the living-room.

Mike stood up. "Eddy's."

"Right on!" Kevin grinned. "Ooow! 'Bout time you wanted to go there. It's been a long time!"

Gary drove Mike and Kevin out on Highway 50 to a topless bar called, 'The Hi-Way.' Eddy had managed to make some tricky deals with the owner, and had his own thing going on in the back.

The three boys paid their five-dollar cover charge and sat down at a table. There was a skinny, bleached blonde doing a routine on stage to Marvin Gaye's "Let's Get It On".

They ordered beer and sat watching, when Eddy came out of the back room and spotted them.

"Hey," he said, walking over to their table. "What are you studs looking for? Dope?" He lit a joint and handed it to Mike.

"No, man," Mike said, taking a hit off the joint and handed it to Gary. "My buddy here needs some stray fuckin' pussy." He grunted, holding in his hit, and then exhaled.

"We all need some stray fuckin' pussy," Kevin said, eyeing the dancer.

Eddy looked over at the dancer. "Right on. You see anything you want, let me know, or come on back. We got a little party already goin' on."

It had been awhile since Mike and Kevin had been to one of Eddy's parties, but they knew the routine. "Let's go in the back," Mike said.

"Seventy- five each," Eddy told them.

"Seventy-five?" Mike asked, taking out his wallet. "What happened to fifty?"

"Cost of livin', man, when your I.D. don't say twenty-one," Eddy answered.

"Shit, fucker," Gary said to Mike, handing Kevin the joint. "You wanna pay for it when you got Jessie, the nymph?"

"Yeah, well, I don't have her right now." Mike felt guilty about that. He'd never even spent that much on Jessie. He wanted to; he just hadn't had the opportunity, yet.

Kevin, of course, only had forty dollars, so Mike and Gary put in the rest for him. They walked through the bar and went in the back room to find chicks, dope, and booze everywhere. All they had to do was sit down on one of the sofas.

Two girls came over to Mike. One was the little, bleached-blonde dancer, wearing nothing but a red G-string. The other girl was a tall brunette, who had a blue, skimpy exercise looking thing on, that barely covered her nipples.

The blonde sat down on Mikes lap while the brunette started kissing her and fondling her breasts. Mike needed to get a little drunker. He hadn't really thought about messing around on Jessie, till this moment.

Fuck it. He thought. *She was probably screwing Luke all afternoon, anyway. It's not like she doesn't do the same to me, every fuckin' day.* He knew it wasn't the same thing, but he needed to justify his actions. After about three more shots of Tequila, and the little bleached-blonde, rubbing herself all over him, it was more than he could stand. He pulled her down on the sofa and started kissing her already naked breasts. He took another shot of Tequila and went back down to her, feeling dizzy. This was a familiar feeling; he'd been there many times.

She and the brunette pulled him into one of the back rooms, and the blonde knelt down in front of him, and started to unbutton his Levi's, kissing his stomach. He looked down at her breasts. They weren't nearly as beautiful as Jessie's. The brunette was rubbing his chest, from behind, trying to kiss his neck, but he wasn't real cooperative.

He wasn't sure if he was drunk, or dreaming, or if he'd really ever met Jessie. They laid him down on the bed, and the blonde put her hand down his pants. Mike was breathing heavy; the room was spinning fast. Jessie kept coming into his head.

"Jessie," he whispered.

"No, I'm Sugar," the blonde said, smiling. "You got a big fuckin' dick, baby; might have to charge you extra for that big thing."

"Jessie," Mike whispered again, while Sugar started to put a rubber on him. His head was spinning.

"It's all right, baby," the brunette whispered in his ear, "I can be Jessie if you want."

He was lying back against her. She was rubbing her breasts all over his face; while she had his shirt pulled up, twisting his nipples between her fingers. Sugar was holding onto Mike when he suddenly sat up. That didn't feel like Jessie. He got up, stumbling around in the room, buttoned up his pants and found his jacket.

"Where you goin'?" Sugar asked.

"I gotta find Jessie," Mike said, leaving the room.

"Where you going, man?" Gary smiled up from underneath a pair of lovely breasts.

"I gotta find Jessie, man." Mike stumbled out of the bar. He walked outside and down the road, not even knowing if he was going the right way. He threw up on the side of the road.

The cold, night air slapped his face, and snow began to fall as he tried to walk straight, toward the lights of town. His mouth was dry, and his drunken thoughts were swimming in emotions. He was getting pissed, thinking. Thinking how Jessie kept tormenting him with Luke. He kept shaking his head, trying to wake up. He was talking to himself, "I can sit there watching two chicks make out, and it seems perfectly normal, but I can't make love to my girlfriend with my god damn brother, and why the fuck would I want to? Why is she so obsessed with it? How long am I gonna have to do this?" He felt like she was becoming a spoiled, little brat. A beautiful, spoiled, little brat that he couldn't let go of. He was breathing and living her, every moment was all about Jessie. There was nothing else in the world that mattered.

~

Jessie climbed under the covers with Luke, like she promised him she would. She was worried that Mike wasn't home, but she didn't say anything to Luke about it. She wanted Luke to know that she loved him. She could tell he'd been feeling down about her coming to Mike's room so much. She wanted to be a good girl and not talk about anything. Just make love with Luke, like before. She'd been missing him terribly and things were changing.

"Bubbles," Luke sighed, as she lay down next to him.

"Hi, Lukiss." Jessie smiled.

"My pretty, little girl." Luke moved over on top of her, holding her face in his hands.

"Remember when we were at the Motel, Luke?"

"I do, baby."

"I miss you, then. Can we make love like that? Like we did then?"

"Mm, I'd love to do that, baby," Luke whispered, rubbing her head with both hands, gently kissing her.

Jessie's eyes beamed up at Luke, longing for him to make love to her.

"Jessie," Luke whispered and smiled, tenderly kissing and caressing her body to the fullness of her longing. The moments in time passed away like ocean waves, quietly rocking back and forth against the warm sandy shore. Luke gently made his way into Jessie's warm cove as she swayed and moaned. Her eyes gleamed in this transcendent euphoria. Jessie's face beamed as she softly stroked his arms.

"Luke," Jessie sighed. "This is how I want to be all the time, Luke," Jessie whispered to him, "'cept when I want you both, together."

Luke had begun to climax just as Jessie said that, so he could hardly pay attention to it just then. He lay there for a moment bewildered, while she continued to gently sway her body.

"Jessie, did you say what I think you just said?" He put his head up to look at her. "That you wanted us both together?"

Jessie smiled, and nodded, holding teddy against her chest.

Luke moved closer to her face and stared into her eyes, trying to see if she was serious. "Do you really mean that, baby?" Luke took her face in his hands.

"I do, daddy." She smiled.

"I don't think that's ever gonna happen, baby." Luke shook his head. "Mike and I are brothers, Jessie. That's not ever gonna happen. It's not possible."

"Luke," Jessie frowned, "I can't stop thinking about it. I think about it all the time…I know I'm a bad girl, Luke…I think there's something in my head, that tells me that's what I want, and it won't go away." Jessie was breathing heavily, and her voice trembled, "I-I need medithine, to make it go away."

"Baby," Luke sighed, rolling over on his side. He pulled Jessie tightly up against him. "You're so impossible, Jessie," Luke said, caressing her body. "I don't see physically, how that would work, baby." Luke chuckled, nervously.

Jessie began to cry. "I dis thought maybe we could try it, you might like it, you and Mikey, and then we could all just be together, and I wouldn't have to pick, and we wouldn't keep making each other so unhappy."

"I don't know what to tell you, baby. It won't work like that, love bug. I'm not gonna make love to you next to my brother, and he's certainly not gonna make love to you, next to me. How would we keep from touching each other, baby? How would I keep from punching him in the fuckin' face? What you're asking is…it's…it's a lot. It's crazy. I know how you think about things, darlin', but some things aren't that easy. They're not so easy as you think, darlin'. Guys have a lot of pride and ego, and dignity, and self-respect. Do you know what that means, baby?"

"No," Jessie answered, softly.

"Well, men want to be proud of their manhood, to be tough and strong, and better than the next guy. For most guys, like me and Mike, it's not natural to do something like that. What's natural is for a guy to be with a woman, alone, and no one else. To love her and cherish her, only her, and for two guys to be like that, with the same woman, well…it's a little weird, especially two brothers. It's even illegal. Mike and I are kind of in a fight all the time over you. We fight a lot over you. We both want to take you away from each other, not do that together, and it's just not something that either one of us could do. I don't know if I'm making any sense to you, Jessie?"

"Well, why do guys like two girls together?"

"What makes you think that?"

"Because they told me that."

"Who told you that?"

"Kevin, and Jenny, and Mikey. They told me that two girls are sexy, and they wanted me to be with Jenny."

"What?! Did you?"

"Dis for a minute, but I didn't like it, and Mikey took me away, because I was scared."

Fuckin' asshole, Luke muttered. "Well, it's scary for me and Mike to think about making love to you at the same time. Does that make sense to you, baby?"

"Luke, I don't mean make love together, that's gross. I mean be together, all together in the Miller House, and you and Mikey could still have your same rooms, and I can have Ricky's room."

"Really, baby? That's what you meant?" Luke said, chuckling at himself.

"Luke, maybe you should dis take me to a place where they put people away; crazy people."

"Jessie, don't be silly. I would never put you away, Jessie, never. I wouldn't even think of doing such a thing. You just didn't grow up in the same world as the rest of us, darlin'. I'm sorry, babe. I thought that's what you meant. Heh, we both thought that. Whew, you kinda scared me, baby. That still wouldn't work out though, darlin'. We'd really be fighting then.

"And I am crazy? That's why you took me to Dr. Colby?"

"No, of course not, Jessie, you're innocent." Luke smiled. "I can understand why you feel like that. I really do. There are rules and laws of what's right and wrong, and sometimes how we feel, doesn't fit into them. Love doesn't always follow rules," Luke said, stroking Jessie's arm.

"Mikey says we have to tell Momma about the wood bin, and we have to tell the cops about Carl...I'm afraid about that, Luke."

Don't be afraid, baby. We're gonna be with you. No one is gonna take you away from us again, and Carl will go to jail."

Thursday, January 24, 1974

Mike came stumbling into the house at two a.m. He was cold, wet, tired, and angry. He went into the bathroom and washed his face and hands. He was a bit more sober, but still spinning. He came out and saw his room empty, then went to Luke's closed bedroom door and opened it. Jessie was lying asleep in the middle of the bed. Luke was just staring up at the ceiling. He looked at Mike as he closed the door.

Luke put his arm up over his eyes. He didn't want to fight with Mike, and upset his parents, or Jessie, but maybe that's what it was going to take for Jessie to understand, and he wasn't leaving. "Get out," he told Mike.

Mike lay down next to Jessie, ignoring Luke. He pulled her to him and kissed her. "Wake up, baby," he said, kissing her with little kisses. "This is what you want, Jessie, Mikey's here to give you what you want."

Luke leaned up and shoved him. "Don't do this, Mike. Get the fuck out." He got up to pull his jeans on.

Jessie stirred, squirming and whimpering under Mike's hand. Mike forced his tongue deep inside her mouth.

"Oh, Mikey," Jessie whined, waking up.

"Isn't this what you wont, baby?" Mike kissed her. "Damn you, Jessie, isn't this what you want? Damn you Jessie, you fuckin' little spoiled brat, you fuckin' little spoiled girl." Mike was panting and breathing heavy. He was out of control and started to cry. He put his head down next to her neck, laying it on the pillow. "Isn't this what you want from me? You want me to be a fuckin' freak, you fuckin' little *bitch*, Jessie."

"Shut your fuckin' mouth and get the fuck out!" Luke yelled, through his teeth, trying to pull Mike away from her.
"You don't know what you're doing! You're gonna wake up Mom."

Mike pushed him and started to be a little too rough.

Jessie tightened up her body, pushing on him. "Mikey," she said, crying. "Stop it."

"Get away from her!" Luke grabbed Mike's arm. "Hasn't she been through enough?!"

"That's right Luke; you protect her, because I fuckin' can't," Mike said crying, putting his head up to look at her face. "This is what she wants so god damn bad! Do it! Come on, Luke; come give it to her, that's what she wants!"

"God damn-it, Mike, knock it off!" Luke looked down at them, not wanting to scare Jessie or fight with Mike, who was obviously drunk.

"No, Mikey," Jessie cried.

"We gotta give Jessie what she wants. We gotta give the fuckin' little spoiled brat what she wants." Mike panted, breathing heavy.

Luke pulled Mike off Jessie. "Get the fuck away from her, fuckin' drunk!"

Mike stumbled, falling on the floor. "Yeah, you just cry, Jessie, cuz it ain't never gonna happen!" Mike stammered, picking himself up and stumbled back on the bed.

"That's not what Jessie wants, asshole!" Luke gritted his teeth, ready to hit Mike in the head, when Jessie yelled.

"You assholes!" She grabbed Mike's arm, pinching it. "You assholes!" Jessie yelled, hitting Mike in the chest. "*You* made me this way!" Jessie panted. "It's *your* fault, Mikey, you asshole, Mikey." Jessie cried, repeatedly hitting his chest.

Mike looked down at Jessie, stunned, in disbelief.

"You made me this way, Mikey!" Jessie cried, sitting up against the head board. "I was never this way. I never knew *anyone*!" Jessie kicked at him, holding Teddy against her chest.

"But you kept *doing* me." She kicked him again. "You and Luke... you kept fucking me and...and teasing me, and
begging me, and taking me, and doing whatever *you wanted to me*! You, you're like Andy! You're already sharing me, you stupid assholes!" Jessie cried big tears, and her body was trembling. "Now you can do what *I* want or leave me alone!" She held her Teddy up over her face and closed her eyes, crying.

"Oh, baby, oh baby," Mike cried, trying to hold her, but she pushed him away. "You're right, baby," Mike said, trying to take her hand. She held it tight against her. "We did this to you, baby. We taught you all this shit. It's not your fault, baby. You been so hurt, then we came along, like two dogs, like two fuckin' dogs."

They both felt paralyzed, like two guilty perpetrators, looking at Jessie, who sat up tight against the headboard, crying and wiping her face with teddy.

After a short moment of silence, Luke sat at the end of the bed. "Bravo, Jessie, good for you. Thank you for telling us what we needed to hear."

"I'm sorry, baby," Mike sniffed, wiping his nose. "Please don't cry," he said, rubbing her leg. She kicked at him.

The boy's dad knocked on the door, scaring the crap out of them. "Luke, what's going on in there?"

Jessie looked up sniveling. She looked at Luke and then Mike, pouting. Her pout turned to a grin and she giggled, sniffing her nose. Luke and Mike both cracked a smile. They all started sniffing and laughing.

"Are you in there, too, Michael?" his dad asked, surprised.

"Yeah, dad, we got a girl in here," Mike answered, trying not to laugh.

"*Damn,*" Tom sighed and walked back to his room.

"*Boy, do we have a girl in here,*" Mike said, smiling down at Jessie, and they all laughed at the old pervert, Mr. Miller. "I gotta go lay down." He stumbled to his room and passed out.

Luke lay down and pulled Jessie tight against him. "I'm sorry, my little love."

"I guess you're right, Luke. You and Mikey fight."

"Yeah, I wanted to kill him just then."

"Don't kill Mikey, Luke."

~

Mike woke up with a headache and got up to get some water and aspirin. He felt like a piece of shit and needed to apologize. He went into Luke's room and quietly lay next to Jessie, "I'm sorry, peanut," he whispered, kissing her face. "I'm sorry I put your through hell."

She was making so many cute faces in her sleep and started to giggle. Mike stopped to watch her sweet, beautiful, little faces. Her giggles woke up Luke, and he leaned up, seeing Mike watching her.

"That one is my favorite," Mike said quietly to Luke, smiling and staring down at Jessie. "That one is when she's reading my fuckin' mind, its scares me to death," Mike said, tracing her lips with his finger.

"The whole room spins around, like we're about to be sucked up in a vortex that goes to some other world," Luke thought, watching her.

Jessie giggled out loud. "Come on, Ricky."

"Uh oh, here comes that pout." Mike frowned. "That damn little pout, now she's gonna start crying, shit. Wake up, baby," Mike said, kissing her face. "Come own, baby, don't cry."

"Ricky," Jessie whined, "Where are you, Ricky?"

"Fuck," Mike whispered. "Baby, wake up." He stroked his hand across her forehead.

"Baba," Jessie pouted. "I thaw Ricky."

"You're just having a dream, darlin'," Luke said.

"Luke," Jessie pouted at him, "We were playing football in the grass, and then Ricky disappeared, and I couldn't find him."

"Remember when we played football, Jessie?" Luke asked.

"Yeah, Ricky loved me." Jessie rubbed her eyes. "He took my picture of me, but I never thaw them."

"I have 'em, baby," Mike said, standing up.

"You have my pictures that Ricky took? Where are they, baba?"

"I have 'em in my room. I didn't think it was a good idea to let you look at them just yet."

"Why, Mikey?"

"Because, he put them in a folder with a story he wrote about you, and I don't want you crying over it."

"I want to thee it, Mikey," Jessie pouted.

"Let her see it, Mike," Luke said, yawning.

"Shit," Mike exhaled. "You're not gonna cry are you Jessie? You know I can't take that."

"I might!" Jessie snapped.

"Go get the fuckin' pictures, Mike. Let her cry if she wants," Luke said. "She has a right to see them, and cry if she feels like it. Stop telling Jessie how to feel and let her cry."

Mike went and got the folder from under his mattress and brought it back in to Jessie. Luke reached over his nightstand and turned on the lamp. Mike lay down on his stomach, with his arms tucked up under the pillow, closing his eyes while Luke and Jessie sat up looking at the folder.

"There I am," Jessie said to Luke. "There's me, Mikey. Remember when he took the pictures, Mikey? You were there."

"Yeah, baby, I remember."

"Mike was there?" Luke asked.

"I was in the living room watching football, and Ricky had Jessie locked up in his room with mom's camera."

"You kept bothering us, Mikey."

"That's because I was jealous, baby." Mike smiled, with his eyes closed.

"They're pretty good pictures, darlin'. Ricky did a good job," Luke said, smiling at the photos.

"He said he needed them, so he could still see me when I was gone away from him."

"Do you wanna read the letter, baby?" Luke asked.

"Read it to me, daddy."

Luke began to read Ricky's letter, and she laid her head on his shoulder. Jessie giggled when he got to the 'Angel' part and being from another planet. "He used to call me that," Jessie said, smiling.

After Luke read the letter, she closed her eyes, holding onto Luke's arm. "I think Ricky's right, Luke. That's why I feel like I do; because I'm not from here. That's why I feel like I don't belong."

"Ricky's not right," Luke answered. "It's a beautiful little story, and sometimes I've thought the same thing, but you're right where you belong, darlin'."

"You mean in the Miller house?" Jessie pouted.

"Yeah, in the Miller house." Luke kissed Jessie's forehead.

"I'm going to go get ready for school now, baba."

"Aright, baby." Mike took the folder and went to his room.

Luke helped Jessie put her pajamas on and carried her home.

~

"Who's this girl the boys have been seeing, Mama?" Mr. Miller asked Meg, leaning over her in their bed.

"It's Jessie, Tom." Meg got up and walked to the bedroom window, wrapping her blue silk robe around her. She looked over at her husband. "Come see."

Tom got up and looked out the window just as Luke was carrying Jessie home. He put his arms around Meg from behind her. Meg bit her thumbnail, watching Luke. "The boys are both in love with her."

Tom laid his head down on her shoulder. "Sounds like a familiar story, doesn't it, darlin'?"

Meg reached up behind to put her hand on his face. "Yeah, Daddy." They both watched Luke kiss Jessie good-bye on the front porch.

Luke drove Mike with his fat hang-over back to Gary's to get his car. He was going to be sick all day, but he was determined to take Jessie to school.

Chapter Twenty - Home Alone

Mike pulled Jessie against him, in the front seat of his dark, metallic-blue, *'70 Chevelle Super Sport.* Gently, he stroked her little, pixie face. "I'm sorry I'm an asshole, baby."

"Why do you have to keep telling me sorry, Mikey?"

"I told you, baby, I'm an idiot. You're the farthest thing in the world from being anything like a bitch. In fact, you're the opposite of a bitch, if there is such a thing. You're a princess. You're beauty and I'm the beast, and I didn't mean to hurt you. I was drunk and scared. I'm sorry if I scared you. I didn't mean to. I didn't mean to call you that."

"I know you didn't, Mikey, but I meant to call you asshole." She smiled, leaning her face against his big, strong arm.

"That's okay, bunny." Mike smoothed back the hair on her head. "You're too little to call me that, but I'll let you. I can't share you with Luke in the same bed. I know that's what you want, but it's never gonna happen, Jessie."

Jessie looked up at him. "Mikey, I don't know why you and Luke think that. I don't want thex with you and Luke, both. Mikey, that's disgusting. I dis wanted all of us to be together in the Miller house, and I could live in Ricky's room, so we could always be a family."

"Really, Jessie? That's all you…"

"Really, Mikey; but I guess we can't."

"No baby, we can't." Mike kissed her nose, and tried to explain, while she looked up at him. All she could do was listen as he held her face in his hands.

"I keep forgetting how you are. I never met anyone like you, Jessie. I guess I just have to learn to shut my mouth and start asking you things better and listen to you. I'm a selfish, jealous, bastard. I have a hard time remembering that-that it's all about you, baby, not me. I know I need to let you express your feelings. You've earned that more than anyone, and I'm sorry, baby. I love you so much. I wanna be good for you, baby. I wanna do the right things by you. I try, but I get so afraid. Afraid I'm gonna lose you. I don't want to lose you, Jessie…I can't stand you bein' in love with Luke, baby, but there's nothin' I can do about it, except wait. It's tearin' me up, and I know it's hard on you, too. I love you, Jessie, you forgive me?"

Jessie nodded. "I love you, Mikey."

Mike smiled, caressing her face. "You want a *Slurpee*, peanut?"

"Yes, please, baba."

~

The morning went well, though Mike was sick as a dog. He didn't eat lunch, just coffee. When they got back to school from Denny's, they sat at a table in the courtyard, with Maddy and Aimee, before the bell rang.

"Momma's planning a big birthday party for you, Jessie," Maddy unwittingly, blurted out. "I suppose I'm not supposed to tell you."

"You're not," Aimee said, giving Maddy a dirty look.

"What kind of party?" Mike asked, playing with Jessie's hair.

"We don't know, but all she's been talking about is Jessie's sixteenth birthday next month," Aimee answered, a bit jealous. "I'm gonna be sixteen in August."

"Sweet sixteen." Mike smiled, kissing Jessie's neck.

Jessie was busy reading all the writings carved on the table through the light blue paint and wasn't really listening. Suddenly she gasped and then fainted, falling backwards off the bench. Mike caught her just before she smacked her head on the concrete.

"Jessie!" he said, pulling her up in his arms. Aimee and Maddy ran over to her.

"Jessie," Aimee said, rubbing her cheek. "Are you okay?"

Jessie came to, looking at everyone.

"What's wrong?" Maddy asked.

Jessie sat up dazed for a moment, and then pointed to a carving on the table.

It was a heart shape, and inside was written: "Ricky loves Jessie."

"Oh," Aimee sighed, looking mournfully at Jessie.

"Shit," Mike said. He took out his pocket knife and started to scratch it off.

"No!" Jessie shouted, pushing his hand away. "Leave it there, please, Mikey."

He put his knife back in his pocket. "Come own, baby, let's go get a drink of water." He picked Jessie up, and she wrapped her legs around him, squeezing his neck as he carried her to the drinking fountain.

Aimee frowned, watching Mike carry her away. "Poor Jessie."

"What do you mean, poor Jessie?" Maddy snapped. "Look at her. Does that look *poor* to you?"

"Stop being so jealous, Maddy. How are you ever gonna get a boyfriend if you don't stop thinking about Mike? And why would you tell Jessie about her surprise, party?"

~

On the way home from school, Jessie sat next to Mike, holding his arm.

"Tomorrow's our day, baby. We're goin' to Reno." Mike bent down and kissed her head. "What do you want for your birthday, bunny?"

"To live in the Miller house," Jessie answered glumly, looking out the window. "I want to go to *7-ll*."

Mike grinned. "*Seven-Eleven*, is it? For your birthday, so you can have a *Slurpee*."

"I like *7-11*. They have a lots of stuff. I'm going to wear a dress tomorrow, Mikey; a pretty dress."

"Mmm." Mike smiled, rubbing her leg. "I was thinking of asking Kevin if he wanted to go."

"No!" Jessie frowned, looking up at him. "I don't want Kevin to go. Dis me and you, Mikey."

"Aright, baby, I don't care."

"I want us to buy a motel after, so I can wear my new pretty." Jessie pouted, rubbing Mike's arm.

"*Mmm yeah*, that sounds even better. I wanna buy you a black one." Mike stopped the car on the side of the road and attempted to make out with Jessie, pulling her close and rubbing his hands all over her, kissing her face and neck.

Jessie squirmed, not really in the mood. "I want a *pink* pretty, Mikey."

"Well, we'll buy a pink one and a black one."

"Why do you want Kevin to go, anyway?" Jessie frowned, being rather uncooperative.

"I didn't really. He's just been moping around since Jenny got all freaky on him."

"What did she do to him?" Mike didn't answer. He was busy with his hands up her shirt. "Mikey, listen to me." She squirmed, trying to stop his roaming hands and get his attention.

"Well, obviously, she's decided she likes girls, not guys," Mike said, unable to release his mouth from her.

"Oh? ... Is that why she liked me?"

"Guess so. If I were a girl, I'd like you. I'd have to be a lesbian, just so I could be with you."

"I wouldn't like that, Mikey. I like you to be a boy. I would miss your big muscles around me. Stop it, Mikey. Behave, and listen to me, now."

"Aright, baby. I guess I better git your little bossy butt home."

As they neared Pinewood Drive, Jessie put her head up and pointed to a small boy walking home from school. "See that little boy right there?"

"Yeah, what about him?" Mike asked, parking in front of his house.

"I saw the lady that lives there be mean to him. It made me sad. He's tho little. She was making him take the garbage can to the street, but it was too heavy for him, and she yelled at him, and hit him on the head. What's his name, Mikey?"

Mike looked at Jessie, who was watching the little boy go in his house. Her face looked so sad. He pulled her close, again.

"Calvin, I think. We always had to take out the garbage, Jessie. Mom beat the crap out of us, and I'm still alive. You gonna come see me tonight, baby? I wanna makes lots of bunny-lovin's to you."

"You mean your mommy hit you when you were little, Mikey?"

"Well, yeah. We were little assholes."

"Did you cry?"

"No. She didn't really *beat* us."

"I'm not ever going to hit my baby. You won't hit our baby, will you, Mikey?"

"Never, Jessie."

"Do you have to work, baba?"

"No, don't you remember, I'm off on Wednesday and Thursday."

"Those are stupid days off."

Mike chuckled. "I'll call you, and talk to you on the phone, and say lovin's to you, okay, bunny?"

Jessie looked at him, pouting.

Mike opened the car door for her. "Don't forget to wear your pretty dress in the mornin', bunny."

"I won't, Mikey."

He wanted to kiss her, but she got out and walked to her house. He watched her walk up the stairs, and go into the front door, carrying teddy and her backpack. She seemed so sad. He didn't know how to fix it. He didn't know how to fix himself.

"We're all home alone, tonight!" Eli yelled at Jessie, as she walked in the door. He was wearing his A's baseball cap and playing with his ball and glove.

Jessie looked out the window at Mike, going into his house. "What do you mean, Eli?"

"Mom and Dad, and Mr. and Mrs. Miller are all going out tonight, to a party or something," Eli answered.

"Oh," Jessie sighed. She wondered why Eli was so excited about that.

"We're home alone, tonight!" Aimee exclaimed, skipping down the hall from her room.

Jessie smiled at the apparent joy in their faces. "Why are you guys so happy about that?"

"Because, we can do whatever we want!" Aimee answered, jumping around the living room like an idiot.

"What are you going to do, Aimee?" Jessie asked.

"I don't know, stay up late, and watch scary movies, and eat junk food."

"The Millers are having some banquet down at the hardware store," Maddy said, coming out of the kitchen. She was scarfing down a *Ho-Ho*.

Debbie came from the hallway, with her hair up in hot curlers.

"It's the stores twelfth Anniversary since the Miller's owned it. Are you kids going to be able to fix yourself something to eat, or are you sure you don't want to go? Why are you eating that right now, Madison?"

"I'll cook, Momma!" Jessie answered excitedly, still holding her backpack. She followed Debbie into the kitchen.

"Well, I didn't take anything out. There's some frozen pizza's you can make," Debbie said, looking in the freezer.

Jessie was anxious to help. "No, Momma, I can make eggs and fried potatoes."

"Well, sure Jessie, if you'd like. Thank you, Sweetie. I have to go get ready, now." Debbie hurried back down the hall. "You kids get your homework done!"

Eli stayed on the couch watching television, while Aimee sat down at the bar and phoned Courtney. Maddy went to her bedroom, and Jessie sat down at the table taking out Mike's homework assignments from her backpack and started to work on them.

"Aimee, get off the phone," Maddy said, coming back into the dining-room. "I'd like to call Jenny sometime, *tonight*." Maddy sat down next to Jessie, watching her. "Why are you doing his homework for him? The teachers know you are."

"I don't know, because I like to do homework."

"You're so weird, Jessie. Wanna do mine for me?"

Jessie looked up at Maddy. "Your hair looks pretty like that. Have you been getting any boyfriends yet, Maddy?"

Maddy laughed. "Not yet, Jess, but thank you."

Aimee finally hung up the phone when immediately, it rang, and she answered it. "*Maddy, it's for you,*" Aimee said, all googly and smiling. "*It's a boy.*"

"Yeah, it's probably Mike, wanting some ignorant favor." Maddy grabbed the phone from Aimee. "No more favors, Mike," Maddy snapped at the person on the other end.

"Favors? Who's Mike?" the voice chuckled.

Maddy's eyes got as big as saucers, and Jessie looked up at her, curious.

"Hello?" Maddy answered nervously, as she looked at Jessie.

Hi, Maddy, it's Bryce."

"Bryce?" Maddy grinned, excitedly. She jumped up and down, waving her hand in front of her face, looking at Jessie, who was smiling at her.

"Yeah. I was wondering if you wanted to go to the movies with me, Ty, and Jodi, tomorrow night."

"Me?" Maddy asked, about to pee her pants and biting her fist.

"Yes, you," Bryce answered. "I've been meaning to ask you for a while, but...you know you looked really nice today."

"Thank you, Bryce. Yes, I would like to go." Maddy's heart was racing. She sat down and began talking on the phone with Bryce, twirling the phone cord, with her feet up on the bar. They were talking about some really dumb stuff.

Maybe that's what Mikey was talking about when he said girls talk about stupid shit. Jessie thought. Maddy was smiling from ear to ear, and she kept nervously giggling.

Debbie and Harry left, and Jessie got right to work, peeling potatoes. After a while, the dogs started barking their heads off, and someone knocked at the door.

"Shut up!" Eli yelled, pushing the dogs away from the door with his foot. "Oh, Hi, Mike." Eli was a bit surprised at seeing Mike at the door. He told the dogs to shut up, again. Mike picked up one of the little dogs, playing with it.

Maddy was still gabbing on the phone as Mike walked into the dining room and put the dog down. He leaned on the bar next to Maddy and watched Jessie peel potatoes over the sink. He stood smiling at her, but she was so busy, she didn't notice him.

"Hi, beautiful," he said after a minute.

Her eyes twinkled up at him. "Mikey! What are you doing here?" she asked, going back to her potato.

"Watching you cook my dinner, tit…cute little thing. Luke called and said he's been trying to call over here for an hour, but *the phones been busy all damn night.*" He turned looking at Madison.

"Are you home alone, Mikey?" Jessie asked.

"Yeah. What are you cookin', baby?"

"Fried potatoes and eggs. We're home alone, too."

"I love fried potatoes and eggs. Can I have some?"

Jessie nodded, smiling. "Yeah, Mikey, you could have dinner with us, Mikey. What did Luke want?"

"He wants you to call him." Mike looked at Maddy. He walked into the kitchen and stood behind Jessie.

Jessie leaned her head up to Mike and whispered, "She's talking to a boy named Bryce."

"Bryce?" Mike took Jessie's hips and kissed her neck. "He plays quarterback for the JV team. He's pretty good."

Maddy felt giddy all over. Mike put his arms on either side of Jessie, leaning his hands on the sink over her.

"I think they're talking about stupid shit," Jessie whispered.

Mike chuckled, kissing Jessie's neck, again.

"You better not be here doing that, Mikey," Jessie said, leaning her head down.

"Why, tittie girl?"

"Because I don't want to get in trouble, I'm a good girl."

Mike smiled and kissed her neck, again. "You ain't no fu… um, good girl."

"Mikey, I *am* a good girl," Jessie pouted.

"Aright, good girl, let me help you." Mike took the potato peeler and the potato from Jessie and started to peel it. "How come you're always peeling potatoes around here? You cut, and I'll peel, baby. Did you get my homework done?"

"Most of it," Jessie answered, taking a knife from the drawer.

"Most of it? I want it *all* done."

"Okay, Mikey. Mikey, you're going to have dinner with us," Jessie giggled, slicing a potato.

"I know, baby." Mike grinned. "I was gonna take you out for dinner, but this looks like more fun."

Maddy finally hung up, and Jessie went over to call Luke. "What's the number, Mikey?" Mike gave her the number and Luke answered.

"Damn, darlin', who's been on the phone all night?" Luke asked, irritated.

"Maddy."

"I been tryin' to call you, to see if you wanted to come down here to this stupid banquet? I kept forgetting to tell you about it."

"No, I told Momma I would cook dinner."

"Well, I miss you, pretty girl. How was school today?"

"Okay, I fainted."

"What? Why did you faint? Have you been taking your pills?"

"Yeth, daddy. I thaw something at school. I saw Ricky loves Jessie on a table at school and it made me faint."

"Baby, I'm sorry. Are you okay?"

"Yeah, I'm cooking dinner now, Luke."

"All right, Bubbles. I love you."

"I love you," Jessie replied with her cute little voice, and her cute little face, holding the phone to her ear. Mike watched Jessie, with a painful look on his face. He didn't know if he could ever get used to that.

He helped Jessie make a big mess in the kitchen. After dinner, they all played Monopoly, laughing, cussing and having a great time. Jessie felt so happy to have Mike in her own house, eating dinner with them, and being a part of the family, and so did Mike…and so did Maddy. She was going out on a date with Bryce Baker!

Mike didn't want to leave. He kept trying to make out with Jessie, who was not cooperating, but finally at ten o'clock, he realized he better go. He gave Jessie a big, long kiss at the door.

"You better come see me tonight, bunny," he whispered in her ear, tickling her neck.

Jessie giggled. "I will, Mikey."

Aimee and Eli were watching Creature Features, eating greasy popcorn. Their eyes were glued to the TV and, the *Creature from the Black Lagoon*. Maddy was cleaning up the kitchen.

"Maddy!" Mike hollered to her.

Maddy couldn't wait for Mike to leave so she could tell Jessie all about her phone call with Bryce. "What, Mike?" she asked, irritated.

"Come here," he said, pulling her over to him. He whispered in her ear, "I don't want Jessie watching that."

Maddy looked up at him, curiously. "Okay...Come in my room, Jess, I have to tell you about Bryce!"

"Okay, Maddy." Jessie turned not even saying good-bye to Mike. He left out the door, feeling slightly thwarted, as usual, chuckling to himself.

"He said he liked me for a while, but was kind of afraid to call me," Maddy began telling Jessie, as they walked to Maddy's bedroom. "He *has* been smiling at me lately. *And*, he said 'hi' to me last Friday. Anyway, then he said when he saw how my hair was dyed blonde, he thought I looked really foxy, and decided to work up the courage to call me."

"How did he get our phone number?" Jessie asked.

"From Jodi. Oh, Jessie, he's really cute. He said I looked foxy! I don't know if you've seen him yet. He plays quarterback."

"I know, Mikey said so."

"Jessie, he's sooo sweet. He was really nice on the phone."

"Do you think he wants to have thex with you?"

"Jessie! He said he *likes my body...*"

"Yeah, he wants to have thex with you. Maddy, Mikey is taking me shopping tomorrow, and we're not going to school."

"You mean you're ditching?"

"Do you have a dress I can wear?"

"Sure," Maddy answered and went to her closet, talking about Bryce all the while. Maddy pulled out a black dress that was too small for her, now. It was sleeveless and buttoned down the front, with a V-neck lapel and collar. Jessie tried it on.

"Wow," Maddy said. "You look really nice in that dress; older." Maddy found a pair of black, slip-on shoes from when she was in the sixth grade. Jessie slipped them on. They looked adorable on Jessie's little, feet. Jessie gave Maddy a hug.

"Thank you, Maddy, for being tho nice to me."

"You're my cousin, Jessie. I love you."

Jessie was surprised to hear that from Maddy. "I love you too, Maddy."

She took the shoes and dress and carried them to her room. She hung the dress up on the drawer pull of Aimee's dresser. She put her *Black Sabbath Vol. 4* record on, turning it down low, and lay on her bed, imagining herself at the

Rock Fest. It was the first time she'd been able to listen to it since Ricky died.

Chapter Twenty-One –
Beauty and the Beast

Friday, January 25, 1974

"Mm, my baby," Mike whispered as Jessie cuddled up inside his big arms. It was midnight, and he was leaned up against his headboard, looking at Ricky's pictures.

"My little playboy bunny." He smiled, caressing her body.

"Mikey?" Jessie asked, looking up at him.

"What baby?"

"I love you, Mikey Miller." Jessie began to cry and become upset.

"I love you too, baby. Why do you always start your little cry baby motor, peanut?" Mike squeezed her against him.

"Because, I love you tho much, Mikey Miller," she answered, squeezing his big arms. "It dis starts."

"Baby," Mike said, kissing her lips. "I love you so much too, my little Jessie Miller...Baby?" Mike asked, "You don't really think I'm like Andy, do you?"

"Oh Mikey," Jessie answered softly, "No. I don't think that."

"I never saw your face look so miserable, baby."

"Because, you were scaring me."

"I'm so sorry, Jessie. I scared myself. You know I would never hurt you, don't you? Didn't I beat Andy up for you?"

"Yes Mikey, my big, strong, boy." Jessie closed her eyes, wiggling under Mike's big body.

"You feel safe with me now, beautiful?" Mike eyes were worried, and anxious as he stroked Jessie's face.

"I feel tho safe, I feel tho loved and safe, like I'm inside you, Mikey. I want to be inside you, where no one could see me or hurt me. You make me feel tho safe and pertected. You're tho strong, Mikey…You're a big strong man, and you're… you're tough and people do what you tell them, because

you're the boss…And you're tho tough, Mikey. You're my boss and I'm your baby girl…and you make me feel like I was tho safe with my big man."

"Jessie," Mike kissed her. "I have to keep remembering how you think, you're so innocent. My thoughts are so dirty sometimes, I forget you don't think that way. I know you're so good and loving, and you don't do anything to hurt anybody. I know how much you want to be loved. I know how lonely and alone you've always been. I have to keep telling myself you didn't grow up like me, seeing the same things that I saw. There was nothing for you to see, so you had to make up what you needed. I have to keep remembering that your world was so different from mine, that there was no one to show you about love, or life, or people. I'm sorry, baby, when I get stupid. I don't mean to. I don't mean to make your life so hard or try to make you fit into what I believe is right or wrong. I want you to be happy when you're with me. I don't want you to cry, baby. I want you to smile and be my beautiful little bunny girl, that I love so much. It seems like when you're with me, that you're mostly unhappy instead of happy. I wish I knew how I can make that better. I want to be better, Jessie."

"Because I don't want to leave you, and I always have to leave you. I always have to go, and I can't ever stay. I just want to stay, to stay with you, and be Jessie Miller, and live in the Miller house where I belong. I don't want to just remember, I want to live here, and be here, and feel safe, and loved, and happy."

"Marry me, Jessie. Baby, marry me, and you'll never have to leave me, again. Just marry me, Jessie. You can live in the Miller house with me."

Jessie had big tears going down her face. "I want to live in the Miller house, Mikey. Your Momma loves me, and your daddy loves me…and I can cook you eggs and fried potatoes, and I'll never be mean to my little boys, and I'll always give them kisses, and I'll call them Ricky, and Mikey, and Juliana, and never make them afraid. And you can buy them presents at Christmas and toys…and you can love them and not-not make them take out the garbage, Mikey. You can be a cop and take care of me, and get all the bad guys, Mikey."

"Marry me, baby, so I can take care of you."

"Who will take care of me when you're at work?"

"Marry me, Jessie."

"Mikey, can I still make love to Luke, then?"

"*No*. I won't share my wife with Luke, Jessie."

"You mean I could never hold him, or love him again?"

"No."

Jessie closed her eyes and let the tears run down the sides of her face. She couldn't bear the thought of never being able to love Luke or hold him.

"I know you don't understand, baby. But it's the right thing. I know it doesn't fit into what you understand, but it's the right thing. Luke's a big boy, and he's tough. He'll get over it and love someone that he doesn't have to share with anyone. Don't you want Luke to be happy, too, baby?"

"But you won't let me love him no more, or hold him, or let him love me."

"Jessie," Mike exhaled, frustrated and exhausted with her. "I don't know what else to tell you baby, except that you'll get over it after a while."

"No, no I won't…I know I won't," Jessie whimpered, closing her eyes and holding teddy against her face.

Mike took Jessie's face in his hands. "I almost had sex with another girl last night, Jessie."

Jessie opened her eyes, looking painfully up at him. "You did, Mikey?"

"Two girls, actually."

"Two together?"

"Yep."

"Why, Mikey?"

"Cuz, we got drunk. Me, Kevin and Gary. We went to a bar. A bar where there's a lot of girls. Girls that have sex with guys. There was two girls there, making out, and rubbing all over me."

"Why did you go there, Mikey?"

"Because, I was mad. Mad at you, Jessie. How does that make you feel, Jessie, if I have sex with someone else?"

"It makes me cry, and feel sad, and-and…*mad!*"

"Does it make you feel really sad and really mad?"

"Yeah." She pouted, looking up at Mike. "Because I'm *mad* at you, now!"

"Well, that's how you make me feel when you want Luke. Do you want me to have sex with other girls, Jessie?"

"No." Jessie pouted.

"I'm not tryin' to hurt you, baby, and I know you don't mean to hurt me, but…I don't want you to have sex with other guys either, including Luke. Can't you see why, baby?"

"Yeah, but I had thex with Luke a long time ago, and he loves me, and he came and got me when I was lonely, and he made me feel better when I was thad…and he took to me good places where I was happy, and he told me pretty things to me, and he loves me tho much. And when I had to go back home, I didn't want to kill myself no more, because I knew Luke would come and…."

"What did you say, Jessie?" Mike interrupted, looking deeply into her mournfully, beautiful, blue eyes.

"I knew he would come thee me at school and take me to places where I wasn't sad. He brought me flowers and told me pretty things about me tho I wouldn't be tho sad at home and feel tho lonely. He loves me, Mikey. I love Luke, he's my life."

"Did you say you tried to kill yourself at home, Jessie?"

"Yeah, because there *was* no one, 'cept the monster and I wanted to be with my mommy."

"How did you try to do that, Jessie?" Mike asked nervously, holding her little face in his big hands, stroking her cheek with his thumb.

"Well, I thought about it. I thought about the big tree in the meadow that I used to climb to the top. And I thought about climbing to the top, and jumping; tho my wings would come, and I would fly up to my mommy. One time, I did climb up, and I was almost going to jump, but my dog was barking at me, and I was afraid the monster would grab me instead, before my wings came. And I heard daddy's truck coming, and he would be mad."

"Jessie, you see this scar on my arm?"

"Yeah, what is it?" She looked intently at the scar, touching it.

"I was climbing a big tree when I was a kid. I slipped and fell out of it and busted my arm up."

"You did, Mikey?"

"Yep, I also hit my head, and was out cold, for a few days. I had a serious concussion. I almost died. But I didn't because there were people there to help me. They took me right away to the hospital. I didn't grow any wings, and fly up to heaven, Jessie."

"Oh, Mikey," Jessie pouted. "Because you weren't ready to fly up to heaven."

"Jessie, what if you jumped, but fell? What if you really hurt yourself, but didn't die, and were just laying there, all alone in pain, with no one to help you?"

Jessie gazed into Mike's eyes, frightened.

"You don't think about that anymore, baby. Please don't think like that. Don't do that, Jessie, please. I couldn't take it. I can't be without you, baby."

"No. No Mikey, I won't do that. I love you, Mikey."

"Jessie," Mike sighed, rubbing her head, pulling it against his chest. "You know there's really no monster, now, don't you?"

"Yeah, I know he's not really there, now. I was just afraid of what Carl told me when I was little, and I forgot for a while. Because you remember, you were with me when I saw it was really Carl. You and Luke saw him, too."

"Yeah, and do you know I beat the shit outta Carl?"

"You did?"

"Me and Luke. We went and found him, and I beat him up. I told him if he ever touched another little girl, I would kill him."

"You did, Mikey?"

"I told you, I'll hurt anyone that hurts you."

Jessie looked up at Mike, thinking about that. "I know you did. When I was afraid, and you were looking at me breathing, and I know that's what you did."

Mike gazed into Jessie's twinkling little pixie eyes, in awe of her bewitching mysterious insight into his brain. "Sometimes you scare the hell out of me, Jessie. How you know what's in my head."

"Because I live in you, Mikey." Jessie's bottom eye lids were squinting up at him with her magical, little gaze.

"Yes...you do," Mike gently kissed her eyes. *"You live right here,"* he whispered deeply. He took her hand, holding it against his chest. *"You're with me always. You've always been with me..."* Mike was in a trance, intensely looking into the windows of her mind, trying to see inside her head.

"What if the cops came?" Jessie asked, breaking the spell. "Would they think you were a bad guy, Mikey, and take you
away in the helicopter?"

"Maybe, but I wanted Carl to know he didn't get away with what he did to you, and I still want him to go to jail. As soon as you're ready, baby, we'll put him in jail."

"You can put him in jail...when you're a cop, Mikey."

"I hope sooner than that, baby, but I can't do it, unless you tell on him. I can't just say he did it without you telling what happened...can you do that, baby?"

"Yes...I want him in jail," Jessie answered, immediately. "Like Dr. Colby says, so I won't be scared forevermore, and he will never do that to any more little girls."

"Good. You're a good girl, baby."

"Do you still love me, Mikey, even because of Luke?"

"Jesus, Jessie. I'll always love you, no matter what. I'm sorry you were so alone. I'm so damn sorry about that. I know how miserable you must've been up there, all alone. After seeing where you lived, and how you been livin'. It's not fair, not fair how neglected you were, and how spoiled we all must seem to you. That's why I want you to marry me. Because you're part of me, now, and I want to take all that away, and give you a happy life, the life you deserve."

"Mikey, I don't want you to hurt people, even if they hurt me. I don't want you to cuss. I want you...I want you to be good and believe in God."

"Jessie, I don't know about that. People can't get away with hurting you. People, like that creep who hurt you, need to die for what they do."

"They won't get away with it forever, Mikey. God will see what they do, and he will see what you do, Mikey, and you have to do what he wants, so...so you can go to heaven.

"Jessie, I know you believe in all that stuff, but I just don't think I do. How do you know there's a God up there? Why does he let bad things happen, if he's really up there?"

"Because I saw him, Mikey. He came to me when I was scared, and then I wasn't scared no more. And I know...I know my momma's in heaven waiting, and Ricky, and my dog. And I know it in here, in my heart. Mikey, if you had a child who was bad, would you want to kill him, or would you still love him and want him to do better? People do bad things, Mikey, not God. It's because they wanted to. He made us to be good, not bad, and when he's ready, then he will take care of it, and people won't be hurt no more. They'll be happy, again, in heaven.

"Well, how do we know that for sure? How do we know it wasn't just some big cosmic explosion that we came from, little science girl?"

"Because things can't make their selves from nothing. Where would anything come from in the first place? How would they know what to do without a brain? How does my body know it doesn't need three heads, or five arms? Sub-atomic particles and atoms from time and space would be popping and forming without anything to tell it what to make, and there would be all kinds of weird things growing and...and making into strange things all crazy, and how does the sun and the earth know we need it, and all the trees, and water, and food? Something has to know how to put everything together, so that it all works right. And how would we know about love, if there wasn't any to begin with? God is the maker of love *and* science, Mikey."

"Wow, did you just think of that all by yourself, little Einstein?"

"No. How do I know how to draw or play music, if he didn't make me like he is? Mikey, I have to go back to my school on Monday. I'm going to miss you. I want to go to school with you, Mikey. I'm scared to go back to my school."

"Why are you scared, peanut? I thought you said you're not scared when God is with you."

"I'm scared I won't see you again…till we go to heaven."

"That's what's really bothering you, isn't it? You're afraid I'm gonna die and go to hell, aren't you, baby?"

Jessie pouted up at Mike and nodded. Mike didn't know what to say. For the first time in his life, he was speechless.

"I want to go to school with you…Mikey; I'm going to tell Momma about you. I'm going to tell Momma that I love you, and I want you to take me on a date. I want Momma to know how much I love you, Mikey. I'm going to tell her that I don't want to go to St. Thomas no more, with all those mean girls. It's too far away from you."

"What's she gonna think about that, peanut? Someday, baby, you're gonna marry me, and all of this will work out. I think it's just gonna take some time. Until then, I'll try to be strong for you."

"Mikey, are you going back to that bar where those thexy girls are?"

"Baby," Mike laughed. "Those girls aren't so sexy. You're the only sexy girl in the world…and no, I'm not gonna go back there, not as long as you're still with me. I think that's real nice that you wanna tell Momma about me, but, you know what? I think I better tell her myself."

"Why?"

"Because, I need to. In fact, I want you to go to my prom with me, in April. I wanna buy you a pretty dress, and you'll be the Belle of the Ball. Will you go with me to my prom, Jessie?"

"Yes, Mikey, I will. And you will buy me a pretty dress?"

"The prettiest one we can find, for the prettiest girl."

"How many more hours do we have, Mikey?"

"Forever. You know, baby, I do know what it's like. I got girls after me all the time, but sweet little girls like you aren't dick heads like me, who never gave a shit. I know you love all of us. I never told anyone, but I did have a big crush on a girl once."

"What happen, Mikey?"

"When I was in eighth grade. She was a little, bitty, blonde girl, like you. Not near as beautiful, but I did like her. She didn't like me though. I guess I was mean to her cuz I'm an idiot who doesn't know how to be nice. She gave me the idea though, of what I thought I was lookin' for. Then you came along, baby, and BAM! You stole my heart."

♥

The big day had finally come, and they were ditching school to go to Reno. Jessie took a shower and put on Mike's favorite pink panties. She shaved her legs and put on some lotion. She put Mike's chain around her neck. Then she slipped into the dress that was a little tighter around the chest on her than it was on Maddy. She put fresh pink polish on her nails, because Mikey loved her pretty, pink polish. It took forever to dry her hair with the blow dryer, and brush it out, but finally, she was ready. She heard the Chevelle roar at six-fifty a.m. Maddy gave her the black sweater to wear, and she put it on, running out the door. "Bye!" she yelled and ran down the stairs.

She ran over to her side of the Chevelle, and sat on her knees in the seat, facing Mike. He winked at her and closed his door. He drove up the road some ways and then pulled over, shifting into park.

"Let me see you," he said, pulling her over to him. "*I like that dress.*" He smiled and unbuttoned the top button. Jessie's cleavage came spilling out at him and he almost had a heart attack. "Damn, baby, how'd anything so little as you get such big, ole titties?"

Jessie giggled, and he put his hands inside her sweater, caressing her, and kissing her pretty mouth. "Good morning, gorgeous." His *intimidation look* with those dark hazel eyes came out and she felt butterflies in her stomach. That was the look he gave her on the beach, and the look he gave her on the wall, when she first kissed him. The look he gave her when she was sitting on the couch, at Jenny's, the look he gave her at the Steak house, when she had her red dress on. Jessie was in love with that look.

"Look at me again, like that, Mikey."

"Like what?" he grinned.

"Like you dis did when you're trying to be scary to me."

"You mean this one?" he asked, giving her the look, trying not to laugh.

"Yeah, that one. It makes my tummy tickle," Jessie blushed.

"Mm, sit over here, baby," he said, taking his hands out of her sweater. I think I better look at you like that all the time."

"I was good this morning, Mikey. I didn't make a fuss."

"I know you were, bunny.

~

They were in Fredericks for what seemed like hours. Mike wanted to buy Jessie everything. He pointed everything out to her, and kept saying, "Let's get this one."

Jessie found a soft pink nightie and finally agreed on a black nightie that Mike insisted on. Mike also picked out some white lacy panties, a black lacy bra with some black nylon stockings.

"How are these 'pose to stay up?" Jessie asked, holding them up.

"Well, they won't be staying up very long, bunny." Mike smiled, taking them from her.

The lady at the counter seemed to remember Jessie, and gave Mike a horrible, dirty look. She was not very friendly at all.

"I wonder why that lady works here, Mikey," Jessie whispered, looking at the lady. "She's always mad."

"She's mad because she knows she can't wear any of this stuff, like a sexy little girl like you can," Mike said out loud, smiling at the lady as she handed him his change.

"Aren't you going to buy you something, Mikey?" Jessie asked as they walked out of the store.

"I don't think I'd look good in anything in there, peanut."

"I don't mean in there," Jessie giggled.

"No, you're all I want, bunny. I already bought what I wanted. You want somethin' else, baby? You want a toy?"

"No thank you, Mikey," Jessie said, as they walked past the automatic photo booth.

"Come here, baby girl." Mike pulled Jessie into it. "Let's take our picture."

"Make a funny face at it," Mike told her, as they both made a funny face. Mike tickled her on the last one, and they were laughing.

"Look how cute and beautiful you are, baby," Mike said, looking at the pictures when they came out. "I love it when you laugh."

"Look how handsome you are, Mikey," Jessie said, as they walked down though the mall, looking at them. "Let's sit here for a minute." Jessie pointed as they came up to a bench. "I want to look at all the people."

Mike put the pictures in his wallet. Jessie leaned back on his lap, and they sat, watching people go by.

"There's tho many people, Mikey. What are they all doing?"

"Shopping, silly girl."

A young couple went by. The woman was pushing a baby stroller, with a tiny boy walking, holding his dad's hand.

"Someday me and you will look like that, haw, Mikey?"

"Yep, we better go get your chocolate, bunny, so we can have time to go to the motel," Mike said to her, getting up.

Mike dropped everything on the floor after closing the motel door behind them. He pulled Jessie against him and leaned down, kissing her. He picked her up and laid over her on the bed.

"How many hours do we have, Mikey?" Jessie asked, still holding her arms around his neck.

"A few."

"Remember, last night, when you came to my house and cooked dinner with me, Mikey?" Jessie smiled up at him.

"Mm hm." Mike said, kissing her neck.

"I like you to come to my house, Mikey."

"Me too, baby." Slowly, he unbuttoned Jessie's dress. He kissed her belly and slipped her shoes off her feet, kissing her toes. He rubbed her little legs as he climbed back up her body, moving her dress a little to expose part of her breast. He looked up at her face with his 'look'. His intimidation look, that gave Jessie butterflies. Mike felt a wave of electricity go down his stomach to his groin. "Jessie, I can't tell you in words how beautiful you are," he said, leaning over her. "Every minute you get more... damn, Jessie." Mike looked in her eyes. "I can't believe you're real sometimes."

Jessie looked up at Mike, holding his arms. Her face was so sweet, and her hair was all ruffled up in long, wavy, strands of smooth silk.

"I love your hair, baby," Mike said, looking down at it. He gently ran a strand of it in his hand. He sat up against the headboard. "Come here and lay in my lap," he said, pulling her into his lap. Gently, he took up her hair into his hands, running his fingers through it, staring into her eyes. "It's so soft and silky. Your eyes are so beautiful blue, like a Siamese cat, or a beautiful, fairy princess," he said, stroking her cheek. His eyes were lovesick. "You have a spell on me, Jessie."

Jessie began to feel the passion she felt the first time Mike came to her at Jenny's, enticing her, wanting her. Her stomach was fluttery, and her heart was racing. Mike pulled Jessie's chin up toward his mouth and kissed her lips. He stroked his finger down her arm. "You sure are a foxy little chick, you know that?" he asked, looking in her eyes.

Jessie felt a bit timid and put her head down. Mike pulled her face to his again and kissed her. Her heart was racing, her hands felt sweaty. "You sure are pretty," Mike whispered, stroking her chin. "Don't be shy, I dig you."

Jessie grinned for a second, and then turned her head away.

"I wanna make love to you, Jessie," Mike whispered, caressing her ear lobe with his mouth. "*You turn me on ...*" Mike put his hand up the back of Jessie's neck, and ran his fingers up through her hair. Jessie took a deep breath and swallowed the lump in her throat.

"You sweet young thing, I *want you,*" Mike whispered, kissing Jessie's face.

Jessie sat up on the bed, while Mike slipped the black nightie on over her head. He let her down, kissing her, and then slowly pulled the stockings up over her legs.

"Am I pretty now, baba?"

"Yeah, baby, you're so pretty. Your legs are so beautiful."

"What about my panties?"

"We don't need no panties, baby," Mike answered, kissing her legs, caressing his hands along the silky nylon. He lay down next to her, pulling her leg up against him so he could caress it. Jessie smiled, squirming her body all over.

"I like to be pretty for you, baba."

He gave her his special kiss that always made her smile. "Do that again, Mikey." She smiled.

"I love to kiss you, Jessie. Your lips are so sensual."

"I want you, Mikey. I want you, I want you, baba."

♥

"How many more hours do we have, Mikey?" Jessie asked from under her arm. She rolled over to look at him.

"Baby, we have our whole life, bunny." Mike petted Jessie's face, looking at her. He was imagining himself as Ricky, trying to imagine what Ricky saw when he looked at Jessie, and how he felt when he was with her.

"Mikey, don't think about Ricky," Jessie pouted.

"Damn-it Jessie," Mike said, completely amazed. "I wish you wouldn't fuckin' do that."

"Mikey…Mikey, if I died before you thee me again, will you promise me you'll get a girlfriend, and be nice to her?"

"I'm not promising anything like that, and why are you asking me that right now?" Mike snapped, getting up to look down at her.

"Sometimes, I feel like I might die. I dis—feel like that, sometimes." She thought a lot about dying, since Ricky's death. She just didn't realize how much at times. It was difficult understanding how one minute he was there, and the next, he was gone. She worried so much about Mike. She knew he wouldn't be strong if something ever happened to her.

"Well, if you died, then I would die, and we'd both be dead, so don't fuckin' think like that." Mike rolled over on his back and held his arm up over his face. He exhaled, "Jessie, everyone thinks like that, sometimes."

"Did Ricky?"

"Baby, don't talk about that. Then you just remember it all over again. Please, don't do that, now."

"I'm sorry! I won't!" she snapped, trying not to cry. She didn't want Mike to get mad and yell at her some more. She got up and went into the bathroom, because she had to cry, just for a minute.

"Fuck," Mike cursed to himself. "Damn-it Jessie, are you in there crying? Do you want me to come give you something to cry about?" he yelled, looking up at the ceiling.

"Yeth!" she yelled through the door. "Come in here, *athhole,* and make me cry! I'm not crying, I'm going to the BATHROOM!" Her little voice was as cute as it could be.

"Don't fuckin' cuss! I don't like it." He smiled to himself, thinking how cute she was.

"You do it," she said, wiping her face off.

"Get the fuck out here! I don't wanna yell at you through the damn door!" He grinned.

"Well, stop yelling, then." She opened the door. Jessie stood naked, in the doorway.

"Where's your nightie?" he snapped, leaning up on his arm, trying to sound serious.

She pouted, and pointed to the floor in the bathroom, looking towards it, like it was a piece of garbage or something.

He gave her a stern look. "Why is it on the floor?"

"Aren't we done with it?" she asked, innocently looking at him.

"Come over here!" he said, really mean, desperately trying to *look* mean and not laugh.

"Well, I don't want to now," Jessie pouted.

"I'm gonna get you." He tried to look serious, and got out of bed to chase her.

She screamed and ran over to the corner of the room. She dropped down on the floor when he got in front of her, screaming, NO, NO, NO, Mikey! She covered her head with her arms.

"I'm not gonna hurt you, you dumb little girl. Come here." He picked her up and carried her back to bed.

"Don't call me dumb!" she pouted, holding on to his neck, and pinched it.

"Ow, baby. I'm sorry. No, you're not, dumb. You're my brilliant, adorable, little baby girl, and I would never hurt you." He lay her down on the bed. "I'm sorry, peanut. You can cry if you really want, but I'd rather have you fuck my idiot brains out, though."

"It doesn't make me horny when you talk like that." She scowled at him.

"It really turns me own when you call me, asshole." He smiled, holding her hands up on her chest. "You're too little to call me that."

"Athhole." She grinned.

"Mmm, baby. Turn me own."

"Fuckin' athhole," she snorted, giggling.

"*Damn,* you're cute."

Jessie pushed him up and got down off the bed. "Athhole," she giggled, running over to the other side of the bed. "Come get me, Mikey."

Mike jumped out at her, trying to grab her across the bed, laughing. Jessie giggled and ran out of his way.

"Fucker," she called him, running to the other side of the room.

"Stop cussing." He got up, trying not to smile. He cornered her against the wall and hovered over her. "You have a dirty mouth."

"You do!" Jessie snapped, trying not to smile.

He bent down and picked her up, tickling her. Jessie screamed with laughter as he carried her back to the bed. "I'm not gonna buy you anymore pretties, if you're just gonna throw them on the floor. You want me to put it in the garbage?" Mike asked, lying on her tummy.

"No Mikey, I won't throw it on the floor, no more." She wrapped her legs around him. "I want my pretty. Will you keep it in your drawer, so when I come over I can wear my pretty?"

"Yes, baby. I'm gonna try not to say fuck no more."

"Really, Mikey?"

"Yeah." Mike held Jessie in his lap, for a long while, in ecstasy, just looking at her. He massaged her toes, while she put her feet up on his thick leg, looking up at him.

"Are you still gonna talk to Momma about the date, Mikey?" Jessie sat up, her hair was all messy. "Thoon as we get home?"

"Yeah, but you let me do the talkin', baby. I think it's better if I talk to her myself."

"Okay, Mikey, you talk to Momma."

♥

They stopped and got cheeseburgers on their way out of Reno. Mike took out an eight-track and put it in his player. He looked at Jessie.

"I asked Maddy the other night what kind of music she liked when she was twelve. I was trying to imagine what you might have been listening to. She told me, *The Monkees*, and I went and bought this. I been listening to it, and I didn't think I would, but I love it. Every song kinda reminds me of you. Well, not kinda, really. There's one called, *Sweet Young Thing*, where she tip-toes into his bedroom at night, and especially this one." Mike skipped to the song, *Saturdays Child*, and crooned it out loud, as they drove on. They both sang and laughed to the entire album, twice, on the way home.

Chapter Twenty-Two – Blessings Wear Unexpected Disguises

"We're home!" Jessie shouted, as Mike followed her into the house. He was anxious and felt skeptical as soon as they walked in.

"I'm in the kitchen, sweetie," Debbie answered. She was leaning over the counter, shredding carrots.

They walked to the dining room and Mike cautiously sat down at the bar, facing Debbie.

"Hi, Mike," Debbie said, a little surprised, and now concerned, seeing the look on his face. "How was school?"

Mike didn't have a second to answer as Jessie spoke right out, "Momma, Mikey wants to tell you something." Jessie took Mike's hand.

"I wanna see Jessie, Debbie," Mike said, realizing he was just going to have to say it, knowing that Jessie wasn't going to be quiet if he didn't beat her to it.

"I want to have a date with Mikey, Momma," Jessie announced, squeezing Mike's hand.

Debbie knew this was coming. She wiped her hands on her apron, went over to the table and sat down, lighting a cigarette.

"Please don't do this to her, Mike." Debbie leaned her forehead on her hand looking over at him.

"Deb…" Mike started to say.

Momma, I love Mikey," Jessie interrupted, smiling at him.

"I don't want to hurt Jessie, or do anything to make her unhappy," Mike told Debbie. "I can't help it. I love her. I wanna see her."

"Mike," Debbie exhaled. "She's just a baby, Mike." Debbie rubbed her hand across her face. "I know you can't help it, but she's just a baby."

"I'm not a baby," Jessie interrupted.

"Jessie, what about Luke? Aren't you seeing Luke?" Debbie asked, quite anxious.

"Yeth, Momma, I love Luke."

Debbie looked at Jessie, and then Mike, confused and puzzled. "Jessie, you're only fifteen. Maybe we better wait to let you see anyone, for a while. Mike, why would you want to see Jessie, when you know she's already seeing Luke?"

"No, Momma, please, no," Jessie cried. She went to Debbie, taking her hand. "For a while, till when? When I grow up? I want to see Mikey on a date," Jessie whined, looking anxiously at Debbie.

"Debbie," Mike tried to get a word in, "How will she know what she wants if I can't see her? I don't want to sneak around you."

"Momma, Mikey loves me." Jessie whined again, squeezing Debbie's hand.

Debbie thought to herself wondering if Jessie would ever grow up. "Mike, don't you think that one of you is going to have to do the right thing here? Jessie's not going to be able to make a decision, you know that. One of you is going to have to do it for her."

"I wish it was that easy, Debbie." Mike looked down at his pants, rubbing his hands on them, seeing that this was not going to go well at all. "I didn't know she was seeing Luke, not at first."

"No, Momma, no!" Jessie cried. "Please no, I can't pick!"

"Jessie," Debbie said, pulling Jessie close to her. "You don't have to pick, sweetheart. You're just a child. You have to wait."

"Momma, Mikey loves me," Jessie cried, with big tears now running down her cheeks.

Debbie looked at Mike, who was sitting very nervously. "I suppose if I locked you up you'd find a way to see them, wouldn't you?" She turned to Jessie.

"Locked me up?" Jessie's eyes opened wide. Mike tried to swallow the lump in his throat.

"Made you stay home, Sweetie. I just think you're too young, Jessie. I'm gonna have to talk about this with Uncle Harry."

"Momma," Jessie begged. "I want to thee Mikey, like you let me thee Luke. Mikey loves me, he saved me, Momma. He saved me from the monster." Jessie's voice was trembling, and tears were rolling down her face as she held tightly to Debbie's arm.

"*Shit,*" Mike thought. He wasn't ready to tell Debbie all of that, not without knowing what Luke was doing.

"Luke helped me, Momma, when I was alone. He came to see me, and made me feel better," Jessie cried.

"What monster, Jessie?" Debbie asked, looking at Mike. He was nervously rubbing the side of his face.

"Debbie…" Mike started to say when Jessie interrupted, again.

"The monster in the trees…Momma, I don't want to go back to St. Thomas. I want to go to school with Mikey." Jessie was becoming hysterical, crying and trembling, pulling on Debbie's hand.

"Jessie, I can't make that decision right now."

"Momma, please…"

"*Jessie, please let me talk!*" Mike interrupted her.

"Jessie, go change your clothes, now," Debbie said to her, somewhat sternly, "so Mike and I can talk for a minute."

"Yes, Momma." Jessie reluctantly turned, pouting at Mike, and went down the hall.

"Debbie, I'm not good at explaining things," Mike began. "Luke and I, we…"

"Does Luke know about this, monster, Mike?"

Mike nodded. "We have to talk to you about Jessie, Debbie."

Just then the phone rang, and Debbie answered it. "Hello," Debbie said anxiously, not really wanting a phone call right now.

"Hey Debbie, it's Luke."

"Luke!"

"Yes, ma'am. I have some things I need to tell you about Jessie, important things. I'd like to come over, if that's okay?"

Luke had just gotten off the phone with Dr. Colby's office to find out if what Jessie talked about under hypnosis could be used in court. He discovered that with Jessie's permission, the doctor could testify.

"Yes, Luke," Debbie answered. "Mike is here, and I think you both have some explaining to do."

"Yes, ma'am, I'll be right there."

Elijah came running up the stairs, on his way home from school. "Hey, Mike," he said, out of breath, and closed the door.

"Hi." Mike replied, trying to maintain himself.

"What's going on?" Eli asked, walking into the kitchen, and opened the refrigerator.

Debbie hung the phone up. "Eli, get your snack and go right to your room, and do your homework, please."

Maddy and Aimee came through the front door.

"How did you get here so fast?" Aimee asked Mike, while Maddy went straight to her room, instantly irritated at Mike sitting there.

Mike shrugged. "Do you mind if I smoke, Debbie?"

"No." Debbie shook her head.

Mike sat down at the table and took out a cigarette.

"Do you want something to drink, Mike?" Debbie asked, taking a drink of her coffee. She was trying not to lose her mind or fall apart.

Mike shook his head. "No, thanks."

Aimee went to her room. Jessie was just slipping her pink sweatshirt on over her head. She could see Jessie had been crying.

"What's going on, Jessie? Are you in trouble for ditching school?"

"No." Jessie sniffed her nose, zipping up her jeans. "Why, Aimee?"

"Well, because Mike's sitting at the table and Momma looks upset." Aimee put her back pack down on the floor and kicked off her shoes. "And you're crying."

Jessie sat on her bed and pulled up her thick, warm socks. "Mikey wants to take me on a date."

"Oh," Aimee replied, wondering what her mom was going to think about that. "And he asked her?"

"Yeah, Mikey and Luke have to ask Momma." Jessie went out of the room and sat down at the table next to Mike. Debbie had gone over to the sink to wash her hands and went back to her carrots, waiting for Luke to get there.

"Luke's coming," Mike told Jessie.

Jessie held Mike's arm looking up at him. "Why?"

Mike stoked her face. "Because, we have to talk now, babe."

Aimee went to Maddy's room and told her Luke and Mike were having a talk with Momma.

"Mom, practice for baseball starts this week. Are we still going?" Eli handed Debbie his practice schedule. She couldn't think, now.

"Eli, practices are at three-thirty. How am I going to get you there and pick up Jessie, too?"

"What days are they, Debbie?" Mike asked.

"Saturday, Tuesday, and Thursdays," Debbie said, looking at the schedule.

"I can pick Jessie up from school."

"You'd have to leave school early, Mike. I don't think that's a good idea to miss your last class." She was hoping to immediately detour him.

"I get out at two," Mike said. "I can pick her up."

"I'll think about it, Mike." Debbie rubbed her face.

Jessie smiled up at Mike, squeezing his arm.

"So, I'm still going, right, Mom?" Eli asked.

"We'll see, Eli. Please go to your room now."

Eli went and turned the TV on and sat down on the couch, drinking a root beer and eating a piece of cold chicken. George and Gracie were jumping all over him, begging for food. "Get down!" he snapped.

They heard Luke's Cuda come up the street, and park in front of his house.

"Mikey, what are we going to thay?" Jessie whispered to him.

"We're going to be quiet, Jessie, and let Luke talk, okay?"

"Okay." Jessie nodded, very serious.

Luke ran up the stairs and George and Gracie started barking their heads off as Luke knocked on the door.

"COME IN!" Eli yelled. "shut up, you stupid dogs!"

Luke came in and walked over to the table, giving Mike a dirty look.

"Sit down, Luke," Debbie said, going over to the table. "Would you like something to drink?"

Maddy and Aimee had both come out of their rooms and Aimee asked if they could stay.

Debbie looked at the girls. "Just be quiet," she sighed.

"No, ma'am, thank you," Luke answered, sitting at the other end of the table. "First, I want to tell you, Debbie, that I'm not here to talk to you about me and Mike."

"Oh?" Debbie asked, sitting down in her chair.

"Mike and I know what Jessie's been hiding from you," Luke said, without hesitation. "You need to know, so you can get a hold of your lawyer, and start an investigation right away."

Debbie anxiously looked at all three of them. "What is it, Luke?"

"Mike and I took Jessie to a psychiatrist last week..."

"A psychiatrist?" Debbie interrupted, quite distressed.

"We told him about how she is; how she's, you know, smart but...but, Jessie told Mike about a monster she says has been following her all her life, and she's been getting headaches, and well, anyway," Luke exhaled, nervously.

"Anyway, he did hypnosis on her, and she told us about being molested by a man when she was little."

Debbie gasped, holding her hand over her mouth. Maddy and Aimee both sat down with sorrowful, looks on their faces. Mike looked down, nervously, tapping his knuckles on the table.

"A man that is still hanging out with Hank," Luke continued. "She also told us that Hank locks her in the wood bin at home. That's what she's been hiding, Debbie."

"No," Debbie gasped again, holding her mouth. She looked at Jessie.

Jessie sat quietly, looking at Luke, pouting.

"She told us how she tried to get out. Well, the molestation was bad, Debbie," Luke said, trying to stay together. "It was really bad and…cruel." Luke voice faltered. "The doctor I took her to when she got on the pill says she was mutilated, damaged, and she'll probably never have children."

Mike squeezed Jessie's hand looking at her. He never heard that part.

"The man, and I don't know why I say man, he ain't no man…anyway, he took Jessie out into the pine trees, by her house, when she was five," Luke continued. "He told her if she ever told anyone, a monster would take her back in the trees. Jessie turned the man that molested her into the monster in her head, and she believed he's been watching her all these years. Jessie is, well, I don't know how to tell you, other than just telling you, she's pretty messed up over it."

Debbie held her hand out to Jessie. "Come sit with me, sweetie." Jessie got up quietly and went to Debbie. "Is that what you were afraid to tell me, about your dad locking you up?"

"Yes, Momma. Luke and Mikey said we have to tell you, so I can't go back there no more. But I was scared, because if he found out I told you, he would put me in there again."

"Oh, Jessie…they're right, Jessie. I won't let you go back there anymore." Debbie kissed Jessie's cheek, and held her tightly against her. "Oh, my sweet little girl, I'm so sorry." Debbie had tears running down her face. Maddy and Aimee were both quietly crying, looking at Jessie. Eli came over and stood next to them, very saddened.

"Mike and I went out to Jessie's house that night," Luke said. "We looked at the wood bin and saw the marks that she told us about. How her dog scratched at the outside to get her out. How she hit the front board off with a piece of wood, even duct tape, where he tied her up. We left everything the way it was. I think you should have the Sheriff go out right away and investigate it. I think you should call your lawyer, now, and tell him."

"Yes, Luke, I'm calling him right now." Debbie quickly went to the phone.

"I gotta go to work," Mike said, getting up. Jessie went to him and he leaned over her and kissed her. "I'll call you," he whispered in her ear.

Jessie sat quietly with Luke, as Debbie spoke with Mr. Burke on the phone. Luke gazed at her with loving eyes. When Debbie got off the phone she sat next to Luke, wiping her face.

"Luke, I don't know whether to be mad as hell, or cry with relief, but you helped Jessie and I want to thank you for that. And you, young lady." Debbie smiled, holding her hand out to Jessie.

Jessie went to her Aunt and Debbie hugged her. "Momma, don't be mad at Mikey. It was his idea to make us go to the doctor, so I could get everything out of my head figured out."

"I'm not mad, sweetheart. I'm mad I didn't think of it myself. I'm mad it happened to you, but I'm glad that Luke and Mike helped you and took care of you where I couldn't. I'm sorry you didn't feel safe telling me. I love you, Jessie, now more than ever, and I'm glad for Luke and Mike helping. Everything will work out now, and you'll be here, safe with us always."

"Dr. Colby wants to see Jessie regularly, Debbie," Luke told her. "He says she needs to talk about it. He feels she needs aggressive therapy, and I do to. He said if Jessie is willing, what she told him could be used as evidence, and he recorded it. He also said that Carl, the man who hurt Jessie, can still go to jail, and Mike and I agree. We want him arrested."

"Yes, thank you, Luke. Yes, definitely, and I'll make sure she goes to see this Dr. Colby, you said?"

"Yes ma'am, here's his card," Luke said, handing her the card. "He also wants her to see a regular doctor, to see if she has an eating disorder. She's not eating, and he says that's probably why she gets headaches, and he wants her to have this prescription for anxiety attacks. He said it also might help her eat and gain some weight."

"I'll make an appointment with my doctor, Luke," Debbie said, taking the prescription. "Jessie will get everything she needs from now on." Debbie smiled and started to cry again.

"Don't cry, Momma," Jessie said. "I'm getting better now."

Mr. Burke called the Sheriff's office. Burt and his deputy immediately went out, meeting up with Mr. Burke at Hank's house. They had gotten a search warrant and did an investigation of Jessie's apparent living conditions. They also took pictures of the wood bin. Mr. Burke advised the Sheriff that no charges would be made until his office could get all of the facts together, and meet with his client, Jessie, to get her statement. Burt agreed that Jessie could make her statement at John's office, and that he would not do anything until they were ready. Mr. Burke did not want to do anything that would set Hank off on a tangent, until they knew how they were going to proceed. Jessie was safe in her Aunt's custody for the time being, and that was going to give them the opportunity to pull their case together.

Debbie told the kids to keep Jessie's information to themselves. She then called Harry at work. He told her he would leave work right away and bring home pizza. She just couldn't cook now, and aside from everything else that was going on that day, Maddy was having her first real date, with Bryce Baker!

All attention turned toward Maddy, as she nervously ran around the house trying to decide what to wear. Between more phone calls with Mr. Burke's office and trying to remember to just breathe, Debbie managed to get Maddy calmed down and helped her with her hair. Jessie went into the bathroom with Maddy and Debbie.

"Momma, did you think about it, if I can have a date with Mikey?" Jessie looked anxiously, at Debbie.

Debbie wasn't sure she wanted to answer that, yet. She was sure she was going to lose her mind, any second.

"Come on, Mom," Maddy said, "Let Jessie go on a date with Mike."

"Maddy?" Debbie asked, a bit surprised, "I thought…"

"Mike likes Jessie, Mom," Maddy interrupted.

Debbie sighed, looking at Jessie's face. "Yes, Jessie, but he has to ask first, and tell me where you're going."

"Oh, thank you, Momma! Thank you tho much!" Jessie smiled, grabbing Debbie's shirt. "Can he pick me up at school, too, Momma?"

Debbie looked mournfully at Jessie. "I guess so, sweetheart, just until we figure something else out."

"Thank you, Momma!"

Luke, Jessie and Eli sat on the couch, observing the chaos with Maddy and Debbie. Aimee got on the phone with Courtney and the two of them were amusing themselves with Maddy's drama.

"You don't get like that when I come to get you, do you, Jessie?" Luke chuckled, whispering to Jessie.

Jessie looked up at Luke and shook her head. "You love me, Luke. I know you already think I'm pretty."

Luke pulled Jessie close to him and kissed her.

"You're pretty smart. You're beautiful, baby." He smiled. "You okay, Love bug?"

Jessie nodded. "Yes, Luke."

Bryce picked up a very nervous and anxious Maddy at five-thirty p.m. Maddy didn't invite him in the house. She was terrified her family would embarrass her. She met him out on the porch, while the dogs were barking, wildly. Debbie ran to the door and introduced herself to Bryce on the porch, very unhappy with Maddy. She didn't say anything about it but planned to when Maddy got home.

Uncle Harry finally got home carrying the pizza with the dog's jumping at his heels. Debbie went to her room and collapsed on the bed.

"Luke," Jessie whispered, cuddled up tight against him on the couch. "You and Mikey have to take turns, now. Momma said I can have a date with Mikey."

Luke felt a chill go down his back and looked down at Jessie. His heart began to pound, and he took in a deep breath, feeling like he couldn't breathe, as if Jessie were stabbing him to death. He understood that Jessie was determined to have things her way, no matter what, and there was nothing he could do about it. Not if he wanted to still see her. Jessie was not going to pick, ever, and he would never let go. He was never going to let her go. He didn't say anything. He squeezed her hand and leaned his head down on hers. He felt like he was getting totally PW'd. Something he thought he'd never get, but he took a breath and sighed, "Okay, baby."

"Thank you, for helping me tell Momma today, Luke. I feel better now." Jessie smiled up at him.

"I'm glad, darlin'."

"Are you going to be with me tomorrow, Luke?"

"Yes, love-bug."

Jessie smiled and squeezed Luke's arm. "Luke, I love you."

"I love you too, baby." Luke closed his eyes and put his hand up on Jessie's face.

~

Mike called Jessie at six p.m.

"Hello," Jessie answered softly, getting to the phone.

"Baby, I been thinking about you ever since I got to work."

"Hi, Mikey," Jessie said, smiling. "What are you thinking about me?"

"Bunny stuff."

"At work?"

"Yeah, I sit at work all night and think about you, bunny, my bunny lovin's."

"Do they still pay you money?"

"I don't tell them about it, peanut," Mike chuckled. "I even jack off in the bathroom, sometimes."

"Why?"

"Because, I can't stop thinking about you, tittie girl."

"Mikey! Jessie shouted in his ear. "Momma said you can take me to a date!" Jessie giggled excitedly.

"She did?" Mike grinned. He was sure that wasn't going to happen.

"Yeah, if you ask her, and tell her where the date is."

"That's far-out, baby."

"Mikey!" She shouted again. "Momma says you can get me at school!"

"That's far-out, too, bunny." Mike grinned.

"Mikey, you have to take turns with Luke…Mikey? Are you there?"

"I'm here…are you gonna come see me tonight, Jessie?"

"Yes, baba."

"I miss you, baby. I really had a good time today with you. Thank you, baby girl."

"Mikey, did you put my pretties away?"

"Yes, peanut, they're in my drawer. I'm proud of you, Jessie. You were a brave girl, today."

"Thank you, Mikey, for helping me."

"I love you, baby."

"I love you, Mikey. We have to go now."

"I know. Have a good practice, foxy little Jessie."

"Bye, baba."

"I'll see you, Beautiful."

~§~

~Review Requested~

Thank you, for reading! If you loved this book, would you please provide a review at Amazon.com or Goodreads

FALLEN, is the second Book in the Expecting to Fly Trilogy. Book three tells of Jessie's discovery of who she is, her struggle to become part of her beloved family, her spiritual awakening, and a difficult decision of the heart in INTO THE LIGHT. Available soon from Penakluppi Press © on Amazon.

www.ingramcontent.com/pod-product-compliance
Lightning Source LLC
Chambersburg PA
CBHW071305200626
46813CB00015B/149